THE
BEST IS
YET TO COME

BY JUDITH GOULD

SINS
THE LOVE-MAKERS
DAZZLE
NEVER TOO RICH
THE TEXAS YEARS
FOREVER
TOO DAMN RICH
SECOND LOVE
TILL THE END OF TIME
RHAPSODY
TIME TO SAY GOODBYE
A MOMENT IN TIME

JUDITH GOULD

THE
BEST IS
YET TO COME

timewarner
books

A *Time Warner* Book

First published in the United States of America by Dutton,
a member of Penguin Putnam Inc., in 2002

First published in Great Britain in 2003
by Time Warner Books

Copyright © Judith Gould, Inc., 2002

The moral right of the author has been asserted.

A CIP catalogue record for this book
is available from the British Library.

ISBN 0 316 85618 5

Typeset in Minion by Palimpsest Book Production Limited,
Polmont, Stirlingshire
Printed and bound in Great Britain by
Clays Ltd, St Ives plc

Time Warner Books UK
Brettenham House
Lancaster Place
London WC2E 7EN

www.TimeWarnerBooks.co.uk

With love,
to the RGF,
who taught me so much
about forgiveness

ACKNOWLEDGMENTS

So many friends offered their unstinting support during the writing of this novel that, for fear of leaving someone out, I have to say a collective thank you. I trust that you know who you are.

I do have to single out two individuals without whose help this novel would not be what it is. First, for her gracious hospitality, time, and help in Amsterdam, the Netherlands, I would like to thank Marion Bienes, whose contributions to this work – and my life, and the lives of countless animals through her dedication to antivivisection and animal rights – have proved to be a godsend to man and beast. Finally, although I'm superstitious about thanking editors (they seem to disappear after I do), I have to express my gratitude to Genny Ostertag for her ideas and diligence and her diplomatic and constructive criticism, all in an effort to make my work better. Please stay put.

Judith Gould
February 2002

Tout comprendre
c'est tout pardonner.

'To know everything
is to forgive everything.'

—Attributed to Germaine de Staël

1

'Where's Richie?' Lyon asked. He pulled off his sweatshirt, balled it up, and tossed it onto a chair.

'He went to a movie after school with Jeff Adler,' Carolina replied. She wrapped a vintage silk kimono around her lithe nude body and tied it at the waist. There was a conspiratorial smile on her brightly painted lips.

Lyon saw her smile, and he grinned, exposing his even white teeth. 'Did you bribe him or something?' He slid his sweatpants down and pulled them off, balling them up and tossing them onto the chair atop the sweatshirt.

Carolina laughed. 'No, I didn't have to,' she said. 'He called from Jeff's while you were at the gym and asked if he could go.'

'That was very thoughtful of him,' Lyon said, turning to her and taking her into his arms. 'Leaving us alone like this.' He leaned down and kissed her lips. 'He's his father's son, all right.'

'I think he has got just a little bit of his mother in him, too,' Carolina replied.

JUDITH GOULD

He nuzzled her ears with his lips. 'You're right,' he said. 'It was very thoughtful of you to take the rest of the afternoon off.'

'Hmmm.' Carolina held his sweat-slick back. She loved the feel of his hard body against hers and the strength of his powerful arms about her. 'How could I let you leave without a proper good-bye?'

'I wonder,' Lyon said teasingly, 'whether you were being thoughtful or just plain greedy.'

Carolina drew back and punched him lightly in the gut. 'You!'

'Watch it,' he said, grabbing her hand and holding it in his.

'Call it what you want to, buster,' she said, 'but I want to have some more fun before you go.'

He pulled her hand up to his lips and kissed it. 'Why don't I jump in the shower for two minutes, then we can play all we want to?'

Carolina nodded. 'That's a wonderful idea,' she said, looking up into his eyes.

'Back in two,' he said, slapping her on the butt and then letting her go.

'Hurry,' she said, 'my meter's running.' She sat down on the bed and watched as he pulled off his jockstrap and flung it onto the chair. *His body's still so great,* she thought as he disappeared into the bathroom.

She lay back against the pillows, smiling with anticipation when she heard the shower and then his tuneless voice, humming some unidentifiable melody that was barely discernible over the powerful blast of the jets. Extending a long, slender arm, she picked up the glass of mineral water on the bedside table and, sitting up slightly, took a long sip; then she set the glass down.

She fell back against the pillows again and glanced about the room, her eyes coming to rest on his custom-made suit. It was hanging on the back of the bathroom door in a cleaner's plastic bag. Carolina sighed wistfully. She hated to see Lyon go – she always did – and seventeen years of marriage had never changed that. *Two weeks,* she thought. *Two long weeks of working and being a mother*

2

and everything that goes with the vast territory that covers. And the waiting. Yes, there is always that, too, she had to admit unhappily. *Waiting for Lyon to return.*

But even worse than his absences, she'd decided, were those times when he was home but was distracted and inattentive, his mind elsewhere and his body unresponsive to her needs. He certainly wasn't that way every time he was in New York, she told herself, but the instances seemed to be more and more frequent lately. When had this neglect started, she wondered, and was it merely a passing phase? The result of business worries, maybe? Or perhaps, she thought, it was simply the inevitable path down which so many marriages went, no matter how solid they were.

She reassured herself now, as she had repeatedly in the last couple of years, that this was not the case with her and Lyon, and when the blast of the shower suddenly stopped, she smiled, knowing that he would soon join her in bed. This lovemaking before departures had become a ritual. No matter how busy she'd been over the years, she had always tried to make certain that the two of them could spend some time alone like this before he left.

He appeared from the bathroom, roughly toweling his hair. His body had never failed to excite her, and at forty-five its musculature was defined and hardened by the gym. He'd always professed to hating exercise, but the last two or three years he'd worked out relentlessly, wherever he was, to keep the ravages of time at bay.

He dropped the towel on the floor and looked over at her. 'I'm going to get you,' he growled.

'Promise?'

He was on the bed beside her in an instant, taking her into his arms and smothering her in kisses, his fresh scent intoxicating to her, the feel of his body against hers reigniting the excitement she'd felt before he'd taken the shower. Carolina returned his kisses, stroking his solid back with her hands, relishing the feel of his breath on her neck, his lips and tongue at her ears as he teased her mercilessly.

One of his hands went to her kimono's silk belt and loosened it, and then slipped inside and fondled a breast tenderly, his fingers brushing the nipple. He kissed her then, his mouth over hers, his tongue delving and exploring, and Carolina responded, kissing him hungrily as he pulled her closer to him. He ran his hand up and down her torso, from her breasts to the mound between her legs and back up again, feathering his fingers against her skin.

She gasped as he pulled back and helped her slip out of her kimono. His mouth went to her fully exposed breasts, licking and kissing, and Carolina ran her fingers through his hair and across his powerful shoulders, her excitement increasing. He slipped a hand between her legs and groaned with passion when he felt the dampness there, his fingers exploring the softness within.

Carolina felt his powerful manhood pressing against her and reached down and encircled it with her hand. Lyon gasped at her touch and slid up onto his knees and positioned himself between her legs, spreading them wide with his hands. He leaned down and kissed her hungrily, and she put her arms around his shoulders as he moved down onto her body and entered her slowly. She moaned with the exquisite sensation of him inside her and couldn't help but thrust herself against him, eager to have all of him.

Lyon plunged to the hilt of his cock, unable to wait any longer, and began moving against her, slowly at first, then faster and faster, moaning with pleasure as she did, relishing the feel of her soft and welcoming femininity on his engorged and rigid masculinity. As his passion mounted, he placed his hands under her buttocks, one on each cheek, and began driving himself into her with abandon.

Carolina clasped him against her, knowing that she was about to reach orgasm, but she couldn't wait another instant. She held on tighter and tighter as she felt the inevitable contractions begin, and cried out as she felt the first of innumerable waves wash over her, lifting her up, up, up to some ecstatic place of sensation and emotion that brought tears of joy to her eyes.

Lyon felt her tremors beneath him and could hold off no longer, letting out a yelp of pure bliss as he exploded inside her, his release so great that he shuddered from head to toe before collapsing against her, gasping for breath. He held her firmly and peppered her face with little kisses.

'I . . . love you . . . Carolina,' he uttered between breaths.

She clung to him with all her might, her heart and soul buoyed as if on a heavenly cloud and sustained by their love. This love, she felt, was so powerful and all-encompassing that nothing and no one could ever threaten or change it in any way.

'And . . . and . . . I love you,' she whispered in breathy gasps, hugging him.

When their breathing had returned to normal, Lyon gently rolled off her and put one arm around her shoulders, his free hand stroking her stomach, his fingers lightly brushing up and down her torso. He tenderly kissed her neck and ears, her face and hair, repeating his declaration of love for her.

Carolina turned on her side to face him, putting an arm across his shoulder, and looked into his eyes. 'I'll miss you,' she said with a smile.

'I'll miss you, too, sweetheart,' he said, 'but it's not for too long.'

'I hope you'll be back for the birthday party I'm having for Matt,' she said.

'Wouldn't miss it for the world. You know that.'

She hugged him. 'It'll mean so much to him for you to be there.'

He kissed the tip of her nose. 'I promise I'll make it,' he said. 'You can count on it.' He drew back and looked at her. 'But when're you going to have time for a birthday party?' he asked.

'I'll find the time,' she replied. 'It's on my calendar, and believe me, nothing's going to interfere with it. Not even a major party.'

'You're getting to be quite the businesswoman,' he said, nuzzling her under the chin. 'Does this mean I'm going to be left in the dust while you get to be more and more famous as New York's greatest party decorator?'

Carolina reached down and pinched his ass. 'No way,' she said. 'And if that's wishful thinking on your part, forget about it. You know I would never let my work interfere with *us* or my family.'

He kissed her lips. 'You've got it all figured out, don't you?'

'I try,' Carolina said. 'I have to at this point. We're so busy I may have to hire somebody else to help out at the shop.' She looked thoughtful for a moment. 'Only I'm not sure about that,' she went on. 'Summer's coming, and business usually slows down with customers going away. I'm not so sure about that this year, though.'

'What's so different about this year?' he asked.

'Business,' she said. 'That's what's different. It's picked up so much that even if it tapers off, it's still going to be crazy as hell.'

'It's because everything you do is so beautiful,' Lyon said. 'You always go that extra mile and make sure everything looks perfect.'

Carolina kissed him. 'You're sweet to say so,' she said, 'but that's not the whole story, and you know it. Anyway, enough about me and my nutty business. What would you like to eat before you have to leave for the airport? I can make one of my famous omelettes, or—'

Lyon shook his head. 'No, I'm just going to have some cereal and a banana or something. I'd better get a move on.'

'I know,' Carolina replied. There was a note of sadness in her voice that she failed to hide. Sometimes, he seemed awfully eager to get away. She quickly sat up and put a smile on her face. She didn't like Lyon seeing the pain she felt every time he left for his sojourns in Europe. 'The suit you're going to wear's ready,' she said. 'Bag's packed. All set?'

'I'm all set,' he said, sitting up. 'How about putting on some really strong coffee while I get dressed?'

'Make-your-hair-stand-up-straight coffee?'

'Exactly,' he said.

'You got it,' she said, getting out of the bed. She picked up her kimono and slipped into it. 'It'll be ready in a jiffy.'

They had finished eating and sat drinking more of the strong coffee at the loft's big dining table. Carolina looked across at her husband over the rim of her coffee mug.

'What are you thinking about?' she asked.

He turned to her, and saw the adoring expression on her face. *Jesus Christ,* he thought with an inward cringe of self-loathing. He averted his eyes, afraid that she would be able to see the guilt that was gnawing away at him. *I still love her so much. I hate to hurt her – and I know it's going to hurt like nothing else in her life has ever hurt her – but I've got to tell her about what's going on when I get back from this trip. Besides, I can't go on living with this secret. It's going to eat me alive.*

'Nothing,' he said at last, trying to make his voice casual. He cleared his throat. 'Well, I was just thinking how it's strange that Richie's not here to say good-bye. There was a time when he wouldn't have missed being here for anything.'

Carolina sighed, and then smiled. 'It's called being sixteen,' she said. 'He's busy making a life of his own, Lyon.'

'What movie did he go see?' he asked, feeling the rebuke in her answer. He knew that he didn't spend as much time with Richie as he should, and this served only to compound the guilt he felt about his secret life with Monique in Amsterdam.

Carolina shrugged. 'I don't know,' she replied.

'You don't know?' His voice held more than a slight edge.

She shook her head. 'No,' she said peevishly.

'Don't you think he could use a little more supervision than that?' he said with a hint of irritation. 'I mean, he's just a kid. It could be some awful trash or something.' The words were no sooner out of his mouth than he felt like a hypocrite. How could he criticize her when he was never around to supervise Richie himself?

7

'That *kid* will have his driver's license soon, Lyon,' she said heatedly, staring daggers at him. 'He's already taking out girlfriends, for God's sake. And he knows more about sex and drugs and disease and all the dangers out there than I knew when we got married.'

'That was different,' Lyon said, softening his voice, trying to backpedal, lighten up a bit. He certainly hadn't set out to offend her, but there was no doubt that he had.

She drew a deep breath, trying to calm herself. 'He also has his own integrity and principles, Lyon. And good judgment. It may not be infallible, but he's very mature. Besides, he and I have talked a lot about all the terrible things that are out there, and I trust him implicitly. He trusts me, too.'

Lyon stared at her for a moment, consumed with guilt. 'I'm sorry, Carolina,' he said. 'I was way out of line, criticizing you. But I do worry about him sometimes. Being gone so much, I guess I feel like I don't do enough. It's like I'm out of the loop.'

'I'm sorry, too,' Carolina said, 'because I know that when you are here you try to spend time with him. He idolizes you, Lyon. He really does. But he's growing up, becoming his own man.' She set down her coffee mug. 'It's a little scary. It seems like yesterday that he was playing with toy cars, and now he wants to drive. Wants a motorcycle, too.'

'He wants a motorcycle?' Lyon said, staring at her in amazement.

'You got it,' she said with a wry smile.

'Jesus,' he said. 'They're so dangerous, and he's so young. And—'

'And he's seen the pictures of you on your old bike,' Carolina said.

Lyon shook his head, as if coming to terms with a new reality. 'Yes, but . . . but that was different.'

'What was different?' she asked. 'You were only a few months older than he is now when you got your first bike. You didn't stop to think about danger. You were a male. You wanted adventure. You had raging hormones.'

'Raging hormones?' he repeated quizzically, almost as if he were talking to himself.

Carolina burst into gales of laughter. 'I think it'll be a good idea if you and Richie spend some time together in the country when you get back for Matt's birthday party.'

'I think you're right,' he said. 'I thought it was still all about skate-boards.'

'That was yesterday,' Carolina said. 'As in kid stuff.'

Lyon smiled. 'It's unbelievable,' he said, shaking his head again. He looked down at his wristwatch. 'Damn, I'd better get going.' He stood up and retrieved his briefcase off the counter that separated the dining area from the kitchen, and then picked up his suitcase.

Carolina got up and walked with him to the vestibule, where the elevator opened onto the loft. Lyon set the suitcase and briefcase down, pressed the elevator button, and took her into his arms, looking down into her eyes. 'I'll miss you,' he said. He kissed her lips and hugged her.

'I'll miss you, too,' she said, trying to sound cheerful. She hugged him tightly to her. She hated these partings, but the ritual itself – like their always making love beforehand – was very important to her. If anything ever happened to him, she often thought, she could never live with knowing that they hadn't had a farewell kiss and a hug.

'It won't be long,' he said, 'and I promise I'll make it back for your birthday. It'll be a good opportunity for Richie and me to spend some time together. I've obviously got some catching up to do with my son.' *And with my wife,* he thought uneasily.

'Uh-huh,' she said, nodding and smiling. 'We all have some catching up to do.'

The elevator arrived, and he kissed her again. 'Bye,' he said, letting her go and picking up his suitcase and briefcase. 'I'll call you, so don't—'

'I know, I know,' she said. 'You're going to be difficult to get hold of, so you'll call me.' He always stayed in the Minervaplein apartment that the company owned, but was seldom there except to sleep.

From the elevator cage, he puckered up his lips into a kiss. 'Love you,' he said.

'I love you.'

The doors closed, and he was gone.

2

The shrill buzzing of the alarm clock was an unrelenting and joyless sound to Carolina's ears this morning. She groaned aloud as she slid one arm from under the sheet and reached over, slapping in the general direction of the harsh, unwelcome intrusion. Her fingers grazed glass and, too late, she jerked her hand back.

The sound of her water glass crashing against the floor brought her struggling up and out from under the covers into a sitting position.

'Damn,' she said aloud, her voice barely audible. Her throat was dry and scratchy. With a decisive push of her thumb, she hit the button that turned off the offensive instrument.

The instant it was quieted, the raucous early morning sounds of Chelsea replaced it. It wasn't even daylight yet, but delivery trucks rumbled loudly on the streets, shaking the windows in their frames. A workman was yelling at the top of his lungs. In the distance, the sound of an ambulance siren wailed frenetically.

Carolina smiled slightly at the reassuring cacophony and pushed her bangs away from her face. She eyed the clock as if it were an enemy: five a.m. Yawning loudly, she stretched her arms and legs, trying to fully awaken her leaden body. She fell back against the pillows again, but only momentarily.

'Oh,' she groaned as she finally slid her feet off the side of the bed, 'this is torture. Why did I stay up watching that DVD with Richie last night?'

But she knew why. She had been working long, hard hours, and Lyon was out of town for a couple of weeks, and she didn't feel as if either of them had been paying enough attention to their sixteen-year-old son. That is, when he could free himself from his friends to pay attention to her.

She stood up, careful to avoid the broken glass, and padded into the bathroom on bare feet. *My mouth!* she thought, grimacing with distaste. *Why on earth—?* Then she remembered. Last night she and Richie had eaten a mountain of popcorn, which they'd buttered and salted lavishly. *Ugh! Never again!* she told herself, knowing full well that she couldn't wait until next time with her son.

She quickly performed her morning ablutions in the shiny marble and glass bathroom, and then dashed to the loft's big open-plan kitchen. She smiled wryly, remembering how the cost of renovating this one room had given her such a shock. Sub-Zero refrigerator, Garland stove and ovens, all the stainless steel and black granite surfaces. Lyon had insisted on the best, and she hadn't argued with him. Now it was practically as new as the day it had been finished, it was so unused. The coffeemaker was a different matter, however, and she headed straight for it. All she had to do was push the button. She'd filled it with water and ground the beans last night before turning in.

She rushed back to the bathroom and quickly brushed her wildly tinted red hair, not a difficult job, considering her severe Louise Brooks do with its razor-straight bangs and razor-straight cut all the way around her head, the length just to the bottom of her earlobes. She quickly and expertly applied eyeliner, mascara, lipstick, and blusher, and then looked at her reflection in the mirror.

Not half bad, she thought, knowing that she looked quite snazzy for a sleep-deprived thirty-five-year-old. She tried a bright smile. *A face to meet faces,* she told herself. *Much better. Smoky eyes. Bright crimson lips.*

Most of Carolina's friends chuckled at her careful grooming, no matter the hour of day or night or the occasion. But Carolina had always reasoned that you never knew who might be around the next corner, and she always wanted to look her best – in case. Even she had to admit that the likelihood of running into anyone she'd want to impress at the wholesale flower market in the early morning hours was highly unlikely, but she'd long ago discovered that the vendors working in the market – the Georges, she called them, because they all seemed to be Greek and named George – loved to see her coming and often commented on her early morning outfits and cheerfulness.

So maybe none of them were Rockefellers or dot-com billionaires. So what? Impressing them and gradually developing a rapport with them had translated into countless favors and sweet deals for Carolina over the years. One George might hide away an unusual bunch of lilies until Carolina was able to see them, giving her the first chance at them before a competitor had the chance to come in and sweep them up and away. If a certain type of greenery was in critically short supply, it might be found stashed away in the back of another George's cooler, just waiting for Carolina's use. If she needed a last-minute delivery, one George or another was sure to make the short rumble down to her shop in Chelsea with whatever it was she had to have, only too glad to accommodate one of their steadiest, friendliest, and best-looking customers.

She hurried back to the bedroom and shrugged out of her nightie – one of Lyon's old, worn cotton tee shirts – and tossed it on the bed. She went to the spacious dressing room they shared – all built-in cabinets and closets – and quickly grabbed a navy blue linen tee

13

with long sleeves and cream nylon clam diggers, and then snatched a bra and panties from a lingerie drawer. Finally, she picked up her tiger-striped high-heeled Gucci mules. In five minutes or less, she was dressed. *Almost.* She put big gold hoops in her ears and slipped enormous matching ivory cuffs on each wrist; then she hung a gold chain around her neck. Hanging from it was the catch of the day, a group of different size fish, some gold, a few silver. Quickly dabbing Caron perfume that had been especially formulated for her, then slipping on her watch and rings – engagement, wedding, and three pinkie rings, one set with a ruby, one an emerald, and the other a blue sapphire – and she was set to go.

Back to the kitchen she went, moving like a cyclone now. She quickly filled an insulated plastic container with coffee, stirred in the usual, and then snapped on the lid. She loathed the look of the insulated container – it had been a freebie from Amazon.com for all of her book and CD ordering on-line – but she had to admit it had come in very handy. She would finish her coffee in the taxi, and then hide the ugly container in her carryall.

She gathered up her keys and canvas-and-leather bag. *All set,* she thought. *Except for one very important thing.* She set her things back down and went down the hallway.

She crept to Richie's bedroom door, opened it a crack, and saw that he was sleeping soundly. Skateboards, his bicycle, in-line skates, and tennis rackets were strewn about the room helter-skelter. The light from his computer's screen saver seemed to preside over the scene like a watchful protector. Richie changed it periodically, and she glanced over to see what it was today. Her lips spread into a wry smile when she saw the picture of a little girl – the little sister Richie had always said he wanted. He still talked about it some-times, but only jokingly these days. He'd finally come to terms with the fact that his mom and dad wanted only him.

She tiptoed over to the side of his bed, where she stood staring down at her son. Her heart surged with pride and joy and a love that threatened to overwhelm her as she looked at his handsome, still boyish face. It was blissfully peaceful and innocent and sunburned from his outdoor activities. *He's so untroubled and unspoiled*, she thought gratefully, her eyes still lingering on her son's features. *And I'm the luckiest woman in the world.*

Finally, she reached down and brushed a lock of shiny chocolate hair – identical to his father's, as were his blue eyes – off his forehead, and then brushed her lips across that very spot. *I love you,* she whispered. He didn't stir.

She straightened up, turned, and tiptoed back out of his room, leaving him to sleep. His alarm wouldn't go off for another couple of hours. She retrieved her carryall and keys, and as she walked to the elevator, she thought about last night and all the wonderful, silly laughs they'd shared.

In the vestibule, she checked her makeup once more in the huge elegant mirror over the Art Deco console. *The Georges are going to like it,* she thought.

'Carolina!' one of the wholesale flower vendors called. 'You look beautiful this morning!'

'And you're a handsome devil yourself, George,' she called back cheerfully, blowing him a kiss. Heels click-clacking loudly on the sidewalk, she continued up Avenue of the Americas.

It wasn't yet six o'clock, and the wholesale flower district was thronged with shoppers, as it had been since before daybreak. These days Roxie or Antonio, her right-hand helpers, did the marketing most of the time because Carolina was too busy with planning and designing the flowers for parties. Today, she'd decided to come up herself to find something really special for the important dinner party she was doing tonight. Roxie and Antonio would soon be at the shop, if they weren't there already, putting together some of the arrangements she'd designed. They would be taken uptown for the party later in the day.

Carolina felt exhilarated making her way among the bustle of the early morning crowds. She was reminded of the days when she'd first worked in a little Greenwich Village shop that Jonathan Muller, a newfound friend, had owned. She and Jonathan would sometimes go straight to the flower market from the clubs after they closed at four a.m., still dressed in all of their fancy regalia. Those had been heady days, full of very hard work and equally hard play.

'Carolina! What are you, deaf?'

One of the many Georges finally penetrated the veil of memories that had preoccupied her, and she snapped out of her reverie. 'What?' she asked, fixing him with a gaze. 'Sorry, George, I was on another planet. Daydreaming.'

'I told you,' George said, exasperated, 'I've got something really special stashed away. They're yours if you want them.'

'Oh, what?' she asked excitedly, her eyes gleaming with curiosity. 'What is it you've got that's so special?'

He gestured her toward the back of his shop with his head, a conniving expression on his face. 'Back here,' he said, his voice a highly dramatic whisper. 'Follow me.'

Carolina trailed along behind him toward the rear of the shop, turning sideways in the narrow pathway between plants and flowers. She drew to a halt at a big cooler in the back, where George was opening the door.

He rummaged inside it, shoving around tall metal buckets filled with various types of flowers and greens, some still completely covered by their paper wrappers, until he found what he was looking for. He pulled the bucket out, set it down on the foliage-strewn floor, and then tore a portion of the brown paper wrapper from around the flowers.

'Look, Carolina!' he said, his big salt-and-pepper mustache spreading wide in a proud smile, a hand gesturing to the flowers.

Carolina peered closely at the flowers revealed by the tear in the paper. 'Sterling Silver roses,' she said in a matter-of-fact voice.

George's face fell when he heard her lack of interest. He hurriedly ripped the paper sleeve completely away from the roses. 'Look again,' he said, thumping the paper. 'Not just Sterling Silver roses, Carolina. *Irish* Sterling Silver roses. The biggest and the most beautifully colored roses you'll ever see. I guarantee it.'

'Oooooh, George,' she cried with delight. 'They *are* gorgeous!' While size did not always matter – and these were huge – color nearly always did, and these were a spectacularly beautiful lavender gray mauve.

What luck! she thought. They would be perfect for Lydia Carstairs's dinner party tonight. Her dining room walls were covered in a beautiful grisaille paper with a neoclassical motif – various gods, goddesses, urns – and Sterling Silver roses would look quietly splashy in the room. And quiet splash was exactly what was called for. It was a mood that would please Lydia – no easy task.

Lydia Carstairs had recently become one of Carolina's best customers. Immensely rich and well connected socially, she was always being written about in society columns and was considered an icon of style. Her homes were often photographed for magazines. She was also extremely difficult to please, and had the sort of eagle eye that could differentiate between fifteen shades of pink where most people merely saw two or three. She also frequently alluded to the colors in Old Master paintings to describe what she wanted: 'The red in Caravaggio's *Judith Beheading Holofernes*,' she might say. 'You know, the blood spouting from his severed neck.' Carolina often knew exactly what the older woman was alluding to or would quickly find out, and she had the same color sense that Lydia had – one of several reasons that Lydia had come to rely on her services. Lydia would swoon over these roses, she realized. They would replace the arrangements she'd had in mind for the dining room.

'You want me to send them down with everything else?' George asked, his hurt feelings now mollified by her genuine show of enthusiasm.

Carolina shook her head. 'No, George,' she replied, 'I'm taking these babies with me. I'm using them tonight.'

'You got it,' he said. He scooped the huge bundle of roses out of the bucket and took it up front to a worktable, where he quickly wrapped it in another layer of paper, sealed it, and looked up at Carolina, his bushy salt-and-pepper eyebrows raised in a question. 'What else, beautiful?' he asked.

'That's it today, George,' she said. 'And thanks a million for letting me see these beauties.'

George nodded. 'I knew they were for you,' he said, smiling. 'Glad you came up yourself today.'

'I am, too,' she replied. 'I don't get up here enough these days.'

'You send Roxie or Antonio all the time. You're getting rich and famous so you got no time for us.'

'Rich and famous!' Carolina cried. 'I wish. What a joker you are, George. Maybe I work for some people who are, but I'm sure not. And you know very well that the reason Roxie and Antonio come up is because I'm so damned busy.'

George grinned. 'Yeah, I know, Carolina,' he said. 'You know I'm only kidding. But you were a go-getter from day one. That I know.'

'Have to be in this town,' Carolina replied.

'You can say that again,' George responded. 'It's do or die.'

'Well, I'm going to go *do*,' Carolina said with a laugh. She headed toward the door with her giant bundle and then turned and blew George a kiss. 'See you soon, George, and thanks again.'

He waved a hand, indicating it was nothing. 'See you later, beautiful. And don't be such a stranger.'

Carolina headed down the sidewalk, immensely pleased with this last-minute alteration for Lydia's party. It was just the sort of find that made all the difference. She stopped to eye some promising-looking lilies, but decided against them, as they were a trifle ordinary, something her shop, though small, most definitely was not. She made several stops, purchasing flowers and greens and placing

18

orders for various arrangement supplies she knew the shop was running low on, all the while chatting with the various vendors, catching up on their lives and sharing bits and pieces of her own.

When at last she was finished, she grabbed a taxi and headed the short distance down and across town. She felt a fleeting moment of sadness overcome her. Here in this marketplace was a part of her past that could never be retrieved. She was not the tall, skinny kid who'd forced herself to fearlessly flirt with all the Georges, cajoling them into making her better deals or giving her dibs on their prize flowers. Nor were they the same. All that handsome olive-skinned muscle had gone soft. Jet-black hair was now gone gray. Most of them had sons, but they'd gone into other businesses, leaving only a remnant of the new generation to take over the reins. And it was no wonder. The future looked bleak for the flower wholesalers. A lot of them had already shut down, and more were abandoning the ranks, their businesses ruined by the cheap flowers being imported from South American countries, particularly Colombia. These flowers were flooding the city, skipping the wholesalers and going directly to the retailers, whether full-fledged flower shops or the Korean greengrocers that were sprinkled about every neighborhood.

As the taxi crawled through the bumper-to-bumper traffic, she realized for the first time that an era had drawn to a close. She felt a profound sense of loss – for a time gone by, for her own lost youth. Then the sadness suddenly felt more like loneliness.

What's wrong with me? she wondered. *I should be the happiest woman in the world. I am the happiest woman in the world most of the time. I have a loving, wonderful husband, even if he is out of town half the time, and a wonderful, well-adjusted son. I have a business that's going great guns, a great loft in the city, and a charming house in the country. So why do I feel sad and lonely?*

She shook her head as if to clear it of sticky cobwebs. *Perhaps,* she thought, *it's just that I miss Lyon and that we've seen so little of each other lately.* She wondered anew at his distant, inattentive behavior. Had it grown more removed lately? Yes, she decided, there was little doubt about it. Lyon had been spending longer and longer periods of time away. Worse, he wasn't as interested in her when he could finally get home. There'd been too many nights in the last couple of years when he'd wanted to go straight to sleep, ignoring her obvious advances.

Is it because of his age? she wondered. *Or is it* mine? She worked very hard to keep herself slim and fit, and she knew that she certainly still attracted men. But she also knew that she wasn't eighteen anymore. She sighed again, unhappily perplexed by this change in her husband.

Looking out the taxi window at the crowded streets, she asked herself, *Where's the magic gone?*

3

Carolina paused outside her Ninth Avenue shop's window to view the new display. She'd finished it yesterday and wanted to make certain that the window was as eye-catching as she'd hoped. She'd taken everything out of the display case except the one flower arrangement she wanted to feature, placing it in the center of the window on a small draped kilim rug. Overhead, a diffuse floodlight was aimed at it, washing over it night and day. The display area itself – the backdrop and the field upon which the rug and vase of flowers sat – was covered in black velvet.

Studying the display with a fresh and sharply honed critical eye, she reassured herself that the flower arrangement was as elegant as she'd thought. The large vase was virtually obscured by the enormous bunch of various flowers and assorted greens that it held. There were fat white and pink peonies and full-blown pink roses, luscious red poppies and sepia hydrangeas, uncommon pink geraniums, wildly striped and shaggy parrot tulips, regal lilies, and long stems of tiny Rothschild orchids, among several others, all capped off by a glorious dark orange fritillaria.

Not content to stop with the flowers and greens, Carolina had placed realistically painted insects, made of wood, paper, and wire, among the blossoms. A black-spotted butterfly, with its burnt orange, brown, and white, seemed to hover at a peony, and a dragon-fly appeared to have paused midflight on a hydrangea's leaf. An observant grasshopper perched on a grapevine. At the foot of the vase sat a small blue-and-white delft bowl full of dark red fresh cherries, and a beautiful bird, feathered in reds and whites and blacks, pecked at them with its long beak. Strewn about the kilim were a few pieces of fresh fruit – lemons, pears, and peaches – ripe and succulent, begging to be eaten, some still on the stem.

Carolina couldn't help but feel pleased with her handiwork. The window was sure to excite the attention of passersby. *God knows*, she thought, *I worked on it hard enough.*

Over the years, her windows had become a destination in New York City. Not quite so famous as the Christmas windows at stores like Tiffany, Barneys, Lord & Taylor, or Bergdorf Goodman, but Carolina's were beginning to draw curious people from all over the city, many going out of their way to stop by and see what magic she'd wrought. She had grown accustomed to newspaper and maga-zine photographers coming by to take pictures. Even the major networks had sent cameramen down to get footage for their local news segments. The window display had always been important to her – it was the face of the shop, after all – and her passion for making it interesting had translated into free publicity for the shop and an untold number of customers.

She took one last look at the tableau, remembering when the idea for it had initially occurred to her. The inspiration had come several months ago when she was traveling with Lyon and Richie. She'd been traipsing through room after room at the Rijksmuseum in Amsterdam. As she had many times before, she was admiring some of the Dutch and Flemish Old Master paintings of flowers and fruit.

Back in New York, she'd beefed up her collection of art books, adding several devoted to the Dutch and Flemish Old Masters. Flipping through one of them on a lazy Sunday, the idea recurred. It had seemed both brilliant and simple at the time: Why not create arrangements similar to those of the paintings? Countless floral decorators over the years must have had the same idea, she'd thought, but nobody in New York that she knew of was currently doing anything even close. She'd immediately run out to the market and bought lots of fruit, rifled through the shop's refrigerators for suitable flowers and greens, and found insects and birds in various shops and among her own Christmas tree decorations. The kilim had come out of her own dressing room at home, and the delft bowl had been borrowed from a console where it was filled with potpourri.

Creating the arrangements was time consuming but relatively easy, and the results were truly magnificent. Antonio had photographed several of the completed tableaux for Carolina's portfolio, a growing body of work that she always kept on hand for customers. She'd sensed that these arrangements would appeal to some of her well-heeled clientele, and she was being proved correct. In fact, several of these arrangements would be used at the party she was decorating tonight. Predictably, Lydia Carstairs, who was probably her wealthiest client, had fallen in love with them.

Her hand was on the doorknob when a reflection from the window caught her eye. Light struck the glass at a certain angle, and she saw a small but noticeable area of it that was dull, in this case because it was dirty.

'Damn,' she said to herself. 'This is inexcusable. Absolutely inexcusable.'

With that, she opened the door, setting off a loud tinkling of goat bells she'd brought back from a trip to Greece, and marched into the shop, the huge bundle of Sterling Silver roses still in her arms.

'Oh, look what the cat's dragged in,' Roxie said with delight from

23

behind the counter. She was busy poking flowers into a vase, and there was a huge smile on her golden cocoa face. Holding a long-stemmed French lilac in the air, she made a show of looking at her watch. 'Why, it's almost seven o'clock. I'm so glad you could come help us.'

Carolina looked at Roxie quizzically. 'Where's Antonio?' she asked.

Roxie nodded toward the back of the shop with her head. 'Talking to somebody on the telephone,' she said with a lift of her eyebrows.

Carolina saw him then, remote receiver in hand, his back turned to her. She could see that he was whispering with his hand held over the receiver, as if speaking with a conspirator. He seemed to be on the telephone an awful lot lately. That or spending an inordinate amount of time flirting with the shop's most beautiful young female customers. *Oh, well*, she thought, *never mind*. He was doubtless an asset to the shop. His sexy macho appeal and dark good looks drew women like flies, many of whom had become regulars just so they could see Antonio. Plus, he had been a faithful employee all these years.

She put the big bunch of roses down on a worktable behind the cashier's counter and set her carryall down alongside it.

'What did you get at the market?' Antonio asked, coming up behind her. He sat down on the stool at his worktable, picked up his knife, and began deftly making long slits in thick rose stems. These cuts would enable the flowers to better drink their water. 'I thought we had everything we needed.'

'Whose turn was it to clean the display window this morning?' Carolina said calmly, ignoring Antonio's question.

'Mine,' Antonio replied, continuing his work without looking at her.

'Then stop what you're doing and please go clean it again,' Carolina said. 'I want it shining. And I do mean *shining*.'

'But I just told you I cleaned it already,' Antonio protested.

'No, you didn't,' Carolina said firmly. 'You cleaned ninety-five percent of it, and that's not good enough.'

24

'Yes, ma'am!' he said, snapping his hand in a salute to her. He looked miffed for a moment, his black eyes flashing angrily, but he immediately put down his knife, slid off his work stool, and went in the back of the shop to get the Windex and paper towels for spot-cleaning. He knew that Carolina didn't make unreasonable demands, and he also knew that if she wanted the window cleaned again, there was a reason. He must have missed a spot.

'Who's he always talking to?' she asked Roxie.

'I don't know,' she answered. 'Some new girlfriend, I guess.'

'How's it going with the party preparations?' Carolina asked.

'Fine,' Roxie replied. 'We'll be ready in plenty of time for the party. I've even got a group of small bouquets ready to put out in the sidewalk rack.'

'Oh, great,' Carolina said, going over to one of the refrigerators to have a look. On a shelf sat several large metal buckets filled with small bouquets in transparent sleeves, each tied with a colorful bow. She smiled with satisfaction. These small bouquets made for the sidewalk, though relatively inexpensive, had carried the shop through lean times after she'd first opened it, and she'd never stopped making them up and putting them outside, except in severest weather. They were time consuming to produce, but her markup was high. Most of New York's very successful florists wouldn't stoop to making such small, inexpensive bouquets for a mass audience, regardless of the potential profits. Carolina, however, had no such snobbish prejudices. It may be like selling penny candy, she'd often told Roxie, but pennies add up to dollars.

She loved to watch them being snapped up in the late afternoon by business people on their way home from work, usually taking them to a husband or wife or lover. Later, customers stopped by on their way to dinner parties. The bouquets provided a quick and easy solution for a host or hostess gift. On special occasions, such as a recent Mother's Day, they could hardly make them fast enough to keep up with the demand. They would start the day before, the three of them – sometimes joined by a talented part-timer or two helping out – and work incessantly, making the bouquets, securing them with rubber bands, and then wrapping them in sleeves.

The bells on the door rang, and she looked around, expecting to see Antonio. However, it was Seth Foster, resplendent in what appeared to be a custom-made suit and shoes shined to a high gloss. His neatly cut hair was brushed slickly back, and he sported a healthy tan. In one hand, he carried an expensive-looking leather briefcase.

'Hi, Seth,' Carolina called out to him. *How well put together he always is*, she thought, *and . . . well, good-looking, too.* He was a regular customer, although he didn't come into the shop more than once or twice a month. When he did, however, he usually spent quite a bit of money. More important, he was responsible for her introduction to Lydia Carstairs, the well-known society matron for whom she was decorating tonight.

'Hi,' Seth said, revealing even white teeth when he smiled warmly. *She looks ravishing*, he thought. *Even at seven o'clock in the morning.* 'Hope I'm not bothering you, but I saw Antonio outside cleaning the window and he said I could come on in and place an order. I know it's early and you're not open yet, but—'

'Anytime I'm here,' Carolina said, 'the shop is open for business.' She smiled up at him, and their eyes met. He held her gaze, and she suddenly felt unnerved, as if her heart had skipped a beat. 'W-what can we do for you?' she stammered, feeling a blush rise to her cheeks. *How silly*, she thought. *Why does he have this effect on me? I guess it's his money and social connections and sophistication. Yes*, she told herself, *that must be it.*

'I want to send some flowers,' he replied in his easy manner. 'I have the name and address written down here.' He fished around in his jacket pocket for a moment before producing a small calling card that he handed to Carolina.

She glanced down at it. His name was engraved in thick black script on the heavy ivory vellum: E. William Seth Foster III. She turned the card over and another name with an address was written in black ink: Ms Payton Fitzsimmons, 2 East 77th Street, Apt. 15A. Carolina almost gasped aloud when she saw the name.

I'll be damned, she thought. *Payton Fitzsimmons. He knows them all. Another social column name. Another beautiful heiress to another great fortune who spends more on clothes in a year than I'll make in my lifetime.* But Payton Fitzsimmons wasn't just any young, beautiful, rich socialite. For hadn't it been only a couple of weeks ago that Carolina had heard the news? That the bored Ms Fitzsimmons – like so many of contemporary Manhattan's trust-fund babies who didn't have to get a job – had decided to roll up her silk shirtsleeves and go to work. And as a floral decorator and party planner, no less.

She's the enemy, Carolina couldn't help thinking. *Or soon will be.* After all, they were aiming for the same customer base – Manhattan's richest and most social – and Payton Fitzsimmons was part of that very group. A card-carrying blue blood who, like Seth Foster, knew everybody who was anybody. *I won't mention anything to him*, she thought, *or ask him about it. That would be prying. Besides, he has come to me for flowers, and he is one of my best customers.*

Carolina stifled a grimace and looked back up at Seth with a smile. 'We'll have to have the telephone number,' she said, 'to make certain someone will be there to accept the flowers.'

'That shouldn't be a problem,' Seth replied in his mellifluous voice. 'They can be left with the doorman.'

'You know we always take the telephone number in case the person is out of town or something,' Carolina said. 'We don't want the flowers to wither and die in a package room while someone's gone.'

'She'll definitely be there,' Seth said with a knowing smile, 'and I want this to be a surprise. So I don't want her to be alerted to it by a phone call.'

'Oh, I see,' Carolina said. 'Okay. In that case we won't call first.'

She decided not to persist about the telephone number, but in her experience the people who were *definitely* going to be there to receive the flowers were sometimes unexpectedly called away or had a last-minute change of plans, the result being a very brown and very dead bouquet to greet them on their return. 'Did you have something particular in mind?' she asked.

The bells rang at the door, and Carolina glanced over at it. Antonio was coming back inside, the Windex and roll of paper towels in hand.

'I'm not sure,' Seth said. 'I thought I'd see what you've got and go from there.'

'Smart man,' Carolina said. 'Why don't we have a look in the cooler, and you can decide. There are some beautiful lilies in different colors and lots of roses. Lilacs. Fabulous tulips. Alliums. Orchids. Lots and lots of things. I guess you don't want us to arrange them?'

'No,' Seth replied, following her to the cooler. 'Just a big bunch of flowers – then she can do whatever she wants with them.'

He's of the old school, she thought appreciatively. *Some people thought that sending an arrangement implied that the recipient was incapable of arranging them herself.*

There was a frown of concentration on his face as he studied the plethora of flowers in the cooler; then he turned to her. 'I think those huge roses,' he said. 'The pale pink ones. They're really extra-ordinary.'

'They are beautiful, aren't they?' Carolina replied. She slid the cooler door open and reached in with both hands to take the roses out. The container was heavy, and as she heaved it out, she brushed against his jacket sleeve. Without warning, that fluttery feeling of being unnerved swept over her again, and she felt a blush rise to her face.

'Oh, Seth, I-I'm s-so sorry,' she stuttered, setting the container on the counter. 'I didn't hurt—?'

He jerked back a step and looked at her as if he'd been scalded. 'You're a very dangerous woman, aren't you?' he said. Then he laughed. 'Of course I'm not hurt.' *She looks genuinely concerned*, he thought. *As if she honestly cares about my well-being. How refreshing. Why can't Payton be more like that?*

'I am sorry,' Carolina said again. 'I'm not usually such a klutz.'

'Those things must weigh a lot,' he replied. 'I should've gotten it out for you.'

'Oh, I'm used to it,' she said, waving her hand airily. 'Now, how many do you want to send?'

'Oh . . . say about three dozen.'

'Fine,' Carolina said. 'We'll send them uptown the first thing this morning. Is that okay?' Out of the corner of her eye, she noticed that Antonio had picked up Seth's card and was looking it over.

'That's perfect,' Seth replied. He set his briefcase down and extracted a black alligator wallet from his trousers. Flipping it open, he pulled out an American Express card and handed it to Carolina.

Platinum, of course, she thought. 'Thanks, Seth,' she said, smiling up at him. 'I'll just be a moment.'

'Take your time,' he said, returning her smile.

Carolina processed his card and then handed him the receipt to sign. He took it from her, and their hands touched. In that instant, she felt a sudden self-consciousness. 'Do y-you want to enclose a card?' she asked, feeling the heat of a blush rising up her neck to her face.

'Oh, yes,' he said, observing her closely, aware that his touch had made her somehow uncomfortable.

He cleared his throat. 'Glad you mentioned it.' He folded up the receipt and put it in his wallet.

'Plain or something else?' she asked.

'Plain, please, if you have it,' he said. 'I forgot to bring a card with me.'

Carolina retrieved a small plain ecru card and envelope from a rack on the counter and handed it to him. 'There,' she said. 'How's that?'

'Fine, thanks, Carolina,' he said. He took a pen from his jacket's inside breast pocket and wrote a quick note on the card. He put Payton's name on the envelope, then put the card inside, and sealed it. 'There you go,' he said. 'And thanks a lot, Carolina.'

'Thank you, Seth,' she replied. 'We'll make sure that she gets them this morning.'

'That would really be great,' he said. 'I'll get out of your way now. I know you're busy.' He hesitated a moment, as if he didn't want to leave quite yet, but then he reached down and picked up his brief-case and headed toward the door. 'Thanks again.'

'I'll see you later,' Carolina said.

'Bye,' he said, waving when he reached the door. The bells jangled as he left the shop.

'Well, well, well,' Roxie piped up from the work area, 'that's a good way to start the day. A quick few hundred bucks' worth of roses before opening time.'

'Yes, it is,' Carolina agreed. 'I wish every day were like that.' She looked back into the work area. 'Thanks for doing the window, Antonio,' she said. She saw that he still had Seth's business card in his hand.

'You were right,' Antonio said. 'I'm sorry I missed a spot.'

'Don't lose that calling card,' she said. 'He wrote the address of the first delivery of the day on it. What's the fascination with it, anyway?' she asked.

'Nothing,' he replied. 'It's just that I've seen pictures of this Payton Fitzsimmons, that's all. She's one hot chick, and rich to boot.'

'Well, you may get to see the lady in person,' Carolina said. 'Because you're going to be taking flowers to her this morning.'

'Cool,' Antonio said, flipping the card onto his worktable.

'Oh, and please try to keep that window shining,' Carolina said. 'It's like I've told you a thousand times – that window is the face we show the world, and we don't want it to be dirty.'

'No,' Antonio said with defiance in his voice. 'We want it scrubbed and bright and shiny like Mr Moneybags Foster, don't we?'

'He's always perfectly groomed, isn't he?' Carolina said.

'And perfectly divine, if you ask me,' Roxie said. 'I can see why you blush like a girl when he comes in,' she added.

'Who, me?' Carolina asked in surprise, looking over at Roxie. She unwrapped the bunch of Sterling Silver roses and got a knife to start cleaning them.

'Yes, you,' Roxie replied. 'You start blushing and get nervous every time he walks through that door.'

'You're crazy!' Carolina exclaimed. 'I'm a happily married woman, for God's sake.'

'You're probably upset because he's sending flowers to a hot rich uptown babe,' Antonio said.

'You're crazy, too,' Carolina said, slipping on her work gloves. Why should I care if he sends flowers to half the women in Manhattan?'

'You care,' Antonio said. 'It's obvious. And he's got the hots for you, too.'

'He is *not* interested in me,' Carolina said firmly.

'Ha!' Roxie said. 'You must be wearing blinders, girl. He's always a little nervous around you.'

'Roxie!' Carolina exclaimed. 'That is such crap.' She sliced several inches off the bottom of the roses with a resounding thump against the cutting board and then began making slices up the middle of each stem.

'No, it's not,' she replied. 'I ask you. Why would a busy man like Seth Foster, who can pick up the telephone and order whatever he wants and have it sent wherever he wants, bother to go out of his way to come into this shop?' She stood, arms akimbo, staring at Carolina.

'She hit the nail on the head,' Antonio said. 'Him? Trust me. He's

31

so glad to see you when he comes in here he can hardly keep it in his pants.'

Roxie and Carolina both laughed. 'You are so bad, Antonio,' Carolina said.

'Yeah, well, there's definitely more than a little tension in the air,' Roxie said.

'You're both crazier than I thought,' Carolina said without looking up from her work. 'Seth Foster's a very nice guy, and that's that.' She continued cutting flowers, hoping they would drop this line of conversation. She was happily married with a teenage son, and Seth knew it.

'You're the one who's crazy,' Roxie said. 'He's a very sexy man.'

'Yeah,' Antonio agreed. 'Plus, he's a real sharp dresser. Isn't he, Roxie?'

She nodded in agreement as she positioned a full-blown peony in the arrangement she was making. 'I think he has real class.'

'I don't care what either one of you think,' Carolina said.

'Jesus, Carolina!' Antonio exclaimed. 'If it wasn't for Seth Foster, we wouldn't be decorating for this party tonight.'

'I know,' she assented. 'But it was sort of an accident. Lydia Carstairs just happened to be at the wedding party Seth had when his mother was remarried. And Seth just happened to ask me to do the flowers. That was only the second or third time he'd ever been in the shop.'

'I remember he'd just moved into the neighborhood,' Roxie said.

'That's another thing,' Carolina said, curiosity on her face. 'Why on earth does he live in Chelsea? Doesn't he belong on the Upper East Side with all his stuffy society friends?'

'Ewwww,' Antonio said. 'You are being nasty, and you know there's no one neighborhood for society people anymore. Lots of uptown people have moved downtown and vice versa.'

'That's true,' Carolina said. 'But I still wonder what drew him down here among us more common folk and why he doesn't live uptown with his rich friends. Which reminds me. Antonio, drop whatever you're working on and get three dozen of those big beauties' – she pointed at the pale pink roses Seth Foster had selected – 'ready to deliver. Then I want you to shoot uptown with them. Make his rich playmate's day.'

'Huh,' Antonio grunted. 'I could use a playmate like that. A total babe. And rich. The combination is perfecto.' He put down his knife and brought the huge bucket of roses to his worktable, where he started choosing the most beautiful of them to take uptown. He worked very quickly and efficiently.

'How on earth could you ever afford her?' Roxie asked.

'Maybe she'd think I was so hot she'd take care of me,' Antonio countered. 'It could happen, you know.'

'Yes, and I could wake up tomorrow morning and be a billionaire,' Roxie said.

'Stranger things have happened,' Antonio said. 'I sure wouldn't mind a few free weekends at one of her houses. Palm Beach. Southampton. Places like that. I could soak up some sun. Some gin. And some major action.'

'You'd be bored silly,' Carolina said, although she knew that a lot of rich women out there would pay to have Antonio around. He was of average height, around five feet ten inches, darkly handsome, with black hair and dark eyes, and powerfully built. He was always well dressed, and he could also be charming when he wanted to be, which was one of the reasons she'd hired him, aside from the fact that he had a passion for flowers. She often thought that his interest in flowers accounted for his frequently sharp tongue and macho posturing. It certainly was not an interest shared by most of the Hispanic boys he'd grown up with.

'Oh, I think I could get used to being bored with somebody like her,' Antonio said. 'But I guess Seth Foster's beat me to her.'

'Her and about a dozen others, if you believe the social columns,' Roxie said.

'See?' Carolina exclaimed. 'You two talk about how nice he is and all that, but Seth sounds like he might be a real womanizer.'

'Oh, for God's sake, Carolina,' Roxie replied, 'just because he's seen going out with different women doesn't mean he's some kind of creepy womanizer.'

'Maybe not,' Carolina said, 'but he could be a real smoothie, a love-'em-and-leave-'em type.' She looked over at Antonio. 'No greens with those roses at all, Antonio. None. People like Payton Fitzsimmons don't like that. Just wrap them in that pale pink tissue, then put them in a transparent sleeve, and tie it up with an extravagant pink bow. And don't forget to attach the card.'

'No problema,' Antonio replied jokingly.

'Then hurry back here,' Carolina went on. 'It's going to be a busy day. We're all going to head uptown to Lydia Carstairs's about five o'clock. We've got to place the flowers properly and touch up any damage. I want to make sure everything looks perfect.'

'So we're closing up early?' Roxie asked.

'No,' Carolina said with a shake of her head. 'Mercedes has offered to come over to watch the shop. She'll be here about four-thirty or so.'

'Mercedes!' Roxie exclaimed.

'Yes, Mercedes,' Carolina said.

'Jeez, Roxie!' Antonio said. 'What's wrong? You like good-looking men, but you don't like beautiful chicks? Afraid of the competition or something?' He stapled the sleeve closed over the roses and then tied the big pink bow with a flourish.

Roxie took a deep breath. Antonio didn't know how close to home he'd hit. Ever since Roxie had begun dating Leland Mountcastle, Lyon's younger brother, Mercedes had been a thorn in her side. Needling her about little things every time they came into contact, especially behind other people's backs. As far as Roxie was concerned, there was no doubt that Mercedes was resentful of her relationship with Leland, if not downright jealous. She knew that

Leland and Mercedes had dated a few times some years back, but Leland assured her it had amounted to nothing more than a few dinners. The situation was further complicated by Mercedes being a friend and neighbor of Carolina's. Roxie didn't feel at liberty to discuss her true feelings about Mercedes with Carolina. She didn't want to put Carolina in the middle.

'I don't know what you mean by that,' she replied to Antonio. 'I'm just surprised that she's helping out, that's all. I thought she was busy on some kind of project or other.'

'She is,' Carolina said, 'but she offered to help out when I told her what was going on. So I said yes, why not? She's helped out before. Besides, she's extremely stylish and very beautiful to look at, and you know how that can draw in customers.'

'She chain-smokes those awful cigarettes,' Roxie said, twitching her nose.

'I've asked her to step outside or in the back to smoke,' Carolina said. 'And she'll use some of that Floris room spray to get rid of the odor.'

'Her perfume makes me so horny she could smoke cigars and it wouldn't bother me,' Antonio said.

'Antonio,' Carolina said, looking at him. 'Get uptown. And fast. Then get back here, even faster.'

'I'm on my way,' he said, but before he could get out the door, old Mrs King came in with Mrs Bevacqua.

'Oh, Antonio,' Mrs King said, 'how are you?'

'Fine,' he said politely, eyeing her with suspicion.

'We're on our way to the church, Antonio,' Mrs Bevacqua chimed in. 'Would you part with just a few flowers for Our Lady? Just a little something.'

Antonio glared at them, but before he could answer, Carolina called to them from behind the counter, where she was practically hidden by flowers, 'Back here, ladies. Antonio, you run on. I'll take care of them.' She could almost see smoke coming out of Antonio's ears. He had grown to despise these neighborhood ladies who stopped by every week wanting free flowers for the church, and although she'd told him repeatedly that it was good free publicity to give them what they wanted – and more – he bristled nevertheless.

He turned and came back to the counter to get the flowers and leave.

'The package looks gorgeous,' Carolina said. 'Simple but elegant. You've put them together and wrapped them perfectly.'

'Thank you, madam,' Antonio said, bowing dramatically. He swept out of the shop with the huge bundle of roses on an arm, casting a sidelong glance of disdain at the two elderly ladies. The bells on the door jingled as he closed it behind him.

'What can I get you today?' Carolina asked them when they'd finally shuffled to the counter.

'Oh, anything, Carolina,' Mrs Bevacqua said. 'You're such a dear.'

'The Holy Mother will bless you,' Mrs King said. 'You're always so kind, Carolina.'

Carolina quickly gathered up several different kinds of chrysanthemums, some irises and greenery, sleeved them, and put a ribbon around it. 'Here you go,' she said.

'God bless you,' Mrs Bevacqua said. 'God bless you.'

'I don't know what we'd do without you,' Mrs King added.

The two of them shuffled back to the door, turned and waved, and then left the shop, their prize in hand.

'Those two come in like clockwork,' Roxie said.

'Ever since I first opened my door,' Carolina said with a laugh.

'They know a sucker when they see one,' Roxie said. 'Do you think you've ever made a sell because of them?'

'I don't have the faintest idea,' Carolina said, 'but what have I got to lose? A handful of flowers, that's all. So what does it matter if it makes them happy?'

Antonio approached the uniformed doorman at 2 East Seventy-seventh Street, the huge bundle of roses in hand. 'I have flowers for Ms Payton Fitzsimmons,' he said.

'You can leave them in the package room,' the doorman said, swinging the lobby door open. 'It's to your left just inside the lobby.'

'I can't do that,' Antonio protested. 'I have strict instructions from the sender that they must be taken to her apartment.'

'Well, we have instructions that gifts are to be left in the package room,' the unflappable doorman replied.

'You are going to have a very unhappy tenant,' Antonio said, 'and a very unhappy boyfriend on your hands. Seth Foster. He told me in no uncertain terms to hand these to her personally.'

The doorman's ears perked up when Antonio used Seth's name. 'Here,' he said, letting the lobby door swing shut. 'Wait a moment while I call upstairs,' he said.

He turned away from Antonio and dialed a number on the inhouse telephone. Antonio's eyes hungrily swept the vast marble-and-mahogany expanse of the lobby. There were expensive-looking Oriental carpets on the floor and fancy gilded consoles over which were hung ornate gold-framed mirrors. In a seating area, silk-covered sofas and chairs were grouped around coffee tables with flower arrangements. A crystal chandelier hung from the coffered ceiling, and its light was reflected in the mirrors. Every surface was pristine, as if the lobby and its contents were polished every night so that the inhabitants of this extravagant building would never have to see a speck of dust.

Jesus, he thought. *It must cost a fortune to live in a place like this.* He'd seen a lot of fancy places while delivering flowers, but this was one of the nicest.

'You may take them up,' the doorman said, turning to him. 'Apartment Fifteen A. The service elevator straight ahead and to your left.' He indicated the direction with a nod of his head.

'Thanks,' Antonio said. He pressed the button for the service elevator and entered the car when it arrived. When he stepped out on the fifteenth floor, he was in a vestibule with two doors. A and B. *Damn*, he thought. *Only two apartments to a floor. They must be huge.*

He walked to the mahogany door with its highly polished brass *A* and pressed the shiny button for the bell. After a moment the door was opened by the stunning woman whose picture he'd seen in the newspapers many times. Payton Fitzsimmons in the flesh. And more beautiful in person than in her pictures, if that was possible. Long blond hair. Cool blue eyes. A nice tan. And she looked like she had a great body beneath the pale pink silk robe that was tied loosely about her waist. Her feet, he noticed, were bare.

'Hi. I'm from Carolina,' Antonio said. 'The florist. I have flowers for you.'

'Hi there,' she said, looking him up and down. 'Come in, won't you?' *No wonder Carolina does so well*, she thought. *With a stud like him working for her she must have all the women in Manhattan ordering from her.*

'Sure,' Antonio said as he stepped confidently across the threshold.

'I'll run and get a vase for those,' Payton said, 'if you don't mind waiting a minute. Okay?'

'I don't mind at all.'

'Just take a seat,' she said, her eyes trailing up and down his muscular body again. She swept her hand about the vast hall. 'Sit anywhere you like.'

'Thanks,' he said.

He watched as she crossed the gleaming inlaid wooden floor of the entrance hall and disappeared into a room off to her right. In the center of the hall was a large round table, and placed on it was a mammoth orchid plant with dozens of blooms. *A thousand bucks, easy*, he thought. *For one plant.* From his vantage point, he could clearly see into two vast drawing rooms, both furnished with ornate chairs, sofas, and tables and decorated with what looked like very expensive paintings. The palette was pale and cool – *like Payton*, he thought – with a few dabs of hot, spicy color here and there that drew his attention. *Maybe like Payton, too.*

She sashayed back into the entrance hall, empty-handed. 'Do you mind?' she asked. 'The vase I want to use is so heavy I can hardly pick it up. Could you help me with it?'

'I'd be glad to,' Antonio said.

'Sure you have the time?'

'I've got all the time in the world,' he replied.

'Good,' she cooed. She beckoned to him with one long slender finger. 'This way.'

Antonio put an extra degree of macho in his strut as he followed her down a hallway and into a large butler's pantry. It had floor-to-ceiling mahogany cabinets and shelves with marble counters for workspace.

'It's the big lead crystal one up there,' she said, pointing toward a neoclassically shaped vase on a shelf.

Antonio put the flowers down on a counter and reached up for the vase, easily taking it down and setting it beside a sink. When he turned around, he could see that she was staring at his body. There was a blatantly appreciative and greedy look in her eye.

'You're so strong,' she said. 'You lifted that as if it were made of paper.' *God*, she thought. *He exudes sex from every pore.*

'Want me to fill it with water?' he asked.

'Oh, that would be great,' she said. 'You see, all the help's out running errands, so I'm all alone.' There was innuendo in her voice that any red-blooded male would have immediately picked up on.

Antonio filled the vase with water and then turned to her. 'I'll put the flowers in it for you, if you'd like.'

She nodded. 'I would like,' she said.

She watched as he untied the ribbon and took out the card inside. He handed it to her, and she opened the envelope, read the card, and tossed it down on the counter, her eyes immediately returning to Antonio as he took the enormous bunch of roses out of their sleeve and slipped them into the vase.

'Perfect,' she said as he shifted stems this way and that, positioning them so that they were seen at their best advantage.

'Where do you want it?' he asked.

'Oh, follow me,' she said.

They went down another hallway and then into a huge bedroom decorated in several shades of white. Its primary feature was an enormous canopied bed hung with lace and silk. She pointed to a silk-draped table on one side of the bed. 'Over there, I think,' she said, a fingernail thoughtfully poised at her lips.

Antonio placed the vase where she'd pointed and then turned it in place, making certain that the roses looked their best. He stepped back against the bed to get a different view and nodded to himself. 'How's that?' he asked her.

She walked over to him. 'I think they're perfect,' she said. 'Absolutely perfect.' The silk rope about her waist had come undone, and her robe had fallen open, revealing the luscious tanned cleavage of ample breasts.

Antonio stared at them and unconsciously licked his lips. *God, is she built!* he thought. *And oh, sweet Jesus, would I love some of that.*

Payton's lips parted in a smile, and she reached a hand up inside her robe, apparently in an effort to adjust a strap on her nearly sheer gown. Antonio watched as even more cleavage was exposed; then he almost groaned aloud when a nipple appeared above the gown. In another moment her hand slipped inside his shirt, tugging him to her.

Stepping forward, he placed his muscular arms about her waist and then slid them down onto her rounded ass. She was silent as their bodies met, staring into his eyes daringly, as if challenging him. Her silence was short-lived, however, for it was only moments before Antonio had buried his warm moist tongue in her breasts and had her moaning in ecstasy.

When he came up for air, she had her head thrown back, and he sought out her neck, kissing and licking and nibbling at it, enjoying the sighs of pleasure that issued from her full sensuous lips. He brought her mouth to his then, plunging his tongue inside, exploring every surface, kissing her hard, feeling the play of her tongue against his, and all the while his hands were everywhere. Brushing across her buttocks, fondling her breasts, reaching down to between her thighs and the treasure that was tucked between them.

'Let's get undressed,' he whispered, pulling back slightly. Without waiting for an answer, he took her robe off, flinging it to the floor, and then helped her out of her gown. When she was completely naked, his eyes drank in her perfect body.

She smiled at him lasciviously and began helping him out of his clothes, anxious to see what promised to be a heavily muscled sex machine. And that's just what she wanted. A well-built stud to fuck her good. When his shirt was off, she couldn't keep her hands off his rock-hard shoulders and arms, feeling the strength that rippled with his every movement. When he'd shed his jeans and stepped out of his jockey shorts, his cock sprang out in front of him, curving slightly upward.

She almost gasped in delight. *So big and thick*, she thought as she went down on her knees, his hands pressing down on her shoulders slightly. She teased him mercilessly, licking the head, then the shaft, then his heavy testicles, before she finally took him in her mouth and began licking and sucking in earnest.

Antonio thought he would explode. He was groaning with pleasure, but wanted this to last a while. Before he let go completely, he pulled her up and led her to the bed, where she spread out, her legs wide in welcome.

He got atop her and began licking her breasts again, thrumming at her nipples with his tongue, a hand sliding down between her thighs, his fingers discovering the wetness there. Excited by her desire, he slid down her body and began tonguing her sweet mound, driving Payton wild. She clutched his curly raven hair, and thrust herself up against his mouth, a series of loud moans escaping her lips.

'Oh, my God,' she rasped breathily. 'Oh, my God, you're going to make me come.'

Antonio immediately withdrew his tongue and then climbed back on top, positioning himself to enter her. Staring into her eyes, he slowly drove his cock inside her, teasing her once again, moving very slowly in and out, until he couldn't hold off any longer and plunged himself in as far as he could.

She screamed and rolled from side to side, her hands on his hips, then rose to meet his thrusts. Antonio moved harder and faster, and she gasped and mewled. Then Payton screamed again as she felt her body convulse. Contractions seized her as she came again and again.

Antonio went mad, riding her as if possessed, but the ride ended almost as quickly as it had begun. He bellowed in ecstasy as his body went rigid and then trembled its full length as he erupted time and again for what seemed to him like an eternity.

He collapsed atop her when he was finally spent, his cock still in her. They gasped for air and clung to one another tightly. Antonio began planting little kisses all over her sweat-slick face, and at last they both broke out into laughs of pure carnal delight.

'You are one hot chick,' he said when he could speak at last.

'And you're one very hot man,' she said. 'Just what the doctor ordered for a boring morning alone at home.'

'I'll be glad to fill your doctor's prescription anytime,' Antonio replied. He rolled off her and slid an arm under her neck, hugging her body next to his. 'Damn! What a way to start the day.'

'You can say that again,' Payton said. 'I haven't had it this good in a long time.'

'What about Seth Foster?' he asked.

'Oh, so you know that I've been dating him,' she said. 'Aren't you well informed?'

'Well, it didn't take a genius to figure it out,' Antonio said. 'I mean, he ordered the flowers from the shop where I work, and I delivered them.'

'Let's don't talk about him right now,' she said, 'and why don't we keep this between the two of us.' She nibbled at his ear playfully. 'It'll be our little secret for now,' she said in a whispery voice.

'Okay,' he said, 'but he orders flowers from the shop a lot.'

'That's going to change,' she said, twirling one of his raven locks in a finger.

'What do you mean?' he asked.

'Oh, I've started a party-planning service myself,' she said. 'And it includes floral service, of course.' She stopped twirling his hair and looked into his eyes. 'From the shop that I've just opened here in the East Seventies.'

Antonio looked surprised for a moment and then grinned. 'I see,' he said. 'So he's going to have to buy his flowers from you in the future.'

She nodded, smiling smugly. 'In fact, I think quite a few of your boss's customers are going to start coming to me,' she said.

'Uh-huh,' Antonio said.

'And I'm going to be needing help,' she went on, running a fingertip across his chest and then down his treasure trail to the joyous toy that lay at its end. 'Interested?'

'I might be,' Antonio said, feeling aroused again. 'Yeah, sure. But what's in it for me?'

'Oh, for one thing, I think you'd be interested in the money,' she said, stroking his cock lightly. 'And nobody can beat the fringe benefits.' Her hand encircled him then, and she slid down on the bed, her tongue out, greedy for more.

5

'I wonder what the devil's taking Antonio so long?' Carolina said, looking at her wristwatch.

'I don't know,' Roxie replied with a marked lack of interest.

Carolina glanced over at her. She knew that something was bothering Roxie, but she decided not to ask. If Roxie wanted to talk, Carolina knew from experience, then talk she would, but not until she was good and ready.

Finally Roxie looked over at Carolina. 'Do you really think Mercedes knows enough about the shop to run things while we're out? I mean, if somebody's here with her, it's one thing, but leaving her alone? I don't know.'

'I do,' Carolina said, nodding. 'There won't be much for her to do. She'll be fine.' She gazed over at her friend and smiled. 'Roxie, I have the powerful suspicion that you're still bothered by Mercedes because she dated Leland a few times. Am I right?'

'No,' she said in an emphatic voice. Then she shrugged and sighed. 'Oh, I guess I am. A little. I know she and Leland had something special going for a while, even if he says otherwise. I guess I'm just a tad paranoid.'

'Come on, Roxie. They're ancient history,' Carolina said. 'I don't think you need to worry about Mercedes. She's lived downstairs from me for a long time, and we've never even had an argument. I know she's a bit of a snob, but she's also very interesting and creative.'

'All I know about her is that her father was some aristocratic painter, and she used to be a model,' Roxie said. 'Leland almost never mentions her, but I hear she's one of those rich upper-class English party girls.'

'Well, I guess Mercedes has a lot of family money to rely on. She has that expensive loft and all, but she's always busy on some project or other and usually makes a success of it.'

'Like what?' Roxie asked.

'Well, for a while she picked up cheap pieces of furniture at the flea market, painted them in wild patterns, and sold the pieces for a lot of money. She'd paint a table in leopard spots and make it look like a million dollars. She designed rugs that were so beautiful they were shown in a gallery. She's had big decorating commissions from people who saw pictures of her loft and wanted one that looked like it. The list goes on and on.'

'I guess she is pretty rich, then,' Roxie said.

'I don't really know,' Carolina said. 'She lives high on the hog, that's for sure, but I don't know whether she gets much alimony or what. I don't think that German count she was married to for a couple of years had much money.'

She looked at her watch and put down her knife. 'Why don't we do our party inventory now?' She opened a large hardbound sketch-book in which she had written up the plans for tonight's party, as she did all parties, regardless of size, and turned to the page where she'd entered the information about Lydia Carstairs. First the date, name of the customer, address, and number of guests was written in, with the names of the guests if supplied. Then she'd carefully sketched in detailed pictures of all the arrangements needed, with little arrows pointing to the kinds of flowers in each bouquet. Finally, she'd drawn and written a careful description of where every arrangement should be placed in the apartment. She saved these workbooks for future reference. Aside from the fact that they refreshed her memory and gave her ideas, she didn't want to accidentally repeat herself at a future date. Nor did she want to suggest or use the same arrangements for a customer who might have been a guest at a party she'd decorated in the past.

'Okay,' Roxie said, putting down her knife and pulling off her gloves.

'We've got two of my huge Old Master arrangements for the entrance hall consoles. Right?'

Roxie nodded. 'Ready to go.'

'In the living room, there're two identical small bunches for the mantelpiece and six small for various tables. Right?'

'Yes,' Roxie said. 'They're ready to go, too.'

'The library,' Carolina said. 'A big one for the center table and four small for other tables.'

'The small ones are done,' Roxie said. 'Antonio wants to do the large one for the center table.'

'Okay,' Carolina said. 'He can start on that when he gets back.' She looked down at her notebook again. 'One small for the powder room.'

'Done,' Roxie said. 'I did it.'

'Four for the master bedroom and two for the bathroom?'

'I'm working on those,' Roxie said.

'Then another four for a guest room, and two for its bathroom.'

'Not done.'

'I'll do them,' Carolina said. She looked back down again. 'What else? Oh, four small arrangements for hallways within the apartment.'

'Done,' Roxie said.

'And last but certainly not least,' Carolina said, 'the dining room.'

'The two huge ones for the sideboard and console are done,' Roxie said. 'That leaves the flowers for the dining table itself.' She smiled and looked at Carolina questioningly. Carolina always left the dining table for last if the flowers were for a dinner party, and she always insisted on doing the arrangement for the table herself.

'I'll start that in a few minutes,' Carolina said. 'That's what I got the Sterling Silver roses for. They'll be perfect on the dining room table, and Lydia Carstairs is going to love them. People don't use them much anymore, so they'll be unexpected.'

'This is going to be a lot of flowers,' Roxie said. 'More than some people use for a wedding.'

Carolina nodded. 'Thirty-five separate arrangements,' she said. 'No. Thirty-six, because I'm going to do two small ones for the dining table. We'll have a lot of last-minute work to do at Lydia's. Oh, don't forget to put three hair dryers in the big carryall, one for each of us. Lydia likes the flowers to be totally open, at the peak of bloom, so we'll use the hair dryers to force any of them that aren't.'

'I told Antonio not to put any of the arrangements in the cooler, so they'd open more out in the shop,' Roxie said.

'That's always a good idea in a case like this,' Carolina said. 'Besides, customers love seeing them out and sometimes want something like them. Now, let's hurry and get the bouquets out on the sidewalk. People are starting to go to work. Some of them want something for their desk or the boss or whoever.'

Together, the two of them carried the wooden holder from the back of the shop out onto the sidewalk in front of the shop. They placed it under the canopy so that the flowers would be in shade, but made certain it didn't obscure the window. Then they placed buckets, each holding ten to twenty individually wrapped bouquets, on the shelves. Each bucket was labeled with a price, ranging from four to twenty dollars.

Back in the shop, Carolina got two blocks of oasis and green tape from a work shelf and retrieved Lydia's sterling silver bowls from the back of the shop where she'd placed them, each one thickly surrounded in bubble wrap. She placed the heavy bowls on her work counter and placed a block of oasis in each one; then she heaved a sigh.

'What is it?' Roxie asked. 'Something wrong?'

'No, not really,' Carolina said. 'I just miss Lyon. He's been gone so much lately.' She began stripping leaves off the Sterling Silver roses. 'Sometimes I feel like we're becoming strangers.'

'Not the two of you?' Roxie said, looking at her with lifted brows. 'You've got the perfect marriage.'

'I know,' Carolina agreed. 'I guess I'm just missing him more than usual. We've spent so little time together lately.'

'I think you ought to consider yourself lucky,' Roxie said. 'At least you and Lyon have a strong marriage. His handsome, wonderful, perfect, and stinking brother is miles away from committing to me.' She laughed.

'How's it been going with you two?' Carolina asked. 'I haven't seen Leland in ages.'

Roxie turned her huge dark eyes on Carolina and smiled. 'Oh, I still worship the ground he walks on,' she said, 'and he treats me like a royal princess.'

'Come on, Roxie,' Carolina said. 'You still sound like something's not right.'

'Why do you say that?' Roxie asked.

'I know how Leland can get,' Carolina said, 'and I know you. I can see that you're not the happiest camper in the world right now. I know you're in love, but it seems to me that that blush you had is gone. Something's going on, isn't it? Did you two have a lover's spat?'

Roxie nodded. 'He – he . . . I mean, I – I don't know what he's up to. I don't think he's seeing another woman. It's not like that, but he's up to something. He's drinking too much, for one thing, and he gets these phone calls at all hours from strangers – always men – then has to leave for meetings with *clients*, as he calls them.' Tears formed in her eyes and coursed down her exquisite high-boned cheeks. She brushed at them with long, beautifully manicured finger-nails. 'Damn it!' she said. 'I don't understand why he doesn't include me in this . . . whatever it is that's going on with him.'

Carolina put her arms around Roxie's thin shoulders. She hugged her and began patting her back. 'Oh, Roxie. My precious Roxie,' she whispered in a voice fraught with worry. 'It's going to be all right.' She felt the young woman's body convulse with strangled sobs and continued holding her, stroking and patting her back.

In her arms, the beauty began to laugh through her tears. She leaned back and looked at Carolina. Her face was wet, but there was a smile on her lips. 'You're . . . you're the best, Carolina,' she said. 'Your brother-in-law can be a real piece of work, but you always make me feel so much better.'

Carolina returned her smile. From the worktable she pulled some tissues out of the box and began to gently brush the tears away from Roxie's face. 'There,' she said. 'You're as beautiful as always.'

'Thank you, Carolina,' Roxie said. 'I'm sorry. I just couldn't help it. I guess it's getting to be too much.' She turned from Carolina, took some more tissues from the box, and then blew her nose. 'I shouldn't let him get to me like this.'

'That's more like it,' Carolina said with a laugh. They parted, and she pulled on her gloves to get to work, secretly wondering how serious the rift between Roxie and Leland was – and what her brother-in-law was up to. While her relationship with Leland had always been amicable over the years, even warm at times, she'd never really trusted him.

Although he was suave and handsome and could be incredibly charming like Lyon, he was also somewhat aimless, impulsive, care-less, and self-centered in her opinion. She didn't think he was necessarily a bad character, but in his thoughtlessness he'd caused a lot of pain and problems for others. And he'd broken more than a few hearts.

When Roxie had first started going out with Leland a few months back, Carolina had kept her fingers crossed, hoping Roxie wouldn't end up like so many of the vulnerable women he'd courted and eventually spurned in the past. Roxie didn't seem to think another woman was involved now, however. So what could it be?

Her reverie was interrupted by the jangle of the telephone. Carolina reached over and picked up the remote.

'Carolina,' she said in a bright, cheerful tone.

'Bad news.'

'Oh, my God, Lyon.' All the cheer went out of her voice. He seldom called her at the shop, making a point of not bothering her when she was at work. That and his greeting made her extremely uneasy. 'What is it? Are you okay? Is something—?'

'No, no,' he said. 'It's nothing like that, Carolina. There's nothing wrong with me, at least nothing that a few days with you wouldn't cure. It's just that they need me here for a few more days.'

'Oh, no,' she said, disappointed. 'I was hoping that you'd be here for Matt's birthday party. It's been such a long time since we've all been together, and I got everything worked out at the shop so we could.'

'I know,' he said, 'but I can't avoid this. There's just no way out.'

'I understand,' she said, although she really didn't. 'Or at least I think I do.'

'I know it's confusing,' Lyon said in an exasperated voice, 'but it's this new management. You know how it goes with these mergers. Somebody new comes in and thinks he's got to shake things up to get better results, and half the time he doesn't have a clue what's going on. I'm having to run some training seminars for the new people. Anyway, I don't know why they're doing things the way they are. I just hope everything gets back to normal soon.'

'I do, too,' Carolina said. 'We've been like ships passing in the night lately. A few days here and there. And Matt's really going to miss you being there.' She forced a cheerful note into her voice. 'I've got an idea. If this keeps up, maybe what we should do is switch cities. We'll move to Amsterdam, and I'll open a shop there.'

Lyon laughed. 'Yeah, in a city swamped with flowers.'

'It was only a joke, silly,' she said.

'I know, and I appreciate your attempt at humor under the circumstances. Listen, I hate to cut this short, but I'd better run. I'm going to meet some of these new management guys for drinks.'

'Okay,' she said. 'I'll let you go. And Lyon?'

'Yes?'

'I miss you, and I love you.'

'I miss you, too, Carolina, and Richie,' he said. 'And I love you both.'

'Bye-bye.'

'Bye, honey. Talk to you again soon.'

She replaced the receiver in its cradle and exhaled a deep sigh. *Damn,* she thought, putting her elbows on her worktable and her chin in her hands. *Richie's going to be disappointed, and Matt's going to be disappointed. But, nobody's going to be as disappointed as I am.*

Lyon hung up the telephone and sat with a frown on his handsome features. *I hate lying to her,* he thought, *but I don't really have any choice right now, do I?* He sighed, knowing that he should tell her the truth. He looked out toward the deck where Monique sat, watching Anja play with one of her favorite dolls. Monique's long blond hair shone in the sunlight. It was so beautiful, he thought. Like all the rest of her. Her long, lithe dancer's body, lean and strong yet sexy. Her big blue eyes, sensuous lips, and perfect complexion. Her youth, so fresh and vibrant.

The doors and windows were open, and he could hear Anja gurgling with delight. He got up and went out to join them.

'Daddy,' Anja said in English, holding up her doll for him to see.

'Oh, she's beautiful,' he said with a smile, and Anja returned her attention to the doll, whose hair she was combing with a little pink plastic comb.

'I'm off,' he said, sitting down on the teak settee next to Monique and sliding an arm around her shoulders.

'Is everything okay?' she asked.

'I think so,' he said with a nod. 'I told her that I was staying here awhile longer.'

'I don't suppose that made her very happy.'

'Well, she's really busy,' Lyon said. 'With her shop and everything.'

'Still . . . ,' Monique said, her voice trailing off into thoughtful silence.

Lyon gave her shoulder a gentle squeeze. 'It's going to be all right, Monique,' he said. 'I know it is. Just give me a little more time.'

'I am,' she said, looking back at him.

He saw the doubt and worry that lay behind her cool, beautiful facade and knew that she needed reassurance. 'Look,' he said, 'this is where I belong now, Monique. I know it, and you *should* know it. You've got to believe me. I'm going to make sure that we can be together all the time. You and me and Anja.'

The little girl looked up at him when she heard her name, all huge eyes and grinning lips. She held the doll up again, her hand rosy and chubby. 'Look, Daddy,' she said again.

'She's beautiful, sweetheart,' he said. 'Just like you.'

Anja giggled and then squeezed the doll to her chest.

He turned to Monique. 'How could I give this up?' he said. 'There's no way I could leave the two of you.'

Monique sighed. 'Maybe so,' she said in a soft voice, 'but I don't have to point out that you have the same thing in New York, Lyon.'

'No, Monique,' he protested quickly. 'It's not like this at all. You don't understand.'

'What don't I understand?' she asked, staring at him quizzically.

53

'It seems clear to me. It's simple really. You have a wife and child there. Here you have a girlfriend – or whatever you want to call me – and a child.'

'No,' he repeated. 'It's . . . it's not the same. Carolina has her work.' He looked as if he were struggling for words. 'She's . . . she's married to it,' he finally said. 'Not me. She'd hardly notice if I was gone. And Richie . . . well, Richie's nearly grown up. He'll be off on his own soon. Don't you see? It's *not* the same.'

Monique looked at him with a serious, knowing expression. 'Maybe it's not quite the same,' she agreed. 'But the only difference in the situations, as I see it, Lyon,' she said in a voice of certainty, 'is that she and your son are acknowledged in the eyes of the law and society. And they're . . . respectable. And me? I'm . . . I'm the other woman. A nobody, a nothing. And Anja? She's—'

'No, Monique,' he said, taking her into his arms and hugging her. 'Stop talking that way. That's not the way it's going to be. I'm going to make it right for us. You'll see. This is going to work out. Believe me. That's what I want. I'm going to fix it. And soon.'

Anja looked up at them; then she got up, dropping her doll on the deck, and toddled over on chubby legs. She hugged her father's knees, pressing her chocolate-haired head against them. 'I love you, Daddy,' she said.

He ruffled her hair with his hand. 'And I love you, too, Anja.'

'Here, Anja,' Monique said, holding out her arms. 'Why don't you come and sit in Mommy's lap for a minute?'

Anja went into her arms, and Monique lifted the girl onto her lap and began brushing her hair out of her eyes.

'I love you, too, Mommy,' Anja said.

Monique hugged her close. 'Oh, and I love you so much, Anja. So very much.'

Lyon leaned across Anja and kissed Monique. 'And I love you,' he said. 'And I'm going to make this right. I promise.'

6

Carolina placed a blue-and-white delft bowl on the marble-topped console and then filled it with ripe red cherries. This was the finishing touch on one of her still-life arrangements inspired by Flemish Old Masters. She took a few steps back, eyed it from a distance of a few feet, and then moved right and left, trying to decide if it was in its proper place in relation to the huge vase of flowers. After carefully observing the tableau, she stepped back to the console and moved the bowl about an inch toward the front of the marble top. She backed up a few steps again, repeating the process until she was satisfied that the picture was well balanced, complete, and pleasing to the eye. It was identical to the arrangement she'd placed on the matching console about twenty feet down the entry hall, and they complemented each other beautifully.

'Yes,' she said to herself, finally satisfied. 'Just right.' She yanked a big yellow dustcloth out of her carryall on the floor and carefully but quickly wiped the console's marble top clean of any debris. She'd already inspected it for any sign of spilled water, an unforgivable sin in a household where any given piece of furniture might have cost as much as a lot of people made in a lifetime.

'Oh, I see you're finished with the entry,' a lady's voice said from behind her. Carolina heard the traces of the soft Southern accent that the woman had retained even after traveling and living all over the globe for decades.

She turned and smiled at Lydia Carstairs, noting that her silvery white hair was perfectly coiffed as usual, her lily-white skin glowed, and her silk gown – an Yves St Laurent creation with a plunging neckline framed with huge white ruffles, ruffled sleeves, and completed with a long black skirt tied with a huge bow – was a testament to the couturier's art. 'Yes, I'm just finishing up,' she said. 'What do you think?'

'My first thought is that I'm awfully grateful to see that you're making sure the consoles are clean,' Lydia Carstairs said with a short laugh. 'That terrible Payton Fitzsimmons left a watermark on a table that was a museum piece worth a quarter of a million dollars. And still had the nerve to charge me for the flowers!'

Carolina winced. She'd heard this story about Payton Fitzsimmons, and found it difficult to believe that the rich social set would still hire her. The young socialite was just starting out in the business – and starting at the very top since she was part of that circle – and Carolina could only assume that her terrible blunders would be overlooked because of who she happened to be. She was glad to hear that Lydia Carstairs, for one, wasn't going to tolerate the spoiled and beautiful heiress's mistakes.

'Now I have to have that miserable bitch sitting at my dinner table,' Lydia went on. 'She'll probably break a cherished wine goblet or something. I don't care who she is. I would never allow her back in my home were it not for Seth.'

Carolina didn't respond other than to nod. She made it a practice never to disparage the competition in front of customers. She thought that it made her appear to be less confident in her own abilities and jealous to boot.

She watched as Lydia took several steps up and down the long entry hall, her high heels resounding on its black-and-white marble floor. Lydia paused to study the two enormous arrangements atop the marble-topped gilt consoles from various angles with a critical eye.

After what seemed to Carolina an unduly long period of inspection, Lydia turned those famous blue eyes on her and nodded. 'There're absolute heaven,' she said, her elegant hands folded in front of her.

Carolina couldn't help but notice the huge rings on Lydia's fingers and the bracelets on her wrists. And the enormous diamond that hung suspended just above her cleavage. They flashed in the light with the least bit of movement, serving as a reminder of the economic gap that separated the two women. As much as they shared an aesthetic sensibility, she thought, their lives couldn't be more different.

Lydia took another turn up and down the entry hall, and as Carolina watched her, she couldn't help but reflect on the older woman's dramatic life. She knew that Lydia had been married three times. At an early age she'd married an adventurous oilman who took her on safaris and endless trips to exotic places. After he was killed in a fiery car crash, she married an Italian noble who actually had a fortune and thus she entered the world of European aristocracy and international society on the highest levels. Shortly after he was killed in a skiing accident near St Moritz's Corviglia Club, she met and married Carstairs, an enormously rich and somewhat crass garment manufacturer and chain-store owner who promptly had a massive coronary. Throughout her three marriages, the beauty from the hills of Kentucky had studied and absorbed the lifestyles of the very rich. Now, having inherited the bulk of three considerable fortunes, she spent her time visiting her equally wealthy friends around the globe, traveling to galas and parties at the drop of a hat, and she entertained on a lavish scale herself.

'Would you come to the butler's pantry with me?' Lydia asked.

'Of course,' Carolina said.

She followed Lydia through the vast apartment, her footsteps soundless on the antique Savonnerie and Aubusson rugs that were spread like rich tapestries on the antique parquet de Versailles floors. On the way she saw Roxie, working quietly in the living room, and Antonio, intent on an arrangement in a hallway. When they finally reached the butler's pantry, which was a large room off the kitchen, Lydia turned to her.

'I want your advice about something,' she said, looking Carolina in the eye.

'My advice?'

Lydia nodded. 'You have impeccable taste, and you're very creative,' she said. 'I wanted to see what you thought about the china for tonight.'

'Sure,' Carolina said, flattered that this paragon of taste would ask for her opinion on anything. She glanced around the big room and was amazed by the cabinets that groaned with silver, china, and crystal. It was more than enough for several households, she thought.

'I keep twenty-seven different sets of china here,' Lydia said, a hand indicating the glass-fronted cabinets that lined the room's walls. 'There used to be more, but I sent some to the other houses or sold them at auction because I found that I was never using them. Anyway, I'm trying to decide between two different sets for tonight and can't make up my mind. Look.' She stepped over to a center island and pointed a perfectly manicured fingernail at two plates, set side by side on the island's marble surface.

Carolina looked down. One of the plates was elaborately painted, primarily in blues and reds that covered its entire surface, and was obviously Imari. The other was equally decorative but entirely different. It had tiny pale pastel flowers sprinkled on a field of creamy white, and the plates were molded in a Baroque fashion with curlicues. Meissen, she thought.

'I think both of these are beautiful,' she said, 'but do you mind if I look at some of your other pieces?'

Lydia looked surprised and then smiled. 'No, of course not.'

Carolina stepped over to the cabinets and began studying the china within. There was something for every conceivable occasion, and she enjoyed seeing the many patterns and colors. She stopped when she saw a set that was decorated with a wide mauve band and a smaller gold one. It was rather formally severe but beautiful.

'What do you think of this, Mrs Carstairs?' she asked. 'It—'

'Lydia, please,' the older woman said.

Carolina could hardly believe her ears. *To think that the lioness of international society is asking me to call her by her first name*, she thought.

Producing an appropriate smile, she said, 'Lydia, then. This set would match the roses I'm doing for the dining table and would tie in with the other arrangements in the room. It would even look fabulous with the murals.'

Lydia Carstairs stepped over and looked. She held a finger at puckered carmine-colored lips and frowned thoughtfully. 'I think . . . Well, I think you're absolutely right,' she said. She looked at Carolina and smiled. 'Yes,' she went on, 'you've found the perfect solution, and I wonder why I didn't think of using these before.'

'You hadn't seen the roses I'm using for the table,' Carolina said, 'or you probably would have.'

'I'm so delighted,' Lydia said. 'I haven't used this set in . . . oh, I don't know. I'll have to look at my planning book – I keep a record of the menus and table settings for all the dinners I have, you know – but it's been a very long time. So some of my guests won't ever have seen them before. Oh, and you know what?'

'What?' Carolina asked.

'My heavy Buccellati sterling will go perfectly with this,' Lydia said, 'and I haven't used that in ages either.' She looked at a clock on the wall. 'Oh, my God. I have to tell Normal right away. The guests will start arriving soon, and he and the maids will have to reset the tables at once.'

'Let me see how Roxie and Antonio are doing,' Carolina said. 'We'll be glad to help, if there's time.'

'Carolina,' Lydia said, 'you're a dreamboat.' She reached over and patted Carolina's cheek. 'That would be wonderful. This dinner tonight is very special and important to me.' She gave Carolina a sly look. 'I'm on the board of the Animal Rescue Mission, so I'm wining and dining some of these new, filthy rich dot-com people, along with some of the old, old money. Some of these people haven't learned how to spend their money yet.'

'So you're going to teach them?'

'Exactly,' Lydia replied. 'And believe me, I'm an expert at it. I'll slather on the charm for the most boring coot alive to get his money for these animals. Now, I must go tell the butler about the changes.'

'I'll check on Roxie and Antonio,' Carolina said. 'We'll meet you in the dining room, or I will at least.'

'Great,' Lydia said, sweeping out of the butler's pantry with the rich swishing of silk.

Carolina found Roxie in a guest suite. 'How's it going?' she asked.

'I'm just finishing up,' Roxie said. 'Antonio's doing the bathroom flowers.' She indicated the adjoining room with a nod of her head. 'He should be just about done in there.'

'I hope you don't mind,' Carolina said, 'but I volunteered our help resetting the table.'

'Why?' Antonio asked, coming out of the bathroom with a big carryall. 'This lady has enough help to run Buckingham Palace. We're floral decorators, not servants, remember?'

'I caused her to change her mind about the china,' Carolina said, 'and guests will start coming soon.'

'I don't mind,' Roxie said.

'Well, I don't like it,' Antonio said in a clipped voice. 'That's not part of the job description.'

'Then maybe you don't want this job,' Carolina said sharply. 'I think you'd better remember that this woman is responsible for a lot of the big jobs we've gotten lately, and she might be a lot more help in the future. Besides that, Antonio, if you're serious about doing this as a career, then you'd better learn to roll with the punches. That includes not feeling like you're too damn grand to help set a table.'

Antonio's eyes glittered with anger, and his chin was set at a lofty angle in the air, as if he were about to defy her. 'Okay,' he said at last, 'but I don't like it.'

'Then go on home,' Carolina said, challenging him. 'We're supposed to work as a team, and if you don't want to be part of it, then go.'

His chin lowered a notch, and his eyes lost a little of their spark. 'Forget it,' he said. 'I'll stay and help.'

'Then let's go to the dining room,' Carolina said. 'It won't take any time.'

Later, after the china and silver to be used had been buffed off by Normal, the butler, with the help of two of the household maids, the table had been reset to Normal's exacting specifications. Carolina, Roxie, and Antonio gathered up their work equipment and were in a hallway on their way to the kitchen's service entrance to leave when Lydia approached Carolina.

'Do you mind staying just a minute longer?' Lydia asked her, sotto voce. 'I'd like to speak with you privately about something.'

Carolina turned to Roxie and Antonio. 'Would you take our gear to the van, please? I'll be down in just a minute.'

'Sure,' Roxie said. 'Take your time.'

'I've got a date at eight o'clock,' Antonio said, pointedly looking at his watch, 'and it's almost eight already.'

'Why don't you put your gear in the van, then jump in a taxi?' Carolina said.

'I will,' Antonio said. He and Roxie turned and went on out to the service entrance, which was in a vestibule off the kitchen.

Lydia smiled. 'A little rebellious?'

'I don't know what's gotten into him lately,' she said. 'There was a time not so long ago when it wouldn't have mattered if it was midnight. He would've been happily working away.'

'You seem to handle your business and your employees very well,' Lydia said, 'and that's not an easy thing to do. I imagine it gets very touchy sometimes. Always decorating for somebody else's party.'

'Well, it never bothered *me*,' Carolina replied, 'but I can see how it might get to some people.'

'That's one of the things I like about you,' Lydia said.

'What's that?' Carolina asked.

'Well, you're down to earth and unpretentious,' Lydia said, 'and you're not afraid to get your hands dirty. I like that. I was a country girl myself, and believe me, I've gotten my hands dirty plenty of times.'

'I don't mind. Not if that's what it takes to get the job done,' Carolina said with a smile. She looked at Lydia quizzically. 'But what did you want to discuss?'

'Well, there're two things actually,' Lydia said. 'First, I'd like for you to start doing the flowers for the apartment every week,' she said. 'Not as elaborately as tonight, but flowers in exactly the same places as tonight. Simple bunches will do. Nothing too arranged-looking.'

Carolina's lips quivered as she tried to conceal the elation she felt. She didn't want to start jumping up and down, clapping her hands, and shouting with joy in front of Lydia Carstairs. *Thirty-five or more bouquets a week*, she thought, *and in an apartment that the biggest spenders are into and out of all the time.* This was a major coup. It could translate into even more clients as friends and acquaintances of Lydia's saw Carolina's work.

'It would be a pleasure,' Carolina said. 'I think I know what you like, but we can discuss it when you get a chance if you want to.' In the distance she could hear the apartment's buzzer. The doorman must be announcing guests, but Lydia ignored it.

'Oh, I trust your judgment,' she said, 'or I wouldn't have asked you. You can start next week, if that's all right. I'll expect fresh flowers every Monday unless I'm out of town, and Normal will always keep you posted.'

'I look forward to it,' Carolina said.

'Good,' Lydia said. 'The other thing I wanted to bring up has to do with a magazine. I wondered if you'd like to be profiled in *W*. I let them photograph me here in the apartment recently. It was part of my publicity efforts for the Animal Rescue Mission. Anyway, they're always asking me for introductions, and I thought a profile of you and your business would be ideal for them. You do such beautiful work, Carolina, and a lot of their readers would enjoy knowing about you. What do you think?'

Am I dreaming? Carolina asked herself. 'I – I would love to do it,' she said as calmly as she could. 'It might be good for my business.'

'I would hope so,' Lydia replied. 'It's awfully tempting to keep you a well-guarded secret, but that wouldn't be fair to you.'

'Thank you, Lydia,' Carolina said, forcing herself to use her first name.

'But remember,' Lydia said, shaking a finger at Carolina, 'don't do the same thing for other hosts and hostesses that you do for me.' There was a vibrant smile on her face as she said the words, but Carolina knew she was serious.

'I wouldn't dream of it,' Carolina said.

'I wouldn't hire you if I thought you would,' Lydia said. 'Well, I'd better get to the entrance hall. I heard the buzzer, and I don't want to keep anyone waiting. Thank you for your beautiful work, Carolina. You'll be hearing from the people at *W* soon, I'm sure.'

'Thank you, Lydia,' she replied. 'And should we start with the apartment next Monday?'

'Absolutely,' Lydia said. 'Say about eight o'clock? I'm always up very early.'

'That's perfect,' Carolina said, 'and good luck with your fund-raising.'

'Thank you,' Lydia said. She started toward the entrance hall but stopped. 'Well, look who's here!' she exclaimed.

From around the corner, Seth Foster stepped into view, resplendent in black tie. And on his arm was a stunning beauty: the very blond, blue-eyed, and tanned Payton Fitzsimmons, wearing what was probably at least a twenty-five-thousand-dollar Galliano couture gown from Dior.

'Hello, Lydia,' he said. They exchanged continental air kisses, one to each cheek. Then he looked at Carolina over Lydia's shoulder. 'Hi, Carolina,' he said.

'Hi, Seth,' she said, suddenly feeling uncomfortable. *He and Payton look so great together*, she thought.

'Oh, you're the little flower person from downtown, aren't you?' Payton said, extending a hand to Carolina. 'I'm Payton Fitzsimmons.'

'I'm Carolina Mountcastle,' she said in return. 'Very nice to meet you.' *Little flower person from downtown? What a bitch!*

Carolina was distracted by a commotion behind her and turned around. Antonio was picking up another load of equipment to take down to the van, but he didn't seem to notice Carolina at all. His eyes were riveted upon Payton Fitzsimmons.

She saw that Payton's eyes in turn were fixed on Antonio, and the glance they were exchanging was unmistakably steamy. *Wow*, she thought, *you almost expect to see sparks start flying between the two of them.* The exchange was over almost before it started, however. Antonio picked up the rest of his gear and disappeared.

'Carolina,' Seth said, 'from what I've seen so far, it looks like you've done a beautiful job here tonight.'

'Thank you, Seth,' she said, 'that's very kind of you.'

'Oh, you can count on him to be kind,' Payton said, patting his arm. 'Even when the circumstances don't call for it.'

'Well, I'd better run,' Carolina said. 'Have a wonderful time. Good night.'

'Good night, Carolina,' Lydia said. She blew her a kiss and winked; then she turned to Seth and Payton. 'Come with me. I've got to show you what this Wonder Woman has done.'

'Bye, Carolina,' Seth called to her. 'Hope to see you soon.'

'Bye,' she called back.

'Lovely to meet you,' Payton said. 'A shame you can't stay.'

Carolina ignored her remark, going on through the kitchen, where the cooks were busy preparing for the dinner, and out to the service entrance. She could handle Payton's condescension, but for some reason she was disturbed by Seth's being with her. *I hate to see him with someone who doesn't deserve him.* When the service elevator arrived, she stepped in and pressed the button for the lobby. *Seth needs to be protected from Payton Fitzsimmons,* she thought. *She's a viper, and he doesn't have a mean bone in his body.*

7

Seth looked across the table at Payton, who was chatting with the man on her right, a young billionnaire – something to do with fiber optics, Seth believed – who looked rather out of his element but was enjoying Payton's lively attention enormously. In the candle-light, her eyes sparkled brightly, as did the expensive jewelry she wore. White diamonds at her ears, around her neck, and on her wrists. She wore her Dior gown – a confection in dramatic black frills – with ease, as if she had been born in couture. But then, he reminded himself, that was practically the case.

She was certainly born and bred for this sort of dinner party. She could make small talk with almost anyone, and could be amusing, tactful, and interesting. She was also stunningly beautiful. In short, she was the perfect wife for a man like himself. Her remarks to Carolina earlier in the evening, however, had disturbed him. He had noticed Payton's haughtiness in the past and her inclination to bitchiness, but this time she hit a nerve.

They had finished dinner, a delicious feast beginning with fois gras, going on to grilled quail with truffled wild rice and asparagus, followed with a light dessert of mango-papaya sorbet. Now they chatted over espresso.

'We'll have drinks or more coffee in the library,' Lydia announced from her end of the table as she rose to her feet. The other guests began to rise, following suit.

As Seth took the arm of his dinner partner, Marcella, the wife of an Italian auto manufacturer, and walked toward the dining room door, he overheard Payton talking in a loud and shrill voice. Had she had too much to drink? he wondered.

'I'm surprised, Lydia,' she was saying, a pointed finger indicating the roses that decorated the table. 'They're really déclassé. Sterling Silver roses. Ha! Has anybody used them since the fifties?'

'That's one of the reasons I think it's so clever to use them,' Lydia said, moving toward the door. 'Nobody uses them anymore. Besides, I think they're extraordinarily beautiful in this room,' she went on. 'They're also exceptional Sterling Silver roses, and I really don't care that you think them déclassé, Payton, darling. I myself prefer to think of them as retro.'

'Oh, I see what you mean,' Payton said. 'Well, they certainly are retro.' Then she swept a hand in a circle, indicating the rest of the room. 'And these others that Carolina did,' she declared. 'The ones that are fashioned to look like Old Master paintings. Isn't that a corny idea? And so *yesterday*. Maybe they'd work in a cheap piano bar or—'

'Payton,' Seth called in a firm voice, 'why don't you tell everyone about your new business?'

She started at him momentarily and then smiled. 'Why, what a wonderful idea. Thank you, Seth. As soon as we're settled in the library I'll do just that.'

In the magnificent mahogany library, its shelves lined with thousands of leather-bound volumes, the guests circulated on the rare and colorful Herez carpet. Antique brass Dutch chandeliers were suspended from the ceiling, and there were several tables with chairs for reading, in addition to numerous comfortable leather-covered couches, chaises longues, and chairs. No sooner had they begun chattering, as the footmen circulated with trays of drinks, than Payton, a brandy in hand, tapped the crystal snifter with one of the diamond rings she wore. She stood in front of the huge fireplace, with a gilt William Kent mirror over it. When she had everyone's attention, she cleared her throat and looked around the room.

'I've started a party-planning business, everyone,' she announced, 'and I'm opening a flower shop right here in the East Seventies. So I hope you'll come to see it, and see what a real decorator can do.' She cast a malevolent eye on the beautiful bunch of parrot tulips on the table in front of her. 'I know most of your friends, of course, so you can trust me and my helpers to take very good care of them. Thank you.'

After a light smattering of applause, congratulatory murmurings, and nods of approval, chattering began anew. Payton crossed the room to Seth. 'How was that?' she asked.

'It was fine,' he replied, 'although I don't know that I would've made an announcement about it.'

'You told me to,' Payton said, scowling.

'Well, what I had in mind was circulating among the guests and telling them one or two at a time. This party is for the Animal Rescue Mission, after all, and that should be of primary importance.'

'Not to me, it isn't,' Payton said. 'My new venture is more important than a bunch of starving mutts.'

'Nor do I think it was particularly attractive watching you disparage the work that Carolina has done here,' he added.

Payton's eyes glinted with anger. 'You can't possibly mind what I say about some absolute nobody from downtown who's trying to invade my territory!'

'She's been at it for years, Payton,' he said mildly, 'and I don't think she's trying to invade anybody's territory. She's simply been offered work by uptown social types who've seen her work and like it. She's very creative and refreshingly down to earth. Even if she's not part of this social set, they're beginning to appreciate her.'

Payton threw her head back and laughed. It was an ugly laugh without any humor. 'Well, she's not going to get much more work like this if I have anything to do about it,' she spat out. 'I'm going to start a real blitzkrieg, and take all of her uptown business away from her. You just wait and see. I'll ruin her.'

Seth was astounded by the vehemence in her voice. 'Why would you want to ruin her?' he asked. 'There's plenty of room in this business for both of you.'

'She's the competition, isn't she?' Payton replied. 'And a nobody besides. What right does she think she has to decorate for people like us? People like *us* decorate for us.' She tapped her chest with a hand. 'When my mother wanted the house redone, she called Sister Parrish because Sister was in the *Social Register*. Nowadays, you might call Mica Urtegun or some other member of good society. You certainly would not call in some interloper.'

Seth had heard enough, and he really didn't know how to reply without getting into a big argument, something he didn't want to do at Lydia's. One thing he did know, however, was that he didn't want to spend any more time with Payton tonight. 'Are you about ready to leave?' he asked. 'I have an early day tomorrow and ought to get going.'

Payton shrugged her lovely tanned shoulders. 'That's fine with me,' she said. 'I have lots to do myself. You know how it is with us working girls. In fact, I was going to ask you to get me home early.'

'Good. We'll leave, then,' Seth said.

Marcella approached them and took Seth's arm. 'Such a divine man, Payton,' she said. 'You mustn't let him go.'

Payton laughed. 'You're a terrible matchmaker Principessa,' she replied. 'I heard it was you that introduced poor Count Volpicelli to that terrible actress who took him for nearly all his money.'

Marcella laughed gaily. 'But she knows how to spend it, doesn't she?'

'Sorry to break this up, but we must go, Marcella,' Seth said, taking Payton's arm in his. 'We both have early mornings.'

'Oh, dear,' she said. 'Such a pity. Anyone under fifty should be able to kick up his heels all night without worrying about the morrow, don't you agree?'

'Exactly,' Payton said, 'but Seth's a fuddy-duddy.' She waggled a good-bye to Marcella.

They moved across the room toward Lydia, who was in conversation.

'We have to run,' Seth said, taking her hand and squeezing it.

'So early, darling?' she said. She held a cheek out, and he air-kissed her. 'So glad you could come.'

'Thank you, Lydia,' Payton said. 'It was really lovely.'

'Glad you enjoyed yourself,' Lydia said. She would have loved to say something biting to Payton Fitzsimmons, but she decided to hold her tongue, for Seth's sake. 'Normal will show you to the door.' She turned back to other guests, and Payton and Seth made their way toward the entrance hall.

When they reached the street, Seth turned to her and asked, 'Do you really think I'm a fuddy-duddy?'

'No,' she said with a laugh. 'I was only joking, Seth.' *He may be a stick in the mud as far as I'm concerned*, she thought, *but he may be a very useful one, so I don't want to burn this bridge.* She squeezed his arm. 'How could anybody think that? You're handsome and a gentleman and . . . well, you have all the things a woman wants in a man for a husband.'

He didn't reply to her, and they walked in silence up Fifth Avenue to Seventy-seventh Street, where they turned east toward her apartment. When they arrived at her building, he went upstairs with her, feeling that it was his obligation to show her to her door.

At the doorway, Payton turned to him. 'Want a quick nightcap?'

'I don't think so, Payton,' he said. 'I don't think it's a good idea for us to see each other again.'

'Why do you think that, Seth?' she asked in a hurt voice. 'I don't understand. Is it something I said or did?'

'I don't like the way you disparaged Carolina's flowers at Lydia's party, and right in front of Lydia,' he said. 'I think it was insulting to Carolina and Lydia both, and I think it was very rude . . . and mean. I didn't know you could be so spiteful.'

'I certainly wasn't mean on purpose,' Payton said in a girlish voice. 'I think you're just hypersensitive about them, that's all. Anyway, I don't want this to spoil our . . . our friendship, because I think the world of you, Seth.' She kissed him on the cheek, but he drew back from her.

'Good night, Payton,' he said. He turned and started to the elevator.

'Good night, Seth,' she said. 'Give me a call, won't you?'

He didn't answer her for a moment, then said, 'I haven't changed my mind, Payton. I don't think we ought to see one another for a while, so I don't think I'll be calling.'

The elevator car arrived, and he stepped in.

Fuck you, too, she thought, watching until he'd disappeared. She closed the door to her apartment and quickly grabbed the cell phone from out of her jewel-encrusted evening bag and punched in a number.

One ring. Two. Then, 'Hello?'

'It's me, Payton,' she said breathily. 'Can you come up right now?'

'I'll be there in fifteen minutes tops,' he said.

'Good,' she said. 'I'll be waiting for you.'

Her Galliano gown from Dior lay sparkling in the middle of the living room floor, and Antonio's worn jeans and tee shirt were tossed haphazardly next to it. They stood naked, staring at one another's bodies with burning desire in their eyes. He made the first move toward her, cupping her shapely breasts in his hands. She gasped aloud as shivers of excitement ran up her spine and shot out all over her body, like tiny electrical shocks. It was incredible what his touch did to her. She gasped again as his mouth found first one nipple, then the other, licking them.

Reaching down, she ran her hand along the shaft of his engorged cock, then lightly stroked his balls, taking delight in her effect on him. She began stroking it very slowly, listening to his quickened breath.

He surprised her, suddenly picking her up and placing her on the couch as if she weighed nothing in his arms. He was atop her at once, panting like an animal, and entered her in one hard thrust, shoving himself in up to the hilt. She almost levitated off the silk damask and began to tremble, with both the suddenness of it and his brutal entry, and in another moment she was moving rhythmically with him, pounding against him as he did against her.

Oh, my God, she thought, *I drive him crazy*. The way she excited him, the way she elicited the crude beast that lay within his well-defined musculature, drove her to new heights of carnal pleasure. She began to convulse almost immediately, her body trembling from head to toe as wave after wave of contractions sent her into a frenzy.

'Oh, Jesus! Antonio!' she yelled. 'Antonio!' She sank her nails into his back, holding on for dear life as he plunged into her as no one ever had before, his body like a heaving machine, until with a roar, he abruptly arched back. He drove himself into her with a final thrust and then exploded, his body taut and trembling, until at last he dropped atop her.

'Oh, Antonio,' she gasped. 'Oh, my God, it's never been like this.' She held on to him tightly, unwilling to relinquish her hold.

For a while they lay there, clutching one another as they caught their breath. Antonio broke the silence after rolling off her and snuggling close. 'Damn, I'm glad you called me,' he said, running a finger down her nose and then kissing it. 'It was so hard to see you coming into that party and not be able to put my hands all over you. Not even be able to speak to you.'

She smiled and squeezed one of his biceps. 'I felt the same way,' she said, 'but it's better this way. Better for both of us in the long run.'

'I don't see why,' he said.

'Because if nobody knows about us,' she said, a fingernail tracing a circle around one of his nipples, 'then nobody will know that you're helping me work out a little plan I have.' She smiled mysteriously.

'What kind of plan?' Antonio asked, returning her smile. His hands began gently stroking her perfectly curved buttocks.

'I'll tell you all about it,' she said, 'but you have to promise me that nobody will know about it but you and me.' She ran a finger down his chest to the thatch of raven hair between his thighs. 'And that means nobody.' She grasped his cock in her hand, and Antonio gasped.

'I don't have much of a choice, do I?' he said, kneading her sweet cheeks harder.

'No,' she whispered, squeezing his cock. 'Not if you want to remain a man.'

'Ouch!' he exclaimed with a laugh, and then looked at her seriously. 'I don't like having to sneak around, you know? This is so good I wish we could shout it to the whole world.'

'I feel exactly the same way,' she said, 'but we have to be patient, Antonio. It won't be forever. In fact, with your help, I don't think it'll take us long at all.'

He pulled her tightly to him. 'God, I hope not,' he said. 'This is so damn good. I want to be able to show you off.' He began kissing her with a sudden passion, as if he couldn't get enough.

Payton responded to his kisses, matching his ardor, but her mind was working overtime. *I'm going to have to be very careful handling*

Antonio, she thought. *He's like a kid in some ways, and he likes me too much. But he's the key to making my plan work.*

She moaned as he entered her, and they began moving in rhythm. *And I haven't given up on Seth, because he might be useful. Maybe I should do something sweet for him. I haven't gotten my claws out of him quite yet, and certainly nobody else is going to have him. But come hell or high water, this hot stud and I are going to ruin Carolina Mountcastle.*

8

The taxi pulled under the marquee at the Fifth Avenue entrance to the Plaza Hotel, and a uniformed doorman came down the steps to open the door for Carolina and Roxie. They exited the taxi and started up the carpeted steps to the revolving door that led into the hotel's magnificent lobby. Carolina hadn't been in the hotel for a long time, and when she heard the elegant strains of the string trio coming from the direction of the Palm Court, she was reminded of what a beautiful slice of courtly Old World grace the hotel was in the midst of busy Manhattan.

It was a nostalgic moment as she stood, soaking up the perfumed atmosphere. She could remember having lunch at the Oyster Bar in years gone by with Lyon and dinners in the Edwardian Room with her parents. And often she'd met Matt in the noisy Oak Room for a drink.

The huge flower arrangement on a center table immediately drew her professional eye, and she thought it was magnificently suitable and envied the florist who did the hotel's work. She noticed a few perfectly coiffed and exquisitely dressed women seated in the tapestry-covered French chairs, waiting for husbands or friends, she imagined. The carpet underfoot was so thick her heels actually sank into it, and all the marble, gilt wood, and crystal sconces and chandeliers provided the perfect backdrop for the dramatic events which so often were set here.

'I'd forgotten how beautiful it is,' Roxie said in an awed hush as they headed for the concierge's desk.

'It's the perfect place for a wedding,' Carolina said, 'isn't it?'

'I'll say.'

'Here we are,' Carolina said. She looked at the man behind the concierge's desk. 'Hi, are you Michael?'

The young man nodded his head slightly. His hair was slicked back and gleamed even in the subdued lighting. 'And you're Mrs Mountcastle?' he guessed.

'Yes,' she said.

He smiled. 'Hold on just a moment,' he said, 'someone will be right out to take you up to the Grand Ballroom.' He looked off to his left. 'Ah, here he is now. Mrs Mountcastle, this is Alec. Alec, Mrs Mountcastle. You will be showing her the Grand Ballroom and all of its facilities for a wedding. Please stay with her as long as she requires your services.'

Alec nodded politely. 'Come this way,' he said, indicating the elevator bank with a hand.

Carolina and Roxie followed the young man to the elevator. He pushed the button for ONE, and up they went, then down a plushly carpeted hallway to the Grand Ballroom. Several sets of double doors led into the room, and he unlocked one of them and held it wide for them.

Once inside, Carolina's eyes took in the immense cream-and-gold room, its majestic columns, crystal chandeliers and sconces, the rich red carpeting, and then she turned her gaze on Roxie.

'We have one hell of a job to do between now and tomorrow night,' Carolina said.

'We sure do,' Roxie agreed.

'One smart thing is your idea about using the pergola. It fills a lot of space and takes a lot of decorating, plus its columns will tie in with the ballroom's.' Carolina turned to Alec. 'Can you turn on all of the lights for us? Then we can take care of things from there. If you have something else to do, we could ask Michael to send you up if we really need you.'

'That's fine,' Alec replied.

'Oh,' Carolina said, 'I'll see him before I leave, but please tell Michael that there are going to be several deliveries for the Grand Ballroom this evening and tomorrow.'

'I will,' Alec said, and then turned and left.

'Well, we might as well get busy.' Carolina set down her carryall on a table and then rummaged in it for her big tape measure. She placed it on the table with the sketchbook and notes Antonio and Roxie had done on their own. She'd had an early morning appointment with a client, discussing an upcoming party, and then returned to the shop to discover that Roxie and Antonio had taken on a wedding for tomorrow night.

'Here, Roxie,' Carolina said, handing her the tape. 'Let's start down at the end where the ceremony will be. First the width.' The chandeliers and wall sconces suddenly came on, lighting the room brightly. 'I'm sure all the lights are on dimmers,' Carolina said, 'but remind me to check and make sure before we go.'

'I will,' Roxie said.

They walked down to the end of the huge, elegant ballroom and started measuring, Carolina writing all the measurements down in her book. As they worked, she thought back to that morning with wry amusement. She'd walked in the shop door and found Antonio and Roxie working away madly on arrangements she knew nothing about.

'What's going on?' she'd asked.

'You know that big ballplayer that just signed a multimillion-dollar

77

contract with the Mets?' Roxie had said.

'No,' Carolina had replied, shaking her head. 'Why, should I?'

'It's been in all the papers,' Antonio chimed in. 'Ricky Sanchez is getting married tomorrow to that supermodel, Chrissy Madison. Apparently she threw a fit with the florist, some old bag from Philadelphia, and fired her on the spot. Lucky for us, she saw the mention of you in the *Post* after Lydia's party. She showed it to him, and he called and insisted that you do the wedding tomorrow. Said he wouldn't let anybody else do it. Only the best for Chrissy.'

'Tomorrow!' Carolina exclaimed. 'But that's impossible.' Then she eyed the arrangements they were both working on. 'These are for the wedding, aren't they?' she'd said.

Roxie and Antonio nodded.

'You said I would do it, without asking me, didn't you?'

They nodded again.

'You told us we'd have to work harder and longer hours for our raises,' Antonio said. 'And you said we'd have to assume more respon-sibility and make decisions on our own,' he added imperiously. 'So that's what we're doing.'

Now Carolina, down on her knees with one end of the tape measure in her hand, laughed aloud just thinking about it.

'What's so funny?' Roxie asked.

'I was thinking about how you and Antonio took this job on,' she said. 'Boy, did you ever surprise me.'

'I'm glad you're not mad at us,' Roxie said.

'This wedding is going to receive a lot of press,' Carolina said, 'which will be great for business. It's also going to make the shop a lot of money. Twenty thousand dollars on flowers alone. Besides, you and Antonio were doing what I told you to do.' And it was true, she thought. She'd had a long heart-to-heart with Antonio and Roxie, and after they'd convinced her that they were serious about being a real part of her team and wanted to stay on, they'd discussed the future of the business together.

'What time did you say Antonio and Richie would be coming up here?' she asked Roxie.

'Probably not until about seven tonight,' Roxie said. 'Somewhere in that vicinity.'

They would be driving the van, after filling it up with all the big candleholders and flower stands, the framework for the pergola they'd decided to use, and the many other necessities for the wedding. Everything except the flowers, which would be put in place tomorrow.

'You said Mercedes is going to help out in the shop?' Carolina asked.

'Yes,' Roxie said, looking over at her. 'I didn't know who else to call, and you trust her, so—'

'Good,' Carolina said. 'She'll do just fine, I think, and she and Antonio seem to work together pretty well.'

Roxie nodded. 'She and Antonio are getting along like a house on fire lately.'

Carolina glanced over at her quizzically. 'Do you mean they might have something going on?'

'I don't think so,' Roxie replied, 'but they sure are getting along awfully well. They do a lot of whispering, if you know what I mean, and I don't think they're talking about the news.'

Carolina laughed. 'No, I wouldn't think so.'

Her cell phone bleeped, and she scooted across the floor to her bag and grabbed it. 'Hello,' she said.

'Hi, beautiful.'

'Matt!' she cried, delighted to hear the sound of her brother's voice. 'I'm so glad you called. Guess where I am.'

'Uh . . . swimming around Manhattan in the buff?' he joked.

'No, silly,' she replied. 'I'm sitting on the floor in the Grand Ballroom at the Plaza Hotel.'

'What's up?' he asked. 'You had too much to drink and you fell down and you can't get up?'

'You *are* silly today,' she said with a laugh. 'No, Roxie and I are here getting ready for a wedding tomorrow night. One of those last-minute things.'

'I'm sure you can handle it.'

'We'll do it somehow,' she said. 'Anyway, how's Thad? Okay?'

'He's fine,' Matt replied. 'Busy as usual.'

'Oh, good. So what's new?' she asked. 'I'm going to have to cut this short because I've got to get back to work. We've got a lot to do.'

'Nothing's new,' he said. 'I just wanted to say hello. Sounds like things are really booming.'

'It's unbelievable,' she said, 'but I couldn't be happier. *House and Garden*'s doing a write-up. And *W* wants to do a piece on me, using the loft, the shop, and the country house. I do think I'm going to have to get some more help, though, and the sooner the better. If you've got any bright ideas, let me know. Are you coming into the city soon?'

'Wish I could,' he said, 'but you know how it is. I've got so much work lined up here I don't know how I'll ever get it all done before it gets too cold.'

'All of those beautiful Wall Street dollars,' Carolina said with a laugh. 'Spreading themselves around country houses in Litchfield County. Anything interesting?'

'Most of it's routine,' he said, 'a terrace here, a patio there, landscaping around swimming pools. You know, the usual. But there are a few really cool projects. You know who Sybil Conroy is?'

'Sure,' Carolina said. 'Wasn't she the one that got something like two hundred million from that big leveraged-buyout guy in a divorce settlement?'

'That's the one,' he replied. 'Anyway, she's spending big buckeroos on her place up here. And I mean big. I'm designing a rose parterre for her and an herb garden based on the one at the Cloisters. They're going to be real knockouts.'

'That sounds exciting,' Carolina said.

'It is, but there's a lot of drudge work, too. I have to redo all three of her ponds. The guy who did them originally didn't do them right, so now they're all stagnant. Looks like hell, but we'll fix them up. There's a lot of outside lighting to do, too, so Thad's working his butt off. It's a good thing he was a light designer on Broadway, because he has really fabulous ideas for things I'd never think of. Anyway, we're going to get her place looking fantastic.'

'I'm sure you will,' she said, 'and separate her from a lot of those dollars she got off her ex.'

Matt laughed. 'Don't worry about that,' he said. 'She's really great to work with – she has a lot of good ideas and she knows what she wants – and there's going to be a lot more to do down the road. Anyway, guess what she got all excited about today?'

'You're going to put a little island love nest in the middle of one of her ponds?' she joked. 'I don't have the faintest idea, Matt. What?'

'You,' he replied.

'Me!' she exclaimed. 'What're you talking about? The woman's never laid eyes on me.'

'Maybe not,' he said, 'but she heard about you from some friend of Lydia Carstairs. She likes to work with flowers a lot – always making new arrangements all over the house – so I told her about how my sister was a florist in New York who did a lot of decorating for parties and stuff. Then when I told her who you were, she got all excited. Said she'd heard you were a genius.'

Carolina was thrilled to hear this news, but was so stunned she didn't know what to say for a moment. 'I – I . . . well, that's great,' she finally said.

'It *is* great, Sis,' he replied. 'She's another potential big customer for you. Entertains all the time and spends a fortune on flowers. You're beginning to get the kind of attention for your work that you've always deserved. You're coming into your own.'

'Thanks, Matt,' she said, appreciating her brother's saying this.

He was critical, demanding, a perfectionist in his own work; so, coming from him, the compliment meant a lot.

'I'd better let you go,' he said. 'Just wanted to pass that along.'

'I'm so glad you did,' Carolina said. 'Tell Thad hello for me, and I love you both.'

'Love you, too, Sis,' he said. 'Later.'

'Later.'

She snapped the cell phone shut, tossed it back in her carryall, and then hugged herself. *The word really is spreading*, she thought, *and a lot faster than I would ever have thought.* And Matt was right, she realized. She'd worked long and hard to reach this juncture in her career.

'You look happy,' Roxie said.

'Oh, I am, Roxie,' she replied. 'The word about the shop and our work really is spreading, and it is a good feeling.'

'Why don't we celebrate with a drink or something in the Palm Court after we get the measuring done?' Roxie asked.

'That's a great idea,' Carolina said. 'But first, let's get everything done here that we can. I want to put tape down where all the candle holders and flower baskets are supposed to be set up. When the guys get here later, they can put everything in place. Even the pergola will be ready to decorate.'

'Do you think we're going to have enough flowers?' Roxie asked.

'Between what you and Antonio ordered this morning and what I could beg and borrow from all the Georges, we'll have enough,' she said. 'We already have enough white orchids and greenery to get started, and a lot more are being flown in tonight. Enough to sink a ship. We'll be all right.' She rummaged in her tote bag. 'Aha! My tape. Let's get this laid out on the floor.'

They worked together for another two hours, finally finishing the arrangements in the ballroom. 'You ready for that drink?' Carolina asked.

'You bet I am,' Roxie replied.

*   *   *

The strains of graceful music greeted them as they approached the beautiful Palm Court. They were greeted by the maître d', who seated them at a table for two. They were surrounded by palms and a virtual forest of other plants, all multiplied by the generous use of mirrors framed in gilded wood. Marble columns soared to the glass ceiling high above them, and sconces, their crystals dangling like fat grapes on the vine, enhanced the regal atmosphere of the room.

'This is truly heaven,' Roxie said. 'Like something in Europe.'

Carolina smiled. 'It really is. I've always loved this place.'

The waiter approached their table. 'Good afternoon, ladies,' he said. 'Will you be having tea? Something from our dessert cart, perhaps?'

'I think I'll have a drink,' Carolina said. 'A glass of champagne.'

'Very good,' the waiter replied. He looked at Roxie. 'And you, madam?'

'The same,' Roxie replied.

'Thank you,' the waiter said, disappearing.

'What's that they're playing?' Roxie asked.

'Oh, it's . . . it's . . . I don't remember,' Carolina said. 'I've heard it all my life and can't think what in the world it is.'

Her eyes swept the beautiful room, and she noticed several tables of elegantly dressed ladies taking tea together.

'Don't look now,' Roxie said, 'but isn't that Gloria Towson sitting by the column almost directly across from you?'

Carolina restrained the impulse to look immediately; then she casually glanced that way. Turning back to Roxie, she said, 'Yes, it is, and that's Lulu Riviere, the designer's wife, with her. I'd love to be a fly on the wall. The newspapers have been full of articles about how Towson had to sell off millions of shares of stock to raise cash.'

'It's no wonder, from what I hear,' Roxie said. 'Leland knows the decorator who did their apartment, and he told me that she spent over forty million dollars on furniture. And that doesn't include any of the artwork.'

'I guess that's chump change for them, isn't it?' Carolina said.

Roxie nodded. 'From what Leland says. I bet she's out trying to be seen everywhere, looking beautiful and happy and rich, just to show the press and all the gossips that the rumors about them going down the tubes aren't true.'

The waiter returned with two flutes of champagne and placed them on the table. 'Thank you,' Carolina said. She picked up her flute and took a sip of the golden, bubbly liquid. 'Ah, this is so good,' she said, savoring its taste on her palate. Then, from the corner of an eye, she thought she saw a familiar face waiting for the maître d', but before she could say anything, Roxie did.

'Look,' she said, setting her champagne down, 'there's Seth Foster and some woman.'

'So it is Seth,' Carolina said.

'I wonder who the blond beauty is?' Roxie said.

'I don't know,' Carolina replied. 'But she sure is a beauty, and she sure isn't Payton Fitzsimmons.'

Seth saw them as the maître d' led him and his companion to their table. He said something to the maître d'; then he and the woman walked toward Roxie and Carolina.

'What a surprise,' he said, beaming.

Carolina immediately felt that fluttery feeling he seemed to cause every time she saw him. 'Hi, Seth,' she managed to say.

'This is Cosima von Anhelt,' he said. 'Carolina Mountcastle and Roxie Davis,' he said, introducing them to his friend.

'How do you do?' Cosima said in accented English. She smiled ever so slightly, one manicured hand playing with the strands of pearls she wore with her Chanel suit.

'Cosima's an old friend from Amsterdam,' he said.

'Yes, since the Dark Ages,' Cosima volunteered with a little laugh. She squeezed Seth's arm, with affection, Carolina thought.

'Amsterdam's a lovely town,' Carolina said. 'My husband's there now.'

'Not on vacation without you, I hope?' Cosima said playfully.

'No, he works in airline management,' she said, 'so he has to spend a lot of time there.'

'It's a wonder I haven't run into him,' Seth said, his eyes studying hers. 'I spend a lot of time there, too. Working for the Netherland-American Bank.'

'It is a small world, isn't it,' Carolina said. She still felt uncomfortable when his gaze rested upon her, and didn't know how to interpret the frisson of excitement that rushed through her body.

'Well, we'd better get to our table,' Seth said. He hesitated a moment before turning to leave. 'It's nice to see you both,' he added.

'See you again soon,' Carolina said.

'Jeez,' Roxie said, 'he does know how to pick them. I'll give him credit for that. She looks like she's wearing more on her back than I'd make in a year, and she wears it well, too.'

'Yes,' Carolina agreed, 'doesn't she?' She glanced their way once again as they took their seats. They fit into this setting perfectly, she thought. Like Lulu Riviere and Gloria Towson, they were as refined and as civilized as all the marble, mirror, gilt, crystal, and silver that sparkled in the Palm Court. It didn't hurt that they were extremely attractive either.

'We'd better drink up,' Carolina said, suddenly wanting to leave the beauty of the Palm Court and its music behind. 'We're going to be up half the night as it is. I want to make a quick swing by the shop to make sure everything there's okay and see how the guys are doing getting the van loaded. It's going to take several trips, I think. We can order food for everybody, too,' she went on, 'and bring it back up here with us.'

Roxie studied Carolina's face for a moment, wondering why she was abruptly in a rush, but there were no clues to be read in the fixed expression that her boss wore. 'Okay,' she said. She finished her champagne and set down the flute. 'I'm ready when you are.'

On the way out, Carolina smiled and waved in the direction of Seth and Cosima. Seth waved in return, and Cosima, turning slightly, smiled. *The perfect couple,* Carolina thought with a tinge of envy, *but then he and Payton seemed to be the perfect couple, too. I wonder who it's to be?*

9

'Don't worry, Leland,' Mercedes said, nearly breathless with excitement, her aristocratic British accent less staccato than usual. 'Antonio will cover for me. We just have to be quick.'

Leland's hand was easing up her slim thigh, beneath her skirt, while his tongue licked at her exposed cleavage with ardor.

'Oh, God, don't stop,' she rasped excitedly, one of her hands moving down to the obvious bulge in his trousers. She rubbed against it in anticipation, and was rewarded by his moan of pleasure.

'Come on,' he said, loosening his belt. 'Quick.'

He watched as she shed her high heels and then stepped out of her skirt and panties. She wanted to do it right at her front door.

'I like high-class girls like you that get down and dirty,' he said.

He was so aroused that another minute of foreplay was out of the question. He let his pants drop and with his hands on the twin orbs of her ass, he pulled her against him, hoisted her up against the door, and entered her with a growl of passion.

Mercedes cried out in ecstasy as he began pumping away at her, hard and fast, as if his life depended on it. Only moments passed before she began to writhe wildly from side to side. She felt her floodgates open and contractions seized her in waves of pure physical pleasure.

Leland couldn't wait another second, so excited was he by her release, and he thrust into her with a final heroic effort and let out a loud groan as he exploded inside her. Finally spent, he set her back down on the floor.

'Ah, Jesus,' he said in a gasp. 'Mercedes . . . you are one wild lady.'

'Not so bad yourself,' she said with amusement. She ruffled his hair. 'A shame we don't do this more often.'

There was a sly grin on his lips and mischief in his eyes. 'Yeah, it is, isn't it? Maybe we ought to do something about that, huh?'

'Maybe,' she said, 'but right now I've got to get back to that damn shop of your sister-in-law's.' She bent down and started gathering up her clothes.

'Why're you helping her out, anyway?' he asked, watching her get dressed. 'You can afford to stay home and do your own thing.'

'Oh . . . I'm getting a little experience in the flower business,' Mercedes said. 'And pocket change never hurt a girl, either.'

'Just think,' he said, 'if you weren't going back to the shop, we could fuck the rest of the day away.'

'You seem awfully preoccupied with your precious little Roxie for that,' she said, looking at him with an arched brow.

'Somebody's got to pay the rent,' he said.

'Oh, right. Give me a break,' she said. 'You're making a fortune in the market from what I hear.'

'I'm doing all right,' he said.

'So why the starry-eyed Roxie?' she asked.

'She's convenient.'

'I see.' She looked at him with curiosity. 'We'd better hurry,' she said impatiently. 'You don't want your Richie or Carolina to see you leaving here.'

'You said he's at the shop, and she's uptown.'

'Yes, but one of them might stop by here for all I know,' she said.

'Okay, I'm going,' he said. He quickly pulled up his pants and took her in his arms. 'Hmmm,' he said, pressing her to him. 'I'll have to come by this way more often.'

'You do that,' Mercedes said. 'In the meantime, let's go. You first, then I'll follow in a minute.'

'All right,' he said. He released her and headed toward the elevator vestibule. 'See you later.'

'Later,' she said, watching him go, wondering why he was interested in her again, more than he had been for a while at least. They'd always been attracted to one another sexually, but sex with Leland had always been like an after-dinner drink. A potent one, to be sure, but nothing more. Perhaps it was because they were so much alike, she thought. Neither of them wanted a commitment, and both of them were after the goose that laid the golden egg.

He's up to something, she thought, *but I wonder what it is. And how do I figure in, if I do?*

The bells on the door jangled. Antonio looked toward the door, and Mercedes said something into the telephone, then quickly hung up.

Richie bounded into the shop, baseball cap on backwards, sneakers smacking loudly against the floor.

'Hey, dude,' Antonio said with a grin.

'Hey,' Richie said. 'Mom back yet?'

Mercedes shook her blond hair. 'No, Richie,' she said. 'She's still up at the Plaza, I assume. Anything I can help you with?'

'No,' he said. 'But the van's already got a load in it, so we wondered if we should go on up to the hotel or wait for her.'

'Why don't I ring her cell phone?' Mercedes said.

'Okay,' Richie said. 'I'll be outside with the van, trying to fit some more stuff in.'

'Right,' Mercedes said, watching him go back outside.

'What's up with Payton?' Antonio asked.

'I told her I might be willing to become involved in your little game,' Mercedes replied. 'But I also told her we'd have to sit down and discuss money. Helping her ruin Carolina's business is going to cost her, but she's got the money. No problem there.'

'No, I don't think so,' Antonio said with a bark of a laugh.

'And if the two of us go to work for Payton full-time in the future, then she's going to have to come up with contracts for us.'

'Contracts?'

'Why not?' Mercedes said. 'We should get some sort of guarantees from her in black and white. After all, you'd be giving up a very good job here, and I'd be devoting my time to her instead of all my other projects. Besides, Payton stands to make a killing in this business.'

'You don't trust her, do you?' Antonio said worriedly. He was counting on Payton to be his meal ticket.

'It's just that if Payton should decide to drop you or me after she's got what she wants, she's going to have a hard time doing it.'

'Why's that?' he asked, still miffed. 'What do you mean?'

She glanced at him slyly. 'We'll know Payton's nasty little secret, won't we? And she certainly wouldn't want us spreading the word, would she?'

Antonio frowned. 'You're talking blackmail.'

'Call it what you will,' Mercedes said, 'but I call it covering your ass.'

The bells on the door jangled again, and they both looked toward the front of the shop.

'Hi, everybody,' Carolina called to them. 'How's it going here?'

'Fine,' Mercedes said lightly. 'I was just going to ring your cell phone. Richie's looking for you.'

'Did you see him outside?' Antonio asked.

Carolina nodded. 'Yes,' she said, 'he and the guys are on their way up to the Plaza with the first load.'

Roxie came in behind her and closed the door.

'Hi, Roxie,' Antonio said.

'Hello everybody,' Roxie said, avoiding Mercedes's cool, aristo-cratic gaze.

'We're going to order out Chinese for everybody,' Carolina said, 'and work on arrangements until everything has been taken up to the Plaza. Then we'll go up there and get everything in position tonight, ready to be decorated tomorrow.'

'Sounds cool,' Antonio said.

Carolina placed her carryall on her worktable and sat down on the stool. Roxie did the same and immediately occupied herself with the take-out menu.

'Catch me up,' Carolina said. 'What's been going on here?'

'Several people rang up,' Mercedes said, 'and I have a list of them here. Some of them doubtless important in one way or the other.'

'Give me a rundown,' Carolina said.

'Let me see,' Mercedes said, consulting the list in her hand. 'Oh, an editor from *Country Style Living*, that terrible cutesy magazine. They would like to do a piece on you.' She paused and looked at Carolina with a frown. 'One must be careful where one allows oneself to be exposed, you know.'

Carolina simply nodded. She didn't want to debate the qualities of the various magazines with Mercedes, but she happened to think *Country Style Living* was a good one. 'Okay,' she said, 'I'll get back to them tomorrow sometime. Who else?'

'Payton Fitzsimmons, that piggish young socialite, rang up to place an order, a rather extravagant one, I might add, which I took.'

'That's great,' Carolina said, 'but why on earth would she be placing an order with me? She's setting up her own business.'

'Perhaps it's because the order is to go to someone in this neigh-borhood,' Mercedes said. 'And maybe she's not actually set up to do deliveries yet.' She shrugged. 'I don't know, Carolina. I just took the order.'

'Where's it going?' Carolina asked.

'To an art opening at the Matthew Marks Gallery,' Mercedes said. 'Apparently Payton is a friend of the artist and the flowers are for the reception.'

'I see,' Carolina said. 'But why did you call Payton Fitzsimmons piggish, Mercedes? I've met her, and she's really beautiful.'

'Didn't you know?' Mercedes said, looking at her with surprise. 'Everybody who's anybody knows that Payton is an absolute sexual pig. Simply can't get enough, from what I hear.' She didn't notice the angry look that flashed on Antonio's face.

'Oh, I see.' *So the perfect Mr Seth Foster is or was running around with a woman everybody says is a nympho,* she thought.

'She also wants to speak to you personally about a cocktail party she's giving at a club in the next couple of weeks or so,' Mercedes went on. 'Wants you to do the flowers, of course.'

'I don't get it,' Carolina said. 'Why on earth wouldn't she do it herself?'

Mercedes shrugged again. 'As I said, I don't know. I assume she's not set up for it yet.'

Carolina looked thoughtful for a moment. 'You've got the numbers and names and everything?'

'Naturally,' she said sweetly. 'You know I wouldn't forget something that important. There were also calls from a couple of other magazines. Here, I'll give you the list.'

'Thanks, Mercedes,' she said. Her eyes scanned the list quickly. 'Beulah Davenport,' she said to herself. 'That name rings a bell, but I can't think who she is.'

'Oh, you know who daft old Beulah Davenport is,' Mercedes interjected. 'She's that fruit juice heiress. Lives in that magnificent house near here. On the seminary block.'

'Oh, right. I remember,' Carolina said.

'She ordered flowers for Millicent Percy,' Mercedes said. 'Send a bunch of mimosa, is my advice. Milly loves mimosa, and it doesn't matter if they're dead. The drier the better.'

Carolina laughed. 'I'll send mimosa, but I don't think I'll send it quite dead,' she said. Mercedes could be a very good friend, she thought, always loyal and ready to help out in a pinch. And her knowledge about the various social circles in Manhattan was encyclopedic. If she didn't know someone personally, she might nevertheless know about them. That kind of knowledge could be very useful. *Perhaps*, she thought, *I might be able to persuade Mercedes to come to work for me full-time. I think she would be a real asset to the shop.* But she decided to tackle that situation after the wedding was over tomorrow night. There was too much to do right now to let any other considerations sidetrack her.

'Anyway, is there anything else vital for me to know? We should get busy on arrangements until we leave for the Plaza.'

'No, I don't think so,' Mercedes said, her silky blond hair swinging as she shook her head. 'Oh, one thing. Two people called from Southampton and wanted to know if you would deliver out there this summer. I told them they would have to speak to you personally.'

'Deliver to Southampton?'

'Why not,' Mercedes said, 'if you have enough orders. Make them outrageously expensive. You'd start a contest with the social climbers out there. See who could spend the most.'

It is food for thought, Carolina decided. 'Thanks, Mercedes,' she said. 'Okay, let's decide what we want from the Chinese restaurant. We'll order food and get busy on arrangements. Then when the guys have delivered everything to the Plaza, we'll head up there.'

Roxie called from her worktable. 'Carolina, you're needed over here,' she said. 'We have a minor disaster on our hands. Some of these orchids are shot.'

Carolina hurried to Roxie's worktable and looked at the orchids she had been talking about. 'These will be fine for filler,' Carolina said. 'Where they won't be noticed as anything except as color.'

'Okay,' Roxie said. 'If you say so.'

'Okay, team,' Carolina said. 'Antonio will take your food orders and call them in. Okay, Antonio?'

He looked as if he was going to argue for a moment, but then his face smoothed out into a placid and handsome mask. 'Sure, no problem,' he said.

'What say I start on the bride's bouquet and get it out of the way?' Carolina said.

'We knew you'd want to do that,' Roxie said, 'so it's up to you.'

'Tons of white orchids,' Carolina said, 'with oodles of white violets.'

'Oooooh,' Roxie crooned. 'I'd like a bouquet like that if I ever get married.'

'Maybe you will,' Carolina said. 'If Leland had any brains, he'd pop the question tomorrow.'

10

Carolina stepped off the elevator into the entry vestibule and crossed the loft in her stiletto heels, making a beeline for her dressing room. Sitting down on a chair, she removed first one crystal-encrusted shoe, then the other, and wiggled her toes before massaging each of her extremely tired feet. She'd been on them half the night and all day, but the effort had been well worth it. The wedding in the Plaza's Grand Ballroom had been extraordinarily beautiful – everyone had said so – especially considering the time limitations, and the bride and groom had been very pleased.

The press had been out in full force owing to the celebrity of the young couple, and Carolina was certain to be mentioned in more than a column or two as the wizard who'd transformed the Plaza into an orchid-laden paradise overnight. *I'd better be*, she thought, as she continued to rub her feet, *after all the work this took.*

Out of the corner of her eye, she glimpsed the clock on one of the built-in cabinets, and abruptly stopped massaging her feet and stood up. *My God*, she thought with alarm, *it's after eleven o'clock.*

Where's Richie? Then she sighed with relief. *He had said he was going to see a movie with his best friend, Jeff Adler.*

Nevertheless, on bare feet she went through her bedroom and down the hall to his door to make certain. His door was closed, and no sound came from within his room. Opening the door as quietly as she possibly could, she peered into his room. In the eerie glow of his computer's screen saver, she could see that his bed was empty. She threw his door wide open and then switched on the light. *No Richie.*

She switched the light back off, closed the door, and returned to her dressing room. *Damn,* she thought. *He should be home by now.* She had told Richie they were going to the country in the morning.

She carefully undressed, hanging her golden Mary McFadden empire gown with its Fortuny-like pleated skirt and exquisitely embroidered bust on a padded hanger, and dispensed with her undergarments. Grabbing one of Lyon's old tee shirts, she pulled it on and then slipped into her vintage silk robe, tying it at the waist. Only then did she realize she'd forgotten to take off her jewelry – the diamond earrings, necklace, and bracelet that Lyon had given her on their tenth anniversary. She removed them, placing them in their suede-lined boxes, which she put in the jewelry box on one of the cabinets.

After pouring herself a glass of wine, she settled down on a couch in the den to wait up for Richie. The novel she'd been reading was on the table next to her, but she didn't pick it up. She knew that she couldn't concentrate enough to get anything out of it. Not now. Not until she knew what was happening with Richie. *Maybe I ought to call the Adlers,* she thought. Then she decided against it. She didn't want to sound like an overpossessive, hysterical mother. Besides, the boys probably went to see the late movie. He was fine, she assured herself, but she couldn't help but watch the clock.

A while later, she heard the whir of the elevator in the distance. She glanced at the clock on the bookshelf again. Twelve o'clock.

She set down her wineglass as she heard the elevator door slide open and Richie's sneakers pound like elephant's feet on the oak floors. When he peeked around the corner, she smiled up at him. 'You went to see a movie?' she asked.

'Yeah. It wasn't bad,' he said, slowly taking the baseball cap off his head. 'Great car crashes.'

'Sounds like it was intellectually stimulating,' she joked.

'Yeah, it was pretty mindless,' he said with a shrug, 'but it was fun.'

She patted the couch beside her. 'Come sit here just a minute before you go to your room,' she said.

He immediately looked guilty, and an alarm bell went off in her head. 'I'm really tired, Mom,' he said. 'I think I'll hit the sack.'

'Just for a minute,' she said more firmly. 'I want to talk to you.'

He reluctantly crossed to the couch and sat down beside her. 'What's up?' he asked without looking at her.

'Your eyes look glazed,' she said. 'I'd like to know why.' She thought she detected the smell of beer, but wasn't certain.

He shrugged again. 'We just went to a late movie,' he said, his head hanging, his eyes still averted.

'You can do better than that, Richie,' she said. 'I'm not a complete fool.'

He was silent, shuffling his sneakers slightly on the floor. She was certain she could smell beer now.

'Come on, Richie,' she said, impatient. 'Where were you? What did you do?'

'Not much of anything,' he said. 'Kicked around with Jeff and some guys.'

'Have you been drinking?' she asked.

He frowned. 'Why are you asking me that?'

'You're avoiding the question,' she said, 'but to answer you, it's because you smell like a brewery.'

'I . . . we . . .' His voice trailed off, and he stared at the floor glumly.

'You can talk to me, Richie,' she said. 'You know that. Just tell me the truth.'

'Ah, shit!' he cursed.

'Without the expletives, if possible,' she said sternly.

'Where do you think I learned them?' he asked heatedly.

'I'll take all the credit,' she replied, 'but I still want to know the truth, Richie.'

'Yeah,' he said at last, nodding his head. 'I had a beer. One. That's all.' He finally looked at her. 'Satisfied?'

She nodded, wanting to believe him. She feared this was a reaction to the news that his father had canceled yet again on coming home – for Uncle Matt's birthday this time. Her stomach was twisted up into a knot of fear and loss and sadness. The days of his innocence were fast disappearing.

'Are you doing this because your dad couldn't come home?' she asked when she could trust herself to speak. 'I know you're disappointed that he hasn't been around much lately.'

Richie turned away petulantly, staring at the floor again, not deigning to answer her question.

She studied him for a moment, the unresponsiveness in his face. It was pointless to discuss the drinking now, she thought. She drew a deep breath.

'I know we're going to have a great time in the country,' she went on. 'With Matt's birthday party and all. Even if your dad can't be there, it'll be fun. You'll see.'

Richie kept studying his sneakers before finally lifting his head and saying, 'I think I'll hit the sack.'

'Okay, sweetie,' she said. 'That's a good idea, because we're leaving bright and early.'

He got to his feet and started for the door.

'Aren't you forgetting something?' Carolina asked.

He stopped but didn't turn around.

'Just a good-night kiss for your mom,' she said. 'Please?'

Richie shuffled over, leaned down, and brushed her cheek with his lips, then turned and left the room.

Carolina's shoulders slumped. *If only his father were here,* she thought. *But he's not, and I've got to work this through with him the best way I can.*

She let out an audible sigh. *Where is Lyon when I need him? When Richie needs him?*

11

C arolina turned off the highway and onto the narrow dirt road that led to the Mountcastles' weekend cottage in northwestern Connecticut, near Kent. The forests that bordered both sides of the road were leafy, the foliage lush with countless shades of green. Wildflowers of various types thrived alongside the lane, and in the morning sun she could see that the wild raspberries had already begun to form, although they weren't yet the plump, juicy red they would become.

Just ahead, the cottage, with its white clapboards and dark green shutters, came into view. Her heart lit with affection as it always did when she caught her first glimpse of the rambling old house. Roses in blazing reds, pristine whites, and golden yellows climbed all over the lattice entry porch and meandered along the white picket fence that enclosed part of the garden, giving the cottage a storybook appearance. She felt herself relax, as if this small piece of the country held some magical curative powers.

Crossing the tiny bridge that traversed the rocky stream bordering the property on one side, she pulled into the grassy lane that led to the garage, which had once been a coach house. Richie, who'd fallen asleep in the backseat on the drive, instantly woke up when she killed the engine.

'We're here,' he said, sitting up and rubbing his eyes.

'We sure are,' Carolina said. 'If you'll help me unload, I'll make us something to eat first thing.'

They quickly piled the groceries and their small bags on the old pine table in the kitchen.

'What's to eat?' Richie asked.

'We're going to have some of that curried chicken salad I got at the gourmet grocery,' Carolina said, 'and some mesclun greens and that fab bread they have. How's that?'

'Cool, Mom,' he said.

'You want to take your bag upstairs and drop mine off on the way? This'll only take a few minutes to get together, then we can hit the road. Start your driving lessons if you want to.' She looked over at him with a smile.

'Supercool,' he said, returning her smile. According to New York's peculiar driving rules, Richie could drive in the country at age sixteen, but not in the City until he was eighteen. Carolina had held out, saying he didn't need to learn to drive yet. But Richie had badgered her for months until, after his sixteenth birthday, she'd finally given in. Every time they came up, he got another lesson.

He took his small gym bag and her overnighter in hand and headed to the master bedroom and then to the tiny, enclosed stairway that led up to the second floor. *What a difference a day makes*, Carolina thought as she set the table. She was relieved to see that Richie's hostility of last night had dissipated with the morning light. Now, it was almost as if last night had never happened, and she had to remind herself that she and her son were going to have to have a sit-down and discuss his drinking.

When she was finished in the kitchen, she went around the

downstairs rooms, opening windows to the fresh air. Sunlight flooded the large dining room, and she looked around, admiring the botanicals that adorned the walls and the old blue-painted fireplace mantel. Through the small entry foyer she went on into the living room. Its knotty pine bookshelves and paneling glowed warmly in the sunlight, as did the old wide-board pine floors. She opened another window there before passing through the small sunroom and going on into the master bedroom with its big canopied bed. She opened a window that overlooked the pond in the back garden and inhaled the heady perfume of roses that came in on the air.

She retraced her steps to the kitchen, where Richie had turned on the small television set. 'What're you watching?' she asked.

'Nothing,' he replied. 'Just surfing.'

She served their lunch, and they ate hungrily, talking about what they would do the next couple of days.

'What time is Uncle Matt's birthday dinner?' he asked.

'Around eight,' she said.

'Maybe he and Thad'll ride their motorcycles over.'

'I don't know,' she replied. She took a sip of the pinot grigio she'd found in the refrigerator and set the glass back down. 'I thought we could do your driving lessons right here,' she said. 'I like that there're almost never any cars coming down this road. What do you think?'

'Sound good to me,' Richie said.

They finished lunch and cleared the table together. 'Give me a few minutes to put my things away,' she told Richie, 'then I'll meet you outside.'

'Cool,' he said, going out the kitchen door.

She went to the bedroom, where she quickly unpacked the few things she'd brought and put them away; then she took a couple of new magazines back into the living room, where she put them on the coffee table, and looked around.

The old pine-paneled room, its shelves stuffed to overflowing with books, CDs, videos, and bric-a-brac, never failed to fill her mind with memories. On one of the shelves, she eyed the photographs of her parents. Her mother was in her seventies when the picture was taken. Her gray hair was pulled back rather loosely into a bun at the nape of her neck, and her cool eyes stared into the camera's lens as if she were superior to it. Pearl earrings adorned her ears, and the single strand of pearls that she'd perpetually worn hung around her long slender neck. The photograph of her father was taken at the same time. His receding hair was also gray, and he wore a jacket and tie. There was almost, but not quite, a smile on his face. It was as if he'd seen too much of the world to allow himself the luxury.

Carolina turned away. The cottage often evoked her parents' spirits, as if they were ghosts that refused to leave these few rooms. Here, their voices were distinct, as they were nowhere else, and she could see their idiosyncratic mannerisms in her mind's eye, as though they stood before her.

Carolina had been thrilled to inherit the family cottage rather than money, which Matt got, and she still was. As a child she'd been free to explore the woods, swim in the pool, play games with anyone she could round up, and gather treasures from the forest and stream and gardens. Almost as important to her had been the wondrous shedding of her city clothes and the donning of her tomboy outfits: old jeans and tee shirts and sneakers. She'd been allowed to roam free as a bird without supervision, and she'd reveled in that freedom.

Puberty had quite naturally changed her interests. Gone was the tall skinny tomboy. She blossomed into a strikingly beautiful young woman with an avid interest in discovering the opposite sex. Overnight her appearance counted for everything – as did satisfying the desires that her mind and body told her were only natural. Carolina began to experiment with makeup and shopped for clothes that she felt lent her a sexual appeal. Thus armed, she began her incursions into the more adult world of parties and dating.

Her parents became harshly overprotective, threatened by her growing sexuality. Their behavior, in turn, only made Carolina all the more rebellious. Her friend, Millie Weiss, whom she would never forget, came to her rescue, inviting her to stay over so often that the Weiss apartment became a second home. They allowed the girls to wear makeup and dress the way they wanted to and let them stay out late, no questions asked.

When they were only fifteen years old, they hit the latest and trendiest clubs, only to be refused entry. Undaunted, they got fake IDs. In these clubs they met a fast-living, hard-playing, and fun-loving set that experimented with sex and drugs. For the most part, the people she got to know best were trying to be artists of some sort or another, and, like Carolina, many of them were searching for an adult identity and a place to fit in.

It was in one of these clubs that she met Lyon. She glanced up at the photograph of the two of them that had been taken soon after their marriage. She'd been only eighteen and Lyon had been twenty-eight. They were looking into each other's eyes, smiling widely, the perfect picture of youthful happiness and desire. *Damn him!* she thought. *Why isn't he here now?*

'Mom! Mom!' The voice that interrupted her reverie was an urgent plea, and Carolina hurried from the living room into the kitchen.

'Aren't you coming?' Richie asked, standing at the back door, holding it open.

'Let's go,' she said. She tossed him the car keys, and he caught them with one hand.

They went outside and got in the big Jeep Grand Cherokee. She thought that Richie might be a little nervous. 'There's nothing to be afraid of,' she said, to ease any anxiety he might be feeling.

'I'm not afraid,' he said, looking at her.

'Good,' she said. 'Is the seat adjusted okay for you?'

'It's perfect, Mom,' he said.

'Okay. Fire it up.'

Richie started the car.

'Now then,' Carolina said, giving him a route he'd done before, 'I think the best thing to do is back out of the driveway, then go on up the lane to Pump House Road. You can make a left there, then circle back around to here. Why don't you try that a few times, then we'll go toward the general store on back roads? So, without giving it any gas, put it in reverse.'

Richie did as he was told and then sat waiting.

'Using your rearview mirror and the side mirror, make sure nothing's coming, then give it a little gas and back out.'

'There's nothing coming, Mom,' he said. 'There never is on this road.'

'We'll play like this is a high traffic area,' she said, 'so you'll learn to do the things you'll have to do in the city.'

Richie patiently looked behind him, using both mirrors, turned in his seat to look out for good measure, and then gave the car gas. They glided back perfectly and turned into the road, where he stopped, shifted into drive, and then drove on up the road ahead, keeping his speed down. All like an old hand.

'That was perfect,' Carolina said enthusiastically. 'You're doing this like you've done it a thousand times.'

'I have,' he said, looking straight ahead.

'What do you mean?' Carolina asked in surprise.

'I mean that I've done it a lot,' Richie said. 'Maybe not a thousand times, but a lot.'

'Richie!' she exclaimed. 'We've only done this a few times. Have you gone out with your dad and you didn't tell me?'

'No,' he replied, slowing to a stop at Pump House Road. He put on his turn signal, looked both ways, and then turned left. 'The last few times we've been up here, after you were asleep I'd get the keys and take the car out for a spin.'

'You what!' she said, outraged. 'But you could've been killed or something!'

'I just drove around here on back roads,' he said defensively.

'I don't believe this,' Carolina said. 'I don't *believe* it.'

Richie stopped at the highway, put on his turn signal again, turned left, and drove toward the little dirt lane that led to the house. He drove with quiet concentration.

'I thought I could trust you,' Carolina said. 'I did trust you, and now you've broken that trust.'

Richie turned into their lane after signaling, and drove toward the cottage. 'I'm sorry, Mom,' he said. 'I really am. But I kept asking, and you kept not wanting to go. And Dad is never around.'

Carolina's shoulders slumped. She could certainly understand what Richie was saying. It was true that Lyon had repeatedly promised to teach him to drive, but had never found the time. Nevertheless, she felt betrayed. Her trust in Richie had been shattered, and now she wondered if she would ever be able to trust him again. And compounding the problem was his drinking last night.

He pulled over into the lane that led to the garage behind the house and put the car in park. 'I know you're upset, Mom,' he said, turning and looking at her, 'and I really am sorry. It's just that . . . I got tired of Dad's always making excuses.'

'That doesn't excuse you from doing what you did, Richie,' she said. 'We're alone a lot, just you and me, and I have to trust you. If I didn't trust you, I wouldn't let you go off with Jeff to the movies or wherever, staying out late. You know what I mean?'

He nodded, but didn't say anything.

'And I guess if I didn't trust you,' she said, 'you wouldn't have been out drinking last night. Right?'

He nodded again.

'I trusted you on that count, too, Richie,' she went on. 'We've talked about alcohol and drugs, and you know that I think you're too young to be experimenting. But I trusted you. Let you go out and do whatever you wanted to. What if you didn't get to do those things?' she said. 'You'd start to feel like a prisoner, wouldn't you?'

'I already was,' he said in a small voice.

Carolina sat there, momentarily stunned by his words. She could feel herself flush, in part from anger, but in large part from embarrassment. Richie, she suddenly realized, was feeling exactly the way she'd felt all those years ago when her parents had refused to let her stay out late or use makeup or dress the way she wanted to. *Damn!* she thought. *I don't want to be like them. The last thing I want to do is be like they were. I'm liable to run him off. But* . . . She felt helpless and uncertain what she should do.

She finally turned to Richie. 'Will you promise not to take the car out like that again?' she asked. 'Tell me whenever you want to go. If you want to wake me up in the middle of the night to go with you, I don't care. Just promise me you won't take it out again by yourself.'

'I promise,' Richie said somewhat sheepishly.

'That was a very dangerous thing to do,' she said. 'It could have gotten us all into a lot of trouble if something had happened.'

'I know, Mom,' he said, 'and I really am sorry.'

'And you'll promise not to go out drinking while you're underage?'

He nodded.

She looked over at him and wanted to believe that what he'd said was true. She needed to believe him. 'Okay,' she said. 'Let's start over. We'll go toward the general store this time.'

Richie put the car in reverse, backed out, and headed up the dirt lane as before.

'How did you know what to do?' Carolina asked when he stopped at Pump House Road again. 'I mean, how did you get to be so good at driving? Was it just watching us?'

'I . . . well . . .' His voice trailed off, and then he fell silent as he drove down the road.

It was obvious to Carolina that he wasn't telling her something. 'Come on, Richie,' she cajoled. 'You can tell me whatever it is.

107

Remember, we have a deal, the two of us, and part of that deal is being honest with each other.'

'I promised,' he said.

'Promised what?' she asked.

'Oh, man,' he said.

'What?'

'I promised Uncle Matt I wouldn't tell you and Dad,' he said, stopping at the highway again.

'Tell us what?'

'He's . . . he's been letting me drive around his place in Connecticut when I'd come up on weekends,' he said.

'You mean he let you drive that big Land Rover?' she said.

'Uh-huh,' he said, 'and I drove the pickup truck, too.'

'That too,' she said.

'It's just like driving the Jeep, Mom,' he said, turning onto the highway and heading toward the general store.

Oh, shit! she thought. *I should've known. I'll have to have a little talk with my big brother tonight.*

12

Carolina was in the kitchen when she heard her brother's Land Rover in the lane and the screen door bang loudly as Richie ran out to greet him and Thad. Smiling, she covered the lobster salad with Saran Wrap, put it in the refrigerator to chill, and took out the bottle of champagne that she'd put there this morning. She was so grateful that Richie liked – no, was crazy about – Matt and Thad, and that they doted on him the way they did. With the exception of his brother, Lyon had almost no relatives on his side of the family, and Matt was the only relative, other than some cousins, on her side.

'Hey, Sis,' Matt called out, coming through the kitchen door.

'Hi, sweetums,' she said as she filled a champagne bucket with ice cubes.

He gave her a kiss on the cheek. 'You must be psychic,' he said. 'Why's that?'

'Because you knew I was bringing a bottle of bubbly.'

'For your own birthday party?' she said.

'Sure, why not? I wanted something extra special.'

'Oh, let me see,' she said.

He produced the bottle from behind his back.

'Oh, Cristal!' she exclaimed. 'Forget my lowly Veuve Clicquot.'

'We can have both,' he said with a laugh. 'It *is* my birthday. We'll start with mine and finish with yours.'

'It's a deal,' she said. 'Is it chilled?'

'Yes,' he said. 'I brought it over in a cooler.'

'Silly me,' she said, 'asking such a question of you. I should have known. Always the Eagle Scout. Prepared and all that. But I am surprised you sprang for something so extravagant.'

'Well, I have to tell you the truth,' he confided. 'It was a gift from Sybil Conroy. She gave me a whole case.'

'Oh, my God, you're kidding,' she said. 'That's a king's ransom – but I guess she can afford it. How's the project going?'

'Really well,' he said. 'We've drawn up some plans for next spring, too. She wants some major landscaping done.'

'Then it's her good fortune that she found you and Thad,' she said. 'Where *are* Thad and Richie, by the way?'

'They ran to the general store,' he replied. 'Thad was out of cigarettes.'

'And left you, the birthday boy, here to help get his own party ready?'

'I told him to go on because I wanted to catch up with you,' he said.

'I guess the hypnosis didn't help him stop smoking.'

'For a few weeks.' He shook his head. 'I wish he'd give them up, but I'm not going to say anything.'

She looked at him and smiled. 'I don't think either one of us had better say anything since we used to practically chain-smoke.'

'No,' he agreed. 'I think that would aggravate the situation anyway. Here, why don't you let me open that bottle? We can get an early start.'

'Wonderful idea,' she said. She handed the bottle back to him and got a corkscrew out of a drawer. 'Want to sit outside?'

'Why not?'

'Good, I'll take some glasses down to the pool,' she said.

They walked down to the swimming pool together, glasses and champagne bucket in hand, and then sat down on chaises longues. Matt put the bucket on the stone patio between them and poured each of them a glass.

'Cheers,' he said.

'Ditto,' Carolina replied.

They touched glasses; then she spread out on her chaise lengthwise. 'I'm glad they went to the store,' she said, 'because I wanted to talk to you about something.'

'Fire away,' he said.

'I gave Richie a driving lesson this morning,' she began.

'Great,' Matt said. 'How'd he do?'

'Why don't *you* tell *me*?' she replied, looking him in the eye.

'What—?'

'Don't play games with me, Matt,' she said. 'I know you've been letting him drive around your place. He didn't want to tell me because he'd promised you he wouldn't, but I finally got it out of him.'

Matt took a quick sip of his champagne. 'I'm sorry, Sis,' he said quietly. 'You have every right to be pissed off at me, but the kid was desperate to learn. And I thought, why not? My place is perfect for it with the roads going to the greenhouses and up into the woods and everything.'

'I wish you'd told me,' she said, 'or better yet, asked me beforehand.'

'I know I should've asked you first,' he said, 'but I didn't see any real harm in it.'

'I'm his mother, Matt, and I don't like the idea of you two conspiring together behind my back. Not about something like this.'

111

He nodded. 'It won't happen again,' he said. 'I promise.'

She saw the regret written on his face and immediately softened. 'What you did was very special to him, Matt,' she said, 'and I appreciate that. I just think that I should've known.' She took a sip of her champagne and then looked back over at him. 'Did he tell you that he'd taken the car out at night after we'd gone to bed?'

'What?' he said. 'You've got to be kidding.'

She shook her head. 'Nope. He confessed that, too. He's been doing that when we've been up here.'

'Aw, Jeez,' Matt said. 'It's too bad Lyon . . .' He paused a moment, choosing his words carefully. '. . . Well, it's too bad he can't spend more time with Richie. He's such a great kid, and it's a critical time in his development, you know?'

Carolina nodded her head solemnly. 'You've taken the words straight out of my mouth,' she said. 'It's really been worrying me lately, especially with all of Lyon's broken promises.' She paused and took a sip of champagne. 'In fact, I'm beginning to get really pissed off, Matt.'

He knew his sister well, and could see that she was more concerned than she would admit. 'Want to talk about it?' he asked.

She shrugged. 'What can I say? Lyon's gone for longer and longer periods of time. Then when he comes home he doesn't seem to be able to find the time for either me or Richie.'

'You surely don't think . . . well, that maybe something's going on, do you?' Matt asked.

'No. I don't think so,' Carolina said, 'but sometimes I do wonder. You know, I looked at that picture in the living room. The one of Lyon and me right after we were married. And I thought about how happy we were. How devoted we were to each other. How he would practically move mountains to get home to me.' She looked into Matt's eyes. 'That's gone,' she said sadly. 'We're still in love, but . . . well, I guess Lyon just doesn't care as much as he used to.'

Matt reached over and patted her arm. 'It's probably just his work,

Sis,' he said. 'Lyon loves you as much as ever. Remember, the company's going through a rough time and a lot of changes.'

'I know all that,' Carolina said, 'but I also know that in the past all that business-related stuff would've taken a back burner to me and his son. He's started acting more like Leland, if you know what I mean. Everything's all about Leland, no matter what the situation is.'

Before Matt could respond to her, they heard the car pull into the driveway and doors slamming. He squeezed her shoulder. 'We'll talk some more later,' he said, 'if you want to. Now wipe that glum look off your face. It's my birthday, remember?'

Carolina grinned. 'Time for party talk?'

Matt laughed. 'Yes, definitely. Nothing important or meaningful allowed. Just party talk.'

Richie and Thad came down the bluestone steps to the pool area. 'Hi, you two,' she called to them.

'Hi, Mom,' Richie said. 'Hey, Uncle Matt. Happy birthday!' He rushed over to Matt and gave him a high five.

'Thanks, Richie,' he said as their hands smacked together loudly in the air.

'I see you two got a head start,' Thad said. He kissed Carolina on the cheek and then sat down on a chaise.

'You can catch up,' she said. She held a glass while Matt poured champagne for Thad. 'Richie, do you want something?'

He shook his head. 'No,' he replied. Then he grinned. 'Unless you let me have some of that.'

Carolina and Matt exchanged glances and then laughed. 'You can have a tiny sip of mine,' she told Richie.

He took the glass from her and had a sip, then looked thoughtful for a moment. 'Not as good as beer,' he said.

Matt and Thad looked at him in surprise, but Carolina used the comment as a welcome opener. She wanted Richie to open up about drinking. 'Not as good as beer, huh?'

113

'I've drunk a few times with Jeff,' Richie said with a dismissive shrug. 'No big deal.'

Maybe. Maybe not, Carolina thought, *but it has the potential to be. Cars and booze! This really is a critical time. I'll have to have a serious talk with Lyon about this the next time he calls, or better yet the next time he's home.*

'Want a refill?' Thad asked.

'Why not?' she replied. 'One more before we go in for dinner.'

'That was really delicious,' Thad said as he helped clear the table.

'Mercedes's recipes,' Carolina said.

'How did such a rich, aristocratic English girl ever learn to be such a good cook?' Matt asked, carrying empty dessert plates with their spent birthday candles to the kitchen. 'You can't go wrong with her recipes.'

'They never fail to impress,' Carolina said. 'She would have approved of the lemon cake I made for your birthday, but the lobster salad wouldn't have come up to her expectations.'

'Why not?' Thad asked.

'Because I didn't do it from scratch,' she said, 'and she'd be able to taste the difference.'

'What wasn't from scratch?' Matt asked.

'I bought frozen lobster,' Carolina said. 'Mercedes would never do that.'

'Well, I sure couldn't taste the difference,' Matt said, 'and I don't see how Mercedes has any taste buds left. Not with the way she smokes.'

'It's odd, isn't it?' Carolina said, glancing at Thad. 'But I made a salmon soufflé, and the minute she tasted it she told me I should've marinated it in lemon before cooking it. I couldn't believe it.'

'That is unbelievable,' Thad said.

'Lemon is the speed of cooking, she told me.'

They all laughed. 'In that case, I'm going to start putting it in everything,' Matt joked.

'How's she doing? Working on some kind of project?' Thad asked.

'I don't really know,' Carolina said. 'But she's been a real friend, helping me out at the shop, which is really great because we've been so busy.'

Later, they took their coffee into the living room, and Matt opened his birthday presents. A silly leopard print bathing suit from Thad brought merry laughter.

'I dare you to wear it,' Thad said.

'You're going to lose this one,' Matt replied.

Playing cards with motorcycles on them from Richie. 'I promise I'll teach you to play poker,' Matt said. 'And we'll use these cards.'

'That's why I got them,' Richie confessed.

From Carolina he received a rare old book on the gardens at Vaux-le-Vicomte. 'Ah, Sis,' he said. 'This is so special. You know me so well.'

He'd begun talking about his greenhouses and the landscaping business when Carolina had a sudden inspiration.

'You know about my Lydia Carstairs connection,' she said, 'but I didn't tell you the latest.'

'What is it?' Matt asked.

'She's on the boards of a bunch of charities,' Carolina said, 'and she called me the other day to ask me if I thought I could handle a big benefit in the fall.'

'Wow, what an opportunity!' Matt exclaimed. 'How big?'

'Around a thousand people,' Carolina said.

'Oh, my God,' Thad said. 'That's enormous. But isn't this awfully short notice?'

Carolina nodded. 'Boy, is it ever. But the guy who was supposed to handle the decorating, Jimmy Josephson, just backed out. He had to go to rehab, and from what I hear he's having financial difficulties.'

'You're kidding,' Matt said. 'I was looking at pictures of his new town house in *Architectural Digest* just the other day. I would've thought he was rolling in dough. He's the one practically everybody uses for those big benefits.'

'Yes,' Carolina agreed, 'and he's really fabulous at what he does. Which means that if I accept this plum, I'll really have to do an incredible job.'

'You can do it, Sis,' Matt said.

'Yeah,' Richie said, 'you can do it, Mom. I'll help you.'

She looked at her son. 'Thank you, sweetie,' she said. 'You may have to. And you're right, I think I can do it, too,' she said confidently. 'I guess if the shop can do a wedding like Chrissy Madison's and Ricky Sanchez's virtually overnight and survive it, we can do almost anything. I'm going to need a lot of help. I'll be using the part-timers I always do for party cleanups and such, but I'm going to need a lot more. There're a thousand things to think about. The flowers aren't even the half of it. Make that a tenth of it. First, I'm going to have to think about space, not necessarily for the shop, but space for props and storage. Lighting design and the equipment. All kinds of things I haven't done before except on a tiny scale in comparison.'

'Is there a theme for this party?' Thad asked.

'Lydia's going to discuss it with me this week,' she said, 'if I agree to do it. She was going to call other people on the board first to get their okay to hire me. A courtesy, she told me. There'll be a contract and everything.'

'What's the charity?' Matt asked.

'It's the Animal Rescue Mission,' she said.

'Where's it going to be?' Thad asked.

'The Metropolitan Museum of Art,' she replied, 'but not in the Temple of Dendur space where most parties are. It's going to be in the Medieval Court.'

'That's fantastic,' Matt said. 'Really beautiful.'

'Well, it has its good points and bad points,' Carolina said.

'You can sure use the architecture in your favor,' Matt said.

116

She nodded. 'I've been giving that a lot of thought, but it depends on the theme.'

'My God, we could get a whole forest of huge trees, shrubs, or whatever in there,' Matt said with excitement.

Carolina smiled. 'I see you get what I'm driving at,' she said. 'I figured since you know all about landscape design and you know all the wholesale nursery people, and Thad knows everything in the world about lighting and a lot about props . . . I mean, what a combination. Right?'

The two men nodded and smiled.

'I know you're busy, but I was thinking that maybe you'd be interested in helping me out. For a share of the profits, of course.'

Matt looked at Thad, and a silent signal passed between them. He turned his gaze back to his sister. 'I'm pretty sure we can work something out,' he said. 'But you should call us the minute you know what the theme is so we can put our heads together. As far as storage goes, I know it's a long way, but if you want, you could always use one of the barns on our property. Temporarily, at least. Leasing storage space in or around Manhattan would cost you an arm and a leg.'

'Thanks, Matt,' she said. 'I appreciate it, and I'll keep your offer in mind. But if this pans out, I'm going to have to have space close in, so that it's readily accessible any time. What if I had three benefits like this in a week?'

'You're thinking really big time,' he said.

She nodded. 'Why not? I've got the introduction, and there's a gap to be filled.'

'What about the shop?' Thad asked.

'The way I see it,' she replied, 'the shop would turn into a sort of showcase for my work. Well, it already is to some extent. It wouldn't cease functioning as a shop. No, I want to keep that little place, but my emphasis would turn to managing the party business. Getting the clients, planning the parties, overseeing the decorations – whatever they might be. Sometimes it would mean building elaborate props, designing complicated light systems, that sort of thing. But the shop would stay as it is with the very best floral designers working there. I might expand it somewhat, or have an uptown branch. That remains to be seen.'

Matt sat grinning at her, and she saw the look on his face. 'What are you grinning at?' she asked.

'Oh, I was just thinking how I'm your big, older brother,' he said, 'and I was remembering how I was the one who was always interested in flowers and botany growing up. You didn't pay any attention. You just wanted to swim and hike and play ball and stuff like that. But look at you now! You're going to be the Queen of Flowers in New York City, Sis.'

Carolina laughed heartily, and the others joined in. 'You're right,' she said. 'You'd always be gathering flowers and plants and classifying them or arranging them for the house, always talking about how beautiful or unusual they were and always growing things. I didn't care one way or the other until I went to work in that first shop. I guess some of it must have rubbed off on me without me even knowing it.'

'I'll say it did,' Matt said. 'And royally.'

'Anyway, I'll call you the instant I hear from Lydia Carstairs, and let you know what she has to say. I mean, it could happen that the board won't even approve me.'

'I doubt that,' Thad said. 'Not with Lydia's power.'

'We'll see,' Carolina said. 'In the meantime, you two can do some brainstorming on the subject.'

'We will,' Matt said.

Later, Matt and Thad got up to drive back to their place. 'You can come up whenever you want, Richie,' Matt said.

'That'd be great,' Richie said.

'And the next time,' Carolina said with a smile, 'maybe you guys will let me know what you plan on doing *before* you do it. Like driving big Land Rovers and pickup trucks.'

'We will, Sis,' Matt said.

'Promise,' Richie added.

'Good,' Carolina replied, 'because I don't want to hear about Richie running around on a motorcycle after he's done it.'

Matt, Thad, and Richie exchanged uneasy glances that were not lost on Carolina. 'Sure thing,' Matt said. 'The next time we'll ask you first.'

Carolina was silent for an instant, staring at them with narrowed eyes. 'He's already done it, hasn't he?' she finally said. 'Richie's already actually driven one of your motorcycles, right?'

Matt and Thad stood motionless as Richie shifted from one sneakered foot to the other. 'Well, it's like this,' Matt started to say.

'Just go on home,' she said, waving them away. 'Happy birthday. Now go.'

'Sis, we didn't lie to you about that,' Matt said defensively, yet hardly managing to hide the smile that hovered on his lips. 'You didn't ask—'

'That's a sin of omission,' she said. 'Now, *out*!'

'We're going, we're going,' Matt said as he and Thad backed out the door.

'I'll ring you this week,' she called after them.

'Okay,' Matt said. 'Can't wait.' Before he started the Land Rover, he called, 'And thanks for my birthday dinner. The food was great.'

'Bye.' She and Richie stood at the door, waving at them as they left; then she turned to go back into the kitchen. Richie walked on ahead of her, obviously heading upstairs to his room.

'Richie,' she said.

He turned around. 'Yes, Mom?' She could see that he was preparing himself for a lecture. 'Which motorcycle did you ride by yourself?' she asked. 'Thad's Sportster or that monstrosity of Matt's?'

'Neither one,' he replied. 'They've got an old Triumph Bonneville, totally restored like new, and that's what they let me ride.' His voice had become more excited with each word.

'Wonder what they got that for?' she asked.

Richie shrugged. 'Maybe . . . they just needed a small bike around the place. You know . . . for . . . I don't know . . . maybe just running errands or something.'

She looked at her son and instantly knew the answer to her question. 'I see,' she said. 'Well, are you going to give your blind and stupid old Mom a kiss good night?'

Richie kissed her cheek and hugged her. 'Night, Mom,' he said.

'Night, sweetie,' she replied.

She watched him start up the stairs to his bedroom and then went on into her own. *I guess there'll be a helmet and leathers joining all the other stuff in his bedroom clutter*, she thought.

13

When the telephone's persistent ringing finally penetrated the thick veil of sleep that held her in its grip, Carolina rolled over and cast a bleary eye at the clock on the bedside table.

'Oh, damn,' she swore aloud. Her throat was parched from drinking champagne, and her voice was a dry rasp. 'Who the hell is calling here at one o'clock in the morning?' *Lyon*, she thought. *Has to be. Probably calling to see how the birthday dinner was.*

She reached over and picked up the receiver. 'Lyon?' she said.

'Mrs Mountcastle?' a man's voice asked. His English was almost perfect, but she could hear the faintest trace of an accent.

What the devil? she wondered. 'Yes?' she responded, sitting up and flipping on a lamp.

'You are the wife of Mr Lyon Mountcastle?' the man asked.

'Y-yes,' Carolina replied in a stutter. Fear suddenly twisted her stomach into a knot, and she felt her heart begin to race. 'W-who is this? What do you—?'

'Mrs Mountcastle,' the man went on in a slow and methodical

manner, 'I am Kees Verhoeven.' Kees, pronounced like *Case*.

Kees Verhoeven? Who the hell is Kees Verhoeven? She felt as if her already racing heart had lurched into her throat and would surely suffocate her.

'With the police department in Amsterdam,' she heard him say. 'I regret to inform you that your husband, Mr Lyon Mountcastle, has suffered a fatal heart attack.'

She heard a gasp, barely audible above the stranger's continuing drone, but didn't realize it was her own. Later, much later, when she tried to remember his exact words, she became aware that nothing after those few words had registered. Nothing. It was as if a steel door had clanged shut in her mind, closing it off to any further perception.

She didn't remember that she failed to respond, that she'd dropped the receiver on the floor and let it remain there, the man's voice a little squawk calling to her, 'Mrs Mountcastle, Mrs Mountcastle,' time and again.

Nor did she remember that Richie rushed into the bedroom, frantic, when he'd heard the crash of glass shattering against the floor, the dull thunks of missiles slamming against the walls, and the mournful wail that sent gooseflesh racing up his arms.

He found her amid the wreckage of broken lamps and glasses and bottles, of mirror shards and slivers of glass that had covered framed pictures on the walls, of a dented clock and splintered radio, of flung books and magazines, of strewn pillows and sheets and clothing, oblivious of him and the havoc she'd wrought. He'd simply stood and stared at her, wide-eyed, his mouth agape, terrified by the picture that she and the once-beautiful room presented. Then he'd rushed to her and flung his arms about her.

'Mom,' he cried. 'Mom, Mom, Mom!'

She didn't respond. She wasn't aware that he was even there, but continued to wail as if she were an animal that had been caught in a trap from which it couldn't extricate itself, mortally wounded and alone.

Richie saw the telephone receiver on the floor and reached over to pick it up. He responded to the stranger's voice and listened as he repeated his terrible message; then he let go of his mother long enough to rush into the kitchen, grab a pen and piece of paper from a notepad, and take down the telephone number that Kees Verhoeven wanted to give him.

He held his mother then, rocking her as if she were a child – as if their roles had been reversed by the act of an unloving God – and cooed to her tenderly, trying to reach through the utter despair that had engulfed her. When he saw that his efforts were useless, he reached for the telephone again and dialed the number for his uncle.

Uncle Matt will know what to do, he thought in desperation. *He has to know. He has to.*

Richie went back to his mother after the telephone call and continued to try to console her, whispering to her from time to time, 'Uncle Matt is coming. He'll fix it.' But even Richie, at sixteen years of age, knew that Matt couldn't really *fix* anything. Nobody could.

Carolina's wails eventually turned to sobs that shook her entire body, then as she gradually wore out, to spurts of tears, punctuated with long periods of silent dead-eyed staring into space. Richie tried to move her, but she wouldn't budge.

Matt arrived at last, and he and Richie together picked up Carolina and laid her on the living room couch. Matt had brought a small bottle of Ativan, and he slipped one onto her tongue, giving her a swallow of water. After a while, she calmed down enough to listen and then finally to talk. Matt realized that he had to take over because his sister wasn't capable of handling the situation in her present state or of making even the simplest plans.

'Richie,' he said, 'I'm going to make a couple of telephone calls in the kitchen. You're okay to stay with her for a few minutes?'

Richie nodded his assent.

'Be right back,' Matt said, glancing at his sister.

As good as his word, he returned to the living room in a very short time. He pulled a chair over to the couch and sat at Carolina's side.

'I talked to Kees Verhoeven,' he said, 'and I also called the airlines. I've made reservations on a flight out from New York late in the day,' Matt said. 'I'll have plenty of time to drive you and Richie back to New York, get you settled in, then catch my flight.'

'What about Leland?' she asked. 'Shouldn't he be called?'

'I'll call him when we get into the city,' Matt replied. 'There's no need to wake him up now.'

'When will you be back from Amsterdam?' Carolina asked.

'The day after tomorrow,' he said. 'A couple of days at most.'

'That quickly?' Carolina said. 'I mean . . . don't you have to . . . to see . . . him . . . and all that?' Her words were somewhat dulled and slow, but her agitation was calming down considerably. The Ativan that Matt had given her was beginning to take effect.

'I've already cleared everything with this guy Verhoeven,' Matt said. He didn't want to give her all the details unless she asked, but he would indeed have to identify the body before it was cremated and then pick up the ashes before returning to New York with them. There was also a great deal of paperwork to handle and who knew what else?

'You don't have to worry about it,' Matt went on. 'Verhoeven told me that they'd be ready for me when I get there. They're even meeting me at Schiphol.'

'That . . . that seems nice of them,' Carolina said.

'It is,' Matt said. 'They've been extraordinarily helpful. Right now, I think what we'd better do is get ready to go back to New York. Get anything you might need, and we'll put it in your car. Thad's bringing by an overnight bag for me, and he'll pick up my car later on.'

Carolina nodded, not really knowing what to do, such was the fog she was in, and she willingly submitted to his orders. Within the hour, she and Richie, with Matt driving, were on their way into New York City.

'I want to go with you,' Richie blurted out. They were seated in the loft's big living room, waiting for the driver who would pick up Matt and take him out to Kennedy.

'Well . . .' Matt cast an uneasy glance over at Carolina, where she lay on one of the long couches, but she didn't seem to be listening. 'I think I'd better make this trip alone, Richie,' he said. 'There's going to be a lot of paperwork, and that's about it. I'll be coming straight back, and I think you should stay with your mom.'

Carolina sat up and took a sip of water. 'I . . . I think it would be best if you stayed here,' she said at last, setting the glass down. She looked over at Richie and attempted a smile that didn't quite succeed.

'But why, Mom?' Richie asked in a frustrated voice. 'He's my dad. I've got my passport and everything and—'

'No,' she replied in a more authoritative voice than she'd intended. The fiery glint in her eyes died almost immediately. She patted the couch, indicating to Richie that he should come and sit next to her.

He got up from his chair, crossed the expanse of rug between them, and sat down next to his mother reluctantly.

Carolina put a hand on his shoulder and squeezed it lightly. 'I . . . I need you here, Richie,' she said. 'Please. Roxie and Antonio are going to help out at the shop, but . . . but I'll really need someone here to help.'

Richie's face reddened with barely concealed anger. 'What am I going to do?' he asked. 'There's—'

'Answer the telephone,' she broke in. 'Answer the elevator buzzer. Run errands. There're going to be all kinds of things to do. Matt'll be gone until day after tomorrow, handling things in Amsterdam.'

Richie heaved a dramatic sigh of exasperation. He stared at his sneakers, his face a stony, expressionless mask, but it was all he could do to control the volatile mix of emotions that whirled around in his mind.

He was almost afraid to be alone with her now. For the first time he'd witnessed a vulnerability in his mother that he didn't know she'd possessed. He'd told his uncle, 'She's lost it, Uncle Matt. Like, totally.' This new and very fragile mother frightened him.

He finally lifted his gaze from the floor and his sneakers, looking off into space. 'Okay,' he said. 'I'll stay here and do the flunky work, but Uncle Leland said he could help out, so I don't see why I'm really needed.'

'Because your mother needs you, number one,' Matt said. 'What you'll be doing is very important, Richie. Not flunky work. Your mom doesn't want some total stranger, not even your uncle Leland, coming in here invading her privacy once the word gets out. And the news is already spreading around town. You know how small New York really is. Word spreads like wildfire.'

He cleared his throat before continuing. 'Look, Richie,' he said, 'you're the man of the house now, and you'll have to be here to help take care of your mom.'

His words had the immediate effect Matt had hoped for, even if he had reservations about placing such a heavy responsibility on a sixteen-year-old. Richie stood up and went back to his chair. He didn't sprawl or slump dejectedly, but sat upright, expectantly.

He looked at his uncle. 'Okay,' he said. 'I'll stay here.'

'I think you're going to have a lot to do,' Matt said. 'I have a feeling the buzzer and telephone are going to start any time now. Better to have everything shipshape first.'

The telephone rang, and the intercom buzzed at the same moment, cutting Matt off. He looked over at Richie. 'You want to get the intercom, and I'll take the phone until I have to go?'

Richie nodded, got to his feet, and then headed to the intercom in the kitchen. Matt picked up the remote receiver on the table next to his chair.

'Hello,' he said as Carolina watched his face.

'Yes, Mercedes,' he said. 'It's true.' Carolina sat all the way up on the couch and mouthed, 'No,' while waving her hands, indicating to Matt that in no uncertain terms did she want to talk to Mercedes.

Matt finished the conversation and pushed the OFF button on the receiver. 'Don't worry,' he said, 'she's not coming up here now. She sends her sympathy and love and says to call her if you need anything.'

'Thanks,' Carolina said. 'It was sweet of her to call, but I don't want to talk to her right now.'

They both turned toward the entry vestibule as Richie came toward them with a huge bunch of flowers. They were the pale pink roses that Carolina was so crazy about, and there must have been four or five dozen of them.

'My God,' she said. 'Who sent those, Richie?'

He laid the bundle of flowers down on the coffee table and removed an envelope from within the sleeve. 'They're from Seth Foster,' Richie said, handing her the card.

She looked down at it. 'My deepest sympathy,' it read. 'If there's anything I can do, please don't hesitate to call me.' He'd enclosed one of his calling cards and written his home telephone number on it. 'That's awfully nice of him,' she said. 'Why don't you . . . No, I'll do it.'

'What, Mom?' Richie asked.

'I'll put these roses in a vase of water,' she said, getting to her feet.

'I can do it,' Richie said.

'No,' she said. 'I need to keep busy, too. And this I can certainly do.' She picked up the flowers and went to the kitchen with them. When she returned, she placed the roses, in a huge crystal vase, in the center of the coffee table.

'I think I'll go get some clothes on now,' she said. 'Be back in a few minutes.'

The buzzer sounded again, and Richie went to answer it while Matt fielded telephone calls. When Carolina came back into the living room, she'd put on fresh makeup and brushed her hair and changed into slacks and a linen tee shirt. She sat down on the couch, and her eyes locked on to the pink roses. *They're so beautiful,* she thought.

Matt was heartened by Carolina's attention to her appearance. It was a sure sign that his sister was beginning to get a grip on herself. Keeping busy was probably the best thing for her now.

Richie headed in from the entry vestibule with two more enormous bunches of flowers. 'They're bringing up a lot more, Mom,' he said.

'Why don't you put them on the kitchen counter for now?' Carolina said. 'I'll put them somewhere later.'

'Here're the cards, Mom,' Richie said, handing them to her.

She took the cards from him and opened them, one at a time. 'Lydia Carstairs,' she said, placing the first card back in its envelope. She stared at the second card and then looked over at Matt. 'My God,' she said. 'They're from Sybil Conroy.'

'Thad must've told her,' Matt said.

'But which is which?' Carolina asked.

'The roses are from Mrs Carstairs,' Richie said, 'and the orchids are from Mrs Conroy.'

'Do you mind putting the cards back on the flowers, sweetie?' she asked Richie.

'Why don't I just write the kind of flowers that the person sent on the envelopes?' Richie asked.

'Smart boy,' she said with a little smile. 'What did I ever do to deserve you?'

Richie rolled his eyes. 'Yeah, like it took a brain surgeon to figure that out.' He turned and went back toward the kitchen.

'Have you got everything you need for the trip?' Carolina asked Matt.

He nodded. 'The car should be here in a couple of minutes,' he said.

'I . . . I really appreciate your doing this, Matt,' she said. 'I don't know what I'd do without you.'

'It's okay,' he replied.

'Will everything be all right at the nursery and the landscaping business while you're gone?'

'Of course,' he said. 'Thad's going to stay put and make sure we stay on schedule. But he said to tell you that he'd come down if you want him to.'

'No,' she said, shaking her head. 'He needs to stay up there and take care of things.'

Richie came back into the living room. 'Uncle Matt,' he said, 'the driver's downstairs waiting for you.'

Matt kissed Carolina good-bye and then walked to the elevator with Richie.

My men, she thought. *So sweet. So thoughtful. Trying to take care of me.* Her eyes abruptly filled with tears. *Minus one. The most important one.*

14

The urn that held the ashes – Lyon's ashes, she reminded herself – was small and made of gray marble, carved into a neo-classical design. It was tasteful, Carolina thought, but she knew she could trust Matt to make the correct choice. Perhaps it would eventually weather in the garden, where she'd placed it earlier in the center of one of the formal parterres. She hoped it would take on an appropriately mossy hue and lose some of its – to her eyes – tacky luster.

Almost the moment she thought about it, she chided herself for focusing on such a trivial thing at a time like this. However, Lyon would have understood her thinking these thoughts of hers, Lyon above all others. His sense of aesthetics had been almost identical to her own. That had been one of the many things that had held them together.

Carolina, Richie, Matt, Thad, and Leland stood at the arched entrance to the parterres, while a group of friends and acquaintances stood in attendance behind them, waiting for the short memorial service to end. The minister, a local nondenominational pastor whom none of them actually knew, had agreed to lead the service after conferring with Matt. Carolina would make a donation to his congregation, and he would conduct a short, not overly religious service.

Reverend Biggs, standing inside the parterre arch, closed the small book he'd been using and asked them to recite the Lord's Prayer with him. Carolina joined in, though she wondered now if it meant anything to her. She didn't have any connection to a church. She only had moments she could call spiritual, for lack of any other name to give them.

At the end of the Lord's Prayer, holding Richie's hand in her own, she stepped forward in the simple black linen suit she wore, and the minister stepped aside to let them pass. She and Richie walked to the parterre where she'd placed the urn earlier, and she bent down and removed the lid. Richie reached in first and scooped out a small portion of his father's ashes. His eyes welling up with tears, he opened his hand and let the wind spread them about the garden that Lyon had loved so much.

Carolina scooped out the remainder and did as her son had, opening her hand wide near the ground. She watched as the ashes drifted on the air and settled among the roses, the thyme and geraniums, the rosemary and butterfly bushes, the lamb's ears and the artemisia.

When Richie began to sob, she took his hand, held it tightly, and then wrapped her arms around him. Richie put his arms around her and held on with all his might. They stood like that, until Richie's tears had been exhausted.

They turned at last to face the waiting friends and acquaintances, Richie's eyes red and swollen, Carolina's sad but dry. She still felt oddly detached from the proceedings somehow. Even the ritual itself had seemed unreal. It was almost as if it were happening in a movie, she reflected, and wasn't happening to her at all. It couldn't be that

Lyon was gone. Dead. That she would never see him again. It was all an impossible joke. Too much for her to comprehend.

She led Richie back through the parterre's rose-covered, arched lattice entry and out to greet the assembly of mourners. They each shook the minister's hand, and he said a few consoling words and began to mix with the other guests. Matt and Thad, their eyes red and swollen like Richie's, hugged Carolina and her son, and then they stood close by, helping greet guests. She noticed that Leland, whose resemblance to Lyon was a constant reminder of Lyon's absence, had wandered away after speaking to one or two people.

The few local people who came – the man who mowed the lawn and his wife, several workmen, a handful of village folk who had known Carolina and Matt's parents – quickly said their good-byes. They weren't family and weren't friends really, but they had come to pay their respects, and Carolina appreciated the gesture.

Seated at a table on the stone terrace in the distance, Carolina was surprised to see Lydia Carstairs chatting quietly with Sybil Conroy and Seth Foster. *What on earth?* she wondered. *They didn't know Lyon, and they hardly know me. Why are they here? An hour and a half from Manhattan?*

As if to answer her question, Matt touched her elbow. 'Sybil Conroy called and asked me if it was all right to come and bring her guests,' he said. 'So I told her it was okay. I hope you don't mind.'

'No, I don't mind,' Carolina said. 'I just don't . . . well, I just don't quite understand. Sybil Conroy doesn't know me at all.'

'Yes, but she does know me,' Matt replied. 'And she wanted to pay her respects and meet you at the same time. She's a great admirer of your work, Sis. I mean she is a real flower person.'

'I understand,' Carolina said doubtfully.

'Lydia Carstairs and Seth Foster were spending the weekend with her and wanted to come along, too.'

'It's fine,' Carolina said, recovering some of her humor. 'At least we've got some good wine. Thanks to you, I might add. I doubt if these people have ever tasted anything but French. A lowly domestic has probably never passed their lips.'

'Oh, I think you'd be surprised,' Matt said. 'I think that underneath all the jewels and clothes and manners, some of them would be just as happy with a cold beer.'

Carolina managed another smile, more faint this time.

'Want me to take you over to say hello?' he asked.

'Sure,' she replied. 'I'm getting weary of all the heartfelt condolences. Lyon hated that sort of thing.'

'It won't take but a minute,' Matt said.

He took her arm, and together they walked over to the distant terrace where the threesome sat sipping wine and chatting quietly. When they saw Carolina and Matt approach, they got to their feet in unison.

Lydia Carstairs was the first to extend her hand. 'I'm so sorry, Carolina.' She leaned forward and brushed her cheek with a kiss. 'We couldn't stay away when we realized the service was so close by. We didn't know your husband, of course, but you've been like a shot of new blood to our tired little group. We want you to know how much we've appreciated all your efforts.'

'Thank you, Lydia,' Carolina said. 'I really appreciate it, but you shouldn't have gone to so much bother. The flowers were beautiful.'

'It's no trouble at all,' Lydia said with her slight drawl. 'I want you to meet my friend, Sybil Conroy. She's a bona fide flower lover like you, and your brother is working wonders at her house in the country.'

'How do you do?' Sybil said, extending a long, slender hand. 'I'm so sorry to meet you under these circumstances, but I'm very glad to get to do so at last. I love your work, and your brother's. I think you're quite a family.'

'Thank you,' Carolina replied. 'I appreciate this so much.' She was surprised to see that Sybil Conroy was even younger-looking than she appeared in her pictures. Thirty-five at the most, with raven hair cut at her shoulders, carefully arched brows, bright blue eyes, an enviably creamy complexion, a little ski-jump nose, and perfect pearly white teeth. A truly heart-shaped face with prominent cheek-bones. The billionaire who'd married her had settled a couple of hundred million on her when they divorced. She was a stunning beauty and seemed genuinely nice, too.

Seth extended his hand. 'I'm glad I could pay my respects,' he said. 'I happened to be up at Sybil's this weekend, so I came over with them. I hope things get better for you soon.' *My God, even in mourning she looks so beautiful,* he thought. *And she's so poised, in complete control of herself.*

'Thanks, Seth,' Carolina said.

'Carolina, I adore your cottage and the gardens,' Sybil Conroy remarked. 'Everything is perfection. It's a storybook kind of place.'

'Thank you, Sybil,' she said. 'This was my father and mother's weekend place. They worked on it for years, and I keep adding my little touches. There's still so much that I'd like to do.'

'Well, I think it's perfection just the way it is,' Sybil said. 'I would love to pick it up and transport it directly to my backyard.'

'Another couple of years and a little maturity,' Matt said, 'and your property is truly going to be a showplace, Sybil.'

'I hope so,' she said, looking at Matt and smiling. 'I can see now where you've gotten so many of your ideas. I wish I'd grown up surrounded by such beauty. My parents were so poor, and the neighborhood was so bad that the only grass that would grow was crab-grass.'

Everyone laughed at her comment.

'I think my brother can certainly make your grass grow,' Carolina said. Her eyes quickly scanned the crowd for Richie, but she didn't see him anywhere. 'If you'll excuse me, I have to go look for my son. I hope I see you again before you leave.'

'Of course, dear,' Lydia said. 'We'll say good-bye before we get on our way.'

Carolina turned and began walking toward the house, and Matt caught up with her. 'Are you okay?' he asked.

'I'm . . . I'm okay,' she said, not breaking her stride. 'I just want to find Richie.' She paused a moment, looking back toward the table where Seth and the others were sitting. 'There's Mercedes,' she said. 'I didn't realize she'd come up. How sweet of her.' She looked at Matt. 'Who did she come with? Do you know?'

'I think Roxie and Leland,' he said. 'Interesting, huh?' He smiled.

'It is that,' she said. 'Well, I'm off to find Richie.'

'You want me to come with you?'

'No,' she said. 'It's okay. I just want to be alone with him for a few minutes.'

She strode on determinedly, nodding at the people around her, slipping past their well-meaning greetings and looks and outreaching hands. When she got to the house, she went through the living room and den, back to her bedroom and bathroom, and then retraced her steps and checked the powder room, the dining room, and finally the kitchen. He was nowhere to be found, but in the kitchen, Roxie sat at the table talking to Thad.

'Have you seen Richie?' she asked them.

'No,' Roxie said.

Thad shook his head. 'He's probably outside, Carolina.'

'Are you—?'

'Yes,' Carolina said with a smile, 'I'm okay.' She wanted to scream. She turned and fled the kitchen. *One more solicitous question, and I'll explode*, she thought.

In the dining room, she noticed for the first time that the door to the staircase which led up to his room on the second floor was shut. Opening it, she called up to him. There was no answer, but she climbed the steep stairs anyway, pausing at the top to catch her breath.

The door to his room was closed, and she walked to it and knocked. When there was no answer, she called to him softly. 'Richie? Are you there?'

There was still no answer, but she thought she heard something. 'Richie?' she called again.

Still no answer.

She tried the door and discovered that it wasn't locked. Pushing on it gently, she opened it a crack and peered in.

Richie was sprawled facedown across his bed, still in his suit and tie, his face in a pillow, his hands grasping another pillow over his head, holding it down tightly to muffle the sobs that racked his body.

Carolina stepped into the room and closed the door behind her. 'Richie?' she said softly. When he didn't respond, she walked over to the bed and sat down beside him. She placed a hand on his back and began to stroke him. When he still did not respond, she encircled him with her arms and pulled him close.

'Oh, Richie, Richie,' she began to cry. 'My baby. Please let me comfort you. Please. I know I can't replace your dad. Nobody can. Nobody. Ever. But please let me love you.'

He let go of the pillow over his head and, without looking at her, returned her hug, throwing his arms around her. He sobbed against her, his body shaking violently, and she held him tight, tears streaming from her eyes.

'We'll get through this, Richie,' she said. 'We'll get through this somehow. With each other.'

She began to rock him gently in her arms. 'It'll get better, baby,' she crooned through her tears. 'Someday. The pain will go away.' But she wondered if the agonizing pain she herself felt would ever go away, if life would once again hold any joy for her. It was unthinkable now. Unimaginable.

Oh, Lyon, she prayed, *wherever you are, please protect your son and give him peace.*

15

'Payton, darling.' The bone-thin, heavily made-up woman wearing huge chunky gold jewelry air-kissed her on both cheeks.

'So good to see you, Yvette,' Payton said. 'You know Champers, of course.' Wilson Davenport 'Champers' Whitbey III was a harmless older cousin of hers whom she used as an occasional escort.

Yvette Kasanov, a fixture in the art world, extended a bony hand. 'How are you, Champers?' she said.

'Very well,' he replied. 'And you?'

'Where's Sasha?' Payton asked. She could hardly wait to see the hot young painter she'd met last summer in the south of France. He was the talk of the art world and a hunk to boot.

'You can't miss him,' Yvette said. 'He's basking in all of his glory in the next room. Just follow the camera flashes.'

'We'll run along and say hello,' Payton said. 'See you later.' She and Champers began moving through the crowd toward the next room.

'Oh, Payton,' Yvette called to her.

Payton turned on her heels. 'Yes?'

'Darling, the flowers you sent. You must see them.'

'Why?' Payton asked. 'What is it?'

'They're an embarrassment,' Yvette said sotto voce. 'Everyone's commented on them, darling. Even Sasha.' Her harsh laugh was that of a four-pack-a-day smoker.

'I don't understand,' Payton said. 'You know I used that floral designer everyone is talking about, Carolina. She's supposed to be the best.'

'Well, see for yourself,' Yvette said, waving a hand in the air.

'I will,' Payton said. 'I know her husband died, and I hear she's having a hard time of it. But that shouldn't have anything to do with the flowers.'

She and Champers headed into the thick of the chic-looking crowd that milled about in the large open spaces of the Matthew Marks Gallery. It represented a cross section of Manhattan society – from immensely rich buyers down to the lowliest, struggling up-and-coming artists – but they all had an avid interest in contemporary art, as well as a penchant for dressing in black.

Payton's eyes quickly assessed the crowd. Comme des Garcons, Prada, Gucci, Issey Miyake, Yoshi Yamamoto, and other of the more adventuresome designers were more often favored by this crowd than the staid Oscar de la Rentas and Valentinos seen at charity balls. She was glad that she'd dressed as she had. To descend to the Chelsea gallery from her luxurious Upper East Side apartment, she'd donned one of her most provocative dresses, a metallic Gucci see-through that barely hid her most valuable assets. With it she wore stiletto heels, and in one hand held a Fendi baguette. Champers held the other.

Through an opening in the crowd, she could see Sasha standing proudly in front of one of his paintings. His long black hair fell below his big shoulders. He was wearing a black tee shirt, black sports jacket, and, even in this wonderful weather, slick, shiny black leather pants. He was sex personified, as far as Payton was concerned.

Tugging Champers along, she strode purposefully toward Sasha. He turned and looked at her as she approached. The smile on his sensual lips turned to a frown.

'Did you think this was an Addam's family party?' he asked in a booming, thickly accented voice. 'Did you think I'd like your idea of a joke?'

Heads turned from every direction and an abrupt quiet came over the crowd in the immediate vicinity, but the cameras kept flashing.

'What do you mean, Sasha?' Payton asked innocently as she tried to kiss him.

He pushed her away and pointed toward a distant corner, where the flowers had been stashed away. 'Look at that,' he yelled, walking toward them. 'Look at it! This is what you think of me? This you send me for my big opening?'

Payton followed after him, as did a number of the crowd, and approached an enormous cross of white poms with a sash of red roses, set on a stand.

'Oh, my God, Sasha,' Payton gasped. 'I certainly didn't send those. I hired Carolina Mountcastle,' she said loudly, so all could overhear. 'You know I wouldn't do a thing like that.'

Before she could finish what she was saying, Sasha rushed to the funeral cross, picked it up off the stand, and threw it facedown on the floor. There were screams and shouts as the crowd moved back out of the way. Cameras flashed everywhere, and the entire scene was recorded for posterity.

Payton threw her hands up to her face, which was contorted into a mask of surprise and rage. She swiped at the tears that had abruptly sprung into her eyes.

Grabbing Champers by the sleeve, she began weaving through the crowd back toward the entrance. 'Come on, Champers,' she growled. 'We've got to get out of here. And quick.' He helped her push, and they were soon out the door and on the sidewalk.

'Hurry,' she said, pulling him along with her, in the direction of Ninth Avenue. 'We've got to hurry.'

When they reached the next corner, she began laughing uncontrollably.

'What is it?' Champers asked. 'Payton, what the hell is so funny?'

'Oh, nothing,' she said, still laughing. 'You wouldn't understand, Champers. Let's go back uptown and get a drink.'

Mercedes burst out with laughter, nearly sputtering wine all over her big canopied bed. 'I know I shouldn't be laughing,' she said, 'but I still can't get over it.'

Leland, who was pulling his jeans on, turned and looked at her with a smile. She looked like an exotic princess, he thought – an exotic, evil princess – piled up on her luxurious bed. Its pillows, spread, and hangings, all brightly colored prints from India, blended in with the rest of the loft's haute bohemian air.

'I thought the picture in the *Post* was hilarious,' he said. 'Payton Fitzsimmons looked like she'd seen a two-headed dog. Carolina's really in pretty bad shape, so this must be driving her fucking nuts.'

'Of course it is,' Mercedes said. 'She's been functioning. Going through the motions and all that, but you can tell she's really grieving. Anyway, she pitched a fit at the shop today.'

'There was a time when she would've laughed off something like this,' Leland said.

'Well, not in the shape she's in now,' Mercedes said. 'She lit into Antonio, but he said it was a mix-up. Sure, it was weird taking a funeral cross into an art gallery, but he thought it was intentional because – get this – he says, "All artists are weird."'

'"Fashionable florist and party designer Carolina sends funeral flowers to big art opening."' He barked a laugh. 'I can't forget the headline on the gossip page. They're having a field day with poor,

poor Carolina.' He sat down and started pulling on his socks. 'Only she isn't so poor. That's for sure.'

He fell silent, and Mercedes rose to a sitting position. 'What are you looking so glum about all of a sudden?' she asked.

'Nothing,' he said. 'I was just thinking about Lyon.'

'Do you miss him?' she asked. 'I thought you hardly saw him.'

'Jesus, Mercedes, we were brothers,' he said, shooting her a cross look. 'I didn't see him a lot, but I miss him. He was always there when I needed help, you know?' He shoved his foot into a sneaker. 'And now? It's a hell of a lot different now. I know I can't depend on Carolina for a damn thing.'

'Maybe he left you a bit of cash,' Mercedes said, taking another sip of wine.

'I won't know about that till tomorrow when they read the will,' he said, 'and somehow I doubt it.'

Mercedes studied his face. She'd never seen Leland look this unhappy. Perhaps she'd even detected a bit of fear in his voice. In his attitude, too.

'You're in some sort of trouble, aren't you?' she said.

He glanced over at her. 'Yeah,' he said. 'You might say that.'

'What is it, Leland?' she asked, swirling a finger around in her wine. 'Money?'

'You've got that right, too,' he said.

'Gambling?'

He was silent but nodded.

'I wish there was something I could do to help.'

He stood up and stretched his arms wide. 'If you've got about a hundred grand lying around that you don't need, you can help.' He laughed and looked back at her.

She shrugged. 'Sorry, darling,' she said, 'but I'm broke.'

He looked at her in complete surprise. 'Broke? You?'

She nodded and smiled. 'Totally.'

'But how could that happen?' he asked. 'Everybody in the world knows you're from a famous family with all kinds of connections and money. You can't pick up a magazine without seeing something about you.'

'Famous maybe,' she said, looking up at him, 'but the money's gone, darling.'

'Jesus, Mercedes, I don't believe this,' he said.

'Believe it,' she said, 'because it's true.'

He was still baffled by her revelation, and stood staring at her.

'Maybe we should put our heads together,' she said. 'Perhaps we could come up with something that would benefit us both.' She looked at him with mischievous eyes.

'Like what?'

'I'm not sure,' she said, 'but why don't you sit back down? Let's talk it over.'

Leland sat down. 'I'm all ears,' he said.

'You say they're reading the will tomorrow?'

'I have no idea how the mix-up happened,' Carolina said into the telephone, 'but believe me, it'll never happen again.' She'd been spread out in bed, hoping against hope that sleep wouldn't elude her tonight when the telephone had rung.

'I've tried to call you several times today to discuss this with you, but couldn't get hold of you, Payton. I don't think you could be more distressed by this than I am.'

'I want you to know that it's ruined my relationship with Sasha,' Payton whimpered with a hint of tears in her voice. 'He was one of my dearest friends and a very sensitive artist. This was to be such a special occasion. And the press!' She gasped before continuing. 'I've never been so embarrassed in my life. Think of my family. My friends. How could you allow this to happen to me?'

'I told you that I would get to the bottom of it,' Carolina said in frustration. She thought that she might break down and cry herself, so sick at heart was she about the entire matter.

'So it was a mix-up by that deliveryman of yours?' Payton asked. 'The sort of dark . . . Latin type?' She ran a hand down Antonio's thigh and looked at him with a smile. He responded by licking her naked breasts, making Payton shiver with delight.

'I can tell you that when he left the shop, he had the right flowers,' Carolina replied firmly. 'The cross was supposed to go to a funeral, and these beautiful sprays were going to the art gallery. But the cards somehow got mixed up.'

'Well, whatever happened,' Payton said, 'I can't possibly have you doing the flowers for my party at the club. It's out of the question now.'

'I understand,' Carolina said, 'and I'm terribly sorry about this.'

'Sorry doesn't help me, Carolina,' Payton replied, her hand on Antonio's head as he licked and kissed away. 'You've destroyed a treasured friendship and made me the laughing stock of New York. I can never forgive you.'

She slammed the telephone down so loudly that Carolina jerked back from the receiver. *Oh, my God,* she thought, looking up at the ceiling in vain. *What am I going to do?*

Incidents like this could ruin her business. Certainly, any grand plans for expansion and doing important social events would be out of the question if any more mix-ups happened. She still couldn't believe Antonio had been so stupid.

She turned off the bedside light. *I don't need this right now,* she told herself. *If there was ever a time I didn't need this, it's now.*

16

The room was surprisingly small, even claustrophobic for a law firm that was so large, Carolina reflected as she took a seat on one of the leather chairs that Bernard Goldsmith indicated. Richie sat down on her right, and Matt was already sitting on her left. Next to Matt sat Leland Mountcastle, who shifted in his seat nervously. *He looks a little hungover*, Carolina thought. He'd been unusually silent and withdrawn today, and she put it down to grief.

She watched as Bernard picked up what she assumed to be the interoffice telephone and, swinging around with his back to them, began to speak sotto voce into the receiver.

From far below them on Fifth Avenue and Forty-sixth Street, she heard the sound of traffic, punctuated by New York's ubiquitous sirens. Today, for some reason, the cacophony from below gave her a kind of solace, perhaps because it meant that there was still a world out there, removed from this room where she really didn't want to be.

She hadn't been surprised when Bernard told her that he'd sent a letter to Richie requesting his presence at the reading of Lyon's will since he had been named a beneficiary. She had argued with him that she thought Richie should be spared such an emotion-laden event, but Bernard had been intractable, insisting that Lyon would have wanted Richie to be there. She'd finally caved in to his wishes and brought Richie along. She put her arm around her son's shoulders and hugged him. His lips formed an attempt at a smile, but he was obviously in pain.

Matt took her hand and squeezed it reassuringly. He had called Carolina to express surprise at being asked to be here because it hadn't occurred to him that Lyon would leave him anything. Perhaps, he'd said, Lyon had left some token of goodwill such as a watch or cuff links.

Bernard cleared his throat, and the four of them faced forward as he sat down behind his rather messy mahogany desk. He'd done legal work for Carolina and Lyon several times over the years, but she didn't feel that she knew him well. Their relationship was cordial but strictly professional. She longed for someone close, Matt perhaps, to read Lyon's last will and testament. It seemed almost an invasion of privacy that Bernard would be the one to read Lyon's wishes aloud.

'We'll start in just a moment,' Bernard said. 'There are still two people to arrive, and I'm told they're on their way up.'

Two more people? Carolina thought. *But who could they be?* Then she distinctly remembered that Bernard had mentioned six people being asked to come to the reading. She'd gotten so caught up in arguing with him about Richie's presence that she'd completely forgotten to ask him who the other two people were. She started to ask him now, but she heard the office door open and turned to look.

A tall, lean young woman, startlingly beautiful, with long, straight, naturally light blond hair, huge blue eyes, rosy-hued lips, and a perfect creamy complexion stepped into the room. She wore an

145

elegant black pantsuit that contrasted dramatically with her pale hair. In one hand, she held the chubby hand of a little girl, about three years old, Carolina thought. The child had chocolaty hair and huge eyes, and she was holding a doll.

'Who on earth are they?' she whispered to Matt.

'I don't have any idea, Sis,' he said, staring at them.

The young woman sat down quietly in a chair to the side and slightly behind them; then she brought the child up onto her lap.

'Who the devil?' Carolina whispered. 'Haven't they come to the wrong place or something?'

Matt looked at her worriedly. 'Bernard said there were going to be two more people.'

'Yes, but I never saw that woman in my life,' she replied.

Matt shrugged. 'Bernard will handle it,' he said.

Carolina was aware that Richie had turned and was staring at the woman and child. She leaned down and whispered to him, 'I think they're in the wrong place. Don't pay any attention to them. Bernard will straighten it out.'

'I won't waste your time,' the lawyer said in his raspy baritone, looking at them over the little tortoiseshell half-glasses perched on the end of his nose. 'We'll get right down to business now that everyone is here.'

So they are supposed to be here! Carolina thought. *These perfect strangers that I've never seen in my life are going to listen to the reading of my husband's will?* She started to interrupt Bernard, but Matt squeezed her hand as if to say, *Let it go. Let Bernard go ahead.*

Bernard pulled a legal-length document from a folder and flipped open its cover of heavy blue paper. 'I'll ask you to let me read the entire will from start to finish before you ask any questions,' he said. 'Please do not interrupt me. This is a very short will and to the point, so it won't take long.'

He cleared his throat again and then began to read slowly but clearly. The introductory legalese took only moments; then Bernard paused and looked up from the will. 'I'm going to read Lyon's specific bequests now.

'"To my brother-in-law, Matthew Ross Banford, in appreciation for his unflagging friendship and support from the earliest days of my marriage to his sister up to the present, I leave the sum of twenty-five thousand dollars, with the proviso that he do with it whatever he wishes."'

Matt was stone-still, and Carolina patted his arm affectionately.

'"To my younger brother, Leland Montgomery Mountcastle, in appreciation for his faithfulness as a brother, I leave the sum of fifty thousand dollars, hoping that he will use the funds to clear up whatever debts he has incurred at the time of my demise."'

Like Matt, Leland remained silent, though Carolina could see that he appeared to be gritting his teeth and clenching his fists. *Is he angry?* she wondered. *Or simply excited and nervous?*

'"To my beloved son, Richard Banford Mountcastle, I leave the sum of one-half million dollars, to be held in trust for him by his mother, Carolina Banford Mountcastle, until he reaches the age of twenty-one. It is my sincere hope that he will use the money wisely and that he remember it came from a father who loved him unconditionally."'

Richie squirmed in his seat slightly, but his face was impossible to read, and Carolina wondered what was going through his mind.

'"To my beloved wife, Carolina Banford Mountcastle, I leave all of my real and personal property in the United States of America, including our loft, located in New York City, the contents of our safety deposit boxes at Citibank, the monies in both individual and joint accounts, including checking, money market, brokerage, and savings. She is to receive all stocks, bonds, and mutual funds held in my name only or our names jointly. In addition, she is the sole beneficiary of insurance policies held by Northwestern Mutual Insurance Company, the present worth of which is in excess of two million dollars."'

Carolina couldn't help the tears that formed in her eyes. It was as if Lyon was with her, and the love she'd always felt for him – the love they'd always shared – almost overwhelmed her now in its intensity.

Bernard Goldsmith cleared his voice rather loudly, and Carolina looked at him.

"'To my beloved friend, Monique Lehnert, I leave the house we have shared and to which I own the title, located at Twenty-nine Buiksloterwec, Amsterdam Noord, the Netherlands, and—'"

Carolina gasped, then cried, 'What . . . who the hell . . . Bernard?' She turned and looked at Matt with complete puzzlement. Matt was staring back at her with similar bafflement. Then in unison, they turned in the direction of the young blond beauty and the child. 'Who is that . . . this . . . Monique whoever?' Carolina stammered loudly.

'Please,' Bernard Goldsmith said, 'wait until I've finished reading the complete last will and testament before you talk among your-selves. I'll be happy to answer your questions then.'

The blankness in Richie's face had disappeared, although, like the others, he was mystified by the lawyer's words. His curiosity about the woman and child was even more pronounced than it had been before. He listened intently now to what the lawyer had to say, while turning to glance at the woman and child.

"'– any other real or personal property I own in Amsterdam, the Netherlands, including a Smart Car. In addition, I bequeath to her the contents of a safety deposit box at NetherlandBank, and the cash in checking, savings, money market, and brokerage accounts at the aforesaid bank, and all stocks, bonds, and other funds that I currently hold in Europe, administered by Artur van Brakel, Twenty-six Huidenstraat, Amsterdam, the Netherlands. She is also the sole bene-ficiary of a life insurance policy valued at approximately one million dollars U.S., held by Benthem-Vink, Ninety-four Kalverstraat.'"

For a moment Carolina thought that she might faint, and she

gripped Matt's hand in hers, as if holding on to a lifeline. Her mind swirled with a thousand questions, and she couldn't sort any of them out, being by turns repulsed, intrigued, and furious. More than anything, furious.

'What in the name of God is going on, Bernard?' she stormed. 'What are you talking about? And who are you talking about? I want to know.' Her eyes turned accusingly to the woman and child, and the woman, her pale complexion reddening, returned her glare.

'Please, Carolina,' Bernard said patiently. 'Let me finish, then I'll answer whatever questions you have.'

'But—!'

'Please!' Bernard said emphatically, looking at her over the rims of his glasses.

Matt held her hand tightly in his own. 'Wait, Sis,' he whispered.

'"Finally, to my beloved daughter with Monique Lehnert, Anja Maria Lehnert—"'

Throwing her hands over her mouth, Carolina stifled the scream that threatened to arise from her throat. *Daughter? What—? What filthy lies was this man spewing from his mouth now?*

'"—I bequeath the sum of one-half million dollars U.S. to be held in trust for her until she reaches the age of twenty-one. As with my son, I trust that she will use the money wisely and remember that it came from a father who loved her unconditionally."'

Bernard Goldsmith put the document down on the desk and looked over his half-glasses at the six people sitting before him. 'Are there any questions?' he asked.

There was absolute silence in the room, but only for a moment. 'What the hell is going on here, Bernard?' Carolina shouted, shaking a pointed finger at him. 'And what the hell is this stranger doing here?' She turned her glare on the blonde once again.

Bernard looked at her, his face a mask of calm concern. 'Carolina, this is Monique Lehnert. She was Lyon's mistress in Amsterdam, and this is their daughter, Anja.'

'I don't believe you!' Carolina said, although she knew that what Bernard was saying must be true. She turned on the blond woman. 'Get out of here!' she said in a low voice filled with fury. 'Get out!' she said more loudly. 'You don't belong here!'

Matt grabbed at his sister's hand. 'Sis,' he said, 'calm down.'

Carolina pushed away his hand and then ignored him, her attention still trained on the other woman. The blonde hadn't moved or said a word, but Carolina could see that she was crying.

Leland abruptly got to his feet. 'Excuse me,' he said in a small voice, seemingly aloof to the proceedings. 'I have to go.' Without waiting for any reply, he hurried to the door and let himself out.

Ignoring him, Carolina turned to Bernard. 'I'm going to contest this will!' she cried. 'She's not getting a dime! Not a cent!'

Monique flipped her hair out of her face and wiped tears from her eyes with a long, slender finger. She had never really thought about what would happen in the event of Lyon's death, but the reading of the will reminded her of what a kind and generous partner he'd been and of how much she missed him.

'Get out, I said!' Carolina shouted, turning her attention back to Monique.

Monique looked over at her, her eyes first widened with alarm, but then turning defiant. 'He loved me, too,' she said heatedly, 'and he adored our daughter. I think he loved us as much as he did you and your son. Why would our affair have started to begin with if he'd been so in love with you? Why would he have left us anything if he didn't love us?'

Carolina was almost blind with rage. 'I'll fight you to the death,' she screamed.

Monique lifted her chin assertively. 'And I will fight you,' she cried. 'I'm not a greedy person, Mrs Mountcastle, but I have myself and a daughter to take care of. Lyon promised us that he would, that I didn't need to worry, even if he hadn't divorced you yet. I want only what is rightly mine, and I'll fight you tooth and nail for it.'

Carolina felt as if she were going to explode with a rage more powerful than any she'd ever felt before. She wanted to tear this woman limb from limb, then and there. Suddenly, she didn't want to hear another word from her. Nor did she want to have to see that bastard child in her lap. She rose to her feet and took one of Richie's hands in hers.

'I'm getting out of here,' she shouted. 'I'm not going to stay in the same room with that . . . that woman another minute!'

Bernard Goldsmith merely nodded.

Matt tried to take her hand again, but she jerked it away. 'You can stay if you want to,' she said harshly. 'I'm going.'

Richie's eyes were glued to the child, and he shrugged his hand away from his mother's as she started stomping toward the door. 'I'll stay with Uncle Matt,' he said.

'No, you won't!' she shouted at him angrily, grabbing his hand again.

Richie reluctantly followed her to the door, but his gaze remained fastened on the little girl. It was almost as if he were looking into a mirror. He'd never seen anyone who looked so much like him.

'Come on, Richie!' she said at the door. 'We're getting out of this . . . this . . . hell!' After he walked out, she slammed the door behind her with all her might.

17

The shop was situated on the ground floor of a large, elegant brownstone. Just off Madison Avenue in the East Sixties, it was a choice location for a flower shop and party-planning business, since it was in the very heart of Manhattan's wealthiest and most social neighborhood. The guests at its opening night gala entered through a little iron gate that led into a small but beautiful front garden planted with ivy, pachysandra, and large ostrich ferns. Clipped boxwood pyramids, one on either side of the entrance, lent a formal air to the garden and the shop before one even entered it. A discreet engraved plaque announced: PAYTON.

'We'll only stay a moment,' Lydia Carstairs said to Seth. 'You know how I feel about Payton, but I can't resist seeing what she's done. Everyone's been talking about what a stunning shop she's put together.'

'I don't mind at all, Lydia,' Seth said, although he didn't relish seeing Payton or her shop. He hadn't forgotten her abominable behavior toward Carolina, and he knew that Payton had had almost nothing to do with creating the shop that was being touted as one of the most beautiful to open its doors in ages. Nothing other than write the checks, that was.

From a client of his, Seth knew that under an order of the strictest secrecy, Jacques Liagre, the most sought-after decorator and designer in Europe, if not the world, had been brought in from Paris and given an unlimited budget to create a jewel box from which Payton was to operate.

As they stepped through the door and inside, Payton appeared from the midst of the crowd milling about and greeted them effusively, as if they were the best of friends on the best of terms.

'Lydia, you look absolutely fabulous,' she cooed. 'I wish I knew your secret.'

'Thank you,' Lydia said. 'Your shop looks lovely.'

'And Seth. What a surprise,' Payton went on. 'I'm so glad you could make it. I've worked myself half to death to get this done, so I haven't been circulating at all lately. I've missed seeing you. How are you doing?'

'I'm fine, Payton,' he replied. 'But I did see where you made it to an opening in Chelsea recently, didn't I?'

'Oh, that!' Payton said with a laugh. 'Wasn't it the limit? I still can't believe that I paid Carolina five hundred dollars and she delivered a funeral cross to one of my dearest friends. I don't see how she stays in business.'

'I can't believe it myself,' Seth replied. 'I've used her for some time, and nothing like that has ever happened. In fact, everything has always been perfect.'

'Well, you're certainly the lucky one,' Payton said. 'I'm telling everyone I know about what happened to me so no one will be victimized by her.'

'Good luck with the shop,' Lydia said. 'I'm going over to speak to Tipsy Richardson.' She looked at Seth. 'Coming along?' she asked.

'Yes,' he said. 'Best of luck, Payton. I'm sure you'll do very well with this venture.'

'I hope so,' she said. She reached out and took one of his hands in hers. 'Why don't you call? I miss seeing you, Seth. I thought . . . Well, I thought that we had a lot of fun together.' Her voice became that of a little girl's. 'I know I was unforgivably rude to Carolina that night, but I guess I'd had a bit too much to drink.'

'Maybe I'll see you around,' Seth said vaguely. He couldn't deny that she looked seductively beautiful and that she was certainly the sort of woman he was expected to marry, but Payton had lost her appeal for him. 'I'd better catch up with Lydia.' He extricated his hand from hers, but not before a photographer from the *Post* had taken a picture of the two of them hand in hand. He hadn't really noticed because cameras seemed to be flashing all around the shop. When he reached Lydia, he said hello to Tipsy and politely pretended to listen to the two women discuss the shop's decor, but his mind was elsewhere. On Carolina. Payton had reminded him about the death of Lyon Mountcastle, and he wondered how Carolina was getting along.

'Seth?'

It was Lydia. 'Sorry,' he said, 'I was daydreaming, I'm afraid.'

'Ready to go to dinner?' she asked.

'Yes,' he said.

He took her arm, and they made a circle around the shop toward the front door. From behind a door that was slightly ajar, Seth glimpsed the raven hair and tan skin of what he thought was a familiar face. But who was it? he wondered. By the time they finally made an exit and were out on the street, he'd completely forgotten the handsome features peering from behind the *boiserie* door.

Antonio slammed the bedroom door shut behind him with a loud bang and stood staring at her with his hands on his hips, his square jaw set with determination. His dark eyes were fiery with anger, and his lips were curled into a sneer.

Payton, whose naked body was propped against the bed's down

pillows, pulled the sheet up over herself as if the soft Egyptian cotton would protect her from him. She knew that he would be furious, but his anger excited her like nothing else. Even now she could feel her heart begin to beat rapidly, could feel the tingling, nearly electric charges that swept through her body, and she held her breath in anticipation of what he would do.

Antonio walked slowly toward her, unbuckling his belt as he drew closer, his fiery eyes never leaving hers, his movements purposeful, calculated. At the edge of the bed, he reached out and ripped the sheet from her hands, throwing it to the foot of the bed.

Payton almost shrieked with a mixture of excitement and fear, but she remained silent, her eyes taunting and challenging, as if she was neither afraid nor trembling with desire.

Antonio tore off his shirt, throwing it to the floor, kicked off his shoes, and then pulled off his jeans and socks. He stood over her, his powerful, muscular body dark and proud, his cock bearing witness to his desire. In one swift movement, he was atop her, entering her in a merciless plunge and grinding away at her in the relentless pursuit of his own pleasure, his own release.

Payton cried out and almost instantly began to shudder in ecstasy. Antonio roared like a bull as he burst forth within her, in one hot stream after another. Then his body fell flat against hers, spent and winded.

They lay that way for a long time, silent except for their rapid breathing. At last Payton said, 'That was wonderful, Antonio.' She scraped her fingernails down his back. '*You* are wonderful. Nobody else has ever satisfied me like you do.'

He rolled off her and lay at her side. 'If I'm so wonderful, Payton, then why am I still a secret?' He looked at her quizzically. 'You told me that you would start introducing me as soon as your shop opened. Do you know what it's like to be hidden away like some kind of troll?'

She put an arm across his chest. 'I've told you, Antonio,' she said.

'After I've got my business really running, then I want you to join me. To work with me. Then we can go public.' She ran a fingertip down his nose to his lips. The kiss she expected didn't materialize. 'I'm so sorry that you feel bad. It's the last thing I want.'

'Your shop is open now,' he said, 'and you told me yourself that the telephone is already beginning to ring. You won't have any problem getting customers.'

'Yes,' she said, 'that's true. But it'll take a while before we get really busy. Besides, I want all of the *right* customers, Antonio. The really big spenders. And that means taking business away from Carolina. She's been getting all the press, all the magazine interviews, and starting to get the big charity benefits. She's doing the flowers for too many of the important people in my social circle. Lydia Carstairs and her friends ought to be buying from me, and I'm going to see to it that they do.'

'I think there's plenty of business to go around,' he said.

'I don't care,' she said. 'I want Carolina's business. She ruined my friendship with Seth Foster and then with Sasha.'

'Wait a minute,' Antonio said. 'She didn't have anything to do with ruining your relationship with Sasha. *We* did that, and what did she have to do with you and Seth Foster anyhow?'

Payton looked off into the distance. 'He's the one who introduced her to Lydia, and he . . . well, he thinks Carolina's such hot stuff. I was his friend until she came along.'

'You sound jealous,' Antonio said.

'That's ridiculous,' Payton said, hugging him fiercely. 'I've got you. Why the hell would I want him?'

'You didn't mind being seen with him, did you?'

'Look, Antonio,' Payton said, 'I can't wait to show you off. I'll make all my friends green with envy.' She trailed a fingertip down his chest and stomach; then she let her hand rest between his thighs. 'But for just a little while longer, I want you and Mercedes to work behind the scenes, helping me get a head start.'

'How long?' he asked, rolling onto his side, facing her.

'Not long at all,' Payton replied. 'I'm going to need you both in the shop, so it can't take too long. Besides, you told me yourself that Carolina's been half-crazy since her husband died. So she's really vulnerable right now. Just a couple of slipups on her part – like at the gallery – and she's history, Antonio.' She stroked his cock, relishing the power that she had over it, enjoying the feel of it as it grew larger in her hand.

'You think you've got it all figured out, don't you?' he said, his mouth seeking out one of her breasts.

'I know I do,' Payton said, a tremor running through her as she felt his tongue on her nipple. 'You'll see. We'll . . . get her . . . while . . . she's . . . down.' She moaned with pleasure. 'Ah, yes, Antonio. More.'

'Fifty thousand lousy fucking dollars,' Leland snarled, throwing a worn running shoe across the room. His face was red with rage, and the sweat-slicked cords in his neck stood out in bold relief.

Mercedes watched him quietly, knowing there was nothing she could do to placate him at the moment. He needed to let off steam, and she would sip her wine and listen until he'd finished.

'The fucker's got millions of dollars in assets, and he leaves me chump change.' He threw his other running shoe, and it thwacked against a wall, before falling to rest on the antique Herez rug in her bedroom. He glared at Mercedes, his face still contorted in anger. She returned his gaze, a slight smile on her carmine-painted lips.

'What's so funny?' he asked, his voice a little quieter.

'Nothing,' she replied. 'Nothing's funny.' She shrugged. 'I'm just not surprised. I mean, what did you expect? He had a wife and child.'

'You don't know the half of it,' Leland said.

Mercedes raised her brows questioningly. 'What do you mean, Leland?'

He told her about the reading of the will earlier that week.

When he was finished, Mercedes burst into gales of laughter. 'It's too bloody funny,' she shrieked with amusement. 'Randy old Lyon. Carolina wasn't enough. You've got to hand it to him.'

'Yeah,' Leland said glumly. 'I wish I thought it was as funny as you do. The broad in Amsterdam made out like a bandit, and so did the kid.'

'Carolina must be devastated,' Mercedes said. 'Poor thing.' She laughed again. 'The perfect couple. Everybody said so.' She clapped her hands together delightedly. 'This on top of his death will absolutely do her in.'

'You may be right on that account,' Leland said. 'From what Matt told me when I called this evening, she's in a real state.'

'I can imagine,' Mercedes said.

He studied her face with curiosity. 'You seem to take a great deal of pleasure in seeing her suffer.'

'I never could stand her,' she admitted. 'All these years I've been so bloody nice to her. But then everybody is. Carolina's so bloody well liked.'

'You really do hate her, don't you.' It was a statement, not a question.

'Perhaps *envy*'s the better word, Leland,' she said. 'She had a great husband, or so I thought. A great kid. And she was really going places.' Mercedes took a sip of wine before continuing. 'In fact, everything she touched seemed to turn more or less to gold, while not a bloody thing's worked out for me. Not marriage. Not a career. And I'm the one with all the talent. She's merely a . . . a flower arranger.'

Leland laughed. 'Yeah, and I always thought I was a lot smarter and better-looking than Lyon.'

'You are,' she said, offering him a smile. 'And you're alive.'

'Yeah, but he's the one who had all the success,' Leland said. 'I scrape by.'

'Because you gamble too much,' Mercedes said.

'Yeah, and if I don't do something soon, I'm in trouble. To the tune of a hundred grand.'

'Make that fifty,' she said. 'You just inherited fifty.'

'I hate this.'

'We're in the same boat, darling,' she said, 'as I told you before. I have enough money for another couple of months' maintenance on this loft, and that's it. I'm going to have to beg, borrow, and steal from what few friends I have and try hitting on a couple of relatives.'

'Couldn't you borrow against the loft?' he asked. 'Or sell it?'

'It's mortgaged to the hilt, so I can't borrow against it,' she said. 'I could sell it at a profit, but that could take months.'

'What the hell're we going to do, Mercedes?' he asked, looking over at her.

'You say that you really expected more from Lyon?'

He nodded. 'Yeah, I did,' he said. 'He knew I was always in debt, and he'd always bailed me out, so I figured . . . you know, that he'd make sure I was taken care of.'

She sat in thoughtful silence for a while, sipping her wine. 'Do you remember the time you and I went up to their place in the country and holed up to screw all weekend?'

'How could I forget?' he said with a chortle. 'The time Lyon showed up by surprise and found us there.'

'Do you remember the letter he dictated to me that weekend?' she asked, choosing her words carefully.

He looked at her with complete bafflement.

'I remember it distinctly,' she said, staring off into the distance as she went on. 'Because I'm not so good with typewriters, you see. Imagine no computer up there. At least there wasn't then. So I had to type this bloody letter for him, while you both sat there and watched. I remember thinking what a lovely gesture Lyon was making and what a lucky devil you were to have such a generous brother.'

She turned her bright blue eyes to him and stared at him intently. 'Now, don't you remember, darling?'

His lips slowly spread into a smile as comprehension dawned.

'I thought you would,' she said, 'and I happen to have kept a copy of the letter, since Lyon asked me to keep one. He was worried that you would mislay it or simply throw it away. After all, you scoffed at his generosity, saying that he would outlive us all or something to that effect.'

She looked at him with a lifted brow. 'How am I doing?'

'I think you're doing brilliantly,' he said.

'I think it's a good scenario, too,' she said. 'You can help me fill in the details, but as I remember Lyon promised you something like a quarter of a million dollars should he predecease you. Dated, signed, and witnessed by little me.' She smiled.

'But what about his signature?'

'Oh, come on, darling,' she said, 'I'm sure you can write just like your big brother.' She cleared her throat. 'One thing we do have to find out about is whether or not the old typewriter is still up there. It's been five years or so. If not, grand. We simply type the letter on a similar model. If it happens to still be there, we're going to have to use it somehow.'

Leland walked to the bed, where she was spread out in a silk robe. 'Do you really think this could work?' he asked, sitting down next to her.

'Why not?' she asked. 'Carolina knows about that weekend, because Lyon told her. What Lyon failed to tell her was about his generosity toward you, his younger and much beloved brother.'

'A letter like that might not hold up in court,' he said.

'Yes, but it might present such a nuisance to Carolina that she'd be willing to settle with you out of court.'

'Yeah,' he said excitedly, 'court costs, legal costs, and all that.'

'In the meantime, you must be the heartbroken brother, of course. In a few days we'll mention the letter. We can't wait too long. We want to get her while she's at her most vulnerable. And right now she's a wreck. First Lyon's death, then finding out about the other woman. I think she'll cave in without an argument.'

Leland took her into his arms and kissed her hard. 'Oh, God, Mercedes,' he said, 'why did we ever break up? What a team we could make.'

'Hmmm,' she said, 'maybe we still could.'

18

Carolina didn't remember ever having been so busy, especially when it seemed like every day was an uphill battle. The loss of Lyon was constantly in the back of her mind, and the revelation about his mistress and child in Amsterdam had overwhelmed her. As much as she could, she lost herself in work.

There had been the bad publicity to contend with over the gallery event, and although she was certain she'd lost some business because of it, she felt that she could overcome the repercussions by sheer hard work and perseverance. Still, Payton Fitzsimmons had made some inroads into her client list. That was to be expected anyway.

In the meantime, she showered, put on her makeup, and dressed to the nines every single morning, armoring herself against the world and denying that anything was amiss.

Lydia Carstairs had telephoned her to let her know that she'd received the go-ahead for the late fall benefit for the Animal Rescue Mission.

'It took a lot more work than I'd anticipated to get board approval for you to do it,' Lydia said. 'The silly newspaper reports about the gallery mishap didn't help, and then, of course, Payton Fitzsimmons has opened her shop. Nearly everyone knows her, and I had to argue for you. Several board members wanted her to get the business.'

'I really appreciate your help, Lydia,' Carolina said. 'I'll do everything I can to make you proud of my work.'

'Think nothing of it,' she said. 'Your work has already proved itself to me. Now then, "Winter Wonderland" has been decided upon as the theme,' she went on. 'I know it doesn't show brilliance on the part of the board members, but it was the best we could decide on without a major battle.'

'Winter Wonderland,' Carolina repeated in a noncommittal voice. 'It's certainly appropriate for that time of year, and I can do a really beautiful job with a theme like that, Lydia.'

They discussed various details, and as soon as they hung up, Carolina telephoned Matt. 'Winter Wonderland,' she said when he came to the phone.

Matt burst out into laughter. 'How original!' he cried.

'I know,' Carolina said, 'can you think of anything more well worn? But listen, I've already started drawing the party in my workbook. We're going to have to get together at the museum right away. You, Thad, and myself. Plus, I'll have Roxie and Antonio coming with me, so they can get an idea of the scale.'

'Name the day and time,' he'd said.

They arranged their meeting at the museum and made further plans, and endlessly discussed a number of issues related to the benefit on the telephone.

Next, Carolina searched for the storage space she'd need and finally found it right in Chelsea. It had come at great expense, and she was hoping that she would be able to handle the costs. It was going to be well worth the price, she told herself, if she could keep everything together.

Leaving the shop in the hands of Roxie and Antonio, she spent the next few days shopping for props of various sorts: huge numbers of vases and urns, candleholders of all kinds and sizes, columns and doorways, latticework and arches. The list went on and on. She restrained herself from overdoing it, since she knew that individual themes would dictate certain props, but purchased the basics that she could use time and again.

She also introduced herself to several major theatrical prop rental agencies, making certain that when she gave them a call in the future, they would know who they were dealing with. This entailed going from prop house to prop house to discuss her business and the sort of things that she might be needing.

In the meantime, the shop itself had become a beehive of activity. There had been four big weddings, a number of funerals, countless luncheons, and dinner parties to decorate for.

Today, after they'd closed the shop and Antonio and Mercedes had gone home, Carolina and Roxie sat in the back chatting, having a cup of coffee together.

Throughout the awful first weeks it was Roxie who helped Carolina keep her confidence up. 'Look, Carolina, you've worked for years at getting it right. Besides, you have a creative streak that a lot of florists don't have. Nobody can take that away from you. So, Payton Fitzsimmons or no, you're going to do okay.'

Carolina reluctantly agreed. 'I know,' she said, 'but I still get awfully nervous. That gallery business was really hurtful, and it wouldn't take more than a couple of things like that to turn this shop back into a little neighborhood shop that only sells five- and ten-dollar bouquets. I still can't figure out what the hell Antonio was thinking.'

'I can't figure it out either. He's worked here too long to make that sort of mistake.'

'Do you think we need to hire more help?'

Roxie shook her head. 'No, not yet,' she said. 'Maybe in the fall when all the people away for the summer or on weekends are back.

That's when the heavy-duty party season starts. We'll have to get a full-time delivery person for sure when school starts, because Richie won't be able to help out.'

'You're probably right,' Carolina replied. She looked at her watch. 'It's getting late, and I know you want to get home to Leland. How's he doing, by the way?' Carolina asked. 'I haven't talked to him in days.'

'It's like being on a roller-coaster ride with him lately,' she said. Her voice abruptly became very quiet. 'He's really heartbroken over Lyon's death. It's affected him a lot more than I would've thought. I knew they were close, but I had no idea Leland would be so . . . well, devastated.'

'They were close,' Carolina said, 'and probably shared things we know nothing about.'

'I guess so,' Roxie said, nodding her head. 'I've never seen Leland like this. Anyway, I didn't mean to talk about this now. You're exhausted and need to get home.'

The telephone rang, and Carolina picked up the receiver. 'Carolina,' she said.

'It's Lydia Carstairs, Carolina.'

'Hi, Lydia. How are you?'

'I'm not the least bit happy,' she said in a clipped voice. 'I just walked in the door after a very tiresome fitting at Oscar de la Renta's and a very dull cocktail party, and guess what greeted me?'

'I – I've no idea,' Carolina said, alarm bells going off in her head. Lydia certainly didn't sound like herself. In fact, she sounded as if she were very angry and trying to contain it. 'What did greet you?' she asked.

'Dead flowers,' Lydia said. 'Everywhere. In every single room. Thousands of dollars' worth of dead flowers, I might add.'

Carolina's heart sank, and for a moment her hand trembled on the receiver. *What the hell is going on?* she asked herself. 'Oh, Lydia, I'm terribly sorry,' Carolina said. 'I have no idea what's happened, but I'll certainly find out. In the meantime, I can head straight up there with replacements. I can—'

'No,' Lydia said. 'I'm too angry right now, Carolina. I've had Normal throw out all of the flowers, and fortunately I'm going out tonight. There will be no dinner guests to see the disgrace I saw. I like you and your work very much, but I don't want something like this to happen again. And I don't want to hear of it happening to someone else, either. I'm beginning to suspect that these things wouldn't happen if you were truly on your toes.'

'I'll straighten this out right away, Lydia,' Carolina said, 'and I promise you it won't happen again.'

'Good,' Lydia said, 'because you would lose the benefit at the Met in that case. I can't chance something happening to ruin that party.'

'I understand,' Carolina said.

'I'll expect your people on Monday as usual,' she went on, 'but we'll have no more mishaps, Carolina.'

'No, of course not,' she replied.

'Good evening.'

'Good evening, Lydia,' she said, and then realized that Lydia Carstairs had already hung up on her.

'What is it?' Roxie asked.

Carolina held her head in her hands a moment. Then she looked up at Roxie and told her about the conversation.

'Jesus,' Roxie said. 'We've got to find out what the hell is going on.'

'Who did Lydia's apartment this week?' Carolina asked.

Roxie retrieved their workbook and searched for the entry. 'It was Mercedes who actually decorated the apartment,' she said. 'But Antonio chose the flowers and took everything up there for her.'

'Things are getting too damn crazy,' Carolina said. 'And I don't believe this could be a coincidence after the gallery thing. We could be ruined very quickly. I'm not sure what to do. The two of us can't do everything ourselves.'

She sat lost in thought for a few seconds, and then looked over at Roxie. 'I think we're going to have to have a new rule,' Carolina said. 'Every bouquet or arrangement, even just a bunch of flowers, going out this door get vetted first. It has to be approved. By either you or me.' She paused a moment, thinking. 'No, let's change that,' she said at last. 'Make that just you, because I'm off seeing clients or something too often.'

'Okay,' Roxie said. 'That's a tall order, though.'

'I know it is,' Carolina said, 'but we have to do it. It's called quality control, Roxie.'

'Yes, but Carolina,' she said, 'the flowers have been leaving here in beautiful shape. Whatever happens to them happens *after* they leave here.'

'It's got to be Antonio then,' she said, 'doing something to them.'

'But what about up at Lydia's?' Roxie asked. 'Mercedes actually handled the decorating, not Antonio.'

Carolina slammed her hands down on her worktable. 'Damn!' she cursed. 'Who's behind it and why? And how the hell do we stop it?'

'We'll think of something,' Roxie said. 'We always do.'

Carolina turned and looked at her. 'I hope so, Roxie,' she replied, 'because everything I've got right now is riding on it.'

'How did you find out about the typewriter?' Leland asked Mercedes.

She smiled slyly. 'It was so easy, darling,' she said. 'You wouldn't believe. I was entering an order into the computer and hit the wrong key and made some information disappear. Anyway, I said how that sort of thing could never happen with a good old-fashioned typewriter, and Roxie said that I was so right. Then dear, dear Carolina said she'd often regretted that Lyon had gotten rid of the old typewriter in the country when they got a computer up there because she's never learned to do envelopes on a computer.'

She squeezed Leland's cheeks between her fingers and then kissed his puckered lips. 'See? Our little plan is going to work out.'

'Yeah,' he said, 'it's about time for me to contest the will. I might as well go ahead and hire a lawyer.'

'You might save yourself some expense if you tell Carolina about the letter and offer to settle with her first. Like a good brother-in-law. See what she has to say.'

He looked at her thoughtfully. 'You're right,' he said. 'It would make it look more like my claim's . . . on the up and up.'

'Exactly,' she said. 'And this is a good time, remember. She's very vulnerable, and she's going to be even more so tomorrow after she's found out that all the flowers at Lydia's apartment died.'

'What're you talking about?' he asked.

'Ohhhh,' Mercedes said, drawling the word out, 'I think she's going to be hearing from Lydia if she hasn't already. You see, today Antonio and I did the weekly decorating, and I suspect the flowers died an untimely death after we left.' She looked at him, smiling wickedly.

'Jesus,' he said, 'the poor woman's getting hit from every angle.'

Mercedes nodded.

'I bet Payton Fizsimmons is happy as hell about this,' Leland said. 'Does she already know?'

Mercedes nodded again. 'Yes,' she said. 'I ran into her afterwards.'

'How did you do it, anyway?'

'Oh, it was too easy,' Mercedes said. 'As easy as finding out about the typewriter. Antonio had a big bucket of bleach mixture in the van. On the way up, we gave all of the flowers a good stiff drink of the stuff. Plunge them in for a while. When they were put in the vases at Lydia's, they still looked pretty, but they soon began to fade and die.' She clapped her hand over her mouth and laughed.

He grabbed her and drew her close. 'You are one evil bitch,' he said, grinning.

'You bet I am,' she replied, flipping blond hair out of her eyes. 'And you wouldn't win any awards for your humanitarian deeds, either. I think that's why I like you so much. You're one of the bad guys.'

'And you're a real bad girl,' he said, pressing her buttocks hard against him. 'And that always turns me on.' His lips sought out hers, and they kissed deeply, their tongues exploring and delving.

Mercedes felt Leland tug down the zipper on his trousers. She groaned excitedly when he pulled his cock out, and one of her hands reached down and began stroking it.

'Come on,' he said in a breathy whisper, his hands on her breasts. 'Do it like you used to.'

Mercedes moaned and slid to her knees in front of him, her mouth already open.

19

The bells on the shop door jangled, and Roxie looked out from behind her workstation. A smile immediately came to her lips when she saw Carolina stride purposefully in, her hair bouncing with her step and her face aglow with carefully applied makeup.

'You look great,' she called out, putting down her knife.

'Thanks, Roxie,' Carolina said. They kissed cheeks. 'I had a good night's sleep, and a very busy morning. I've been over to the warehouse, checking on things there. Some new props I ordered came in. I had three appointments with potential clients, all of them representing charity boards, and I had a talk on the telephone with Thad to go over some of the lighting details for the benefit.' She paused and smiled. 'So I'm ready for whatever else the day might bring,' she added. She put down her carryall and looked around. 'I see you've been hard at work.'

'I'm just getting more bouquets ready for the street,' Roxie said. 'We sold everything we made up yesterday, and I've done all the arrangements that we need so far today.'

'Where's Antonio?' Carolina asked.

'He hasn't come in yet,' Roxie said. 'He hasn't called either.'

'If he's not here in a few minutes, then I'll call him,' Carolina said. 'Is there much on the slate for the rest of today?'

Roxie shook her head. 'Not a whole lot, thank heaven.' She picked up her knife and began scraping the bottom leaves off a bunch of chrysanthemums.

'Don't sound so happy about it,' Carolina said.

'You know I'm not,' Roxie replied. 'Not really. But it will be nice having a slightly slower pace around here.'

'Oh, come on, Roxie,' Carolina said. 'I think we do our best work when we're absolutely swamped.' She took a dozen roses out of water and laid them on her worktable. Pulling on gloves, she began preparing them for bouquets, slicing their stems at a sharp angle and then trimming off their bottom leaves.

The telephone rang. 'Sorry, Roxie, we'll get back to this.' She picked up the receiver. 'Carolina.'

'Hi, Carolina.'

The voice was so like Lyon's that a chill ran up her back, and she was momentarily discombobulated. 'Oh, h-hi, Leland,' she finally stammered, looking at Roxie with raised brows. She quickly recovered her composure. 'Do you want to talk to Roxie?'

'I need to talk to you for just a minute,' Leland said.

Was there hesitation in his voice, or was it her imagination? Carolina wondered. And why did he sound so serious? 'Okay,' she said. 'I've always got at least a minute for you, Leland.'

'It's about Lyon's will,' he said.

Gooseflesh broke out on Carolina's arms. 'What is it, Leland?'

'I wish I could speak to you about this personally,' he said, 'but I can't get away from the office. You know how it is.'

'Yes, I do,' she said. 'So, what is it?'

'Well, I guess you don't know about it, or you would've mentioned it at Bernard Goldsmith's office,' he said.

171

'About what, Leland?' she asked in exasperation. *Why is he beating around the bush?* she wondered.

'Remember that weekend a few years back when Lyon came up to your place in Connecticut, and Mercedes and I were there?'

'Y-yes,' Carolina replied.

'Well, that weekend,' Leland said, 'he dictated a letter to Mercedes and had all of us sign it.'

He paused long enough for Carolina to lose her patience. 'What letter, Leland? Would you please get to the point?'

'The letter says that Lyon promises to leave me a quarter of a million dollars when he dies,' Leland finally said in a rush.

Carolina was stunned. *A quarter of a million dollars? To Leland? Without so much as a word to me about it?* Lyon had told her about the weekend and finding Mercedes and Leland there, but he certainly hadn't mentioned anything like this bequest. She could hardly believe that he wouldn't have shared something as important as this with her.

'I – I don't know what to say, Leland,' she replied. She could see Roxie watching her intently. 'I didn't know about this, and I don't even know if there's enough in the estate to honor such a promise. I guess the thing to do is send the letter to Bernard.' *It's odd,* she thought, *that Bernard doesn't have a copy of it. Lyon always did everything through him.* 'I'll let Matt know since he's a coexecutor, unless you want to call him yourself,' she added.

'You can pass the word along,' he said. 'In the meantime, I'll send a photocopy to Bernard Goldsmith.'

'Okay, Leland.'

'I'd have thought that Lyon would've told you about this,' Leland said, 'but as it turns out there was a lot he didn't tell you. Right, Carolina?'

She felt as if he'd smacked her in the face. 'Yes,' she said, 'and how nice of you to remind me.' She hoped he hadn't missed the sarcasm in her voice. 'Listen, I have to go. Work, you know.'

'Okay,' he said. 'I'll talk to you later. Bye.'

'Good-bye.' She hung up the telephone and stood staring toward the shop's door but seeing nothing.

'What is it?' Roxie asked. 'You look like you've seen a ghost.'

Carolina turned to her and, angry as she was, attempted a smile. 'I think I know why Leland's been acting so peculiarly,' she said.

'What?'

'He says he has a letter from Lyon promising him a quarter of a million dollars. Says Lyon dictated it to Mercedes the weekend he caught the two of them staying up at the house in the country.'

Roxie was openmouthed for a moment; then she slammed her knife down on the worktable. 'I don't believe it,' she said angrily. 'Not for a single minute. He would've told me.' She looked over at Carolina. 'Do you believe it?' she asked.

'I don't know what to believe,' Carolina said. 'Not anymore, I don't.' She shook her head as if to clear it of cobwebs. 'Oh, well, it's all for the lawyer to figure out,' she said, trying to sound nonchalant, but she was truly disturbed by Leland's news. She straightened her shoulders and stuck her chin out determinedly. 'We've got a lot to do, Roxie, so we'd better get busy.' She picked up her knife. 'Speaking of which, where the hell do you suppose Antonio is? There's a ton of stuff for him to do. If he's not here soon, I'll have to ask Mercedes to come down and help out.'

'I'll try to reach him,' Roxie said.

Antonio was having the time of his life. He'd never been in Bergdorf Goodman's men's store, let alone its private fitting rooms. He took a sip of the aromatic coffee the salesman had served him and then stretched his legs out, enjoying the feel of the luxurious leather chair where he waited for his salesman to return with more samples. Envisioning Payton's cool, patrician blond looks, he could hardly wait to see her reaction when she saw him in the new clothes that she was buying for him.

They'd finished making love, the two of them still cuddled next to each other in her bed, when Payton had mentioned that he was going to have to have a whole new wardrobe when he went to work for her. Besides, she'd said, when they went public with their relationship, he would have to have a lot of clothes to wear to formal functions.

'I can't possibly get together that kind of wardrobe right now,' Antonio had said.

Payton playfully pinched his ass. 'You don't have to, silly,' she'd said. 'I'll call Bergdorf Goodman and tell them you're coming by. They'll take care of you.'

'You mean . . . you mean, you'd be buying clothes for me there?'

She nodded. 'Sure. Why not? They'd be a business expense for me. You can pay me back later, after you've started working for me full-time.' *Toss the donkey another carrot*, she thought. *Maybe he'll quit pestering me about when this and when that.* She would have to keep him satisfied for a while – as long as she needed him – before she dropped him. So what if he cost her a few grand in the meantime? He was worth every penny of it, and it would make the pain for him a little less when she told him to buzz off.

'You'd do that for me?' he said in amazement, having some idea of what the cost would be at such a fancy store.

'You know it, Antonio,' she cooed, running a fingertip around one of his nipples.

'And what am I going to have to do for it?' he said, smiling as he kneaded her firm cheeks with his hands.

She laughed. 'Oh, I think you're doing plenty already.' She could feel him hardening against her thigh. 'Ahhh, there may be a thing or two more,' she said in a whisper. 'We want to be sure and sink your boss's ship, don't we?'

'Hmmm,' he had said. 'No problem.' He'd slowly entered her, enjoying the look of carnal delight on her face as his hardness filled her softness and she began to move against him, greedy for more.

With a start, Antonio realized that he was becoming aroused in the fitting room. *Jesus,* he thought. *What if the salesman saw me like this?* He quickly tried to dispel the memory of this morning's sexual high jinks and refocus his attention on something else. He looked at his watch and saw that he should have been at the shop hours ago. *Well, too bad,* he thought. *Let her get used to it. If she's pissed off, it's no skin off my back. I'm operating in a whole different league now. Carolina wants to decorate for these people, but I want to be one of these people. And Payton Fitzsimmons is my ticket.*

20

'Antonio's not here,' Carolina said. 'Is there something I can help you with . . . He's up at the Central Park Boathouse doing measurements. He should be back in about an hour or so,' she said. 'Could I take a message . . . Okay.' She hung up the telephone and turned to Roxie. 'What a rude woman,' she said.

'Who was it?' Roxie asked.

'I don't know,' Carolina said. 'Some woman. Maybe he's got a girlfriend we don't know about yet.'

'Maybe,' Roxie said. 'When's he supposed to be back?' she asked. 'We've got a lot of arrangements to do for that party the day after tomorrow.'

'He shouldn't be more than another hour,' Carolina said. She hoped she was right. She'd read him the riot act about coming in so late and not calling. 'I wonder who he could be seeing,' she went on. 'He's been so secretive lately.'

'He won't tell me anything,' Roxie said. 'He's like Leland. He keeps everything to himself.'

Carolina looked over at her. 'What about Leland?' she asked.

'I told him we were quits last night,' Roxie said calmly.

'You did?' Carolina exclaimed in surprise. 'You mean you actually told him to get lost?'

'I did,' Roxie said with a nod. Her jaw was set firmly, and her eyes blazed with determination.

'I can't believe it,' Carolina said. 'What brought this on?'

'What do you think brought it on?' Roxie asked. 'I asked him if he'd been seeing Mercedes. I mean, she's the one who's supposed to have this letter that Lyon dictated. Right? So he's bound to have been seeing her.'

'And?'

'And he lied through his teeth,' Roxie replied. 'He told me that, sure, they'd been in touch about this legal matter, but that's all.' Roxie sighed. 'It was so obvious that he was lying that it was insulting. I don't think he really cares anymore.'

'You mean about you?' Carolina asked.

Roxie nodded. 'About me and about whether or not I know he's been seeing Mercedes.'

'Oh, God,' Carolina said. 'I'm so sorry, Roxie. You must feel awful.'

'I do, but I'll get over it.'

'I can't believe Mercedes would be that treacherous,' Carolina said. 'I mean, we were never close, but she was always so nice to me. To think she's been carrying on an affair with my brother-in-law right under my nose. It's hard to believe. Are you absolutely sure, Roxie?'

She nodded. 'One hundred percent. And you will be, too, soon. Because I bet you a million dollars he moves in with her.'

'No,' Carolina said. 'You don't really think so?'

'You bet I do,' Roxie said.

'Oh, God, Roxie,' Carolina said, 'you must be hurting. I'm so sorry.' She got off her stool and hugged Roxie close. 'Is there anything I can do?'

'No,' Roxie said. 'I'm not going to try to act like it's not a strange feeling to be alone, but I guess I'll get used to it.'

The bells on the door sounded, and they both looked toward it. Seth Foster came in and closed the door behind him. 'The window looks great,' he said when he saw them looking at him. 'I like your tropical jungle theme.'

'Thanks, Seth,' Carolina said. *He looks so wonderful,* she thought. She felt that familiar flutter and realized that she was blushing.

'I hope you're doing well,' Seth said in a solicitous voice.

'Very well, thank you,' Carolina said. 'Roxie told me that you called about having a party that you want us to decorate.'

'Yes,' he replied. 'Listen, I've got to hurry to an appointment, but I was wondering if the three of us could maybe discuss it over a drink after work.'

A drink? Carolina thought. *With Seth Foster? Oh, well, it would be the three of us.* 'Well, I guess so, Seth,' she said.

'I don't mean to be pushy or anything. I just had some ideas and thought I could go over them with you and Roxie.'

Carolina found herself nodding. 'Okay,' she said, 'why not?'

'Is tonight okay?' Seth asked. 'Just a drink and a little planning?'

'How's that with you, Roxie?' she asked.

'Fine,' Roxie replied.

'Then sure,' she said.

'I know you work pretty late, and so do I,' he said. 'Is about seven all right? I could come by for you and Roxie here.'

'Seven's perfect,' Carolina said.

'Great,' Seth said, smiling. 'I'll see you later, then. I'd better run now. Bye.'

Carolina realized that she was looking forward to their meeting, although she couldn't really say why. Perhaps it was simply the fact that she needed a diversion from work. *Yes, that's it,* she told herself. *All I've done is work, work, work.* Of course, the meeting would be work, too, but at least she and Roxie and Seth would be working over a drink.

At a quarter to seven, Carolina went into the shop's bathroom. She looked down at her hands as she scrubbed them. Despite the weekly manicure she always had, they looked like they belonged to a farmer, she thought. Working with pretty flowers was a very dirty business and a scratchy one, even bloody sometimes.

At least she didn't have a Band-Aid on any of her fingers tonight, and the new lipstick and nail polish she was wearing – in a shade called Ultraviolet – looked great with the new purplish silk and linen top she'd put on and tucked into one of her favorite summer skirts, a classic long creamy white linen one.

She dried her hands and picked up the bottle of moisturizing lotion from the counter and rubbed oodles of it into her hands, repeated the process, and then wiped her hands on a towel. *Ready to go*, she thought. *Or at least as ready as I'll ever be.*

She felt strange going out for a drink with a man, for the first time since Lyon's death, and was thankful that Roxie was coming along. There was no rational reason for feeling this way, she told herself – this was strictly business, after all – but she couldn't shake the feeling that it was somehow, if not wrong, then not exactly right, either.

Flipping off the light, she went back out to her worktable and made certain that she had a sketch pad, pens, and pencils in her tote bag in case she needed them for her meeting with Seth.

'You look wonderful,' Roxie said.

'Thanks, Roxie,' she said, looking over at her. 'So do you.'

Just then, Richie walked in, returning from a delivery.

'Hey, sweetie,' she called to him.

'Hi, Mom,' he said. 'Guess what?'

'What?' she asked.

'I just got a ten-buck tip from Mercedes.'

'Ten dollars?' she said, surprised. 'From Mercedes?'

'Yeah,' he said. 'She told me not to spend it all on dope.' He grinned.

Roxie and Carolina laughed. 'Sounds like something she would say,' Carolina said. 'Who sent her flowers?'

'Somebody named Warner Goodman,' Roxie said. 'His secretary called and ordered a big bouquet.'

'Warner Goodman?' Carolina said. 'The name rings a bell, but I can't think who it is. How big was the bouquet?'

'Like three hundred dollars big.'

'That's big,' Carolina said. 'I wonder who he is?'

Roxie shrugged. 'I don't know,' she said. 'I only know the name because of the credit card information.'

'That was my last delivery, Mom,' Richie said. 'I'm going on over to Jeff's now, all right?'

'Okay,' Carolina said. 'I hope you have a good time. I won't be gone long myself. Just drinks. What are you and Jeff going to do?'

'Have dinner at his place, then go to a movie,' he said.

'I'll see you by eleven?'

'Yeah,' he said, turning to go. He stopped and turned back. 'Oh, and Uncle Leland said to tell you hello.'

'Leland?' she said. 'When did you see him?'

'He was at Mercedes's place.' He waved. 'See you later.' He turned and hurried out the shop door.

Roxie and Carolina looked at one another. 'I knew it,' Roxie finally said. 'I just knew it. The weasel.'

'Don't insult weasels,' Carolina said. 'I think he's a lot worse than that.'

'Well, let's forget about it tonight,' Roxie said. 'We've got business to take care of. Richie seems like he's in a better mood, by the way. More like his old self.'

'Thank God,' Carolina said. 'I still worry, though. He has such ups and downs, but I think he's going to be fine. Richie's never been a problem.'

At the sound of the door, they both looked up. Seth Foster. Carolina smiled tentatively at him as he crossed the shop toward them.

'Hi, Roxie,' he said. 'Carolina.'

'Hi,' they both replied.

'Ready?' he asked. 'Or do you want me to wait a bit? If you're busy—'

'No, we're just chatting,' she said. 'I'm ready. Ready, Roxie?'

'I'm all set.'

Carolina picked up her carryall and turned to Roxie. 'I'll lock up. You two go on out.'

'I don't know what I was thinking,' Seth said, 'bringing you two here to talk something over and have a drink. It's so loud, we can't hear ourselves think. Maybe we should go somewhere else.'

'What if we get a table outside?' Carolina said. 'I see a couple that're empty.'

'Good idea,' he said. 'You sure you don't mind?'

'No, not at all,' she replied.

'It's nice out,' Roxie said. 'That'd be fun.'

'Okay.' He caught the attention of the maître d' and spoke to him, mouth close to his ear, the only way to make himself heard above the restaurant's din.

They were immediately shown to a table on the sidewalk, and Seth held their chairs for them. 'Thanks,' they both said.

'You're welcome,' he replied. 'Do you ladies mind terribly?' he asked, holding his tie in his hand as if about to unknot it.

Carolina laughed. 'No,' she said, 'of course not.' She was surprised that the natty Seth Foster would dare to take his tie off.

He loosened the tie considerably and unbuttoned the top button of his shirt. He took a deep breath. 'That feels a lot better,' he said. 'Sorry, but the damn thing's had me in a chokehold since seven o'clock this morning.'

The waiter appeared to take their order, and Seth gestured to the women. 'What'll you have?' he asked.

'I'll have a Cosmopolitan,' Carolina said.

'I'll have the same,' Roxie said.

'Make mine a scotch on the rocks,' Seth said.

The waiter nodded and left.

Carolina smiled. 'You're always so perfectly groomed and dressed,' she said, 'that it's just weird to see you with your tie loose.'

'That's because you always see me either going to work or coming home,' he replied. 'Or at a party. The real me likes old blue jeans, tee shirts, and worn-out shoes, I'm afraid.'

'You're kidding,' she said.

'I don't believe it,' Roxie said.

He shook his head. 'It's true,' he replied. 'I hate having to dress like this, but I don't have any choice. When you deal with big-shot European diplomats and financiers, some of them aristocracy, you really have to. They're much more formal than we are, you know. Very Old World, a lot of them.'

'Yes, I know,' Carolina said. 'Lyon complained sometimes about the same thing. Not just the dressing, but the manners and so on. As long as he was in the apartment in Minervaplein – you know, in Amsterdam – he said he never got to know anyone else in the building. Not really. There were barons and baronesses and so on, and he was always a newcomer to them, he said, and a foreigner to boot.'

Seth nodded. 'I know exactly what he meant,' he replied. 'It's not necessarily that the people are being snobbish, either. It's a matter of introductions. Being formally introduced. Once that happens, you're often treated like part of the family, but until it does, you might as well be a ghost.'

'Do you like your work?' Roxie asked. 'I mean, apart from the dressing?'

'Yes,' he said, 'I really do, Roxie. I meet lots of interesting people and actually get to know some of them well. Their families, too.'

'What is it you do, exactly?' Roxie asked. 'I know you mentioned a bank or something.'

'I invest money here in the States for people who live abroad,' he said. 'Mostly for people in the Netherlands and the U.K., although I have a few clients from other countries. But that's enough about me and my work. I'm sure it's boring to you.'

'Not really,' Carolina said. 'I think it sounds interesting.'

'You're very polite,' he said with a laugh.

'No, seriously,' she said.

'Anyway, we need to talk about this party I'm giving,' Seth said.

'Why don't you tell me what you have in mind,' Carolina said. She took a notepad and pen from her carryall. 'How many people, who or what it's for, all that stuff.'

He explained that the party was to be a formal dinner for about thirty people, most of them aristocratic Dutch clients he knew from work. They would be seated at three separate tables. He wanted the tables decorated, as well as arrangements for several other spots in his loft.

'It would be about fifteen arrangements altogether,' he said. 'Not a lot, I know, and I guess it doesn't give you much leeway as far as creativity goes,' he added apologetically, 'since these people are fairly conservative – make that extremely conservative – and expect things to be a certain way. Including the flowers.'

'That's okay,' Carolina said, having quickly calculated the approximate profit she would derive from the party. 'I can live with that. Don't you agree, Roxie?'

Roxie nodded. 'Yes, we can handle it.'

The three of them discussed the party for another fifteen minutes, Carolina taking copious notes, and Roxie trying to make sure they covered every angle.

'The good news,' Seth said as they were finishing up, 'is that several of these people have apartments in New York, and they entertain a lot. So you might get some future business out of it.' He smiled over at her and sipped his drink.

Carolina returned his smile. 'We should hire you to be my one-man publicity department,' she said. 'You've been such a help.'

'Well, it's only because I'd seen your windows for a long time,' he said somewhat sheepishly, 'and I saw what great work you do. Then when I started ordering flowers for friends and business associates, you always made certain that they were taken care of and that I got exactly what I wanted.'

'Yes,' she said, 'but surely anybody would do that.' She took a sip of her drink and savored the taste on her palate.

'No,' he said. 'You'd be surprised how often I've been let down in the past by different florists. Even big-name ones. The deliveries wouldn't be on time, or the flowers would be of poor quality. Sometimes the arrangements would be awful. Things like that.'

'You seem to know a lot about flowers,' Roxie said. 'I know that when they're gifts, it's very important to get it right, but you seem to be a real flower *person*.'

The three of them laughed at Roxie's remark and then sipped their drinks simultaneously.

'Well, I should be,' he said. 'At least I guess I should be. It's in my blood.'

'Why?' Carolina asked, looking at him with curiosity.

'My mother was a florist,' he said.

'You're kidding?' she said. *This man was full of surprises*, she thought.

'I should've guessed,' Roxie said. 'You know so much.'

'That's why,' he said. 'She had a very small shop, but it was really beautiful.'

'Where was it?' Carolina asked.

'In London,' he replied.

'London,' she said. 'I knew you went there on business, but I didn't know you were from there.'

'Well, I am and I'm not,' he said. 'I mean, I was born here. My father was American, and my mother was British. When they divorced, she went back to London to live. So I spent some time there with her. Sometimes I helped her out in the shop like Richie helps you.'

'That's amazing,' Carolina said. 'I knew from the first time you ordered flowers in the shop that you were very knowledgeable about flowers, just like Roxie said, but I had no idea you actually know as much as you do.'

'Well, I should,' he said, 'because I put in a lot of time in my mother's shop.'

'Where was it?' Carolina asked, imagining that it must have been in some gorgeous mansion and patronized by a top-drawer clientele.

'In a sort of red-light district,' he replied, helplessly grinning.

'A red-light district!' Roxie exclaimed. 'This story gets better and better.'

'Seems like an awfully unusual place to have a flower shop,' Carolina said. *How is it that a man like this managed to get to know people like Lydia Carstairs and company?* she wondered. *The job, maybe, but that, in and of itself, doesn't seem to offer the right credentials – or not enough, anyway.*

'It was,' he agreed, 'and the only reason it was there was because she got a good deal on the location. It was what she could afford after the divorce. It was surprisingly busy, though. A lot of the bar people would stop and buy. A lot of them would see the window late at night on their way home from the bars and then come back the next day. Some of the customers for the prostitutes became good customers of my mother's. They'd see certain women regularly and start sending flowers to them. It was a fascinating place.'

'It must have been, especially for a boy,' Roxie said.

'It was. No doubt about it.' He nodded.

'Do you get back often?' Carolina asked.

'About every six to eight weeks,' he said. 'Because of work. My mother died several years ago, so it's just work that takes me there now.' He abruptly laughed. 'You two have done it.'

'What?'

'You've gotten me to yammer on and on about myself,' he said, 'and I want to know about you. How you're doing. And how Richie's doing.'

Carolina took the last sip of her drink and set the glass down.

'Why don't we have another?' he asked.

'Well . . . I don't know,' she replied, looking at Roxie.

'It's early,' he said. 'Just one more?'

Roxie nodded.

'Okay,' Carolina said with a smile. 'One more, and then we'd better go.'

He motioned for the waiter, ordered three more drinks, and looked back over at Carolina. 'You seem to be coping with things pretty well,' he said. 'It must be very difficult.'

She looked down at the table; then her gaze shifted into the distance. 'It's . . . it's—'

'Oh, God,' he said, reaching over to touch the hand she had on the table. 'I'm sorry. I'm being rude. I didn't mean to pry.'

She looked at his hand on hers. She knew it was simply a gesture of kindness, but she felt that involuntary fluttering in her chest. *Nerves*, she told herself. *I'm just very nervous.*

'I don't think you're rude at all,' she said. 'I guess I just find it difficult to talk about. Sometimes it still doesn't seem real. Sometimes, it seems as if he were off on a business trip and will come home again. Plus, I've been so busy with work that I really haven't thought about it all that much.'

The waiter returned with their drinks, and Seth removed his hand from hers. 'And Richie?' he asked. 'How's he getting along? I see him at the shop now and then, and he seems okay, I suppose. But you never can tell, not really.'

'He's had his ups and downs, just like me,' Carolina said. 'But I think he's getting along really great. He is at a vulnerable age. He's not a boy anymore, but he's not quite a man, either. Anyhow, he seems fine.'

'It's a hard age to be,' he said. 'For a man or a woman, I guess. All those hormones racing around in your body. It's so easy to be influenced at that age, by . . . good things or bad things.'

'Oh, yes,' Roxie said, nodding. 'That's for sure.'

'And I'm not always sure I'm doing the right thing,' Carolina said. 'I work so much and everything, but I'm trying to keep him very busy till school starts.'

'He seems like a well-adjusted kid,' Seth said. 'I wouldn't worry too much if I were you. Does he play any sports or anything?'

Carolina took a sip of her drink before responding. 'Well, he used to skateboard a lot, if that's a sport, and he does some inline skating. Bicycles quite a bit. Oh, and he likes to play tennis.'

'I play tennis a lot,' Seth said. 'Maybe I could get him to play tennis with me sometime.'

'That's awfully nice of you to offer, Seth,' she said, 'but I know how busy you are.'

Seth said, 'I play with some other guys, and a couple of them have sons near Richie's age. They come along some of the time and play, so it wouldn't be like he'd be stuck with a bunch of geezers.'

Roxie laughed. 'You're hardly a geezer.'

'To a kid his age, I am,' he said, joining in her laughter. 'But anyhow, they're nice guys and would only be good influences, I can assure you.'

'If they're friends of yours, I'm sure they are,' Carolina said.

He looked at his watch. 'It's getting sort of late,' he said. 'Would you like to stay for dinner? I don't have any plans and would love to treat both of you, if you're not busy.'

'I think we'd better get going,' Carolina said. 'I've got a million things to do for tomorrow, and we've got what we need to start working on your party. But thanks a million for the offer, and we'll take a rain check.'

'I understand,' he said. 'Thanks very much for meeting with me. I can get the party off my mind now.'

'It was a pleasure,' Roxie said, rising to her feet.

He got up also and shook their hands. 'Until later,' he said, as they turned to go. 'Good-bye.'

'Bye, Seth,' Carolina said.

He watched them go, wishing that they had agreed to stay to dinner. More specifically, wishing that Carolina had agreed to stay. He wanted to spend time with her, to get to know her better. But he knew he couldn't push it too much. After all, she was still grieving. He would have to bide his time.

And she's worth it, he told himself. *She's worth waiting for.*

21

'That was real food, Sis,' Matt said, putting down his knife and fork. 'My favorite.'

'I'm going to my room,' Richie said, getting up from the table.

'Okay,' Carolina said, watching him leave.

'Something bothering him?' Matt asked. 'I mean . . . something besides Lyon's being gone?'

'Not that I know of,' Carolina said. 'He's doing pretty well, I think. What do you say to having dessert a little later on?'

'That's a good idea,' Matt said. 'We should get to that paperwork I brought. Why don't we get some coffee and get busy.'

'Okay,' she said. 'By the way, is everything running on schedule at your end as far as the benefit goes?'

He nodded. 'Yes, and if you ask me one more time, I'm going to get real ugly with you.' He smiled at her.

'I guess I am getting pretty obsessive, aren't I?'

'Yes,' he said, 'but I can't blame you. This is going to be the crowning point of your career so far.'

189

'It really is, isn't it?'

'And a new beginning, too,' he added. 'The beginning of something really big. Maybe huge.'

Carolina looked at him. 'Yes,' she said. 'It gives me goose bumps just thinking about it.'

They poured their coffee in the kitchen and took it into the den, where Matt had put his briefcase. They sat down and sipped quietly.

'The light is beautiful,' Carolina said, gazing out through the windows.

He cleared his throat. He hated to broach this subject, but he had to. 'Sis,' he said.

She turned to him with anticipation. 'Huh? I'm ready. What am I signing today?'

'I have to tell you about some things,' Matt said, 'and it's not good news.'

Matt was coexecutor of Lyon's estate and had been a lifesaver, handling the bulk of the work for her. There had been a million details to see to, and he had spared her from making any decisions so far.

'What is it, Matt? The insurance company is refusing to pay? They're charging double for the urn his ashes were in?'

Her attempts at levity only made his task that much more difficult. 'No, nothing like that,' he said, shaking his head.

'Two things. First, Leland's claim. We've heard from Warner Goodman, Leland's lawyer, and he says that Leland has a very strong case to make against the estate. He also says that we might want to consider settling with Leland out of court.'

'Warner Goodman,' she repeated. 'Oh, yes, the guy who sent the flowers to Mercedes.' She slapped her forehead. 'I don't believe it. Leland and Mercedes are working together against us, and they've hired that fancy lawyer that handled Mercedes's divorce from the German count.'

'We have a choice,' Matt went on. 'We can try to reach an

agreement with Leland, offering him more than the fifty thousand Lyon left him, then hope he disappears. Or we can let him take us to court, where he'll have to prove his case.'

Carolina's eyes were fiery with anger. 'We'll let him take us to court.'

'You're sure about that, Sis?' Matt asked.

'Damn right I am,' she said. 'How dare he come up with some cockeyed last-minute letter like this and try to rip us off. I'm not going to settle with him. No way. Let the bastard sue me. I don't care.'

'Okay, okay,' Matt said, holding up a hand placatingly. 'I'll tell Bernard tomorrow. He'll call Leland's lawyer and deliver the message.'

'Good,' she said. 'The sooner Leland knows where I stand on this, the better. Now, what else have you got?'

'Monique Lehnert, the young woman in Amsterdam—' Matt began.

'I know who she is, Matt,' Carolina nearly roared. 'You don't have to explain every little thing to me as if I were a child.'

'Look, Sis,' he said. 'I'm the messenger, okay? Don't kill me. Let me finish, please.'

'Okay,' she said in a calmer voice. 'What about this Monique Lehnert?'

'You heard the will,' Matt said. 'She is demanding every bequest that Lyon left to her and her child, and she is threatening to sue the estate for more if this isn't settled quickly.'

'Have . . . have you talked to her?'

Matt nodded.

Carolina digested this piece of news for a moment. 'He left her the house?'

'Yes.'

'Whose name is it in?' she asked.

'It's in Lyon's name only,' Matt said.

191

'Good,' Carolina said, a triumphant look in her eyes. 'We'll kick her out of it.'

'Lyon left it to her in the will,' Matt said reasonably.

'I don't give a damn,' she said. 'Her name is not on the deed. His is, and I was his wife! And I'm kicking her out.'

'But—'

'And the car,' she said. 'Was her name on it?'

'Same as the house. It was in Lyon's name only.'

'Good. We'll take that away from her, too,' Carolina crowed. 'I want you to see about this right away. Have it towed. Whatever. But get it out of her sight.'

'I'm going to have to discuss this with the lawyers,' he said. 'The property is in a foreign country where he cohabited with the woman and had a child by her. I can't just kick her out of the house and grab the car.'

'Then I'll find somebody who will,' Carolina snapped angrily.

'Look, Sis,' Matt said calmly, 'the woman is only asking for what Lyon left her. No more. She's not pulling something like Leland. She only wants what she considers hers, and she'll put up a fight for it.'

'Well, she'll be good and sorry,' Carolina said, 'because she's never had a fight till she's fought me. And she'll have to fight me for every-thing she gets. I don't want her to have anything. Anything! Do you hear me?'

'I hear you,' Matt said with a loud sigh, 'but I don't think you're being rational. After all, he had a child with this woman.'

'She's going to get no satisfaction from me – or Lyon's estate,' Carolina snarled. 'I'll fight her every inch of the way.'

Matt nodded. 'Okay,' he said softly. 'Whatever you say.'

'Hey, everybody,' Richie said as he came through the kitchen door.

'Hi, sweetie,' Carolina said, smiling at her son.

'You know what?' Matt said, getting up from the table. 'I'd better get going. I forgot I'm supposed to run over to Sybil Conroy's town house this evening, and it's getting late.'

'What about dessert?' Richie asked.

'No time,' Matt said. 'Hate to pass it up,' he added, 'but I really do have to get going, Richie.'

'Well, Richie, that means the two of us will have it all to ourselves,' Carolina said with a show of cheerfulness as she rose to her feet.

'Bye, Sis,' Matt said, giving her a kiss on the cheek. 'Thanks for lunch. It was delicious.'

'Bye,' she said, 'and don't forget to call me about that business.'

'I won't,' he promised.

Richie and Carolina walked him to the elevator vestibule and waited with him until he was gone. When he'd finally left, Carolina felt her spirits deflate, and her body seemed drained of energy. The news about Lyon's Amsterdam whore had taken its toll. *I have to get a nap*, she thought. She walked back to the kitchen with Richie in an exhausted stupor.

'I have to get some rest,' she told him.

'Sure, Mom,' he said, eyeing her warily. He could see that she didn't look too sharp. She and Uncle Matt had probably talked about his dad, he decided, but he didn't want to ask her about it. He might upset her even more. 'I'll be in my room.'

'Okay, sweetie,' she said, already starting toward her bedroom. 'I'll be up in about an hour.'

Carolina didn't take a nap, after all. Instead she went into the big dressing room that she and Lyon had shared. Lyon, she thought, was responsible for what had happened today. If he hadn't deserted them for that woman in Amsterdam, she wouldn't be feeling like crap.

She opened the doors to Lyon's closet, and quickly began pulling everything out and tossing it onto the floor in a pile. She jerked and grabbed blindly, throwing one article of clothing after another onto the pile, kicking at handsome jackets and shirts and ties. She wanted to inflict as much damage as possible on these remainders of the man she thought she'd known.

When she was exhausted at last, she sat on the floor and cried bitter tears. *Tomorrow,* she thought, *I'll call the Salvation Army. I'll have them pick up everything.* Then she decided against it. *No,* she thought, *I don't want another human being to ever wear any of this filth. I don't want them infected by the hideous betrayal and lies that I have been subject to. I'll put it all out with the trash. Because that's what it is. Trash.*

She got to her feet and started to throw the huge antique box covered in fossilized fish scales that held all his jewelry atop the pile. His precious cuff links and tie pins and watches and other such finery would make a fitting crown for the pile of garbage on the floor.

Thoughts of Richie stopped her, however. He might someday want some of his father's things, though she dreaded the idea that she might have to see him wearing them. But she had to consider his feelings. She didn't want him to think his father had been a monster. Lyon had been a good father to Richie – when he'd been around – and that was important for him to remember.

She replaced the box on the top of the cabinet where it had been, and went into her bedroom, but the thought of Lyon's clothes remaining on the closet floor haunted her. Going to the kitchen, she got a box of garbage bags and went back to the dressing room.

In a frenzy, fueled by a renewed rage, she stuffed everything but the jewelry box into the bags. When she'd finished, there was hardly a square inch of floor space in the dressing room. *Tomorrow,* she thought. *They go. All of them. Out with the garbage where they belong.* The only thing that would give her more satisfaction would be to light a match to them. She closed the door on the room once again, feeling somewhat mollified by the fact that she could see nothing of Lyon's through the ugly black plastic.

Bagging up his clothes made her feel infinitely better. This was a step, she thought, in getting the man out of her life. Even in death he was haunting them as if he were still alive, and the fewer reminders of him that were around, the better.

In the den, Richie leafed through the paperwork in the briefcase and then replaced it exactly as he'd found it. It was written almost entirely in legalese that he didn't understand, but that was not what had drawn him to the briefcase to begin with. Tucked beneath the neat stack of letters and legal documents, lay the manila envelope that he knew held the photographs from Amsterdam: pictures of his father with Monique and Anja.

He slipped the envelope out and opened it, spreading out the pictures on top of the desk. There were several photographs of his father and Monique together. In one, they were looking into one another's eyes. They weren't smiling, but they appeared to be content, with expressions that could only be described as devotion to one another. The picture made Richie feel uneasy, almost as if he were a voyeur, seeing something private that had never been intended for his eyes.

He set the picture aside and picked up another one. Monique and his father had their arms wrapped around each other and their heads together. They were smiling gleefully, looking directly into the camera's lens. Richie couldn't help but smile at the photograph. He'd seen this same smile on his dad's face many times. It was a goofy smile, he thought, and meant that his dad was having a really good time. The lady, Monique, looked very warm and happy, too, as if she and his dad belonged together.

He quickly looked at several others that pictured the two of them in various poses, always looking happy, often with one of Amsterdam's many canals in the background, sometimes in a park, less frequently indoors somewhere. Richie put these pictures aside and picked up several others. These were the photographs that truly interested him. He had no mixed emotions about these pictures, and they didn't make him feel the least bit uneasy. These were photographs of Anja, his little half sister.

It didn't matter that Monique or his dad might be in some of the pictures, both of them in a few. The instant his eyes rested upon Anja, anyone else in the photograph disappeared. Once again, as he had in the lawyer's office, he felt almost as if he were looking into a mirror, so strong was the resemblance of his half sister to him. He stared at her in one photograph after another, fascinated, mesmerized, wishing above all else that he could get to know her, this girl who was his flesh and blood. When at last he had studied every detail of her appearance in every picture, he put the pictures back in the manila envelope and put it away, his mind still filled with images of the little girl, usually in a park, giggling merrily at the camera.

I want to get to know her, he thought. *I have to. She's part of my dad, just like me.* He felt certain that his dad, if he had lived long enough, would've wanted him and Anja to get to know each other. *He loved her, just like he loved me,* he thought. He also knew that his mother couldn't bear the thought that he wanted to know Anja. He understood why she felt that way, but it didn't matter. He was more determined than ever that he and Anja would become brother and sister, sooner rather than later.

The sun came and went as clouds crossed the sky, and the air in the manicured verdancy of Beatrix Park was cool and damp. Monique and Anja had already fed the herons, the geese, and the magnificent black swans with their bright red bills. It was a ritual that gave Anja great delight, much as it did her mother, but for Monique, this simple act had taken on near religious meaning. It was here in Beatrix Park that she and Lyon had first come to know one another, and it was here in this beautiful swath of green that she now found a measure of peace and serenity and felt a closeness to him, despite his absence.

She sat on the bench, basking in the warmth of the pale sun when it peeked out from between the clouds, watching Anja as she expended endless energy doing somersaults on the grass, a performance for her mother that demanded constant reassurance in the form of applause and cheers. Monique supplied it in abundance, although her thoughts were far away, in a place she didn't like to visit.

Adriaan Weber, the lawyer handling Lyon's affairs in Amsterdam, had telephoned her today to give her the latest news from New York. Carolina Mountcastle's threats at the reading of Lyon's will had not been idle ones. Her lawyer, Bernard Goldsmith, had filed the necessary paperwork, officially contesting Lyon's will. The woman was determined, Weber told her, that no expense would be spared to ensure that Monique and Anja received absolutely nothing from Lyon's estate, much less the generous bequests he had made.

The wrath of Carolina Mountcastle didn't end there, however. Weber had informed her that, no matter what decision would eventually be made in a court of law, Carolina Mountcastle could conceivably drag out the case for years on end, depriving Monique and Anja of any funds for the foreseeable future.

Monique shivered involuntarily despite the sun's warming rays, and expelled a world-weary sigh. The scene in the lawyer's office in New York began spinning through her head as if it were a movie reel, one that she had viewed over and over, to the point at which she was sickened by it. Clearly, Carolina Mountcastle had every right to despise her and to want to seek revenge, and Monique cringed every time she thought about the woman's outrage. Nevertheless, she knew deep down inside that she'd never set out to steal Lyon away from Carolina.

If anything, she thought, *I'm guilty of falling in love with Lyon and having his child.*

Anja squealed. 'Mommy, Mommy! Look! Look! Watch me!'

Monique smiled over at her. 'I'm watching, Anja,' she said. 'Show Mommy.'

Anja began trying to do cartwheels, as she'd seen other children do, and they were awkward and never quite complete. Nevertheless, Monique clapped her hands together loudly and began cheering her on.

'They're wonderful, Anja!' she cried. 'You're going to be the world's greatest gymnast! Brava! Brava!'

Anja would fall sideways to the ground and then get up and grin from ear to ear, waiting for more encouragement; Monique would give it to her, keeping up the applause and the cheers until her daughter was satisfied.

'Do you want to go to the swings now?' she asked her.

'Yes,' Anja cried with delight. 'Yes, the swings.'

Monique rose to her feet and waited for Anja to run to her across the grassy verge. Taking her hand, they walked down the gravel path together, headed toward the swing sets, Anja chattering away and Monique supplying appropriate nods and shakes of her head.

All the while, her mind was still in that lawyer's office in New York City on that awful day. She hadn't wanted to take Anja with her, but the lawyer had insisted that the child should be there, even though she wouldn't understand the proceedings. Besides, Monique knew no one in New York, and had no place to leave Anja. She hoped now that Anja would not remember a single detail of that terrible day. She had no way of knowing what the child would retain, of course, but she'd tried to explain away – as lightly as possible, as if it weren't of any importance – the angry lady when Anja had asked about her.

She was certain that Carolina Mountcastle was as protective of Richie as she herself was of Anja and would surely regret having made such a scene in front of the two children. Richie, of course, would come to understand what had happened, if he didn't already. Monique could only hope that he would not suffer psychological scars because of her affair with his father. She wished that there was some way she could explain their love for one another, and how much his father had loved him, despite the way it looked. Now she supposed she would never have that opportunity, and she regretted that because it was as important for Richie to know how much Lyon loved him as it was for Anja.

At the swing set, she lifted her daughter onto one of the swings. 'Hold on tight,' she told her.

'I am,' Anja said. 'Push, Mommy. Push.'

Monique began pushing the swing, using very little force at first and then increasing it gradually, careful not to push too hard. Anja *ooohhh*ed and *aaahhh*ed in the beginning; then she began shrieking happily as the swing rose higher and higher.

Tears came into Monique's eyes, but she continued to push the swing, overjoyed by her daughter's happiness. *Lyon loved this child so much*, she thought, *and he loved me. I know now that he loved his wife very much – that is why he never divorced her – and he loved his son. If only there were some way to work this out, so that Anja can have what is rightly hers.*

When they finally left Beatrix Park, crossing the canal back toward Minervaplein, hand in hand, Anja singing quietly to herself, Monique resolved that she would fight fire with fire. *No matter what it takes out of me*, she thought, *I'll do everything I can for my child.*

22

'You worry too much,' Payton said, running her fingers through his curls. She was sitting on a granite counter in her kitchen, her legs dangling out of her robe. 'Think about what a good time we have together, and then remember that it's only going to get better. Think about all those beautiful new clothes, and think about working uptown with me. There's a lot at stake, Antonio, isn't there?'

He nodded.

'And there's no way she's going to know it's you.'

'It's already looking very suspicious, Payton,' Antonio said. 'I mean, the gallery gig, then messing with the stuff at Lydia Carstairs's place. She's not stupid, and I know she already suspects me. She knows it almost has to be one of us.'

'Maybe she does,' Payton replied, 'but she doesn't know for sure it's you. And she can't prove it.'

'So you think this'll be the last time?' he asked.

Payton leaned into his handsome face and kissed him. 'I think this should be it for a while. Besides, I want you uptown with me

– and sooner than expected, because we're really getting busy.'

'Really?' he asked, stepping in between her legs.

'Yes, really,' she said. 'When you leave and come to work for me, poor Carolina's going to think it was you for sure. Only she won't be able to do anything about it. And what she *won't* know is that we've still got Mercedes working for us for a while. She can handle any nasty little incidents that make Carolina look bad.'

'So this would be the last time I'd have to mess with anything?' Antonio asked.

Payton nodded. 'I think so. Why? Are you afraid, Antonio?' She knew that if nothing else worked, challenging his machismo would get him to do almost anything for her.

'No!' he said angrily, grabbing her arms roughly. 'I'm not afraid. I'll do it. You'll see.'

'Okay, okay,' she said, feigning a frightened little-girl voice. 'I believe you, Antonio.'

'You'd better,' he said. He kissed her forcefully, pulling her hard against him, almost off the counter.

Payton moaned with pleasure, surrendering her body to him. She liked it best when she'd made him angry and he took her with a brute force that most men she knew were afraid to use.

His mouth moved to her breasts, where he teased her before moving down to that blond thatch between her thighs. He began licking and kissing her lustily. She thrust her hips up toward him, her head writhing from side to side as she tried to hold off the inevitable orgasm.

Then he abruptly stopped and slid her down onto his engorged cock, plunging into her with all his might. She cried out in a mixture of pain and pleasure such as she had never known before meeting him.

'Ohhhh, Antonio,' she cried. 'Ohhh, my God.'

Her release excited him beyond control, and with a loud groan he burst forth inside her, until he was spent.

She ran her hands through his hair wildly, then up and down his back. 'Oh, Antonio,' she cooed. 'Nobody does it like you. Nobody. Nobody.'

When he had at last set her back on the counter, Antonio whispered, 'We're a good team, aren't we, Payton?'

'The best,' she rasped. 'The best, Antonio.' *For the time being, anyway.*

'Hello?'

'Hi, Carolina,' a man's voice said. 'I hope you don't mind me calling you at home.'

'N-no,' she said. 'That's fine, Seth. I don't mind at all.'

'I wanted to see if we could have dinner together this week,' he said. 'We could iron out the final details of this party I've got coming up.'

'That's fine,' she said. 'I have some ideas that I'd like to run by you.'

'Great,' he said. 'How about tomorrow night?'

'That's impossible,' she said, 'because I've got a party to do at the Central Park Boathouse.'

'Thursday, then?' he asked.

'Hold on a second, and let me check my book,' Carolina said. She dashed to the kitchen, where she'd left her bag with her planning book. She retrieved the book, looked through it, and then picked up the telephone in the kitchen. 'That would be fine, Seth.'

'Okay,' he said. 'About eight?'

'Eight it is,' she said.

'I wanted to ask you about something else,' he said.

'What's that?' Carolina asked.

'If Richie's home,' he said, 'I thought I'd ask him if he wanted to play tennis this week. A couple of his schoolmates will be there. One of those father-son things, you know, and I thought maybe he might enjoy it.'

'That's so nice of you,' she said. 'He's doing something on the computer, I think, but let me see if he can come to the telephone. Hold on a minute, okay?'

'Sure,' he replied.

Carolina went to Richie's room and knocked on the door.

'It's open,' he called to her.

She opened the door and peeked in. She saw a flash of an Internet site being shut off on Richie's computer. 'Seth Foster's on the phone,' she said. 'He wondered if you'd like to play tennis this week. Says you'll know a couple of the guys.'

Richie drew his eyes away from the computer screen and looked over at her. 'Play tennis? Where? And who'll be there that I know?'

'Why don't you pick up your telephone and find out?' Carolina said. 'He's still on the line. Just let me know when you're finished talking, because I have to talk to him again, okay?'

'Sure.' Richie picked up the receiver as she closed the door.

A few minutes later, Richie appeared at her bedroom door. 'I'm done,' he said. 'I'll hang up when you pick up.'

'Thanks, sweetie,' she said. She picked up the telephone. 'Seth?'

'Hi.'

She heard Richie hang up the receiver. 'What did Richie have to say?' she asked.

'He'd really like to,' he said. 'So we're going to meet Tuesday night.'

'Great,' Carolina said. 'I think it'll be really good for him.'

'I hope so,' Seth said. 'Listen, I have to run, but I'll pick you up Thursday at your place.'

'Night, Seth,' she said. She hung up and lay in bed looking off into the distance, wondering how she felt about this or should feel about it. She didn't really know.

But one thing's for sure. I'll never fall in love again, she told herself. *It's impossible. I can't trust anyone, men least of all. Lyon has ruined that for me. Never, never again will that happen. I won't allow it.*

*   *   *

203

Carolina got up very early the next morning and arrived at the shop before anyone else. The party at the Central Park Boathouse was coming up tonight, and there was still a lot to do. She set her carryall down on her worktable and decided the first thing she would do this morning was go down her to-do list for the party, to make certain that they were running on schedule.

Nobody else had arrived yet, and she enjoyed the peace and quiet. She took her party-planning book out of her purse, and looked at the sketches she'd done for the party. It was not to be big, less than a hundred people, but it was very lavish. Clifford Neal, a Wall Street wizard, and his beautiful wife, Joleen, were relatively new billionaires on the New York social scene, and they spared no expense to impress their friends and acquaintances.

Carolina went down the list for the party, ticking off the things that she knew had been done yesterday in preparation for tonight. Then she began going down the list of arrangements that she knew still had to be done. She smiled to herself, thinking how different the requirements were for this party as opposed to a party at one of her old-money client's homes.

Clifford and Joleen Neal were not content with the full-blown roses and an extravagant number of peonies. No, for the Neals, only the rarest and most expensive orchids would do – and in abundance. Carolina had placed her order well in advance because some of the orchids were difficult to come by, and she'd been exceedingly lucky in managing to get some of them at all. She had her Georges in the flower market to thank for that.

The bells on the door sounded and she looked up. 'Good morning, Roxie,' she called out.

'Hi,' Roxie replied. 'I see you're already busy.'

'Just making sure everything's ready for the Neal party at the boathouse,' Carolina said.

'By the way,' Roxie asked, 'have you decided what you're going to do for Seth Foster's party?'

'I know pretty much what to do,' Carolina replied. 'These people are very rich and very conservative, so I'll do rich and conservative. Rich and conservative Dutch, that is.'

'What do you mean?' Roxie asked.

Carolina smiled. 'Lots of tulips,' she said.

'No!' Roxie said.

'Tons of tulips, but tulips like they almost never see. Huge tulips. And lots of tulipieres.'

'I don't believe you,' Roxie said. 'These people have seen tulips all of their lives.'

Carolina laughed. 'You're right, but not like these. Most of them are exported and never even seen in the Netherlands. They'll be perfect. Just what the occasion demands. They'll love seeing them, and be comfortable with them.'

The bells jangled again, and they both looked over toward it. 'Hello, everybody.'

'Hi, Antonio,' they said in unison.

Roxie put her handbag and a shopping bag down on her work-table, and Antonio sat down on the stool at his.

'So what do we have to do to finish up for tonight?' he asked.

'I was just going over the list,' Carolina said. 'Essentially just the arrangements for the tables. It won't take us more than thirty minutes to do all the wrapping and draping since we've got that ready in the cooler.'

'Well, I'm going to get started,' Roxie said, getting up from her worktable, 'because those designs of yours for the tables are really time consuming.'

'You can say that again,' Antonio said.

'I know,' Carolina said somewhat apologetically, 'but that's what they wanted.'

'I think it's really gilding the lily,' Roxie said as she took a container down from a shelf. 'Here, you want this one, Antonio?'

'Thanks,' he said, taking it from her. He got up to get some oasis and other supplies from a cabinet.

Roxie took another container down for herself. She placed it on her worktable and then walked over to the cooler to take out some of the orchids they would be using. 'Awww, my God!' she screeched, throwing her hands up to her mouth and dropping the bowl to the floor, where it landed with a loud thud.

'What is it?' Carolina asked with alarm, turning around on her stool.

'Roxie, what the hell?' Antonio rushed toward her, then stood staring openmouthed into the giant cooler. 'Jesus, Carolina,' he said.

'What is it?' she asked again as she rushed over to the cooler. The moment she looked through the huge glass doors, she knew what the fuss was about. Every flower in the cooler was dead, including the rare orchids that had been special-ordered for tonight's party. The cooler resembled nothing more than a grisly *tableau morte*, all discolored foliage and flowers, drooping and withered almost to nothing.

Carolina let out a loud groan and threw down her planning book angrily. 'What the hell has happened here?' she asked, looking from Roxie to Antonio and then back at the cooler. 'Thousands of dollars' worth of flowers are ruined. Thousands! Everything for tonight!' She wanted to scream or cry, but resisted the urge and stomped her foot on the floor. 'Damn it!' she said. 'What the hell is going on here?'

Roxie, whose face was crestfallen, simply shrugged as if she didn't have the words to express how awful she felt.

Antonio, however, immediately went into action. 'Let me see if it's been unplugged,' he said, going around to the back of the cooler.

Carolina followed behind him. 'I don't see how that could've happened,' she said. 'That plug is so out of the way.'

Antonio looked up at her from where he had squatted down on the floor. 'It's still plugged in,' he said.

'The breaker box,' Roxie said as she came up behind Carolina.

'I'll check it.' She turned and went to the big panel that was on a wall in the hallway across from the little bathroom. She snapped open the door, and called to Carolina and Antonio. 'Come here and look,' she said. 'The breaker for the cooler's been thrown.'

They went into the hallway to see for themselves. Carolina looked at it for a moment; then she reached over and flipped it back up into place. The cooler immediately hummed into life.

'I don't believe this,' she said in a quiet voice. 'It's never happened before. Never. Not in all the years I've been in business.'

'Maybe there was an electrical surge or something,' Antonio said.

Carolina walked back to the work area of the shop and over to the cooler, where she looked in again. 'I'll have to get on the phone,' she said, studying the awful scene before her. 'First I have to call Joleen Neal and tell her what's happened. Then I've got to call all the Georges and see what they can come up with. That's *if* Joleen Neal still wants us to do the party tonight.'

'There's no way the market's going to have any of the stuff you ordered,' Antonio said unnecessarily.

She turned around and said angrily, 'Don't you think I know that, Antonio?'

He glared back at her. 'Well, don't take it out on me,' he said. 'I can walk out that door if I feel like it. See where you'll be tonight without me.'

'Then why don't you walk out that door?' she said. 'I'm sick of your attitude.'

Antonio stifled a growl, turned, and then went to his worktable, where he began gathering up his personal tools, along with the portfolio of arrangements that he had designed.

'It seems to me,' Carolina said, 'that you don't care very much about what happens around here, Antonio. And it also seems to me that you're around every time something like this happens.'

'Are you accusing me of doing these things?' Antonio yelled, his face red with rage. 'How dare you!'

'I don't know!' Carolina cried. 'I don't know, Antonio. But I wish you'd assure me that you didn't have anything to do with this or the other things that have happened.'

'You bitch!' he shouted. He grabbed his backpack and stormed toward the front door, where he turned and glared at her again. 'See if you ever get my help again,' he said. He turned and went out the door, slamming it behind him.

Carolina let herself into the loft, kicked off her high heels, and left them in the entry foyer where they landed. Walking to the kitchen, she stopped at the dining table, where she dropped her carryall and evening bag, and then went on to the refrigerator. She took out the bottle of white wine that had been opened and poured a glassful. She took a big swallow, poured more into the glass, and took it with her into the bedroom.

Sitting down on the bed, she massaged first one foot then the other. *I don't think I can live through another day like this one*, she thought. *It's getting to be too much.*

She had managed to scrape together enough exotic flowers for the party, though they were 'merely acceptable' in the words of Joleen Neal, and she and Roxie together had done all of the arranging and decorating with the help of a couple of freelancers she'd called in. She knew, however, that she would probably never get more work – or that all-important recommendation – from Joleen and Clifford Neal. Like Lydia, they couldn't afford to accept excuses for anything less than perfection, and while Lydia had given Carolina another chance, it was unlikely that the Neals would.

As she undressed, she wondered whether Antonio would come back to work, and decided that she was better off without him. *If he shows up*, she thought, *I'll tell him he can't work for me anymore.* She had been suspicious of him for some time now, but had steadfastly refused to believe he was capable of betraying her.

It's like the end of an era, she thought sadly. *Antonio's been at my side for quite some time, and it's going to seem strange without him around.*

Despite his macho posturing and hot temper, she had been genuinely fond of him, and knew that she was going to miss him. *There've been so many changes,* she thought unhappily. *So many sad, sad changes.*

23

From the luxurious expanse of her dressing room where she sat numbly in a leather-upholstered chair, Carolina heard the telephone ring. Three rings. Four. Five. Six. The machine, which would have normally picked up, didn't. She'd turned it off. She didn't want to hear from anyone, friend or foe. She wanted no news, good or bad. If she'd been exhausted and sad last night after the party, today the weight of the world had come to seem too much for her shoulders.

She'd tried to hide the way she felt from Roxie today and thought she'd been successful. Richie was spending the night at the Adlers', so she was at home alone. *There's something else,* she told herself woozily. *Something else I'm supposed to do.* But she couldn't remember what it was, and dismissed the thought from her mind. She had finished taking off her clothes and put on her silk robe, and she drank the remainder of the wine in the crystal goblet she held. That, with the Valium she'd taken when she got home, would help ease her way through the remainder of the evening, and, she hoped, allow her to collapse into bed and sleep.

She rose to her feet, scooped up the wineglass, and went into the kitchen to get another bottle of wine out of the refrigerator. She opened it, poured her glass full, and took a large gulp. Fumbling in the pocket of her robe, she got out the bottle of Valium and shook two or three or four into her hand. She wasn't really sure how many, but she popped them into her mouth and took another swallow of wine.

I'm so tired, she thought vaguely. *So tired.*

She walked into the living room and sat down heavily on one of the couches. She downed more wine and then clutched the glass in her hand. Spreading out lengthwise on the couch, her head propped on a pillow, she looked over at the painting on the opposite wall, but it was curiously out of focus. When she tried to concentrate on it, to make it come into focus, she found she couldn't.

She let her head drop against the pillow and dropped the wineglass to the floor, but she didn't even notice. She lay there, inert, in a drug- and alcohol-induced stupor.

In the lobby, Seth rang the buzzer again, wondering why she hadn't answered it. *It's not like her to forget*, he thought.

In the small entry vestibule, he pressed her buzzer yet another time, but there was still no response. *Maybe she's in the shower*, he thought. *Or maybe she's using a hair dryer or something and can't hear the buzzer.*

He looked at his watch and decided to try again in five minutes. He went out onto the sidewalk and looked up and down the block hopefully, in case she might have been held up at work and was coming home late. The block was deserted, however. Looking at his watch again, he decided to try her buzzer one more time.

In the lobby, he pressed on it, but as before there was no response. He took out his cell phone and dialed her number at the shop. He heard Carolina's familiar voice on the machine. He hung up without leaving a message and then dialed her number at home. No one answered, nor was there a machine. *How odd*, he thought. *Surely she has an answering machine.*

He began to worry. *She's seemed all right since her husband's death*, he told himself. He believed that part of that was bravado, however, especially in light of the awful incidents at the shop.

He felt a cold sweat break out on his face and neck and realized that he was beginning to panic. He spread his hand out flat and slammed it against the row of buzzers, not caring who he might bother. He hoped that someone would respond and he could get onto the elevator.

Sure enough, without even asking who it was, someone buzzed the elevator door open, and Seth quickly stepped into it. He pressed seven, wondering what he would do once he got to her floor. If she was at home, she would've surely locked the elevator.

On seven, the elevator bobbed to a halt and the door slid open. *I'll be damned*, he thought. *It's not even locked.* Then he felt goose-flesh rise on his arms. *Why would the elevator be unlocked? There could've been a robbery. Anything.*

Without hesitating another moment, he stepped into the entry vestibule and started calling her name. 'Carolina? Carolina?'

There was no response, and he walked on into the large open space and looked around. In the distance, on a couch, he could see her body sprawled, an arm dangling over the side, a wineglass shattered on the floor.

'Oh, my God!' he said as he rushed toward her.

She lay still as a stone, sprawled on the couch, her old silk robe loosely tied at her waist, partially exposing her breasts. Her hair was a limp mop, and what makeup she wore was smeared and streaked.

She looks like a broken doll, he thought, his heart breaking at the pitiful sight she presented. He went to her and knelt down at her side to make certain that she was breathing. He quickly determined that there was no doubt of that. She was simply in a deep sleep. He saw the dropped wineglass and a medicine bottle that had slid out of her robe pocket. He picked it up. Valium. *The wine*, he thought sadly, *and the pills. I hope she didn't overdo it, and I hope she doesn't need medical attention.*

'Carolina,' he said softly, so as not to startle her awake. 'Carolina. Wake up. It's Seth.'

When she didn't respond, he shook her gently. 'Carolina,' he repeated. 'Come on, wake up. It's Seth.'

She groaned, though it was barely audible, and tried to move her arm away from his hand.

'Come on, Carolina,' he said. 'We've got to get you up. Come on.' He shook her again, less gently this time.

She groaned again and opened her eyes, but immediately closed them against the light. 'I – I've got to call,' she murmured. She slowly moved a hand up to her face, covering her eyes. 'Got to call.'

'Come on, Carolina,' he said, shaking her again. 'Wake up. We've got to get you up and moving.'

She opened her eyes again and saw him kneeling there at her side. Her eyes seemed to gradually focus on him, and slowly she became aware of her surroundings. 'Oh . . . oh . . . Seth,' she moaned. 'What . . . How—?'

'Come on,' he said. 'Let me help you get up.'

He put his arms under hers and began lifting her as he rose to his feet. When she was upright, her head nodding loosely on her neck, she moaned again. 'Let me go,' she said. 'I'm all right. I'm fine.'

He didn't let go of her, but headed her toward the kitchen. 'Come on,' he said. 'Let's walk around a little bit.'

'No, Seth,' she complained. 'Let me go. I'm fine, really.'

He realized that she truly was becoming alert when she jerked from his grasp and started across the room on her own. He followed close behind, making certain that she was capable of walking unassisted.

'Want some coffee?' she asked. 'Or a glass of wine or something?'
'I think coffee is an excellent idea.'

At the table in the dining area, they sat sipping the strong coffee Carolina had made. She had perked up considerably, Seth gratefully noted, and was making conversation now as if nothing were out of the ordinary.

'I just had a little too much to drink,' she told him. 'I've had some trouble sleeping, you know, and thought a little wine would do the trick. With some Valium. I guess I had a little too much. Nothing to worry about.'

She avoided his eyes, he noticed. Perhaps she was embarrassed or maybe she wasn't being honest with him. One thing he was certain of, however, was that she needed help. 'You definitely had me worried,' he said. 'I knew it wasn't like you to miss our dinner meeting.'

'How did you get in?' she asked, the question occurring to her only now.

'I hit all the buzzers downstairs,' he said, 'and somebody buzzed me in. Then when I got to your floor, the elevator opened. You must have forgotten to lock it.'

'I can't believe I did that,' she said. 'I – I don't think I've ever forgotten to lock it.'

How can I offer to help her, he wondered, *without chasing her away? She could have accidentally killed herself mixing alcohol and pills.*

'You've had a very trying time lately,' he said cautiously, 'and it's no wonder you were distracted. Your husband's death was a tremendous blow. And I know you've had some trouble at the shop. Maybe I should mind my own business, but it seems to me that you've worked yourself to death for quite some time now. And . . . I'm no expert,' he went on in a very quiet and gentle voice, 'but I think you've probably been hiding a lot of your pain and suffering. You haven't really given yourself a chance to grieve, Carolina.'

She looked at him over the rim of her coffee cup. *He means well,* she thought, *and he really cares. But he doesn't know the half of it.*

She set down her coffee cup and folded her hands on the table. 'I – I want to tell you something,' she said hesitantly. 'Something very personal. Because I think you should know, and because . . . well, I need to talk about it, I guess.'

She proceeded to tell him everything. About Lyon's awful betrayal of her, and how he wasn't the man she thought he was. About his mistress and child in Amsterdam. About Leland's contesting the will. About her own mission to keep Monique Lehnert and her daughter from sharing in the estate. About her troubles at the shop, though he already knew something of them.

When she finished, he let out a slow whistle. 'You've had more than your share of problems lately,' he said. 'It's no wonder you're beginning to . . . to break down. You're trying to do everything by yourself, Carolina, and you don't have to, you know.'

'I'm a thirty-five-year-old woman who's built up her own business and run it for years, raised her son virtually alone, and I think I'm quite capable of taking care of myself.' There was a touch of defiance in her tone, in part because she didn't think of herself as a woman who would 'break down.'

'You're a thirty-five-year-old woman who's lost her husband, Carolina,' he said. 'Who's found out that husband was leading a double life. And you were here alone, drinking and taking tranquilizers,' he pointed out. 'Maybe you've handled everything by yourself in the past, but maybe it's time you had a little help. Even if it's just letting your friends take some of the load. Or you could even get professional help.'

She shook her head. 'I don't think I need that.'

'And what about Richie?' he went on. 'How do you think he would feel if he knew what had happened tonight?'

She visibly blanched and intertwined her hands nervously.

'He's already lost his father,' Seth said. 'How's he going to feel if you're not there for him?'

Tears suddenly sprang into Carolina's eyes, and she lowered her head and began to weep silently.

'You have so much to live for, Carolina,' he went on, 'so much to look forward to, and I think you just need a little help getting there. I'm sure Roxie's a great listener. I am. And I'm sure there're others.'

He handed her a handkerchief, and she wiped her eyes and blew her nose. Then Carolina hung her head as if ashamed.

'Look at me,' he said softly. He took her hands and pressed them gently with his own.

She lifted her head and looked at him again.

'Let me help you, Carolina,' he said. 'I won't hurt you. I promise you that.'

At that moment she believed every word he'd said, although she had convinced herself that she would never believe in another man again. She nodded. 'Thank you, Seth,' she said. 'I'll try.'

Seth smiled and shook her hands in his. 'I was wondering if you would promise me one thing?'

'What?'

'You're not going to like me for saying this,' he said, 'but quit mixing the Valium and wine.'

'I'll flush the Valium right now,' she said, getting to her feet. 'You can come with me.' She headed toward her bathroom with Seth trailing along behind. She emptied the bottle in the toilet. 'There,' she said, flushing the pills down.

'I think it's a great beginning,' he said. And he thought, *I hope it's the beginning of so much more.*

'I do too, Seth,' she said. 'I do, too.'

24

'Was there any word from Antonio?' Carolina asked Roxie when she got to the shop the next morning.

Roxie shook her head. 'Nothing,' she said, 'so I took it upon myself to call him last night when I got home from work.'

Carolina's eyes widened. 'And did you get him?'

Roxie nodded. 'You're not going to like this,' she said, 'but Antonio's going to go to work for Payton Fitzsimmons. In fact, he couldn't keep his mouth shut. He bragged to me about how he and Payton are having an affair, and she's going to be paying him top dollar.'

Carolina sat in silence, numbed by this piece of news. 'So he's going to work for the competition,' she said at last. 'No big surprise there.' She turned to Roxie. 'You know what?'

'What?'

'It's as if Payton Fitzsimmons has declared open warfare.'

'You can say that again,' Roxie said.

'And you know what they say,' Carolina said. 'All's fair in love and war.'

Roxie looked at her with curiosity. 'And what do you have in mind?'

'Fight fire with a little bit of our own fire,' Carolina said. 'I'm tired of sitting here and just taking it.'

'Yes, but how on earth are you going to fight it?' she asked. 'You certainly don't want to stoop to her level. Hindsight's twenty-twenty, and it tells me Antonio and Payton were conspiring against the shop for some time. But what can we do about it?'

Carolina silently looked at her for a moment. 'Remember Erica Rogers, the public relations person who contacted me a while back about hiring her to get more press for the shop?'

Roxie nodded. 'Sure, but you didn't need her. The magazine people were coming to you. Still are. You don't need a press agent.'

'Well, I do now,' Carolina said. 'I'm going to give her a call, hire her for a month or two, and have her plant some choice articles in the papers.'

'Like what?' Roxie asked.

'Oh, like how Antonio, a former designer at Carolina, has gone to work for Payton Fitzsimmons and how the two of them are having a torrid affair. And how Carolina was going to fire him anyway because of the troubles that started in her business when he started seeing Ms Fitzsimmons.' She turned to Roxie and lifted her eyebrows. 'What do you think, huh?'

'I think you're on to something,' Roxie said. 'Give the papers enough to smear her and Antonio. They'll have a field day, and it won't even look like it's coming from us.'

'Exactly,' Carolina said. 'They'll use all the usual phrases, like, "We heard . . ." and "A little birdie told us . . ."'

Roxie looked at her with appraising eyes. 'You know,' she said, 'you seem like a different person today.'

'How's that?'

'I don't know,' Roxie said, 'but you're more . . . with it. You've been sort of . . . down lately. Not that I can blame you, but I was

218

getting worried. Now you seem to be more like your old self.' She smiled.

'Well,' Carolina said, 'I've done a lot of . . . soul searching, I guess you'd say, and I've come to the conclusion that . . . that . . . well, that I need help. I don't have to go through everything alone, and there's been a lot lately.'

Roxie reached over and put a hand on hers. 'Listen, Carolina, you know I'll do anything I can.'

They talked for a long time, working all the while, as Carolina unburdened herself to Roxie. In the end, she felt as if a great weight had been taken off her shoulders, simply because she'd shared it with someone so understanding.

'There is one thing besides getting on the phone to Erica Rogers that we're going to have to do,' Carolina said, changing the subject at last.

'What's that?' Roxie asked. 'You mean about replacing Antonio?'
Carolina nodded.

'What if you had Mercedes come in and help out temporarily?' Roxie asked.

'I don't know if I could deal with that,' Carolina said. 'Don't forget, she's become like a traitor, too. I mean, she's the one who Lyon supposedly dictated the letter to.'

'But do you really think she's a traitor?' Roxie asked. 'Think about it. There's nothing in it for her, is there?'

'If she's in league with Leland, of course there could be,' Carolina said.

'Stupid me,' Roxie said. 'I've been trying not to think about him or her. You're right. We don't want her around here.'

'There are always the freelancers we know,' Carolina said. 'We'll muddle through.'

The telephone rang, and Carolina answered it. 'Carolina.'
'Hi, it's Seth.'
'Oh, Seth,' she said. 'How are you this morning?'

'I'm fine, but that's not why I called. How are *you*?'

'I'm doing better,' she said. 'A lot better, as a matter of fact.'

'Great,' he said. 'I wanted to know if you'd go to a cocktail party with me. We could discuss my party while we're there and maybe have dinner, if that's okay.'

'Where is it?' she asked.

'Up at the Smithsons',' he said. 'Robert and Evangeline Smithson.'

'I . . . well . . .' She wasn't sure what to say.

'They would be a fantastic contact,' he said, 'and so would a lot of the other people there. You know, people on the museum boards and foundation boards. Like that. Plus, guess who's doing the flowers?'

'Let me guess,' she said. 'Payton Fitzsimmons.'

'Yes,' he replied. 'I know it would be like going into the lion's den in a way, but you could see what she's doing. And don't forget the contacts. You might be able to take some people right out from under her nose.' He paused, and then said, 'Why don't I call you back in a couple of hours or so. I have to take a call.'

'Okay,' she said. 'I'll talk to you later, Seth.'

She slowly hung up the telephone.

'Seth Foster asked you out, didn't he?' Roxie said.

She nodded. 'Yes. To a party at the Smithsons'. Payton Fitzsimmons is decorating.'

'And you didn't say yes right away?' Roxie sighed. 'You really do need your head examined, Carolina. He's the nicest man anybody knows, and it would be good for you.'

'I just feel so strange going out with somebody so soon, even if it is a business opportunity.'

'What's to lose?' Roxie asked. 'You know you can trust Seth. You know it's an excellent networking opportunity, and God knows we want to steal as many potential clients from Payton as we can.' She took Carolina's hands in her own and looked her in the eye. 'Lyon is gone, and he's not coming back, Carolina. And you owe it to yourself to go on, to live, to enjoy life.'

Carolina looked at her thoughtfully. 'You're right,' she finally said. 'I'll tell him yes when he calls back.'

'Good girl,' Roxie said, letting go of her. 'Now, why don't we get hold of Erica Rogers and get that ball rolling?'

'Excellent idea.'

'How was your tennis game?' Carolina asked when Richie came into the den, where she was watching the news.

'Okay,' he said, dropping his bag of gear on the floor with a loud bang.

'Just okay?'

Richie sprawled in a chair and looked away from his mother, his baseball cap on backwards, his sneakers tapping a tattoo on the floor. 'Yeah. I mean, it's, like, just tennis, you know? Big deal.'

'I see,' she said, disappointed that he didn't have a better time.

'At least he doesn't treat me like a real dope,' he said.

'What do you mean?'

'He doesn't play bad and goof up, just to make me look good or feel better. You know, like, oh, the poor kid, his dad died so we've got to make him feel good.'

Carolina cringed at his words. 'I'm glad he doesn't do that,' she said in an even tone, 'and I don't think Seth is that kind of man.'

'What kind of man?'

'The kind you described,' she said. 'The kind of man who would be condescending to you.'

'Yeah, well, he's not a creep like that.'

'No,' she said, 'I don't think so. I don't think he's a creep at all.'

'Are you interested in him?'

She looked over at him, stunned. 'What? How do you mean?'

'Like as a date, say?'

'I'm not interested in dating anybody, Richie,' she said.

'Is it because of Dad?' he asked.

'Wh-what do you mean, Richie?' she asked, sitting up on the couch.

221

'Well, I just meant, are you not interested in men because of what Dad did? Because he had another woman? I mean, I heard about it at the reading of the will. I'm not stupid. And I saw the stuff Uncle Matt left here. Saw her pictures and stuff.'

Her mind swirled in fear and horror. *How do I answer him?* she wondered. *What do I say to my sixteen-year-old son about a situation like that?* She might have come to despise what his father did, but she didn't want him to hate his father.

When she didn't answer right away, he said, 'It was just sitting there, so I looked. I have rights, too, you know.'

'I didn't want you to see those things, Richie,' she said, tears welling up in her eyes. 'I wanted you to remember the good things about your dad.'

'I do,' he said. 'But that isn't all there is, is it?'

'But . . . those things . . . I mean . . .' Her voice trailed off as she searched for the right words. 'I don't want to talk about this now, Richie,' she said through her tears. 'I've really been . . . crushed by this. I'm having trouble talking about it.'

'It affects me, too, you know,' he said, his voice rising in anger. 'You're not the only person around here.'

'Oh, I know it does, Richie,' she said. 'Of course it does.' She went over to him and tried to take his hand, but he jerked away from her.

'Please, Richie. I know it affects you, but I just don't know how to deal with it yet.'

'Well, just think, Mom,' he said.

'What, baby?' she said, wiping her tears with her fingers.

'I've got a little sister,' he said. He smiled, and she remembered all the times he'd talked about wanting a baby sister. 'And she looks just like me.'

25

Monique wanted to throw the telephone against the wall, but she resisted the impulse. She had to listen to old Mr Weber, even if he wasn't telling her what she wanted to hear. After all, he was on her side, and it seemed that nobody else in the world was.

'You must understand, Ms Lehnert,' he was saying, 'these things take time, and there is very little I can do to rush it.'

'But what am I supposed to live on in the meantime?' she cried. 'Air?' She paused and tried to control her voice. 'I'm sorry to yell, Mr Weber,' she said, 'but Lyon took care of everything for Anja and me. I didn't have to work, you know. Now you tell me that woman is trying to take the house away from me and the car. You say she is contesting the will and doesn't want me to have *anything*! I can't get money from his bank account till this is settled.'

Her voice began to rise in anger again, despite her efforts to remain calm. 'I can't even use the damn credit card because they stopped it! You tell me, Mr Weber, what am I supposed to do? Starve? Let my child starve? His child?'

'Please, Ms Lehnert,' he said patiently, 'try to calm yourself. Histrionics will get us nowhere. For one, they can't kick you out of the house yet, nor can they take the car. I'm sorry about the bank accounts and the credit card, but they were in his name only. They got their lawyer to put a stop to the card immediately, before we could do anything even if we would have been able to, and they had the bank account frozen. They are acting within their rights until this is settled. I know that doesn't give you much satisfaction, but at least you have a roof over your head and you can get around.'

'Small consolation,' she said.

'I suggest you take a job in the meantime,' he said, 'or if need be talk to social services. This could take a while to settle.'

Monique swept her hair away from her eyes and sighed loudly. 'Fine, Mr Weber,' she said, 'but I want you to make certain that the woman in America knows she's going to have a real battle on her hands. That it is Lyon's child I'm bringing up on my own, and that he wanted us to be taken care of.' She paused and caught her breath. 'Please make certain she understands these things, Mr Weber, and let me know the minute you hear anything else.'

'I will, Ms Lehnert,' he said, 'and good day.'

She hung up the telephone and looked out the sliding glass door toward the canal. It was a uniformly gray day in Amsterdam, as it so often was, and the water reflected the sky. It was dull, even depressing, she thought.

Turning from the glass door, she went to the bedroom to check on Anja, who was napping. The child, her brown hair so like her father's, was still sleeping soundly. Going over to the dresser, Monique picked up a photograph of Lyon and herself. It had been taken soon after they'd met. They were both smiling happily at the camera, his arm wrapped around her waist.

Tears came into her eyes, and she set the picture down, then quickly left the room. She didn't want to wake Anja should she begin to cry. It seemed that she had done little but cry for weeks. She missed Lyon so much. Often, she thought she saw him walking down a sidewalk along a canal, or she would spot him on a tram, speeding past her in town. She'd even imagined that she saw him jogging past her in Beatrix Park, when she and Anja were feeding the black swans.

Hard as she tried, she couldn't bring herself to be angry with him. Maybe he refused to divorce that woman in the States. Maybe he could have put the house and car in her name, and he could have made certain that they had joint accounts – but she couldn't bring herself to love him any less.

Who would've imagined that he would die the way he had, so young and handsome, so virile and full of life? It had been unthinkable and still was. She was alone with their child, whom she heard crying now in the other room.

She retraced her footsteps to the bedroom, where she picked Anja up and hugged her. 'There, there,' she cooed. 'It's okay. Everything will be okay, Anja.' Her weight was becoming difficult for Monique to carry, but she carried her out to the big living and dining area and sat down in a rocking chair that faced the canal.

'Don't worry, Anja,' she said, stroking her daughter's hair as she looked out at the gunmetal water. 'Mommy will take care of you. I'm going to call Mattias today about work. I'm going to start dancing again. You'll see. We'll be able to eat until we get what is rightly ours. Yes. You'll see, Anja. Mommy will get what your father left us. He loved us and wanted us to have it. Oh, yes. And come what may, we'll get what's ours from that horrible witch in America no matter what we have to do.'

'I haven't heard from your goddamned sister-in-law in a while, and I just ran into her in the lobby,' Mercedes snapped as she stalked into the bedroom, where a nude Leland was spread out atop her canopied bed with a drink in his hand.

'Oh?' he said, raising his brows quizzically. 'And what did she have to say that's upset you so much?'

Mercedes tossed her handbag onto a chair and kicked off her heels. 'Why don't you make me a drink, too, and I'll join you?' she said as she began taking off her clothes. 'I could use one right now.'

Leland set his drink down, slid his legs over the side of the bed, and then got to his feet and walked over to a table where several liquor bottles, glasses, and an ice bucket sat on a tray. 'Come on,' he said, as he poured vodka into a glass, 'tell me what the hell Carolina did that got you so out of joint.'

She stepped out of her panties and glared at him, as if he were the source of her anger. 'I told her that if she needed me at the shop just to ring me up,' Mercedes said. 'God knows, I could use the cash.'

He handed her a vodka and tonic, and Mercedes immediately took a large swallow. 'The bitch told me that she wouldn't be calling me to help out anymore. And when I asked her why, she said something to the effect that I shouldn't ask her idiotic questions. I told her that if she was upset because of the letter I'd turned over, I was only doing what was right and that I shouldn't be punished for it, that we're civilized people after all.'

Leland chuckled. 'She's really pissed that you're the one Lyon supposedly dictated the letter to,' he said, coming up behind her and kissing her shoulder. 'And you're the one who had a copy.'

'Yes, well, she tried to make me feel like a stupid bloody cow,' Mercedes went on, ignoring his kisses. 'And I wouldn't mind so much if I didn't need every penny I can get my hands on.'

She took a smaller sip of her drink and then let her head relax against Leland's shoulder behind her.

'We've got to figure out who we can hit up for money,' he said, nibbling at her ear. 'Got any ideas?'

Mercedes turned to face him and smiled. 'I have one,' she said.

'I'm going to ring up Payton Fitzsimmons.'

'What good's that going to do you?' he asked, as he began fondling one of her breasts.

'Oh, you'll see,' she said, setting down her drink and stepping closer to him. 'Just leave it to me.'

He put his arms around her shoulders and pulled her close against his naked body. 'I will,' he said, as he began kissing and licking at her neck, 'but why don't we have a little fun first?'

'Why not?' she said, running her hands over his muscular ass.

Leland backed her against the bed, and she let go of him and climbed onto it, her eyes drinking in his lean, well-defined physique all the while. He stared at her creamy, voluptuous curves, so unexpected on such a tall, thin woman, and his eyes burned with the heat of a powerful lust. He mounted her quickly then, unable to wait another moment, and entered her at once.

Mercedes held on to him as he drove himself into her deeper and deeper. He was like a drug for her, and she couldn't get enough. Meeting his thrusts with her own, she began grinding against him. Leland moaned aloud and began to move against her with more urgency, faster and faster, harder and harder, until he could control himself no longer and released a flood tide inside her. Mercedes cried out as she began to spasm against him, contractions gripping her in ecstasy.

They lay side by side, breathless from their efforts. 'I'd better make that call,' Mercedes said, when she could finally speak.

'Can't it wait till tomorrow?' he asked, smiling at her. 'We've just gotten off to a start.'

She pinched his butt. 'It cannot,' she said. 'Business first, then we can pleasure ourselves all night long if we wish.'

'Have it your way,' he said.

She reached over and picked up the remote telephone and pressed in Payton's home number.

One ring. Two. Three. 'Hello, the Fitzsimmons residence.'

'Could I speak to Payton, please?' Mercedes asked.

'Who's calling, please?'

'Tell her it's Mercedes.'

'Hold on, please.'

Mercedes held for what seemed an eternity before Payton picked up the line.

'Hello,' she said cheerfully. 'How are you?'

'I'm not doing so well, actually,' Mercedes said.

'What is it?' Payton asked. Mercedes heard the cautious tone in her voice.

'I ran into Carolina today, and she was very nasty to me,' Mercedes said. 'In fact, she told me she wouldn't be calling me to help out in the shop at all. So I can't do you any more favors there.'

'Oh, no!' Payton said in genuine alarm. 'I was counting on you, Mercedes. What did you do to upset her?'

'I didn't do a thing,' Mercedes said, offended. She had no intention of letting Payton know about her pact with Leland and his contesting Lyon's will. 'I don't know what's got into her, but she was awfully bitchy. I think she's always suspected that I might've had something to do with her problems at the shop. All those dying flowers, you know.'

Payton laughed with wicked glee. 'Yes, well, she certainly can't prove anything, can she?'

'Certainly not,' Mercedes said. 'Anyway, I wanted to go ahead and start with you since I can't do anything there.'

Payton was silent for a moment. This had come out of the blue. 'I . . . well, I really think it's a little too soon for you to be starting here, don't you think? I mean, Antonio's just started—'

'Antonio's already working there?' she asked in surprise.

'Yes,' Payton said. 'I would've thought you'd known. He and Carolina had an argument, and he left. So, I've taken him on here, sooner than planned. It might look too strange if both of you come to work for me right away. I don't want to be accused by Carolina's uptown fans of having staged a raid on her business. It wouldn't look good, would it?'

'If I started for you,' Mercedes said, 'I don't think it would matter one iota. After all, most of the people you do work for know only the face of the shop, and that's you. Hardly anyone knows that I've helped out at Carolina's.'

'Still, I don't know . . .,' Payton said, her voice trailing off.

'Listen, Payton,' Mercedes said slowly, 'remember that Antonio and I are the only two people who know anything about the tricks you've pulled on Carolina. We may have been involved, but they were your ideas, weren't they? I think it would be best for all concerned if we were finally working together. You don't want anyone talking about your little tricks, do you?'

'You wouldn't!'

'I wouldn't say a thing,' Mercedes said innocently, 'but what if Antonio did?'

'I don't think Antonio would say anything,' Payton replied, 'but I see your point.' And she did, too. She knew that Mercedes was blackmailing her, plain and simple, and that if she didn't hire her, Mercedes would start circulating rumors about her. Rumors that could really hurt her business. 'Why don't you start tomorrow?' Payton said with delight in her voice. 'I have a party coming up at the Smithson town house, and you would come in very handy for that.'

'Wonderful,' Mercedes said, her voice full of good cheer. 'And by the way, Payton,' she added, 'we should discuss my compensation tomorrow, don't you think? And the length of my contract?'

'Contract?' Payton said, astonished.

'Of course,' Mercedes said. 'I am going to be more or less a junior partner, as I assume Antonio is? I am right, aren't I?'

'I – I . . . well, actually, Antonio and I haven't had a chance to discuss that yet,' she said.

'We can tomorrow, then,' Mercedes said. 'See you about nine? Is that when you open?'

'Well, yes,' Payton said. 'I'm not always there by nine, but Antonio will be and Giselle, the girl who runs the shop.'

'I'll see you at nine,' Mercedes said. 'So good to talk to you. Bye-bye.'

'Bye,' Payton said.

Mercedes pushed the OFF button on the remote and turned to Leland, who'd been listening to her end of the conversation.

'You're blackmailing her, aren't you?' he said.

'Call it what you will,' Mercedes said with a smile. 'But she's going to hire me, and she's going to pay me a lot if she wants me to keep my mouth shut.'

'You're too much,' Leland said, pulling her close to him.

'Miss Naughty Knickers?' she said, relishing the feel of his strong, hard body against her.

'Yeah,' he said, his hands beginning to explore, 'and I like that.'

'Thought you would,' she whispered, her mouth seeking out his.

26

Carolina had resisted shopping for the party Seth had invited her to, thinking that she had plenty of clothes and that any number of her party dresses would be appropriate. In the end, however, she decided she wanted something new, something that wasn't associated with the past, something that had no memories attached to it, whether happy or otherwise. So, it was at Yves St Laurent Rive Gauche where she'd finally chosen the flowing, silk-fringed, leopard print caftan that she now swirled around in before her dressing room mirror.

Tom Ford has done himself proud designing this, she thought as she watched it move, light as air, with her body. The dress was sexy and romantic, but not wanton, she thought, and looked wonderful on her. She had put on dangling gold earrings and wore big gold cuffs on both arms, the perfect jewelry to go with the dress, and wore gold high-heeled sandals.

She was excited about tonight, although she'd reminded herself that it was strictly for business reasons that she was going to this party with Seth. No matter what she told herself, however, she remained excited in a way that she hadn't been for as long as she could remember.

Flipping off the light in the dressing room, she went through her bedroom and out to the kitchen, where she'd left her small gold clutch purse. She opened it to make certain that she'd put her keys in it and her small card case, in which she'd placed a number of her business cards. *There*, she thought. *All set.* She picked up the glass of white wine she'd poured and took a sip; then she started to call good-bye to Richie before realizing that he was over at Jeff's again tonight. He'd been spending a lot of evenings away from home lately.

The buzzer rang, and after she made certain that it was Seth, she pushed the button to let him in. She hoped he thought she looked great, too. She heard the elevator and went to the entry vestibule. When the doors slid open, he drank in the sight of her before stepping into the room.

'You look stunning!' he said.

'Thanks. So do you,' she said, returning the compliment. 'You look great in that tuxedo.'

'Are you ready?' he asked.

She nodded. 'Oh, let me grab my purse. Be right back.' She hurried back to the kitchen, retrieved it from the counter, and then went back to the entry vestibule. 'Now I'm ready,' she said.

He took her arm. 'Allow me, madam,' he said in jest, in part to cover up his nervousness at being this close to someone he so desired.

'Certainly, sir,' she replied, trying not to flinch as he took her arm. *I've got to try to relax*, she told herself. But she couldn't quite control the excitement of going out with a handsome man.

The town house was in Carnegie Hill, the east Nineties, and Carolina had never seen it before. She knew very little about the Smithsons

– they kept a rather low profile – but they were immensely rich and known for their major art collection and their philanthropy. When their driver pulled up to the house – Seth had hired a Lincoln Town Car and driver for the evening – Carolina looked out at the house.

It was double-wide and four stories high, with a limestone facade. Graceful pilasters and urns made the gray stone seem light as air, and the golden light spilling out from its many windows made the house seem warm and inviting.

At the door they were greeted by a white-gloved butler. Then a lovely older woman who Carolina knew from pictures was Evangeline Smithson came toward them, holding out a bejeweled hand. She wore her graying blond hair in a loose chignon, and her gown was a simple but elegant silvery gray. Diamonds of stunning size and clarity blazed at her ears, throat, and wrists.

'Seth,' she said, 'how lovely to see you.'

'And you, Evangeline,' he replied.

They exchanged air kisses; then she turned her attention to Carolina. 'And you must be Carolina Mountcastle,' she said. 'I'm so pleased you could come.'

'Thank you,' Carolina said.

'Make yourselves at home,' she said. 'Champagne and hors d'oeuvres are circulating, but there's a full bar and more filling tidbits in the hallway off the ballroom upstairs.' She looked behind them at new arrivals.

'Thanks, Evangeline,' Seth said. 'We'll find our way.'

'I hope I see you again,' their hostess said.

They moved on into the magnificent entrance hall, all checkerboard black and white marble, huge crystal chandeliers, baroque gilt-framed mirrors, gilt and marble consoles, and three monumental paintings. Carolina almost gasped aloud when she saw a Monet water lily painting, the first she'd ever seen outside a museum.

'This is unbelievable,' she said. 'I've been in lots of town houses, but never one this big. And the art.'

'It is impressive, isn't it?' he replied with a smile.

On the consoles Carolina eyed arrangements that were almost identical to hers, based on Old Master paintings. *Aha*, she thought. *Antonio's work. I'm sure of it.*

Straight ahead was an enormous living room that stretched to a wall of windows at the back of the house. It was filled with eighteenth-century French furniture placed on parquet de Versailles floors overlaid with Savonnerie rugs, and the walls were covered with one painting after another, all by famous artists. She saw a Renoir, a Degas, a Manet, and two Picassos. On two matching Boulle chests, inlaid with tortoiseshell, she spotted another pair of arrangements based on Old Masters.

She couldn't resist whispering into Seth's ear. 'Did you see the flowers in the entrance hall? And look at these on the chest. They're straight from my design book. Antonio had to have done them.'

'He's working for Payton?' he asked.

She nodded. 'Yes,' she said. 'I let him go, but it was more or less mutual.'

'Does this mean that Payton doesn't have too many ideas of her own?' Seth asked in an amused voice.

'I think that's exactly what it means,' she said. 'And some of the guests are going to have seen arrangements like this at Lydia's.'

'That's not going to make Evangeline happy if it gets back to her,' he said.

'I wouldn't think so.'

'And I'm sure it will,' he said with a smile.

'Seth! How nice to see you.'

Although they didn't see her approach them from behind, the voice was unmistakably that of Payton Fitzsimmons. Carolina girded herself for the fray.

'Payton,' said Seth, 'how are you?'

'I'm doing exceptionally well,' she said cheerfully. 'Oh, and it's little Carolina, isn't it? How are you?'

'Very well, thank you,' Carolina said. 'It's so good to see you again.'

'There's a friend of yours here tonight,' Payton said, 'and here he is now.' She reached out a hand and took his, pulling him toward her. 'Antonio, you know Carolina, of course, and this is Seth Foster.'

He had sidled up to her, resplendent in a handsome custom-made tuxedo. 'Hello,' he said with a nod. The smug look on his face was much like the one that Payton wore.

'Hi, Antonio,' Carolina said.

'Antonio,' Seth said. 'Nice to see you.'

'We did the decorations for the party tonight, you know,' Payton said. 'Antonio was no end of help, weren't you, darling?' She looked up at him and squeezed his arm adoringly.

Antonio nodded again, although he didn't say anything.

'I thought I recognized the work,' Seth said smoothly. 'Now I know why. I saw the same sort of arrangements at parties Carolina did some time ago.'

Payton's look of smug self-satisfaction was replaced by barely concealed fury. 'I don't think so,' she said from between gritted teeth.

'Oh, I thought you'd seen my work at Lydia Carstairs',' Carolina said in an innocent voice. 'I must be mistaken. That's where I first did these kinds of arrangements. Don't you remember, Antonio?'

The muscles in his face twitched, and he reddened visibly. Carolina thought that he resembled a bull facing the matador's cape. Then he abruptly turned and stalked out of the room.

'Oh, my,' Carolina said, 'I hope I haven't upset him for some reason.'

Payton's lips formed a smile. 'It was no nice to see you both,' she said, 'but I must mingle.' She looked at Seth. 'When you get tired of slumming downtown, why don't you give me a call?'

'How nice of you to think of me, Payton,' he said, 'but I bet you're too busy with Antonio, huh?' He winked lasciviously and then turned to Carolina. 'Shall we go upstairs?'

'I'd love to,' she said. 'Oh, and good luck, Payton. I think you and Antonio make a great team. So . . . original.'

Leaving Payton standing alone, she and Seth left the room and went to the marble staircase that led up to the ballroom. 'You're a very bad boy,' Carolina said. 'And I enjoyed every minute of it.'

He smiled. 'She deserved it,' he said. 'She's so mean and . . . transparent. She's also tough as an old boot, so she can handle it.'

'I hope Antonio enjoys her,' she said. 'She's the kind of woman I think he's always hoped to find.'

'Then pity him,' Seth said, 'because she'll use him for her amusement, then toss him out like garbage.'

They reached the ballroom, from which spilled the sounds of a string quartet and merry laughter and chatter. 'Oh, this is so beautiful,' Carolina said, looking around the immense room. The fireplace was big enough to walk into, with a limestone mantel that looked as if it had been rescued from a chateau in France, and the highly polished floor was made of various woods, inlaid to resemble a flowered carpet. Crystal chandeliers sparkled overhead, and on one wall was a minstrel gallery, where the string quartet was seated, playing. Here, as in the rooms she'd seen downstairs, the flowers were identical to her Old Master arrangements.

Bartenders stood at attention behind draped tables, ready to make drinks for those who didn't want champagne, and platters of hors d'oeuvres were arranged at other tables. Carolina could see heaps of caviar, smoked salmon, quail eggs, and many other delicacies. There were perhaps sixty people in the room, and all of them were dressed exquisitely. Several of the faces she recognized, but a lot of the people, Seth had told her, kept such low profiles that they were virtually unknown to the general public.

'Do you want something from the bar?' he asked. 'Or some of the hors d'oeuvres?'

'I'm content with the champagne,' Carolina said. They'd taken glasses from the tray of a passing waiter dressed in livery.

'What if I introduce you to some of the people,' Seth said. 'I know a number of them that I think you'd like to know.'

'Sure,' she said. 'Why not?'

They began to circulate, and she met so many people that their faces had begun to blur. In several instances Seth mentioned that the decorations had been copied from Carolina's designs, and he'd cajoled her into giving out her card. She had laughingly resisted – she liked to network without appearing to network, at least not too aggressively – but complied, of course.

After an hour or so, Seth asked if she was ready to leave for dinner. 'Oh, yes,' she said. 'This has been wonderful but a little intense.' Actually, she was looking forward to spending time with him alone.

He laughed. 'It has, hasn't it?' He took her arm, and they started down the marble stairs to the ground floor.

Directly below them, a blond-haired beauty and a handsome man with chocolaty brown hair were climbing the stairs to the ballroom.

Carolina could hardly believe her eyes, and she felt her heart begin to race. It made perfect sense, of course. She had already assumed that the two of them were conspiring against her together, but she didn't know they were actually seeing one another again.

'Oh, God, no,' Carolina said under her breath. 'It's Mercedes and Leland, my brother-in-law. I certainly didn't expect to see them here.'

'We'll make it quick,' he said. 'Don't worry.'

When the two couples met on the stairs, Seth was the first to speak. 'Mercedes,' he said, 'nice to see you.'

'Seth,' she said. 'What a surprise.' Her eyes briefly landed on Carolina. 'Carolina,' she said without inflection.

Carolina smiled. 'Hello, Mercedes. And Leland. I don't believe you know Seth.' She introduced the two of them, and they shook hands.

'Nice to meet you,' Seth said, 'but we have another engagement.' He took Carolina's arm, and they started down the stairs again.

'Oh, thank you,' she whispered. 'I'm really not in the mood to deal with them tonight. I wonder why they're here.'

'Mercedes is asked everywhere.'

'Of course,' Carolina replied. 'I should've known.'

'What's going on?' he asked.

She explained Mercedes's role in Leland's scheme.

'I see,' he said. 'It makes sense, I suppose. You say your brother-in-law's always short of cash, and everybody knows that Mercedes is broke.'

'What?' Carolina exclaimed. 'I thought she was loaded, and so does nearly everybody else I know.'

He shook his head. 'No,' he said. 'In fact, I hear she's in dire straits. Everybody thinks she's rich because she's in international society, knows everybody, and comes from a famous family and all, but she doesn't have any money.'

'I don't believe it,' Carolina said.

They said their good nights to the Smithsons and thanked them; then they went outside to their waiting car. The driver started to come around the car to open the door for them, but Seth waved him off and opened the door himself. Carolina got in, and he followed her, glad to be this much closer to being alone with her.

The contemporary design of Le Cirque 2000, one of the most glamorous restaurants in New York, with its rather acidic modern colors, juxtaposed to the Old World look of its setting in one of the Villard houses at the New York Palace Hotel, offered proof to Carolina that superior designs from any age could be commingled to great effect. Sergio himself had seated them when they arrived, and now, after a wondrous dinner of sea bass, they were enjoying the remains of their dessert and espresso. The party had provided plenty of fodder for conversation, and they had talked about it along with finalizing the details for his dinner party the following evening.

'They say this is the best crème brûlée in New York,' Seth said.

'I don't doubt it one bit,' Carolina said, savoring the last bite of hers. 'I decorated a couple of parties at the old Le Cirque, when it was at the Mayfair, but I haven't done one here yet.'

She took a sip of her espresso and set the tiny cup down. 'I guess you eat out a lot, don't you?'

'More than I'd like to,' he said. 'Mostly work-related dinners or charity functions. It gets tiresome.'

'You don't look so unhappy when I see your picture in the papers escorting some beauty or other to a party,' she said, teasing him.

He smiled. 'I guess not,' he said, 'but that's part of the job.'

'What do you mean, "part of the job"?' she asked.

'Well, if you notice, nearly all of those pictures are taken at charity functions of some kind,' he said. 'Which always means I'm working.'

'I still don't get it,' she replied. 'You're photographed with beautiful young society women all the time, and I happen to know that you're always sending them flowers, too. That's work?'

He nodded and smiled. 'Yes,' he said. 'Absolutely. Because what I'm nearly always doing is building up to the point where I can ask these rich young beauties, who can afford to contribute to charity, to part with some of their cash for the Animal Rescue Mission.'

Carolina laughed. 'You, too?' she said. 'That's what Lydia Carstairs told me about one of the dinner parties I was decorating for her. She was impressing her guests before asking them for their money. Is that how you met Lydia? Working with the Animal Rescue Mission?'

'No,' he said, shaking his head. 'Lydia is a very distant cousin, on my father's side of the family.'

'Oh, really?' Carolina said. 'I didn't know that.'

'In fact, she's about the only person on his side of the family I've ever met,' he said, 'and I didn't meet her until about five years ago.'

'You're kidding?' she said. 'But why not?'

'My parents divorced, as you know, and I went back and forth between them for a while. Then my father died when I was about fifteen.' He laughed. 'Are you sure you want to hear this stuff?'

'Of course I do,' she said. 'I've got an inquiring mind.' She realized that she didn't know much about him, and she really did want to learn all she could.

'Well, my father's insurance money sent me to boarding school. So I was nearly always at school. Anyway, when my mother died, Lydia showed up at the funeral. That was several years ago. She told me who she was, and I was really surprised because she was so nice and down to earth. My father had always told me she was this horrible monster. You know, a gold digger who married one rich man after another. A stableman's daughter who'd forgotten where she'd come from and that kind of thing.'

'Lydia Carstairs, a stableman's daughter? She told me she was a country girl, but I can't believe it,' Carolina said.

'It's true,' he said, 'and she would be the first to tell you. She's not ashamed of her past. My father wasn't much better off. He worked a little farm. They were poor country people.'

'And everyone would've thought you both came from oodles of money.'

He smiled. 'I wish,' he said, 'but I've had to work for everything I've got. Anyway, Lydia and my mother had kept up a correspondence over the years, and I didn't know about that either. They'd always liked each other, Lydia told me, and stayed in touch with each other. So there she was at the funeral. We became good friends, and she got me involved in the Animal Rescue Mission when she found out how much I loved animals.'

He took a sip of his espresso and then sputtered laughter. 'I've let you do it again,' he said. 'I don't believe it.'

'What?' she asked.

'Talk about myself,' he said. 'This happened the last time we went out together.'

'I'm glad,' she said, 'because I didn't know anything about you, and your life has been much more interesting than I would've thought.'

The driver pulled up to the curb outside Carolina's loft building and quickly jumped out and opened the door for them. Surprisingly,

Seth dismissed him. 'I'll walk home from here,' he told Carolina. 'After that dinner, it'll do me good.'

'We both should've walked all the way back downtown after that food,' she said with a laugh, 'but it was a truly memorable meal.'

'Yes,' he said, 'in more ways than one.' He walked her to the outside lobby door, held it open for her, and then waited while she unlocked the inside door.

She turned to him at the elevator bank. 'Would you like to come up for a nightcap?' she asked.

'I'd really like to, but I'd better not,' he said, resisting the impulse to accept her offer. He still thought it best to take his time. 'I've got a very early morning, and I bet you do, too.'

She nodded with a smile, but he saw genuine disappointment on her face. 'You're right,' she said, wishing that he would stay for a while, but slightly unnerved by the prospect at the same time. 'I've got a very early morning and should be off to bed soon.'

'I had a wonderful time, Carolina,' he said, moving closer to her, wanting to embrace her. 'I can't remember when I've had such a good time, in fact.'

'I did, too, Seth,' she replied, returning his gaze.

'I'd like to see you again.'

'And I'd like to see you, too.'

He reached out and put his hands on her shoulders and kissed her lips tenderly, expecting a perfunctory good-night exchange. But when she returned the kiss, he took her into his arms and kissed her more fervently. Stroking her back, he loved the softness of her silk dress against his hands – and the promise of what was beneath its softness. Realizing that he was quickly becoming aroused, he drew back for a moment and looked into her eyes again.

Carolina relished the feel of his body against hers, of feeling his arms embrace her tenderly and protectively. She loved his scent, something indescribably masculine that drew her to him, and she already dreaded the moment that they would have to part. She wouldn't have thought what was happening possible as recently as earlier in the day, but she found that she didn't want to resist this man for any reason. She might feel guilty tomorrow, she thought, but for the time being she didn't care. What they were doing seemed natural, beautiful even, and she wanted their evolving friendship to take its course, whatever that might be.

'I really should go,' he said, wanting desperately to stay, but knowing it was too soon for her. 'But I hope we're together again very soon.' He leaned down, kissed her lips again, and then drew back.

'Oh, yes,' she said. 'Very soon.'

He relinquished his hold on her and pressed the button for the elevator. The doors slid open immediately, and Carolina hesitantly stepped in; then she turned to face him. 'Night, Seth,' she said in a quiet voice.

'I'll call you tomorrow, okay?'

She nodded. 'Please.' She sketched a wave in the air as the doors closed, and he disappeared from sight.

27

'I really don't trust that bitch Mercedes,' Payton said two days after the Smithson party. 'I don't even like leaving her in the shop alone.' She and Antonio were sitting in the sun-drenched, glass-enclosed conservatory on her terrace, sipping coffee, the remains of breakfast still on the table.

'I don't blame you,' Antonio said. 'I wouldn't either.'

'She's practically blackmailed me into hiring her, and I've got to have her around almost all the time. Plus she's costing a lot. I think it's best if you're always there when she is so you can keep an eye on her.'

Antonio sighed. 'Okay,' he said, knowing that he shouldn't disagree with Payton, at least not this early in the game.

'Good,' she said. 'We'll think of some way to get rid of her.'

Antonio sipped his coffee and looked out over the expanse of Central Park in the distance. It was a beautiful day, but he didn't like the way it was starting out. He glanced at Payton as she leafed through the newspaper. She was sexy and classy, but she was mean as hell and spoiled beyond belief, he'd discovered. *Oh, well,* he told himself. He could put up with her as long as he thought of her as a stepping-stone.

'Damn it!' Payton swore, throwing the newspaper she was reading to the floor as if it were a poisonous snake. 'I don't believe this!' She glared at Antonio, an expression he was becoming all too familiar with.

'What's wrong?' he asked, alarmed.

'Look at Page Six,' Payton said, pointing to the offending paper.

Antonio set down his coffee cup and picked up the newspaper. He found Page Six and immediately saw the article that had upset her so much.

Copycat Decorator at Smithson Soiree?

Wagging tongues report that billionnaire philanthropists Evangeline and Robert Smithson are furious with a certain society party decorator who's new on the scene and charges exorbitant prices for her services. Word has it that the blue-blooded debutante, who just opened a flower shop on the posh Upper East Side, not only stole drop-dead gorgeous Latin lover Antonio from downtown party decorator Carolina but stole her ideas, too. Seems that more than a few guests at the Smithsons' latest soiree had spotted identical decorations at parties Carolina did some time ago, a no-no in Manhattan's lucrative party business. More on the party decorator wars later.

Antonio put the newspaper on the table and smiled at Payton. 'How do you like that, huh? They call me a Latin lover.'

'Screw you!' Payton said angrily. 'Things like this could ruin my business, and all you can think about is that you got your name in the paper?'

'I'm sorry,' Antonio said. 'I just thought it was funny.' He worked to control his boiling fury. Nobody talked to him like that and got away with it – but Payton, unfortunately, wasn't just anybody. She was his meal ticket. He would have to grin and bear her nasty temper and filthy tongue for the time being.

'Well, one thing it's definitely not, Antonio, is funny,' Payton spat. 'Especially not with people like the Smithsons. Now *I'm* going to have to go crawling to them with some kind of story to try to do damage control.'

'You don't have to do this at all,' Antonio pointed out. 'You've got all the money in the world. What difference does it make to you?'

'I'm not a quitter,' Payton said, 'and I'm not a loser. Once I start something, I finish it, and I finish it on top.'

'Okay,' he replied in an even voice, not really grasping why she was so competitive. He'd always wanted to get ahead, to make a better life for himself, sure. But Payton? Where did she have to go? What did she have to prove?

'I'm not going to sit still while some nobody like Carolina Mountcastle comes along and gets all the clients that should be mine *and* sweeps Seth Foster off his feet.'

'So this is about a *man?*' he said.

Payton looked at him as if he were a crippled child to be pitied. 'Never mind, Antonio,' she said. 'We've just got to think of some way to get back at her. I want to ruin that party she's doing at the Metropolitan. Then she'll never get a job again. Not like that one anyway.'

'That ought to be easy,' he said.

She looked at him with suddenly glittering eyes. 'How?' she asked.

Roxie put the newspaper down on her worktable and laughed until tears came into her eyes. She didn't know when anything had ever struck her as so funny. So infectious was her laughter that Carolina dropped the flowers she was trimming and joined in.

'I bet she's livid,' Roxie said when she could finally speak.

Carolina nodded. 'What's so great is that we called Erica Rogers when we did. The timing couldn't have been better.'

'I know,' Roxie said. 'Along comes the Smithson party, and Payton gives Erica all the fodder she needs to get the gossip columnists interested.'

'I was hoping she could be helpful,' Carolina said, 'but I never dreamed that she'd be this great.'

'I think the only thing that comes close to being as funny is you seeing Leland and Mercedes together, then finding out that she's broke,' Roxie said with another snort of laughter.

Carolina hadn't wanted to tell Roxie, but didn't think it was fair not to. After all, Roxie had been in love with Leland, and she and Roxie were too close to keep it a secret. Roxie's reaction had surprised her, however.

She'd flapped a hand dismissively and looked at Carolina. 'They deserve each other is all I can say.' Then she'd grinned mischievously. 'Besides, I've met somebody.'

'You have!' Carolina said.

Roxie had nodded. 'Nothing serious. But we're having fun dating.'

'Who is it?' Carolina had asked.

'A guy named Gerald,' Roxie'd replied. 'He just moved in upstairs, and he's a real cutie.'

They'd talked about Roxie's new friend and discussed Leland and Mercedes, working all the while.

As summer fast became a memory, and the weekenders returned to Manhattan from their houses at the beach or in the country, the fall social season was beginning in earnest. Orders began to pour in, and the demand for Carolina's services increased exponentially. Weddings, luncheons, dinner parties, funerals – every social occasion imaginable – began to fill the shop's schedule book to the extent that Carolina, for the first time in all her years as a florist, had to start turning away customers. She had yet to replace Antonio, but made use of freelancers whose work she knew well.

The telephone rang, and Carolina picked it up. 'Carolina,' she said. 'Guess who.'

She laughed, knowing immediately that it was Seth. 'I was just thinking about you,' she said.

'You were? Wicked thoughts, I hope.'

She laughed again. 'Nooo,' she said.

'Well, you might after I tell you what I've done.'

'What?' she asked.

'I gave your name to several of my guests,' Seth told her. 'They were amazed and wanted to know who my florist is and if you were some kind of closely guarded secret in New York.'

Carolina laughed. 'That's so funny, coming from a bunch of Dutch people. Especially considering that all I did was use a zillion tulips.'

'Not really,' he said seriously. 'Almost nobody ever sees tulips like the ones you used. Even in Holland.'

'That's because they're so hideously expensive almost nobody ever orders them,' Carolina said. 'Even uptown florists and wholesalers don't usually carry them. I had to special-order them.'

'Well, it was a great success,' he said. 'I was astonished when I walked into the loft after work and saw what you'd done.'

'Thanks, Seth,' she said. 'I was astonished when I walked into your loft, too, but that was *before* I did the decorating. It's so handsome and . . . serene.'

'Do you really like it?' he asked.

'Oh, yes,' she replied. 'All the new stuff mixed with the old. All the styles and periods. Extremely well put together.'

'Lydia helped me a little,' he confessed. 'It's all stuff that I picked out or got from my mother's place, but Lydia helped me put it together.'

'Well, it's beautiful,' she said. 'Roxie thought so, too. We both just wandered around swooning for a while.'

247

He laughed. 'I think you're exaggerating now,' he said.

'No, I'm not,' she said. 'By the way, how did you make out with the dinner. Any donors for the Animal Rescue Mission?'

'Yes,' he said enthusiastically. 'A few people actually wrote checks then and there, and a few more promised to consider it, so we'll see.'

'That's great, Seth,' she said.

'Say, would you like to have dinner again sometime soon?' he asked. *Like right away*, he thought. This was the perfect opportunity to ask her out again, and he wanted to see her. The night of the Smithson party – their kisses, their mutual desire – was imprinted on his mind. 'It would be my way of thanking you for helping me impress my guests.'

'You don't have to do that,' she said, wanting to be with him as soon as possible.

'It's not that I have to,' he replied. 'I want to. I'd really like to. I enjoy your company.'

Carolina felt that familiar tightness in her chest. She could no longer fool herself into believing that this feeling was anything other than excitement generated by him and her desire to be with him.

'Yes,' she said, 'I'd like that, but I'm really busy right now. Going over plans for the big benefit at the Metropolitan and a thousand other things. Let me check my book. Can you hold on a second?'

'Sure,' he said.

Carolina thumbed through her schedule book for the rest of the week and the week after. *Ridiculous*, she told herself. *I want to see him, so I'll make the time right away.* 'How about . . . no, wait a minute . . . let me see . . . how's Thursday after eight o'clock? Or is that too late for you?'

'No,' he said. 'That's fine. I'll see you Thursday. Say, at eight-thirty?'

'Perfect.'

'Okay,' he said. 'Pick you up at your place?'

'Great,' she said. 'Bye.'

Seth had just buzzed the loft, and Carolina told him that she would meet him downstairs. 'How do I look?' she asked Richie.

'Great, Mom,' he said.

'Thanks, Richie,' she said. 'Don't forget I've got stuff in the fridge for you, sweetie.' She retrieved her purse and keys from the kitchen counter. 'Give me a kiss before I go?'

Richie gave her a quick peck on the cheek.

'Bye-bye,' she said. 'I'll be back before too late.'

'Have fun, Mom,' he said, 'and tell Seth hello.'

'I will,' she said. She turned and left, feeling secure in the knowledge that Richie was doing much better lately.

She's gone! Richie thought. *Thank God! I didn't think she was ever going to leave.*

He made a beeline for his bedroom, dashing through the loft with single-minded purpose.

I've got a lot of work to do, he told himself. *And I don't have much time. I've got to work fast. Real fast.*

They had another delightful evening together that became more charged with their mutual attraction as the evening wore on. Their conversation centered on Richie later on, since Seth had devoted a great deal of time to Richie and their tennis playing. They played on a regular basis now, and seemed to be getting to know one another very well. While Richie hadn't discussed his relationship with Seth or their tennis playing – he was recalcitrant about answering his mother's questions – she was grateful that her son respected and liked Seth.

At the end of the evening, they necked like teenagers in the lobby of her building, the two of them reluctant to say good-bye.

'This feels so good,' Carolina whispered.

'Yes, it does,' he said, kissing her tenderly about her ears and neck. 'It feels wonderful.' Then he began kissing her with more urgency, and Carolina hugged him to her all the closer, wanting to feel his powerful, hard body next to hers.

They kissed and explored with their hands, until they had worked themselves up into such a state it was now or never.

'W-we'd better stop,' Seth said at last, gasping for breath.

She looked up into his eyes. 'I know,' she said. 'I don't want to, but I know we should.'

With great reluctance they finally let one another go in the lobby. All the way up in the elevator, Carolina had to recover from her rapid breathing. She caught sight of her reflection in the mirror over the console in the entry foyer and stopped. She was startled by her appearance. It was true what Seth had said tonight. She did look wonderful, and it was due to more than the new outfit she was wearing.

It's an aura about me, she thought whimsically. *Or maybe it's knowing that somebody cares about me, and that I care about him.* Whatever it was, she decided, it suited her.

She reached down and slipped out of her high heels, one at a time, knowing that they would clack loudly on the polished oak flooring. *I don't want to wake Richie up,* she thought. He hadn't greeted her at the sound of the elevator, and the loft was quiet, so she assumed he was in bed asleep.

She went across the floor on her stocking feet, and went through her bedroom into the dressing room. She undressed, slipped into her favorite old silk kimono, and went into the bathroom, where she washed her face and brushed her teeth.

Ready for bed at last, she told herself, and then immediately amended the thought. *I've got to kiss Richie good night first.* She went to his room and listened at the door. Complete silence. *He's sound asleep,* she thought, smiling to herself. Opening the door a crack, she peered in.

His bed was – empty. Carolina's heart lurched into her throat as she panicked.

Where—?

What do I do? she asked herself. *Who do I call?* She felt her heart racing, and sweat suddenly beaded her forehead. *The Adlers. Maybe he and Jeff did something together, and he didn't tell me.*

She dialed their number quickly, her fingernails clicking against the receiver. Then, like a suffocating poison, a thought choked her: *Why would he lie to me? He said he was staying in tonight.*

''Lo?' a sleepy voice answered.

'Jeff?' she asked. 'Is that you?'

'Yes.'

'It's Richie's mom. Have you seen him tonight?'

'No,' he answered.

'Do you have any idea where he could be, Jeff?' she asked.

'No,' he said. 'He's gone?' His voice seemed to perk up.

'Yes,' she said, her heart sinking. 'You're sure you don't have any idea where he might be?'

'No.'

'Okay,' Carolina said. 'If you hear from him would you give me a call? Please.'

'Sure,' he replied.

'Thanks, Jeff,' she said. 'Sorry I woke you up.'

'It's okay.'

'Night.' She pressed the OFF button again, about to burst into tears. *Where the hell is he?* she wondered anew. *And why did he lie to me?*

With a trembling finger, she called Matt's cell phone and let it ring eight times. Maybe Richie had called him, and he would know something. No answer. She did the same with Thad's. Nothing. She called both of their pagers and put in her number; then she stood in the kitchen, waiting. Five minutes. Ten. Fifteen. Nothing.

Tears sprang into her eyes. *What do I do?* she asked herself over and over. She realized that in her panic she wasn't thinking clearly, that her mind was swirling in a dozen directions at once. *Think*, she told herself, making a conscious effort to control her emotions. *Where would he be?*

Then, from out of the blue came the realization that she hadn't even looked in his room to see if he had left any clues to where he might have gone. *What a fool I am!* she thought, heading down the hallway.

She opened his bedroom door and went in. The screen saver on his computer cast an eerie glow, its constantly moving pattern giving the room a surreal air. She went over to his desk and put her hand on the mouse, jiggling it slightly.

The screen saver disappeared, and a simple message appeared in its place.

MOM, I'VE GONE TO SEE MY LITTLE SISTER.
LOVE, RICHIE

Carolina stood, hunched over, staring at the screen for a long time, even when she could no longer read the message clearly. For tears, unbidden and bitter, began to course down her cheeks in rivulets.

She wiped her eyes at last and rose to her full height. She glanced around his room, her heart aching in a way it had never ached before. It was a physical pain, this heartache, wrenching, almost unbearable. Sitting down on his bed, she stroked the comforter with her hand.

Finally, she pushed herself up off his bed and walked back to the kitchen. Matt and Thad hadn't answered their pagers, and at this hour she knew they weren't likely to check them until morning.

She picked up the remote and dialed a different number. It was answered on the third ring.

'Hello?'

'Seth, it's Carolina,' she said in a quavering voice.

'What's wrong?' he said.

'It's R-Richie,' she stammered. 'He's – he's run off to Amsterdam.'

'I'll come right over.'

28

At an ATM in Schiphol Airport, Richie was immediately engulfed in the tide of travelers and not certain which way to go. He'd been here before, but he'd always been with his parents and had never had to pay any attention. His dad had always taken care of everything.

He looked around in confusion, and for the first time since planning this adventure he felt fear begin to crawl up his spine. The people crowding the concourses – everyone in a hurry, many scowling in their determination to get into the city – took on a threatening aspect, their babble an unintelligible mix of many languages, none of which he understood. Even the occasional word or phrase overheard in English gave him no comfort, as he was universally ignored by these travelers intent on getting to wherever they were going.

He'd begun to search frantically for an ATM machine as he chose a concourse – the right one? he wondered worriedly – not really certain it would take him where he wanted to go. Suddenly this place seemed like a no-man's-land, more alien to him than anyplace he'd ever been, despite his having been here before. Nothing was familiar.

Finally, he spotted an ATM in the distance, and he headed toward it, relieved that no matter what happened, he would at least have some money.

Using his card, he counted the strange-looking bills. This single act felt like a small triumph of sorts. He knew it wasn't much, the equivalent of about forty-five or fifty dollars, but he didn't think he'd need much money today. Besides, he reasoned, he could always stop at another ATM. He started off down the concourse again and saw a sign indicating the direction to the train into town. It pointed downstairs. He eventually found himself on a platform where a train would take him to Centraal Station in Amsterdam, about twenty minutes away.

On the crowded platform, he was uncertain that he was getting on the right train, but he boarded it anyway, too shy to ask a stranger, the fear like a lump in his throat that he couldn't dislodge. Once on the train, he unharnessed his backpack, setting it on the floor between his legs. He hadn't brought much with him, an extra sweater, a couple of tee shirts, a pair of jeans, socks, and underwear. He knew how unpredictable the weather in Amsterdam could be, cold and rainy one minute, especially if there was a wind off the North Sea, then fair and mild the next, so he'd carried his favorite leather jacket. He had to put it on now.

He looked out the train's window. The sky was a uniform gray, but it wasn't raining. The linden trees and the birches had already lost some of their leaves. In the distance, he could see numerous construction cranes, and as they neared Centraal Station he could see the cranes that loaded containers aboard ships along the docks of Amsterdam harbor.

When the train pulled into Centraal Station, he once again stood in confusion about which way to go. Finally, he followed the crowd, heading in the same direction as the largest number of people, not certain what else to do. Eventually, the concourse led to the front of the station, looking out toward Amsterdam.

So far, so good, he told himself nervously, trying to buck up his sagging spirits. *I've been here two minutes,* he thought miserably, *and I already feel so . . . alone.*

Outside the station, he was surrounded by what seemed like thousands of bicycles, any number of trams and buses, and scores of people on foot, heading in every direction. Still not knowing which way to go, uncertain whom he should ask, he simply started walking toward what looked like the city center.

I'll go to the main street, he thought, *or some place like that. Somebody can tell me where this address is.* He felt the piece of paper in his pocket, his only link to the little sister he wanted to meet.

He walked and walked, crossing several lanes of traffic, dodging bikes and cars and trams, thinking that he was going in the direction of the Dam – the main thoroughfare – but without realizing it he'd veered off to the west and soon found himself gradually descending into a strange little pedestrian street. The tall buildings on the Dam were abruptly blocked from his view by the small three- and four-story structures that lined the quaint cobbled street.

Oh, well, he thought, *if I keep going in this direction, this street's bound to take me toward the main drag. It's only over there, a couple of blocks away.*

The street quickly changed from quaint to seedy. The first two or three buildings on each side of the street had been prettily painted little restaurants, bars, or shops, but as he walked on, the bars became shabby, scary-looking places and the shops became anything but picturesque, with lurid window displays of sexual devices and obscene-looking clothing in some, joined with head shops whose windows were filled with pipes and bongs and tee shirts depicting sexual acts or obscene words and phrases.

He'd taken only a few more steps when he realized that many of the windows were lined with red neon or had a red-globed lamp prominently displayed in them. In these windows women of all shapes and sizes and colors sat or lay, offering their services to the passing men. Richie blushed with embarrassment when a woman with huge breasts blew him a kiss and shook her breasts at him, and he turned away when another woman put a hand between her legs and started gyrating around on it, leering at him lasciviously.

Oh, my God, he thought. *This is one place Dad never brought me.* He felt himself breaking out into a sweat. It ran down his forehead, his chest, and from under his arms, soaking through his shirt, and he felt panic seize him. His heart started beating faster and faster, and he thought he could almost hear it. He had the urge to run as fast as his feet could carry him, but he felt too self-conscious to act as if he were afraid of the spectacle around him. Besides, it was not easy to run with his backpack.

He put his head down, concentrating on the cobbles, trying not to look from side to side where he could glimpse the women continuing to try to lure him in with their obscene gestures. He tried to ignore the dangerous-looking men who tried to interest him in one of the women, describing sexual acts and practices that he didn't know much of anything about.

Richie had never felt so humiliated in his life, nor did he think he'd ever been so scared and lonely. At a corner he started to change direction – anywhere to get off this awful street, he thought – but a man, dirty and babbling nonsensical obscenities, nearly knocked him down as he came falling out of a cannabis bar. Richie wanted to wash off the place where the man had brushed against him, so vile was his appearance and smell.

Fear ran up his spine once again, but this time its grip was tighter, more malevolent. He backed away from the stoned man, almost falling on the uneven cobbles, and then dashed around the corner.

Just ahead on a footbridge over a small canal, he saw a policeman on a bicycle. He rushed toward him, not slowing down until he'd reached his side, and then pulled the piece of paper out of his pocket.

'Sir,' he said breathlessly, 'I need to find this address. Could . . . could you help me, please?'

The policeman looked at him, then turned to the girl he'd been talking to. He said something to her in Dutch. Richie looked over at her and saw that her clothes were dirty, and her hair was a wild purple nest. Up and down her arms were needle tracks. The sight repulsed him so much he felt sour bile rise up in his throat and threaten to choke him.

'Let me see,' the policeman said, turning back to him.

Richie held the piece of paper out for him to look at.

'Twenty-nine Buiksloterwec, Amsterdam Noord,' he said, reading it. 'You know the Centraal Station?'

Richie nodded. 'Yes – yes, sir,' he stammered.

'Go there, walk straight through to the back. There will be ferries there. You take one of those to get to this address. You'll have to ask at the piers which ferry to take. Okay?'

'Yes, sir,' Richie said. 'Thank you.'

The policeman nodded, then turned back to the girl, resuming his conversation with her.

Richie dreaded heading back in the direction from which he'd come. He tried to stare straight ahead, not looking from side to side as before, avoiding the leering prostitutes and their lewd gestures, the stoned and drunken men and women, and the perverted-looking merchandise in the shop windows.

He breathed a sigh of relief when he saw that he was near the end of the street. Just as he picked up his pace, three young men stepped from around a corner and suddenly came to a stop in front of him. They made a semicircle that he couldn't step past. All three had shaved heads, various piercings, tattoos, and were dressed in military fatigues and boots. And all three were huge.

Skinheads! he thought with alarm. He'd seen them in New York, but not like these. Not so huge and ghoulish and menacing.

He backed up a step and started to go around them, but they moved in tandem, blocking his way. He was about to yell for help, but one of them – the biggest one in the middle – grabbed him by his jacket and swung him off his feet and around the corner, into the tiny lane they'd come from. The goon slammed him up against the brick wall of the building and held him there.

'Your rucksack,' he spat into his face. He spoke in accented English, and absurdly, Richie wondered how he knew to speak English.

'My—?'

The skinhead, who towered over Richie, glared directly into his eyes. 'Your fuckin' rucksack, I said. Gert.' He jerked his head to his right, indicating the skinhead who stood watching with a sneer on his lips. 'Get it.'

He eased his hold on Richie for a moment as Gert roughly pulled the backpack straps off his shoulders, one side at a time.

'Got it?' the monster holding Richie asked, his focus still on his captive.

'Yeah,' Gert said. 'His jacket, too.'

The third one, who hadn't said anything, began laughing a weird hyena laugh.

The monster slammed Richie back against the brick wall again, and Richie could hear the awful thump his head made against it. Worse, he felt a sharp pain shoot through his head and down his neck. Then before he knew what was happening, the goon heaved him upward and threw him down onto the hard cobbles.

As he lay there stunned, the one with the hyena laugh viciously kicked at his head with a boot, landing it just behind his ear. Richie yelped in pain and automatically threw up his hands to protect his head, failing to see the hyena back up and kick again, this time landing a shot directly to his knee. He jerked and rolled over, doubling up in pain.

The three skinheads tore off down the lane, quickly running down a side street and around a corner, out of sight.

Richie didn't see or hear them leave, however. He lay there in terror, waiting for the next kick to land he knew not where. The pain in his head was so excruciating that he couldn't think or see beyond it. It was all-consuming in its intensity, like nothing he'd ever experienced before. He held his head, gritting his teeth, hoping that it would go away.

He had no idea how long he lay on the cobbles like that, curled up in a fetal position. All he knew was that the pain's intensity had begun to subside, gradually becoming a constant, dull ache behind his eyes. When he finally became aware of the silence around him, he took his hands away from his head and slowly opened his eyes. They were gone, he saw, not that he really cared much anymore. He'd never felt so defeated and humiliated in his life.

Eventually, he began testing his legs. The pain in his knee was still blaring, but he slowly pushed himself to his feet. His jeans were ripped at the knee, and the palm of one hand was scraped and bleeding. He realized then that he was trembling all over, and he wiped at the hot tears in his eyes with his fingers, feeling ashamed and helpless.

Shit! he thought miserably. *What do I do now? Do I go back to the policeman and report this – and have to answer a million questions about why I'm here alone – or do I go on and try to find the address?*

It was no contest, he decided. He didn't want anything to do with the police, for sure.

He took a few deep breaths and a few tentative steps. His walk was a limp, pain shooting up and down his leg, but he set off toward the Centraal Station again. As he got closer, he tried to run, but his knee quickly forced him to slow down.

I might as well take my time. I don't have anything left to steal, he thought grimly. *Unless somebody wants the rest of my clothes.* They'd taken his leather jacket, but luckily his passport was tucked into a pants pocket.

'I've got to get to this address,' he told a man standing on the pier.

'Take the one over there,' the man said, pointing. 'It leaves every few minutes. When you get off the ferry across the Ij, ask someone there where you can find this address. I don't think it's far.'

'Thanks a lot.'

'You're welcome,' the man said.

He went to the pier on his left, where he saw that several people were already waiting for the ferry, but he didn't see a ticket booth. He approached a young man who stood holding his battered bicycle by the handle bars.

'How much is the ferry?' he asked. 'And where do you get tickets?'

The rosy-cheeked young man smiled. 'It's free,' he said.

'Thanks,' Richie said. *Free*, he thought. *Wow. It's not New York City, that's for sure.* That's when it dawned on him that he didn't have any money. *Damn, what would I have done?* he wondered. *Am I going to have to beg?* He felt a tremor run through his body again, and he fought the urge to cry. *One thing for sure*, he told himself. *I'm not going to call my mom and tell her I've been robbed.*

He saw the ferry approaching, and the small crowd waiting to board it moved toward the edge of the dock but politely moved aside to let people get off when the ferry's sliding glass doors opened. Richie boarded across the small retractable metal gangplank, and rather than take a seat, he headed to the aftdeck to get a better view of the harbor and the Ij channel. The ferry sounded its horn and departed almost at once.

He noticed that there were all sorts of people on the ferry, young and old, some of them well-dressed, others badly. Many of them had bicycles with them, and nearly all of them carried shopping bags. On the channel, he saw small pleasure boats and big yachts, as well as other ferries, barges, and work boats of various kinds.

The ferry pulled into its dock across the Ij in a matter of minutes, and he got off. He was on a concrete pier with several benches that were surrounded on three sides by glass or heavy plastic to protect waiting passengers from the wind and rain. Heading toward land, he noticed that most of the passengers had already mounted their bicycles and pedaled swiftly away. A few were on foot, and he saw two young boys, about ten or eleven years old, he guessed, with fishing gear. Their rods were broken down into sections that were stowed in quivers slung across their shoulders. He started to approach them, but they began to run, apparently in an excited rush to get to their fishing spot. Then he saw an elderly lady laden with shopping bags. She was just ahead of him.

'Excuse me,' he said, approaching her.

The ruddy old woman turned to him. Snow-white hair stuck out at odd angles from under the scarf she wore tied around her head. 'Yes?'

'Do you know where this address is?' He held the piece of paper out so that she could read it.

'Follow this walk along the canal,' she said. 'See where there's a road veering to the left?'

Richie followed her pointing finger. 'Yes.'

'Go to the left,' the woman said. 'Just a few feet along that road, you'll see that street on the right.'

'Thank you very much,' Richie said.

The woman nodded and resumed her slow but steady pace up the walk. Richie immediately passed her as he headed along the canal toward his destination. The canal was lined with boats of every description, from expensive motor- and sailing-yachts to fishing dinghies that were in desperate need of paint jobs. He saw a middle-aged couple having lunch at a table on the deck of their motor yacht.

Veering left where the woman had told him to, he could see an industrial complex of some sort in the distance. Wondering what it was, his question was answered when he saw the logo of Shell Oil atop the high-rise building.

Off to his right a cobbled lane appeared, so tiny it would have been easy to miss had he not been on the lookout. On the side of a little white-painted brick building that housed a bar, he saw a street sign: BUIKSLOTERWEC. Underneath it was a smaller sign: NOORD.

He looked down the tiny cobbled lane. *This is it,* he thought with a surge of excitement that was a mixture of both anticipation and fear.

On his left were a few detached but shabby houses beyond the bar, then a neat row of narrow two- and three-story attached red-brick houses with white trim. To the right was a narrow strip of land that bordered the canal, and on it were a few houses, squeezed between the lane and the edge of the canal. In places, the land led to houseboats or small barges that had been converted into living quarters, the land providing front gardens, most of them planted with evergreens and run rampant with climbing vines and a plethora of flowers.

It looks like something in a storybook, Richie thought. *From when I was a kid.* He knew his mom would call it magical.

Taking a deep breath, he started down the lane. The side with the detached houses was lined with minuscule cars, some of them tiny Smart Cars, and on the canal side, cars were pulled up onto the narrow strip of land off the lane. There was a sidewalk, no more than a foot or so wide, on the side opposite the canal, but he walked in the middle of the lane. A little car approached, and he stepped out of the way, only to have a near-collision with a bicyclist pedaling rapidly by from behind him.

The bicyclist snarled something in Dutch that Richie didn't understand and looked back at him with a furious expression.

Embarrassed again and feeling totally out of his element, he stepped over onto the nearest garden plot, out of the way of any kind of traffic. He looked at the slip of paper he still clutched in his hand. Number 29 was what he was searching for. He put the piece of paper in his pocket and slid the photographs out of the inside pocket of his jacket. He thought he had the faces memorized, but he wanted to see them one more time. He studied the pictures intently: one was of the woman with the long, straight blond hair and the little girl with brown hair like his own, the other of them and his dad.

A weird feeling close to fear coursed through him again. He desperately wanted to meet his little sister, but he was afraid of the woman in the picture. He knew that she and his mother were in a fight over his dad's estate, and she would probably hate him on sight.

I have to do it anyway, he thought. *I have to.*

Sliding the pictures back into his jacket pocket, he glanced up and saw an old woman standing in a second-floor window in one of the detached houses. He realized that she'd been watching him, and it only increased the creepy feeling he already had. He remembered how the custom in Holland was to leave your front curtains open, so that anyone could see into your house, the reason being that it proved you had nothing to hide. It also showed off your tidy housekeeping habits. Nevertheless, the old woman spooked him.

She stepped back, out of his view, although he was certain she was still watching him, and his eye caught the number on the door to her house: 40. So that was the even-numbered side of the street. He was looking for a house here on the canal side. He walked on, negotiating his way around parked cars, motor scooters, bicycles, and huge old trees, searching for house numbers on this side of the lane. Several of the houses were behind high, vine-covered fences that screened them from the street almost entirely, but he saw a number 37 on a gate.

I might've already passed it, he thought. He walked farther, and the next number he saw was 29, on a small plaque attached to a weathered wooden fence about four feet high. Like most of the others, it was overgrown with vines. He came to an abrupt halt, almost stumbling into an overturned garbage can. There was no gate, but a wide opening gave way to stone steps that led about twenty feet down to the house.

He stood and stared for a moment, entranced by what he knew was his dad's second home. Situated on the edge of the canal, it was made of stained wood that gleamed like a freshly varnished boat, even in the overcast. There were almost no windows on this side of the house, but several skylights pierced its gray shingle roof.

Forcing himself to quit staring, he walked on, past more vine-choked fencing and two or three large-trunked trees, to see if he could get a better view of the house from another angle. A few feet down the lane, he came to what must be the end of the property line and the beginning of the neighbor's. The fence ended and a high hedge began. He checked to see if there was a gap in the hedge he could look through. There wasn't, but he soon came to the entrance to the neighboring property and, from there, he got a clear view of the side of the house where he knew his dad had died.

He stood staring again, and saw the same gleaming stained wood, but with windows on this side. On the front of the house a deck ran along the canal. He looked a while longer, then realized that he might seem suspicious to neighbors, like the creepy old woman across the lane he'd seen watching him.

What do I do now? he wondered. He didn't want to go knock on the door and say, *Hi, I'm Richie, and my dad was your boyfriend. Your little girl, Anja, is my half sister.* He abruptly realized how ill-thought-out his adventure was. Now that he was here, he didn't know what to do.

He crossed to the other side of the street and shuffled slowly back the way he'd come. He felt like a fool. *Why didn't I rehearse what to say?* Turning into a side street almost directly opposite the steps leading down to the house, he sat down on the tiny sidewalk, elbows on knees, head in his hands.

What am I going to say? he asked himself again. *What if she doesn't recognize me from the reading of the will and believe me when I tell her who I am and what I know? She might not even let me in,* he thought. *She might call the police or something. She might be a mean bitch and hate me on sight.* He brushed a stray lock of hair from his eyes. *Why didn't I think about this before?* He could kick himself for being so impetuous. He'd known he wanted to meet his sister, and he'd known how to find her. But he hadn't thought beyond that.

Tears threatened to fill his eyes again. *I'm so stupid,* he thought miserably. *First I get myself robbed, and now I'm sitting here like a dork not knowing what to do.* His hand hurt, and he gingerly rubbed blood off it and onto his torn jeans.

From the corner of his eye he saw movement across the lane. He looked over. It was her! The lady with the long blond hair. And the little girl! The woman was holding her hand as they walked up the steps. A lump rose in his throat, and he felt completely tongue-tied. At first he thought she was going to get on the bicycle locked to the fence, but she didn't. In her other hand was a carryall and a fold-up baby stroller. She laid the bag aside, set down the stroller, and then unfolded it. Picking up Anja, she put her in the stroller, retrieved the carryall, and set off in the direction of the ferry. He could hear the two of them talking to one another and could see the little girl pointing at something.

When they'd gone a ways down the lane, he got up, ignoring the pain in his knee, and set off after them, careful to match their pace, keeping distance between them. At the intersection, she took a left, as he thought she would, and headed toward the ferry. She stopped once to shift the tote bag from one shoulder to the other.

At the pier, she pushed the stroller toward the far end and stood just inside one of the shelters, protecting herself and the child from the chilly wind sweeping in off the North Sea. Richie remained at the end of the pier and tried to appear to look in every direction but theirs. The ferry came within five minutes, and the twenty-five or thirty people waiting for it began to embark.

He watched as she wheeled the stroller onboard and took a seat inside; then he walked aboard himself, remaining on deck with two or three other young people with bicycles who were chatting and laughing among themselves. Even from the deck, through the windows and distance that separated them, he could see them clearly.

The woman, Monique, is really beautiful, he thought. *Really cool. But she also looked like she could be real . . . tough. Or mean.* She was very tall and slender, and she sat erectly, just as she walked with the stroller. Her hair was very long, below her shoulders, and pale blond. She had very high, prominent cheekbones, a straight nose, and full lips. Her complexion was pale, like her hair, and she wore very little makeup. She was wearing jeans and a black sweater that was huge and heavy. A woolen watch cap was on her head, black lace-up boots on her feet.

He couldn't see the little girl because the stroller was placed facing her mother, but he could tell they were talking and laughing by watching Monique's face.

In Amsterdam they debarked, and he followed them across the road and into Centraal Station. She pushed the stroller straight through the station and out the front doors, then went to one of the many tram stops outside. Maintaining his distance, he skulked along well behind, trying once again not to appear to be aware of them. Waiting several feet down the sidewalk, he watched as Monique took Anja out of the stroller and then folded it up. When the number twenty-four tram arrived, he boarded it when they did, but by a different door.

There was no conductor on the tram, and he hoped that one wouldn't come along to sell or collect tickets because he didn't have one and couldn't buy one. He'd have to chance it. He found a seat several rows behind Monique and Anja. The tram remained at the stop for a few minutes before pulling out. As central Amsterdam reeled slowly by his eyes in fits and starts, Richie wondered where they were going, and what he would do once they were there.

Should I introduce myself? he wondered. *Or should I just keep following them?* He was torn between the two choices, and he was still afraid that she might make a scene, possibly call the police. On the other hand, he couldn't continue to follow them like this and not meet them. That would defeat the purpose of his trip. *I came here to meet my half sister*, he told himself again, *but how do I do it now that I'm here?*

29

When the elevator door opened, Carolina was standing there with frightened doe eyes, waiting for him. Seth took her into his arms and held her. She nestled against him, needing the security and warmth.

Seth finally kissed the top of her head, then smiled, urging her toward the kitchen to make some coffee. They sat at the table in the dining area as she told him about Richie lying to her and about finding the message he'd left on his computer.

'I know it sounds crazy,' he said, taking her hand in his, 'but I don't think you have to worry about Richie. He's a big boy, Carolina, and he's been to Amsterdam before, several times, you said.' He was worried about Richie, too, but he certainly didn't want her to see that. Like any large city, Amsterdam had its dark, dangerous side.

'I know all that,' she said, her voice rising, 'but I can't help it. I – I . . . he's still a kid and . . . my God, he could be dead, Seth!' Tears came into her eyes, and she wiped them away with her fingertips.

Seth looked at this wristwatch. 'Richie's probably already there,' he said. 'Depending on which flight he took. It's already after nine o'clock their time. It's not too early to call the woman.'

She stiffened slightly.

'I think I ought to tell her that Richie will be showing up on her doorstep,' he said, 'if he's not already there. She should know, and besides, we want to make certain that he's okay.'

'Yes,' she said, nodding, 'I have to make reservations to fly over today. Right away. The first flight I can get on. I can bring him home.'

'*We* can bring him home,' Seth said. 'I'll go with you.'

'You – you would do that?' Carolina asked, looking at him in wonder. 'Oh, Seth, you don't have to. I can do it on my own.'

'I know you can,' he said. 'I don't doubt that for a minute, but you don't have to. I think you could use some company on this trip, and I'd like to go. You know, I care about Richie, too.'

'You . . . you really do, don't you?'

'Yes,' he said, 'very much.' He nodded and smiled. 'So let me get on the telephone and see what I can find out. I'll call about reservations, too. For both of us. If you want to shower, now's a good time to do it. Or start throwing some things in a bag. I'll probably be on the telephone for a while.'

'That's a good idea,' she said. 'I should get myself ready. I'll call Roxie about seven and let her know she's going to be running the show for a few days.' She got to her feet. 'It'll only take me a few minutes.'

'I just need one thing,' he replied, 'and that's something with the lawyer's letterhead on it, and the woman's name.'

'Okay,' Carolina said, 'but I don't think her telephone number is in any of the paperwork.'

'That doesn't matter,' Seth said. 'I'll get it somehow.'

'I'll just be a minute,' she said. She rushed to the den, where she retrieved the paperwork. Then she took it back to the dining area

270

and placed it on the table. 'There,' she said. 'Help yourself. I think you'll find everything here. I'll go get ready.'

'Okay,' he said, already beginning to look through the papers.

'What've you found out?' Carolina asked when she emerged from her bedroom a short time later.

'I've had some luck,' he said. 'I couldn't get hold of Monique Lehnert, but I left a message on her answering machine. I also spoke to Adriaan Weber, the lawyer who's handling matters there. I explained the situation to him. Told him that Richie was probably already in Amsterdam, and that we would be there later today. He's going to keep trying to get Monique Lehnert, and tell her to call him if Richie contacts her or shows up there. He'll keep his eyes and ears open. Richie may try to contact him for some reason.'

'She could be out of town or something,' Carolina said. 'What if we can't find Richie through her?'

'Look,' Seth said, taking her hand, 'the lady is almost definitely in town because Weber spoke to her yesterday. She has to come by his office to sign some papers and has an appointment to do that tomorrow. The other news is that I got us both booked on the next flight to Amsterdam. Thank God the tourist season is over.'

'That's wonderful,' Carolina said. 'I don't know what I would do without you.'

'Now, what I'd better do is get back to my place and throw a few things in a suitcase.' He looked at his wristwatch. 'We should be leaving for Kennedy in about two hours. I've already called the limo service I use, and they'll pick us up here.'

Carolina reached over and put her hand on his. She gently squeezed it but didn't say anything.

'We'll soon find Richie,' he said, as if knowing what she was thinking, 'and I think he'll be fine. I'd better run. I've got to call a couple of people in my office, too. Will you be okay while I'm gone, or do you want to come with me?'

271

'I'll be fine,' Carolina said. 'I've got to call Roxie and try Matt again.'

'All right,' he said, getting to his feet. 'I won't be too long.'

Carolina got up and went to the elevator with him. He pressed the call button and turned to her. 'Just remember,' he said, 'it's going to be okay.'

She nodded; then she put her arms around him and hugged. He hugged her in return, and they stood like that until the elevator arrived.

They parted, and he got on the car. 'I'll be right back,' he said.

30

As the tram headed south, Monique stared out the window with a growing anticipation and, at the same time, sadness. She knew that she would be better off if she didn't come here with Anja, but it made her feel closer to Lyon to visit the park where they'd first met and talked, where they'd first fallen in love, and where they'd often brought Anja together. It was as if he'd left a bit of himself in the park, she reflected, and her coming here had become a ritual of remembrance.

When the tram stopped at Minervaplein, she quickly stood up, lifted Anja, and took the stroller to one of the exits, unaware of the young man who got off at the same stop. On the sidewalk, she unfolded the stroller and placed Anja in it, looking about at the chic boutiques and good restaurants that they had so often frequented together after they'd met. Then she set off across the street and down a road between the neat, clean apartment buildings, passing the door that led up to the apartment where they'd first made love, the apartment where he was supposed to be living.

Before long she crossed the bridge, spanning the beautiful canal beneath, and wheeled the stroller into Beatrix Park. Although the trees were losing their leaves, the park was still an oasis of green with huge rhododendrons and evergreens towering alongside the paths that curved through it. It was almost devoid of people, much as Minervaplein had been, although the occasional jogger would dash past.

Monique soon stopped, picked Anja up, and set her on the path. Here the path was bordered on one side with a little fence, and across it was a lawn leading down to a pond. When she and Anja neared the fence, giant herons swooped down out of the pine trees and approached it from the other side.

Like prehistoric birds, they wobbled on their long legs toward her and Anja, who began squealing with excitement. Monique smiled and laughed, delighting in Anja's joy. The child had become so accustomed to the bedlam they created that she was no longer frightened by it, as she had been at first, and now took pleasure in watching them. Monique took the package of chopped-up chicken out of her satchel, and began tossing it to the herons, watching them jockey for the best position to catch the booty. Squabbles broke out among them over the food, and their noisy squawks seemed amplified in the nearly deserted park.

When the package was empty, she put the bag in the empty stroller and, with Anja in hand, began walking around the fenced-in pond, pushing the stroller in front of her. She stopped again when she came to the spot where she knew the swans would expect her, and she was instantly rewarded when the three black creatures, magnificent with their red bills, made swift progress across the pond toward her and Anja, their joyous noises more like fluting than trumpeting to her ears. Anja laughed and pointed at them, but Monique's attention was drawn by a sound behind them.

She heard crunching on the gravel, and she turned to glance. A boy, his jeans torn, she noticed, stood on the path looking toward her. He quickly averted his eyes, and she turned back to the swans, ignoring him. Then something about him – his familiar looks? a familiar stance? – made her turn back to look at him again. He was still looking toward her, and her eyes caught his. In that instant, she recognized him. She was certain of it. Hadn't she seen his photograph a thousand times? He was the boy at the reading of the will. Her heart began to beat madly. A tremble of anger and fear made her feel unsteady on her feet, and she glared at him malevolently.

'I – I . . .' he began.

'What do you want?' she spat at him nastily.

'I – I'm . . . my name's . . .' His voice trailed off, and he looked toward the swans as if they would give him courage.

'I know who you are!' she snapped angrily, her eyes flashing. 'What are you doing here? What the hell do you want from me?' She grabbed Anja's hand in hers, and the child looked up at her and then over at the boy.

He looked at her with wide, frightened eyes. 'I – I . . .'

'Get away!' she shrieked. 'Get away from us.'

'But – but . . . I want to see my sister,' Richie finally blurted out. 'I – I came all this way.'

She stared at him contemptuously, her eyes still flashing blue fire, her body rigid, her fists clenched. 'You . . . what?' she said between gritted teeth.

31

Seth had a limo meet them at Schiphol, and they passed through customs and were on their way into Amsterdam by evening. 'It's not the greatest apartment in the world,' he warned Carolina as they neared the city center, 'but it's there and convenient.'

'Don't worry about it, Seth,' she said. 'Who cares, anyway? I'm here to see my son. I don't care where I stay.'

Seth had told her on the flight over that they could stay in the apartment his company maintained, and Carolina had readily agreed. It had two bedrooms, he'd explained, so she would be guaranteed her privacy.

'It's in the center?' she asked.

He nodded. 'Yes. In fact, Centraal Station is only a very short walk away.'

The driver turned the car into a very narrow street alongside a canal and slowed to a crawl.

'The house is on the other side of the canal,' Seth said.

At the bridge, the driver turned right, drove over it, and then turned left onto Geldersekade, the opposite side of the canal. On the left, Carolina noticed two or three of the big windows with red lamps that dotted the red-light district in central Amsterdam, and she glimpsed the figures of the women seated in them, displaying their wares for passersby. On down the street, the driver slowed the car and then came to a stop in front of an elegant old house.

'Here we are,' Seth said. He paid the driver, who opened the trunk and took out their luggage.

On the ground floor of the house, the curtains were pulled open, and Carolina could see directly into the apartment. An elderly man was sitting in an armchair, reading. His walls were covered in paintings and drawings, and there was a grand piano in the room. There was a tea service on a table near him, and plants were everywhere.

How extraordinary, Carolina thought. *A scene of such domestic civility and culture, just down the street from the garishly lit windows.*

Carolina took her carry-on bag, and Seth picked up the other two pieces of luggage and took them to the door; then he set them down and opened the big wooden door with his key. He held it for her, and she stepped into the marble-floored hallway. He retrieved the luggage and brought it inside.

'There's no elevator,' he said. 'Almost none of the canal houses have them, but it's only one flight up.'

'Let me take my suitcase,' she said, reaching for it.

'No,' he said. 'I'm an old hand at this, believe me. You can lead the way.'

She started up the staircase. It was narrow and curving and perilously steep. 'This sure isn't like the apartment in Minervaplein,' she said.

Seth laughed. 'No, it's a far cry from Minervaplein. This house is over three hundred years old. Most of Minervaplein was built in the 1950s.'

They reached the second floor. 'It's to the left,' he said. She went down the hallway, and he followed, setting the luggage down at a door. Unlocking it, he flipped on a light, and Carolina went in.

Looking around, she saw that they were in the living room. The apartment had extremely high ceilings, at least eighteen feet, and the walls were covered in beautifully carved paneling. One window at the end of the room overlooked the canal. The furnishings were well worn but elegant, a few Dutch pieces mixed with French.

'Where's the telephone?' she asked Seth nervously.

'Right here,' he said, pointing it out to her. 'I'll call in just a second.' He picked up the luggage again. 'I'll be right back. I'm going to put this in our rooms.'

He went down a hallway, and Carolina wandered around the big room looking at the paintings on the walls and the bibelots that sat on various tables. There were a lot of books on shelves, in several languages.

Seth strode back into the room. 'How about a drink?' he asked, picking up the remote telephone receiver.

'That's a very good idea,' she said. 'After we've called. Okay?'

'Of course.'

She'd been dreading this moment – making the telephone call – and was grateful that he'd offered to do it.

Just before they left New York, Adriaan Weber, the lawyer in Amsterdam, had called and spoken to Seth once again. Monique Lehnert had telephoned Weber from home that afternoon and told him that Richie Mountcastle was there at her house. She'd said that she would keep him with her until she heard from the lawyer, but she'd been nothing less than furious and was eager to be rid of the boy.

'I'll call now,' he said. He pressed the number into the cordless phone.

Carolina made an effort to block out the foul thoughts that swirled in an endless pattern in her mind. She reminded herself that Monique had at least let Richie stay in her house until they got there. For the first time since Lyon's death, she wondered how this woman was coping with the loss of Lyon, and she couldn't help but be curious about whether or not Monique hated her and Richie as much as she hated Monique and the child. She'd certainly gathered that Monique was very unhappy to have Richie there.

As Seth was speaking on the phone, Carolina asked him anxiously, 'Is Richie still there?'

Seth nodded. 'Just a second.'

'I want to speak to him right now,' Carolina said in no uncertain terms.

'Hold on.' He talked to Monique, and after a moment he said, 'Hey, somebody here is very anxious to talk to you.' He handed the remote to Carolina. 'It's Richie,' he said.

'Richie!' she cried. 'Are you all right?'

'I'm fine, Mom,' he said, 'and I'm sorry I worried you so much. But I—'

'I don't care about that now, Richie,' she said. 'We'll talk about that later. I want to come and get you right now. Where is this place?'

'It's okay, Mom,' he said. 'I can stay here tonight.'

'No!' she nearly shouted into the receiver. 'I'm coming to get you now.'

The street lamps had come on when they walked down Buiksloterwec in Amsterdam Noord, and the charms of the little lane were not lost on Carolina. She loved the cobbles, the overgrown gardens, the somewhat shabby houses, and the glimpses of the canal, off which the lights reflected. At the same time, she felt her teeth begin to ache from unconsciously gritting them. From one moment to the next, it seemed that her heart rate shifted, racing up and away or slowing down. If not for Seth's steady presence, she thought she would've turned back at the ferry.

When they reached number 29, she stood and stared at it, Seth's hand in hers. It looked like a romantic hideaway, she thought. Small and tidy and . . . the perfect love nest. As they walked down the stone steps toward the door, it opened, and Monique Lehnert stood in it, tall and slender, her long blond hair brushed out neatly. Carolina could see instantly that she was a dancer. She stood straight and erect, head up, shoulders back, butt tucked in.

There's a lot of steel in that straight spine of hers, she thought. She was certain that Monique Lehnert was not an easy woman to know or deal with, but she couldn't deny that she was also very beautiful.

When they reached the door, Monique put out a hand. 'I'm Monique Lehnert,' she said in barely accented English.

Carolina shook her hand. She could see that she looked very nervous. 'I'm Carolina Mountcastle, and this is Seth Foster.'

Seth shook her hand. 'Hello,' he said. 'I hope you don't mind me coming along.'

Monique shook her head. 'Not at all,' she said. 'Please come in.'

She moved back, and they stepped into the entry. 'Richie's playing with Anja,' she said, closing the door behind them. 'I – I'm a little nervous, I have to admit,' she said, studying Carolina.

'I'm a little nervous myself,' Carolina said, grateful that the woman had admitted her own apprehension about their meeting.

'This way,' Monique said, showing them through the tiny entryway into the spacious living room. There was a deck outside, which was lit up, and the house faced directly onto the canal.

It feels like being on a houseboat, Carolina thought. Then her breath caught in her throat, and her mind reeled. Richie was walking toward her, holding the child by a hand, and Carolina couldn't take her eyes off her now that she got a good look at her for the first time.

'Mom,' he said, 'this is Anja. Isn't she beautiful?'

He looked at Seth and put out a hand. 'Hi, Seth,' he said. They shook hands, and Richie noticed that Seth kept an arm around his mother's waist, loosely but protectively.

Carolina was thrilled to see her son and had wanted to hug him to her, but she was mesmerized by the tableau he and the child presented and continued to stare, momentarily speechless. Astonishingly, the child was a twin to Richie when he'd been that age. The spit and image. The same chocolate-bar hair and eyes. And her resemblance to Lyon was equally as powerful. There was no denying who her father was. She finally noticed that the little girl had extended her hand for a shake, and she bent down and took it.

'How do you do . . . Anja?' she said. 'I'm Carolina.'

Anja giggled and put her hand on her face, then looked up at Richie. 'It's okay,' he said. 'She's my mom. And this is Seth, Anja.'

She put her hand back out, and Seth bent down and brushed it with his lips in the continental manner. 'It's a pleasure, Anja,' he said.

Anja giggled again and stared at him.

'Well, we'd better be on our way,' Carolina said.

'But, Mom, I was going to watch a video with Anja,' Richie protested.

'Maybe another time,' Carolina said firmly. 'We have to go now.' She turned to Monique. 'Thanks for taking care of my son,' she said. 'Maybe we'll see you tomorrow and can talk then.'

Monique nodded. 'That would be fine.'

'It was nice to meet you,' Seth said, his arm still around Carolina's waist.

'You, too,' Monique said. 'Both of you.'

Carolina was still unnerved by meeting Monique and then seeing Anja and Richie together, but she managed to put out her hand. 'Good-bye,' she said in a formal tone.

Monique took her hand and shook it. 'Good-bye.'

'Let's go, Richie,' Carolina said, already going to the door.

'I'm coming,' he said, clearly unhappy.

They left the house and began the walk back down the lane toward the ferry. Carolina wanted to scold Richie for taking off to Europe, but he chattered away so happily about the wonders of his new sister that she hated to bring up the unpleasant subject of his running away. She was so happy to see him and so grateful that he was safe, she decided to let a serious discussion wait. Besides, she needed time to gather her own thoughts and feelings and sort them out. Her head was still spinning in circles after seeing Lyon's Amsterdam hideaway and meeting Monique and Anja, and she needed to digest what she'd seen.

The short ferry ride across the Ij to Amsterdam Noord was invigorating in the cool morning wind that swept across the ferry's open deck, and the three of them walked briskly toward the little cottage on Buiksloterwec. Carolina and Seth weren't fast enough for Richie, however. He ran ahead of them, eager to get there and see Anja. Carolina had called ahead to make certain that Monique would be home.

Seth took Carolina's hand in his, and he pointed out some of the more remarkable boats docked along the canal, some of which were lived in year round by quite hearty or very foolish characters, depending on your perspective.

'I think the boats are incredibly charming,' Carolina said. 'And the lifestyle looks appealing, but it also looks like it would be very cold and very cramped.'

'It takes a special sort of person to live like this,' Seth agreed. 'It's certainly not for everyone.' He was trying to keep her mind off the visit they were about to make, knowing that she was still a bundle of nerves, even if she was not quite so anxious as she had been yesterday.

They started down the cobbled lane toward Monique's and could see Richie running ahead.

'He's . . . he's enthralled with Anja,' Carolina said, 'isn't he?'

'Yes,' Seth said, 'and I can't blame him. I think that if I suddenly discovered a sister or half sister and she resembled me so closely, I would be a little enthralled myself. Wouldn't you?'

'I suppose so,' Carolina replied. She paused and looked over at him. 'I guess I'm having trouble keeping everything in perspective,' she admitted. 'And Richie's feelings are naturally going to be very different from mine.'

By the time they reached the cottage, Richie had already gone inside and was now coming back out again, holding Anja's little hand in his.

'We're going to that park Monique told us about,' Richie said to them, all smiles.

Anja looked up at them and grinned.

'How are you today, Anja?' Seth asked.

The child giggled and looked up at Richie.

Monique stepped outside then. 'Good morning,' she said.

'Good morning,' Carolina and Seth said in unison.

'Richie,' Monique said, 'let me show you how to get to the park.' She turned to Carolina and Seth. 'I'll only be a minute,' she said. 'Please go on inside. I just need to point the way.'

'Be back soon,' Richie said over his shoulder to Carolina and Seth as they went inside.

'Have fun,' Seth said.

'We will,' Richie replied.

'Give your mother a kiss first?' Carolina asked.

Richie backtracked with a grin on his face and hugged and kissed her. 'I love you, Mom,' he said, then turned and went back out to Monique and Anja.

Seth hugged Carolina to him. 'It's going to be okay,' he said. 'You're doing fine.'

She nodded. 'I – I was so surprised by the . . . by Anja . . . oh, I'm so glad you're here,' she said, her nervousness obvious in her voice. 'I'm more startled today than I was yesterday. By Anja, I mean. The little girl is so much like Lyon and Richie that it's eerie.'

'I didn't know Lyon,' Seth said, 'but the resemblance to Richie is uncanny.' He looked around. 'This is a cute place, and the neighborhood is run-down but charming.'

'It is charming,' she agreed. 'Not like the Amsterdam I've seen.'

'No,' he said, 'this is off the beaten track. I guess a lot of artist types and students live out here. Old people, too. Some fishermen and boat people.'

Monique came back through the front door and walked over to them. 'Would you like some coffee or tea?' she asked.

'I would like tea,' Carolina said.

'I'll have some, too,' Seth said.

'It'll just take a minute,' she replied. She walked into the kitchen area which was open to the living room, separated only by a bar. 'I have some green tea,' Monique said. 'I hope you like that.'

'That's fine,' Carolina said.

'For me, too,' Seth said.

'Why don't you make yourselves comfortable?' Monique said. 'You can put your coats on that rack.' She pointed to a coatrack in a corner.

They hung their jackets on it and then sat on the couch together, looking out toward the canal.

When the tea was made, Monique brought it and the condiments to the coffee table on a tray. There were bowls with lemon, sugar, raw sugar, honey, and a pitcher of milk. Monique sat in a chair opposite them, and they fixed their tea.

Carolina had a sip, then took a deep breath, steeling herself for this discussion. 'Thank you for taking Richie in,' she said. 'As you know, he ran away on his own to meet Anja.'

Monique blushed, then in one elegant gesture flipped long blond hair away from her face. 'I was very angry at first,' she admitted. 'I didn't want anything to do with him or . . . you. But I . . . well, I couldn't resist after I saw how much like Anja he is . . . and he was desperate to get to know his half sister.' She shrugged. 'So I brought him home for them to get acquainted. What else could I do?'

Carolina valued her honesty. 'Well, I really appreciate your letting him come here. I was worried sick.'

'He was okay,' Monique said. 'He did tell me something that I told him I wouldn't tell you. But you should know.'

'What is it?' Carolina asked worriedly.

'He had his jacket and backpack stolen,' she said, 'and it had his money in it. He wasn't hurt badly, but his jeans were torn and his hand was cut. I cleaned his hand, and it's okay. Luckily his passport was in his trouser pocket.'

'Oh, my God,' Carolina said. 'I had no idea. I saw that his jeans were ripped, but I was so happy to see him I forgot to ask about it.'

'Where did this happen?' Seth asked.

'In the red-light district somewhere,' she replied. 'Three thugs cornered him. I think they wounded his pride more than anything.'

Carolina felt almost sick, thinking of what might have happened. 'I'm glad he found you,' she said, 'and that you've taken care of him. I don't know what to say . . .'

'Nothing is necessary,' Monique said with another shrug. 'I did what anybody would've done.'

'We both appreciate it anyway,' Seth said. 'He thought his dad had shown him all of Amsterdam, but he doesn't really know it that well.'

'Lyon loved showing him Amsterdam,' Monique said. 'He loved Richie so much.'

Carolina momentarily bristled at the mention of Lyon, but the effect was softened by Monique's words. 'Yes,' she said, 'there was no doubt about that. Lyon loved him so much.'

Monique looked over at Carolina and then down at her own hands as she folded them in her lap. 'Maybe you don't want to hear this,' she said, taking a deep breath and looking back up, 'but when I met Lyon, I didn't know he was married. He didn't wear a ring, and he didn't tell me, at least in the beginning.'

'So you did know,' Carolina said.

'Eventually, yes,' Monique said, nodding. 'I feed some of the birds in Beatrix Park, and I passed by the apartment where he stayed all the time. We started talking one day when I was feeding the herons.'

'Please,' Carolina said. 'I'm not sure I want to hear this.' Seth squeezed her hand reassuringly, and she glanced at him.

'I'm sorry,' Monique said. 'I just wanted you to know what happened.' Tears came into her eyes, but Carolina looked away, trying to ignore them. 'We began seeing each other. He was very lonely, being here by himself. He didn't know anybody but the men he worked with.'

She paused and looked at Carolina again. 'I'm not trying to justify what we did because I know that I can't do that.'

Carolina nodded. 'No, I don't think so,' she said.

'I got pregnant,' Monique went on, 'and that's when he told me he was married. But I wanted to have his baby anyway because I . . . I was madly in love with him, and . . . and I still am.'

Carolina saw tears roll down her cheeks, and as much as she had hardened her heart, a part of her couldn't help but feel something for this young woman. After all, she, too, had suffered – was suffering – because of Lyon's death.

'And I don't regret having Anja for a single minute,' Monique said, looking at Carolina. 'To me, she's like a gift from Lyon. That and more.'

'What did Lyon have to say about that?' Carolina asked. 'You having the baby, I mean?'

'At first he thought I should have an abortion, but I told him I wouldn't,' Monique said. 'He . . . he finally reconciled himself to it. He found this place and got the car. He was very good to me, and once Anja was born he couldn't believe he'd ever wanted me to have an abortion. He loved her so much. Just . . . just like he loved Richie.'

Carolina nodded. Her mind was whirling as she tried to digest all of this information.

'He never stopped loving you, either,' Monique added. 'That I know for certain.'

Tears stung Carolina's eyes at last, and she held on to Seth's hand tightly. She was afraid that she would cry aloud and didn't trust herself to speak.

'He was playing with Anja when he had the heart attack,' Monique said. 'They were out on the deck there.' She pointed through the big windows. 'He stumbled and fell. I saw it. I thought he was going to fall in the canal, and I ran outside. I didn't know what was happening. He grabbed my arm and said, "Carolina, tell her I love her." Then he was dead. Like that.' She snapped her fingers.

Carolina gasped and then took a deep breath. Seth put an arm around her and pulled her to him.

'I know it's hard to hear this,' Monique continued, 'but I want you to know that. No matter what happened here – and I know it must be a nightmare for you – he still loved you.'

Carolina absorbed her words in silence. When she could trust herself to speak, she asked, 'And you? It . . . it must have been awful for you, too?'

Monique wiped away her tears with a tissue. 'It was awful. He was wonderful to us.' She shook her head as if to clear it of some image, and her hair moved from side to side. 'I know the whole thing must sound very sordid to you.'

'I'm . . . I'm glad you told me,' Carolina said.

They sat in silence for a while. The tea she had made sat virtually untouched, and it was Seth who picked up his cup and took a sip.

'This is delicious,' he said by way of breaking the ice.

'Thank you,' Monique said.

'What are you going to do now, if I may ask?'

'I don't know,' Monique said. 'I will probably go back to work. I danced in a modern dance troupe, but I'm not sure yet. I have to think of Anja.'

287

'Do you have family here?' Carolina asked.

Monique shook her head. 'Not in Amsterdam, no. My father is a farmer, and they live out in the country. They are simple people and don't approve of my having a child out of wedlock.'

'Maybe they'll come around,' Carolina said. 'Parents often do in time, especially with a grandchild as pretty as Anja.'

'We'll see,' Monique said, 'but I'm not holding my breath. They've refused to see her all this time.'

'That must be very difficult for you,' Carolina said sympathetically.

'I'm used to it,' Monique said, with a bark of a laugh.

Carolina watched as the young woman took a sip of the tea and then brushed her hair back in that single elegant gesture. *She's trying hard to be brave*, she thought, *but she's really very vulnerable and afraid.*

Richie and Anja came through the front door in a burst of noisy laughter, and everyone looked over at them. The eerie sensation that Carolina had felt on initially seeing the child returned as powerfully as before. The girl rushed to her mother, babbling a charming mixture of Dutch and English.

'We had a great time,' Richie said, 'but Anja's getting hungry. I didn't realize that it's already lunchtime.' He looked at Carolina and Seth, obviously trying to assess their expressions to get a feel for what had transpired while he'd been away.

Carolina smiled up at her son and took his hand. 'I'm glad you've had a good time,' she said.

Richie smiled.

'We've had an interesting conversation,' she said, 'but I guess we'd better head back.' She looked at her watch. 'It is getting to be time for lunch.' She got to her feet, and Seth followed suit.

'I have some leftover stew,' Monique said, 'if you like.'

'No, but thank you,' Carolina said. 'I've got some business to take care of this afternoon, so we'd better get back.'

Richie looked from her to Seth to Monique. He didn't know what to think or what to do next. 'Is it okay if I come back later, Monique?' he asked.

'Of course,' she said. 'You know you're welcome anytime, Richie, but call me first in case I'm out for some reason.'

'It was nice to see you, Monique,' Seth said, extending his hand. 'And nice to see you, too, Anja.' Monique shook his hand, and Anja threw her hands to her face, suddenly shy.

They started for the door, and Carolina turned to Monique. 'Could we have a word in private? For just a minute.'

'Of course,' Monique said. 'Richie, do you mind taking Anja out with you?'

'No.' He took her hand in his and, with Seth, they went out the front door and closed it behind them.

Carolina turned to Monique. 'I'm not going to pretend that I haven't been through hell because of what happened between you and Lyon, because I have. And Richie has, too. Every single moment since I found out about the two of you.'

'I understand,' Monique said, biting her lower lip nervously.

'I don't know if you really do or not,' Carolina said. 'All those years with him – and having Richie. To me, it was sacred, and that's been destroyed.'

Monique nodded and tears came into her eyes again.

Carolina took a deep breath and looked into Monique's blue eyes. 'I don't know if I'll ever be able to forgive you, and I think you want forgiveness. Otherwise, you wouldn't have told me what you did today. It was a gift, and I appreciate it. I appreciate it very much. I think it'll make things a little bit easier for me in the future, but I don't think I'll ever be able to forget what's happened here.'

Tears streamed down Monique's cheeks, but she remained silent.

'I don't mean to sound . . . self-righteous, and I'm not like some kind of priest who can dispense forgiveness, Monique,' Carolina went on. 'God knows, I've done enough stupid things in my time. I just want you to know how I feel.'

She began rummaging in her shoulder bag and then pulled her hand out. 'Here,' she said, handing Monique some tissues. 'Dry your tears. I just hope for the sake of Richie and Anja that we . . . well, that we can come to some kind of . . . understanding.'

'I do, too,' Monique said.

32

After lunch in a Thai restaurant, Carolina told Seth and Richie that she wanted to make some telephone calls in private. 'Do you mind?' she asked.

'No, of course not,' Seth said, looking at her questioningly. *What's she up to?* he wondered, but didn't ask. 'What say we do some sightseeing, Richie?'

'Sure,' Richie readily agreed. 'But I've been to nearly all the museums at least once or twice, and I've been on the canal boat tours, so what do we do?'

'I'm sure I can think of something,' Seth said. He looked over at Carolina. 'We'll walk you back to the apartment, then we'll take off from there. How's that?'

'That's fine,' she said, 'but I can go back alone if it's out of the way.'

'It's not,' Seth said.

They left the restaurant and walked back to Geldersekade, enjoying the nip in the fall air, the loveliness of the canals, and the elegant old houses. When they reached the house, Seth opened the door for her, then handed her the keys. 'The apartment door key is this one,' he said, pointing it out.

'Thanks,' Carolina said. 'You two have fun. This shouldn't take me too long,' she added. 'An hour or so at the most.'

Why is she being so mysterious? he wondered again.

'Bye, Mom,' Richie said.

Seth kissed her. 'We'll see you in a bit.'

He and Richie set off down Geldersekade, and Carolina went up the narrow, twisting stairs to the apartment. Once inside, she picked up the remote telephone. She pressed in the number, pacing about the living room as she did so.

A secretary answered on the second ring.

'This is Carolina Mountcastle,' she told her. 'Mrs Lyon Mountcastle. Is Mr Weber available?'

'He's with a client, Mrs Mountcastle. May I take a message?'

'Would you please tell him that it's urgent? I'm leaving for New York in the morning and must speak with him right away.'

'Hold, please.'

Carolina quit pacing and sat down on the sofa, her fingernails drumming on the receiver as she waited for the secretary to come back on the line. After an interminable wait, she did.

'I'm sorry to keep you on hold,' she said. 'Mr Weber will be with you in a few moments if you can continue to hold.'

'I will,' Carolina said, 'and thank you.'

There was another interminable wait, and she continued to drum her fingernails against the receiver. Finally, a lightly accented voice came on the line. It sounded like that of an elderly gentleman.

'Mrs Mountcastle, this is Adriaan Weber. I'm sorry for the delay, but I was with a client. How may I help you?'

'I have several things to discuss with you,' Carolina said, 'so you may want to have a pen and paper ready.'

'Of course,' he replied. 'Would you mind if we recorded this conversation? That way we'll have a record to refer to. Just to make certain I get everything.'

'No,' she replied. 'I don't mind at all, Mr Weber.'

'Good. Just a moment.'

She could hear noise in the background; then he came back on the line.

'Now I am ready, Mrs Mountcastle,' he said. 'What did you have in mind exactly?'

Carolina told him, and they discussed all the issues involved for a long time. After she hung up, she looked at her watch. Too early for a drink, and she didn't really want one anyway. She picked up the receiver again and punched in the number for the flower shop. It was early morning in New York, but Roxie should be there.

She picked up on the first ring. 'Carolina,' she said.

'Roxie, it's me,' she said. 'How is today shaping up? Everything okay?'

'Oh, my God! Am I ever glad you called, Carolina,' she said. 'I've been waiting for you to call. It's already been a day and a half. No, more.'

'What happened?' she asked, sitting up. Roxie's voice didn't sound good.

'I'm not certain. Not exactly,' she replied, 'but you're suddenly getting telephone calls from a guy in administration at the Metropolitan Museum. His name's . . . uh, Armstrong.'

'What about?' she asked. Her stomach twisted into a knot. The big benefit was only a short time away.

'He won't discuss the *problem*, as he put it, with me,' Roxie said. 'He says that it's a confidential matter, and he can discuss it only with you.'

'What the hell is he talking about?' Carolina asked in exasperation, even though she knew Roxie didn't know the answer. 'We had everything worked out with them, contract and all. Don't tell me they're trying to get out of it at this stage of the game.'

'Your guess is as good as mine,' Roxie replied. 'I told the man who called that I'm acting on your behalf while you're away, and that any problems they have can be discussed with me. But he was adamant about it, so I couldn't find out a thing.'

'Damn,' Carolina swore. 'Did you talk to Matt or Thad?'

'Yes,' she said. 'Matt called about you and Richie, so I caught him up. Then I told him about this. He nearly freaked. He's sitting on thousands of trees and shrubs and flowers for the party, with big truck convoys and a bunch of guys lined up to work. He said to call him as soon as we know what's going on.'

'This Mr Armstrong didn't give you a home telephone number, did he?'

'No,' Roxie said. 'I told him you were in Europe and would probably be back tomorrow. He said to call him as soon as possible.'

'If he calls again, tell him I'll definitely be back tomorrow. Give him my home number, and try to get his, Roxie.'

'Will do,' she said. 'Oh, I almost forgot. Bernard Goldsmith called, too, and said to call him right away.'

'My lawyer? Did he say what this is about?'

'No,' Roxie said, 'but he said it was urgent.'

Jesus, Carolina thought. *What now?* 'All right.'

'Is everything there okay?'

'Yes,' Carolina replied. 'I'll catch you up tomorrow. I don't know what time we're coming in exactly, but I'll either talk to you or leave a message.'

'Okay,' Roxie said. 'See you tomorrow.'

'Bye, Roxie,' she said. 'And thanks.'

Carolina pressed the OFF button and put the receiver down on the coffee table. She ran her hands through her hair nervously. *What now?* she wondered. *I don't think they'd be calling unless they're trying to break the contract. But why? And why now?*

She stood up and began pacing the room. Her business and Matt's were riding on this party, and everything could go up in smoke if something happened to ruin it. She suddenly broke out into a cold sweat and realized that her hands were shaking. Taking a deep breath, she tried to calm herself. *What the hell has caused this problem, whatever it is?* she asked herself. *What . . . or who?*

Nearly all her problems up to now had been due to the nasty machinations of Antonio and Payton Fitzsimmons, of that she was certain, but how in the world could they have caused trouble at the museum? Antonio, handsome and talented though he was, didn't have any clout whatsoever. Payton, on the other hand, might have contacts at the museum. But powerful enough to get the museum to risk suffering the consequences of a broken contract?

She stopped pacing and sat back down. *And Bernie? What does he want?* she wondered. *It has to have something to do with Leland. What else could it be?*

The intercom buzzer sounded, and she nearly jumped out of her skin, so lost in thought was she. She got up and went to answer it. 'Yes?'

'It's your two men,' Seth said. 'Coming to pay a call.'

'Ooooh,' she said, trying to inject cheer into her voice, 'that sounds very promising. Come right up.' She pressed the button that unlocked the front door, then unlocked the apartment door.

She heard them on the stairs, talking and laughing with one another. As they reached the door, she held it wide open. 'Come in, gentlemen,' she said. 'I thought you were going to be a lot longer.'

'It was wild,' Richie said, and laughed.

'And you?' Seth asked. 'Did you get your calls made?'

'Yes,' she said.

'Everything okay?' he asked.

'I wouldn't call it okay,' she said, 'but we can talk about that later. What did you do?'

Seth and Richie exchanged glances. 'Think we ought to tell her?' Seth asked him.

Richie nodded. 'Why not? Only she might be jealous she wasn't with us.'

'What are you two talking about?' she asked, looking from one to the other.

'Well, we went to the Torture Museum first—,' Richie began.

'The Torture Museum?' she exclaimed.

'Yeah, it was really great,' Richie said. 'They had a real guillotine and everything. Then we went to the Sex Museum and—'

'The Sex Museum?' She looked at Richie, then at Seth. 'I trust you with my son for a little while, and this is what you do?'

Seth shrugged with his hands, palms out, facing her. 'What can I say? I thought he ought to see something besides Rembrandt and Van Gogh.'

'Aw, Mom,' Richie said, 'it wasn't anything I haven't seen before, mostly pictures, but it was kinda cool.'

'What's next?' she asked. 'A cruise through the red-light district?'

'We came back that way,' Richie said. 'It's just around the corner from here, and besides, there're those places down at the end of the block.'

She looked at Seth again. 'What am I going to do with you?'

'He's a good kid. Don't worry.'

'Mom,' Richie said, 'I'd like to go out to see Anja again. Monique said I could come anytime.'

'She said to call first, Richie, so you'd—'

'I've already called,' he said. 'On the way back here.'

That suited Carolina. Since her call to the lawyer, she had to talk to Monique anyway. 'Okay, but we're not going to stay long.'

On the way over, Richie walked ahead and Carolina told Seth about her telephone conversation with Roxie.

'Do you want me to see if we can get on an earlier flight?' he asked.

'I would except that I want to see Monique and Anja one more time,' she said. 'And I want Richie to have a little more time with them, too. If tomorrow's not soon enough, then I'm in real trouble.'

'Remember,' he said, 'whatever it is, I'll be there to help.'

*　　*　　*

When they arrived, Richie dragged Seth off to play with Anja, leaving Carolina and Monique alone. The sat at opposite ends of the couch, looking out over the canal and the woods beyond.

Carolina was the first to speak. 'I was dreading our meeting,' she said, 'but now I'm glad that we did.'

Monique nodded. 'I felt the same way. I thought that you were a monster, but I can see that you're not at all. I should've known better.'

'How could you know?' Carolina asked.

'Lyon wouldn't have married a monster,' Monique replied. 'I think it would've taken – did take – an extraordinary woman to attract him, to win his heart enough for him to marry.'

Carolina felt herself blush slightly. 'I could say the same,' she said. 'I . . . well, I wanted to hate you. Did hate you. Even Anja. I realize now that I was all wrong. You and Anja may not have spent as many years with him, but you were part of Lyon's life, too.'

Carolina hesitated a moment before continuing, looking at the teary-eyed young woman. 'I don't think you're really to blame for the mess that Lyon left,' she said.

Monique looked at her with surprise, but she didn't respond.

'He didn't handle this well at all, did he? If he'd been a braver man, more honest with himself and us, maybe we wouldn't be going through this now. But that's not the way it happened. In any case, I hope that for Richie's sake, and Anja's, too, we can be cordial with each other. I think that's very important for the children.'

Monique nodded. 'Absolutely,' she agreed.

'So I . . . I've decided not to contest the will,' Carolina said. 'For the children's sake.'

'Are you serious?'

Carolina nodded. 'Yes,' she said and stood. 'I have to go now. We need to head back to New York.'

'Of course.'

Monique walked her to the front door and they all said their good-byes. Anja at her side, she watched in quiet disbelief as they made their way down the lane. She had been prepared to hate this woman with whom she'd had to share Lyon. But she found she admired her instead.

33

Seth had a car waiting at JFK Airport, and as she rode into Manhattan, Richie on one side and Seth on the other, Carolina was anxious about what lay in store for her. It was ironic, she thought, that this trip, which she hadn't wanted to make, dealing with a matter she hadn't wanted to face, had turned out fine. As the skyscrapers of Manhattan came into view, she glanced over at Richie. He was staring at the distant buildings intently. The coming weeks and months were going to be a test for both of them, she thought. He had now come face-to-face with the beautiful little half sister who so resembled his father and himself, and he would doubtless want to be a part of her life in the future. Carolina hoped that he would be able to settle back into the routine of school and home life after such a dramatic revelation and confrontation. She also hoped that the plan she had set into motion with the lawyer Adriaan Weber would be carried out smoothly.

When the car pulled up to the loft building in Chelsea, Seth's driver pulled in behind a moving van and parked; then he came around and opened the doors. The three of them piled out of the car, while the driver retrieved their luggage from the trunk.

As Carolina stepped up onto the sidewalk, she was surprised to see Mercedes growling angrily at men moving furniture. Mercedes's furniture, Carolina noticed. *What on earth?* she wondered.

Mercedes wore a fierce expression, and when she saw Carolina it only became more fearsome.

'Are you moving?' Carolina asked.

'What does it look like?' Mercedes snapped.

'I didn't know,' Carolina said.

Seth was tending to the driver, and Richie joined them on the sidewalk. 'Hi, Mercedes,' he said.

'Bugger off,' she said, scowling.

Richie looked at his mother, who returned his glance and shrugged wryly. Richie could hardly keep from laughing.

'Oh, here's Seth,' Carolina said.

'Ready to go up?' he asked.

'We're ready,' Carolina said. 'Here, let me have one of the bags.'

'I've got it.'

They started toward the lobby, and Seth said, 'Hi, Mercedes, how are you?'

'As if you didn't know,' she spat at him.

'Well, see you later,' he said politely, wondering, as had Carolina, why Mercedes was so angry.

'Not likely,' Mercedes said.

He turned back to her. 'Oh? Going away?'

'England,' she said. 'Away from this disgusting backwater and its filthy peasants.'

'I see,' Seth said. 'Have a good trip.'

He joined Carolina and Richie in the lobby, and they went up. In the loft, Carolina was delighted to see a vase on the console stuffed with the huge pale pink roses that both she and Seth loved so much. Some of the lights were on, and when they went into the loft's big living and dining area, Carolina could see that Roxie had also put flowers on the dining table and on the living room coffee table.

'What a wonderful surprise,' she said to Seth. 'Roxie's put flowers out for us.'

He set down their luggage. 'It looks beautiful.'

'Oh, she's left a note on the kitchen counter.' Carolina picked it up and sat down at the table to read it. Seth sat across from her. Roxie had left the telephone numbers Carolina needed to call right away – Bernard Goldsmith's and Armstrong's at the museum – and told her she'd be at the shop if needed.

'Mom, Seth, I've got to hit the sack,' Richie said. His eyes were drooping visibly. The trip had been exhausting for him in more ways than one.

'That's fine, sweetie,' she said. 'You have a good nap, and we'll see about food later.'

Richie gave his mother more than a perfunctory kiss. Then he stopped at Seth's chair and shook hands with him. 'Thanks for all the help, Seth,' he said. 'I really appreciate it, and I'm really glad you were there.'

'You're welcome, Richie,' he said.

Carolina smiled at the bond developing between the two of them. The real affection they had for one another was heartwarming.

Her son went on to his room, and Seth looked across the table at Carolina. 'I'd better get going,' he said. 'I've got a lot of work to catch up on at the office, and I know you have those calls to make.'

'Yes,' she said, 'and I'd better get started.'

He got up from the table, and Carolina joined him. He retrieved his suitcase, and they walked to the elevator together. 'Wonder what's up with Mercedes?' he asked.

'I don't have a clue,' she said.

'Said she was going to England.'

'She goes to England all the time.'

'Yes, but she doesn't take her furniture with her, does she?'

'No,' Carolina said. 'I'll have to nose around and find out what's up.'

In the foyer, he put his suitcase down and took her into his arms. 'I'm going to miss you tonight,' he said softly. 'I want to be with you so very much.'

'I want to be with you, too,' she whispered. 'I hate to see you go, but I have to get this business out of the way.'

'I know,' he replied, looking into her eyes. 'Call me if you need me, otherwise I'll call you tomorrow, okay?'

'You'd better,' she said.

They kissed, long and passionately, with a desire that seemed all the more urgent since it couldn't be fulfilled. Not tonight, at least. When they parted at last, he smiled. 'We've got to work something out,' he whispered. 'I can't live without this. Without you.'

She nodded. 'We'll figure it out,' she said, knowing that they were going to have to somehow, because she felt the same way.

When he had gone, Carolina went back to the dining table and picked up the note, then retrieved the cordless.

'Mr Armstrong's line,' a crisp female voice answered.

'This is Carolina Mountcastle,' she said. 'I have a message to call Mr Armstrong.'

'Hold just a moment, please.'

He was on the line almost instantly. 'Mrs Mountcastle,' he said. 'Yes?'

'I'm glad you got in touch,' he said. He cleared his throat. 'We have a little problem here at the museum regarding the benefit you've scheduled. Seems we have a conflict. The space had already been booked for the night you wanted it, so you're going to have to reschedule or find another location.'

'What!' she cried. 'That space has been booked for a very long time,' she said. 'By me.'

He chuckled lightly. 'Well, you know how these things happen,' he said. 'Little mix-ups . . .'

'No, I don't know how they happen,' she said angrily. 'In fact, it's never happened to me before, Mr Armstrong.'

'There's no need for you to be rude, Mrs Mountcastle,' he said chidingly. 'I think we can behave like civilized people about this, don't you?'

'I'm being very civilized about this, Mr Armstrong,' she said. 'I have that mark of any highly developed civilization filed away in my office. It's called a contract, and your people signed it, as did I. If you'll recall, that contract states the date of usage quite clearly.'

'I see,' he said. 'Well, nevertheless, I was hoping we could come to some kind of agreement regarding that matter. You're new to us, and I think you'd probably like to be able to decorate here in the future, perhaps?'

'There are livelihoods at stake here,' she said. 'This has been in the planning for a long time.'

'Yes, well, our other party can make the same case,' he said. 'In fact, she would be devastated to find out that she can't have her party in that space as she'd thought. This is someone who has very close ties with our board, by the way, and I don't think you want to alienate—'

'Your other party is of no interest to me, Mr Armstrong,' Carolina interjected. 'I have a contract, and I don't think you people at the museum want to break it, do you?'

'I think we might have to,' he said in a deep, determined voice, 'if you force us to.'

Carolina was momentarily dumbfounded by the man. Did he think he could simply railroad her into giving up the space for that night? 'I'm not going to give up that space,' she said. 'Not under any circumstances.'

'Very well, Mrs Mountcastle,' he said, 'you leave me no choice but to have our legal department contact you regarding this matter.'

303

'And my lawyer will be contacting you,' she said.

He cleared his throat again, and his voice became mellifluous and charming. 'I was hoping we could handle this amicably,' he said, 'for everyone concerned. The other party has virtually bottomless pockets, if you know what I mean, and will be very difficult to dissuade from exercising her rights. Ms Fitzsimmons and her family have a history of philanthropy associated with the museum, so I think you're going to have a very expensive battle on your hands.'

Carolina could hardly believe her ears, but she knew that what the insipid Mr Armstrong was saying was true. *Why did I not expect something like this?* she asked herself with growing anger. But then, no reasonable thinking person would have foreseen Payton going so far.

She drew a deep breath before responding to the man. 'I realize this could be very expensive, Mr Armstrong,' she said, 'but I will fight it tooth and nail. I'm calling my lawyer right now, in fact, and you can tell Ms Fitzsimmons that I said so.'

'Very well,' he said, and hung up the phone.

Carolina slammed the receiver down into its cradle. She felt like going into the kitchen and emptying the cabinets of all their glasses and heaving them at the walls. *What the hell do I do now?* she wondered. Payton had virtually bottomless pockets, as he had pointed out, and she wanted the space. She also undoubtedly had relatives on the board of the museum who would try to protect her interests.

She decided to call Bernard Goldsmith and kill two birds with one stone. She could find out what he wanted, and ask him about the museum contract at the same time.

Picking up the receiver with dread, she punched in the number. When his secretary answered, she put Carolina straight through.

'Hello,' Bernard said, 'how was your trip?'

'It worked out fine,' she said. 'Has Mr Weber contacted you yet?'

'He certainly has,' Bernard said, 'and everything's being taken care of. You and Matt are going to have to come into the office to sign some papers, or I'm going to have to send them out to you.'

'We'll come in,' she said, 'if that'll save time.'

'Good,' he said. 'I'll get everything ready right away.'

'Now,' she said, 'what was it you wanted to talk to me about?'

'I'm thinking about bringing the police into this claim Leland has made against Lyon's estate,' he said, 'and I wanted to discuss it with you first.'

'The police?'

'That's right,' Bernard said. 'I think this letter that he and Mercedes have is an outright forgery. They're trying to defraud the estate. Now, we have three ways to go here. We can offer to settle with Leland, give him some money, and tell him to get out of town. Or I can tell him we're going to file a counterclaim in court that the letter is false, and we see if he backs down. That gives him an out. But what I'd like to do is teach the man a lesson.'

'How's that?' she asked.

'I'd like to have the letter analyzed by the police. Then if it turns out to be a fake, have Leland and his girlfriend arrested. They're playing a vicious game with you, in my opinion, and I'd like to see them pay for it.'

'Then go for it,' she said. 'I'm tired of being played with.'

'Good,' he said.

'I saw Mercedes downstairs when I came in, by the way,' Carolina said, 'and she had movers here. She said something about moving to England.'

'Don't doubt it,' he said. 'From what I hear, she can't pay the maintenance on the loft, so she's subletting it.'

'You sure are well informed.'

'I keep my ear to the ground,' Bernard said. 'I have to.'

'I wonder if Leland's going with her?' Carolina asked. 'Maybe he'll drop his claim.'

'I don't think it's going to work that way,' he said. 'The two of them have taken an apartment at a residential hotel on Twenty-third Street. Used the security deposit from the person subletting her place to pay the hotel.'

'Jeez, you really do have your ear to the ground,' Carolina said.

'Well, I better get busy,' he said. 'I'll keep you posted, but I wouldn't worry about this too much. I think we can straighten it out in a very short time.'

'There's one more thing I want to talk to you about,' Carolina said.

'Fire away,' the lawyer replied.

She explained the situation with the museum.

Bernard laughed. 'Payton Fitzsimmons has come along and wants that space – after you signed for it. I'll give that jackass Armstrong a call right now and then get back to you later or tomorrow.'

'What do you think my chances are of keeping it?'

'Who are you doing the party for?' he asked.

'It's a benefit for the Animal Rescue Mission,' she replied.

'And who's your contact with them?'

'Lydia Carstairs,' she said.

'Know her well?'

'Fairly,' Carolina said.

'Then get on the horn to her. She's an extremely powerful woman in this city, and I bet she's on the board at the museum, too. She might be able to get this straightened out without you spending a penny.'

'I'll call her right away,' Carolina said. 'And thanks, Bernard.'

'Talk to you later,' he said.

She hung up and slumped forward onto the table. *One more tele-phone call*, she thought, *and that's it*. Picking up the receiver once again, she dialed Lydia's number. The butler, Normal, put her straight through to Lydia.

'I don't want to alarm you,' Carolina said, 'but I've heard from a Mr Armstrong at the museum.'

'What's going on?' Lydia asked.

She explained the situation as briefly as possible.

'I see,' Lydia said. 'Payton Fitzsimmons is clearly out to destroy you any way she can, but I don't think she stands a chance on this one.'

'How's that?' Carolina said. 'My contract?'

'No, not your contract,' Lydia said. 'Fancy lawyers can break that, I'm sure.'

'Then how?'

'I won't bore you with the details now,' Lydia said, 'but I'll get back to you tomorrow.'

'But you actually think we can go ahead with the party there?'

'Absolutely,' Lydia said. 'Don't worry about it at all, darling. I must run. Talk to you tomorrow.'

Carolina hung up and wondered what Lydia had up her sleeve. Whatever it was, after speaking to her and Bernard Goldsmith, she felt that she had allies to fight the forces that were conspiring against her. And Seth on her side to boot.

34

Carolina left the dining room and headed to Richie's room. The door was open, and he was sitting at the computer, engrossed in whatever was on the screen.

'Knock, knock,' she said, tapping her fist against the door frame. 'I thought you were going to bed. Can I bother you a minute?'

He looked over at her. 'Sure, Mom. What is it?' He focused back on the computer screen.

'I just had a talk with Bernard Goldsmith,' she said. 'The lawyer who's handling your dad's estate.'

Richie turned to her again and then back to the computer. 'Just a sec,' he said. 'Let me store this.'

She went over and sat on the edge of his bed; then Richie turned around and faced her. 'Okay,' he said. 'What's up?'

'I want you to know that he's carrying out your dad's wishes. He's doing everything that Lyon wanted done in his will.'

'Does this mean that you're not contesting the will?' Richie asked.

She nodded. 'That's exactly what it means,' she said. 'After I met

Anja and Monique in Amsterdam, I called Mr Weber, the lawyer there, and got the ball rolling. Bernard just told me that everything's about finished. Your uncle Matt and I just have to sign some papers, and your little sister and Monique will be taken care of.'

Richie came over and sat down next to her on the bed. 'Thanks, Mom,' he said, putting his arms around her. 'I love you.'

She kissed him. 'It's only fair,' she said. 'It might take me a while to get used to the idea of . . . of your sister and all, but I want them to have what your dad wanted. And I want you to be able to get to know Anja. Monique, too.'

'Does this mean that you've forgiven Dad?' Richie asked.

'I don't know, Richie,' she replied, shaking her head. 'I can't answer that question yet. Maybe with time . . .'

'He loved us, too, Mom,' he said. 'I know he did.'

She nodded. 'Yes,' she said. 'He did, didn't he?' She looked at him. 'I wish I was as forgiving as you are, Richie.'

Payton ran her tongue down the length of his torso, her breasts brushing against his muscular body, and when she reached his aroused member, she stopped and glanced up at him with a look of naked lust before lowering her open mouth on it.

Antonio gasped aloud and put his hands on her head, pushing her against him. *Damn,* he thought, *she's giving me everything I want.* He was making a good salary at the shop. She was taking him out to parties and being seen with him, and now she was planning a party at the museum, just so all her friends could meet him. Plus she gave great head.

'Oh, yeah,' he whispered. 'Oh, Payton, that feels so good.' He lifted his pelvis up off the bed and ground himself into her, until he thought he was going to explode. 'Oh, wait! Jesus!' he said, trying to extricate himself.

She came up for air, and he pulled her up on top of him, kissing her passionately before rolling over on top and entering her. He began plunging into her rapidly, unable to wait, and Payton thrust herself up against him, trying to match his rhythm.

Just then the telephone shrilled in their ears. She tensed up. 'I have to get it, Antonio,' she said. 'I have to.'

'Aw, no,' he said. 'No way.' He pinned her down, but she struggled against him.

'Let me go,' she said angrily. 'I've got to get that.'

Antonio relaxed his hold on her, but stayed where he was while she reached over for the receiver.

'Hello?' Payton said.

When she heard who was at the other end of the line, she pulled herself away, got up off the bed, and began pacing the bedroom floor.

Antonio watched her, her ample breasts with their strawberry nipples, her well-rounded ass, and her long lean body, as she nodded her head, talking in a soft voice he could hardly make out. He was eager to get back down to business.

But it was not to be. When the conversation was over, Payton heaved the telephone across the room. It slammed into the mirror at her dressing table, shattering it into a hundred pieces, then fell amid the fortune in perfumes atop the table's surface, toppling several of them to the floor.

Antonio's erection went limp, and his expression turned to one of disgust. He didn't know what had set off the spoiled bitch this time, but he knew enough to leave her alone until she had spent the rage that seemed to consume her so much of the time.

She folded her arms across her chest and began stalking about the room's cream-and-rose Savonnerie rug, her eyes angry, her face contorted into a mask of ugliness. She kicked at his clothes, which lay in a heap on the floor, then turned and glared at him.

'What is it?' he asked, unable to maintain his silence when directly confronted by her vicious look.

'Clean it up,' she snapped.

'What?'

'The goddamned mess over there,' she shouted, pointing at the shards of broken mirror and scattered perfume bottles.

Antonio sat up straight in bed and slammed a fist down on the Pratesi sheets. 'Clean it up yourself,' he shouted. 'I'm not your fucking slave.' His face was red, and the veins in his neck stood out in bold relief.

'You don't think so, huh?' Payton sneered and then laughed. 'You'd do anything for my money, though, wouldn't you?'

Antonio was out of the bed and on his feet in a heartbeat. He drew back his arm and made a fist that hovered threateningly in the air before he suddenly deflated and let it drop to his side. He grabbed her arms and pulled her to him. 'What is it, Payton?' he said, shaking her. 'What's made you like this?'

'That was that little fuck Damian Armstrong, if you must know. At the museum.'

'So?' Antonio said.

'We can't have the museum the night I wanted it,' she said.

'But that's crazy,' Antonio said. 'They already said you could have whatever you want. Your family—'

'Can you hear?' she snarled. 'I can't have it that night! That old bitch Lydia Carstairs has threatened to cancel a big contribution to the museum if they break Carolina's contract.'

'Why don't you promise them the same thing?' Antonio asked.

She looked at him as if he were a dolt. 'Jesus,' she said, 'you don't understand anything.'

'What do you mean, Payton?' he asked, pulling her hard against him. 'Tell me.'

'All of my family's money is tied up in trusts,' she snapped. 'I can't compete with Lydia Carstairs.'

She had become petulant, and Antonio rushed to soothe her, fearful that she might turn against him in such a state.

'It's okay, Payton,' he said, running his hands up and down her back, kissing her earlobes. 'We can have a party somewhere else. Anywhere.'

'That's not the point, Antonio,' she said. 'That bitch you worked for is getting what she wants from the museum.'

'Who cares about her?' he said, his hands brushing across her smooth, rounded buttocks. 'We've got each other, and that's all that matters, isn't it?'

Payton stiffened in his powerful arms, and her hands went up to his chest as if to push him away.

'Come on, Payton,' he said softly, one of his hands exploring the softness between her thighs. 'Forget her. We're what matters.' He put his head against her breasts, and began licking the cleavage there.

Payton roughly shoved him away. 'Get out!' she demanded.

'What the—'

'Get out, I said!' she shouted.

'What's wrong with you?' he asked, surprised. She'd never pushed him away like this.

'I'm finished with you. Put on your clothes and go.'

'Why are you doing this?' he implored. 'Why?'

'Get out!' she shouted again. 'I don't need you anymore. You served your purpose. Now go back to Spanish Harlem or wherever it is you come from.'

'Payton, what the fuck? Come on, simmer down. What about our plans? The shop? Us?'

She laughed derisively. 'Us? There is no us. There never was. As for that shop, I'll close it. I hate the place. I'll close the business, too. It's for losers. I'm a *guest* at parties.' She tapped her chest with her finger. 'I *give* parties. I don't decorate for other people. Not anymore, I don't.'

The blood drained from Antonio's face, and he looked at her, crestfallen. He'd known that Payton didn't love him, despite what she'd so often cried out in the throes of orgasm, but he'd been certain she had to have the sex. Hadn't every woman he'd ever dated

312

told him that he was the best lover they'd ever had? Hadn't they all been addicted to him?

He walked over and picked up his clothes. He slowly dressed, his eyes averted. When he was finished, he opened a closet door to take out the expensive leather jacket she'd bought for him. He saw the fortune in clothes she'd paid for hanging in a long luxurious line, and then stared down at the king's ransom in shoes and boots on the shelves. His heart sank. He'd always been called a 'dresser' in his neighborhood, but he'd never owned such expensive clothing before. He wondered if he ever would again.

He shut the closet door and turned to her. 'I'm going.'

'Good,' she said, 'and don't come back.'

He walked to the bedroom door, then turned and looked at her imploringly. 'Why, Payton?' he asked. 'Can't you tell me why?'

'I don't want to play with you anymore,' she said. 'Just go. Now.'

He turned and left, closing the door softly behind him.

She stood looking at the door, her body tense, her arms crossed against her chest. She had been outfoxed by that sly bitch Carolina Mountcastle. There had to be a way to pay her back. Even if Payton was quitting the business, she was not going to be humiliated. She was the one with class. Somehow she would leave Carolina in ruin.

35

Seth was sitting on her sofa, a scotch in his hand. Richie was staying overnight at Jeff Adler's. Carolina had called Seth, and he'd come right over. He brightened considerably when she told him she was letting Monique have the money.

'I think that's the right thing to do,' he said softly.

She glanced over at him. 'I – I guess so,' she said. 'And . . . maybe, in time . . . I don't know, Seth. I just don't know. It's very difficult.' Reaching over, she placed a hand on his arm. 'You helped me so much. You've been so . . . well, you've been everything. Kind and generous and understanding.'

She saw what she thought was a look of utter devotion in his eyes. Leaning forward, she kissed his lips, and without meaning to, let her lips remain there. This intimacy felt so unexpectedly warm and wonderful that she found she didn't want to move away.

Seth put his arms around her, returning her kiss, tenderly, slowly, his lips lingering on hers, as reluctant as she was to break the momentary spell. Withdrawing slightly, he looked into her eyes.

'Take all the time you need,' he said. 'I'll be here for you, Carolina. I'm not going anywhere.' Then ever so gently, he pressed his lips against hers again, and she returned his kiss with more urgency, as if she'd missed his lips upon hers.

What am I doing? she asked herself. *Why am I letting this happen again?* But even as she put her arms around him, she no longer cared, for he felt so good and she needed this so much that nothing else mattered.

'You must be exhausted,' he said, drawing away. 'Do you want me to go?'

'One more vodka?' she asked. 'Just a tiny one, huh? Or am I over-doing it?'

'I don't think you're overdoing it,' he said, smiling, 'and besides, it'll give me a good excuse to have another scotch.'

He picked up their glasses and went to the kitchen, returning in short order with their drinks. He sat down on the sofa and handed her the vodka and tonic. 'Cheers,' he said.

'Thank you, Mr Foster,' she said teasingly. Putting the drink on the table untouched, she leaned over and kissed him, allowing her lips to linger upon his again. Seth put his arms around her gently and stroked her back and her shoulders. 'You're . . . so special,' he whispered breathily. 'So very special.'

Carolina felt a frisson of excitement that crackled up her back and down her arms. It was a feeling she'd virtually forgotten about, a feeling she'd wondered if she would ever experience again. It was frightening in its intensity, and she abruptly drew back and gasped for breath.

'I – I . . . I don't know,' she whispered. 'I don't know why I'm doing this, Seth. I – I'm . . . I'm scared.'

He drew her to him and held her close. 'You have nothing to fear from me, Carolina,' he said softly. 'Nothing in the world. I only want the best for you because, you see, I . . . I love you, Carolina.'

He felt a slight tremor in her body, but he continued to hold her.

He made no attempt to kiss her. He would let nature take its course.

When she pulled away at last, she looked into his eyes. 'I would like to love you, too,' she said. 'I think I do love you, Seth, but I'm afraid right now. I'm afraid of myself and my own emotions.'

'It'll take time,' he said, 'and that'll change. I'm sure of it. I know you well enough to know that you can't live without love, Carolina. In your heart, for yourself and for others.'

'My heart has been so full of rage and vengefulness,' she said. 'So full of poison.' She sighed. 'And it's no good, this poison. These terrible feelings that haunt me day in and day out. I want to get rid of them.'

'You'll find a way,' he said. 'I know you will.'

'You seem to know me so well,' she said.

'I think I do, yes.'

'Even with all the awful thoughts I have?'

'Even with those,' he said, 'because I know they're not really you. They're only temporary. You'll see.'

'I don't know,' she said. 'I really don't.'

'You can learn from your son.'

'From Richie?' she said. 'What do you mean?'

'You can learn a lot about forgiveness,' he said, 'and love.' He kissed her lips and smiled. 'I love you,' he whispered.

The words galvanized her, and she put her arms around his shoulders, kissing him with more urgency than before. Seth returned her kisses, and slowly they became swept up in their mounting passion for one another. His tongue sought out hers, exploring and delving deeper, and she responded with a tremor of pleasure that only increased as he moved to lick her ears and neck delicately.

His very breath upon her drove her to new heights of sensual delight, and when his hands found her breasts, so soft and round beneath her sweater, she moaned with desire. One of her hands slipped between his thighs, and she brushed against his manhood, which strained to fulfill its own carnal need.

316

Seth gasped and kissed her passionately, his urgent kisses inflaming her aching desire to new heights. He drew back abruptly and looked into her eyes, his hands still on her breasts, stroking them tenderly. 'I . . . I love . . . you,' he gasped between breaths, 'and I don't want to do this . . . unless you're certain, Carolina.'

She responded with a kiss of such abandon that he knew she wanted him. Taking her hands, he eased her up off the sofa, and together they went quietly to her room, where he undressed her slowly, admiring the mature lushness of her body as if he were in awe. When she stood before him naked, he hugged her to him, then drew back and began shedding his clothes rapidly, tossing them carelessly on the floor.

Once disrobed, he took her into his arms again and began kissing her with renewed passion. Carolina relished the feel of his strong arms around her and the steely hardness of his manhood, throbbing against her bare thighs. His hands stroked her back and kneaded the taut roundness of her buttocks, before finding her bare breasts, where he gently squeezed her nipples with his fingertips.

Carolina moaned with pleasure and felt a dampness begin to suffuse her thighs. She wanted him so much, desperately, and she could hardly wait to feel him inside her. As if he had read her mind, he led her to the bed and eased her down upon it, then kneeled above her, his head descending to her breasts, where he licked whorls around them and on them before taking her nipples into his mouth.

She ran her fingers through his dark hair, gasping, then felt a jolt go through her as his tongue slid down her torso to her waiting mound. Thrusting herself against him, she cried aloud when his tongue found the sweetness within, but he lifted his head almost immediately and drew back, spreading her legs with his knees. Poised to enter her, he guided himself to the wetness between her thighs, his manhood sliding into her ever so slowly.

Carolina pushed against him, almost swooning in pleasure as she felt his hardness just inside her. Then Seth plunged in as far as possible, as if he couldn't wait a moment longer. They began moving fast and hard, overcome with passion, unable to restrain the forces that compelled them.

Carolina suddenly shuddered against him as contractions engulfed her and she flooded in orgasm. Seth groaned loudly, then plunged a final time, his body stiffening, then quivering, before he fell gently atop her, gasping for breath. He covered her face and neck with kisses. 'Oh . . . Carolina,' he rasped between breaths, 'I . . . I love you.' He held on to her tightly, as if he never wanted to let her go.

'And I . . . love you,' she said, trying to catch her breath. She hugged him, wondering how she could have waited so long to let this happen, wondering why she had denied herself such pleasure and such love.

They stayed wrapped in one another's arms for a long time, and when he finally rolled off her, she regretted his absence inside her. He slid an arm under her shoulders as they lay on their backs and turned to stare into her eyes. She could see in them the adoration that their lovemaking had inspired.

'This is the most wonderful night of my life,' Seth whispered to her, 'and I mean it. The most wonderful night of my entire life.'

She smiled. 'I've loved every moment of it,' she replied. 'I didn't know that I could still feel this way. You've reawakened something in me, Seth. Something wonderful, and I don't just mean sexually. Not that the sex wasn't wonderful, because it was.' She smiled again. 'But this is more than that. I feel alive again and whole. I was like a ghost and didn't know it.'

He held her close. 'You were never a ghost,' he said, 'but I do think you needed love. To love and be loved. You know, I've loved something about you from the very first time I saw you a long time ago.'

'Really?' she said.

'Yes,' he said, 'but I've come to truly love you – I've fallen in love with you – as I've gotten to know you better over the last few months. I can't imagine life without you now.'

'I can't imagine what I would've done without you, either,' she replied. 'You've done so much for me.'

'I can do a lot more if you'll let me,' he said. Then he smiled. 'I'd like to do more all the time, Carolina.'

'I think I'd like that,' she said, 'but I'm still going to need time, Seth.'

'And you can have all the time in the world,' he replied.

She rolled onto her side and kissed him, and he embraced her, pulling her next to his warm body. Within moments, the fires of their desire were rekindled, and they began making love again, only more slowly this time, exploring one another's bodies, discovering delights they hadn't touched before.

When they lay spent at last, Carolina felt that she really had come back from the dead, that the past was indeed the past, and that a new life had begun for her tonight, with this man. The joy was immeasurable and brought tears to her eyes.

'What is it?' he asked her in a whisper.

'I'm just so happy,' she said. 'I can't help it. I didn't think this was possible for me, and I feel . . . joyous.'

He wiped her tears with a finger. 'I want nothing but joy for you,' he said. 'Always. For you and Richie both.'

'That means so much to me,' she said, pleased. 'That you would include him.'

'I couldn't conceive of it any other way,' he said.

'Speaking of which,' she said, 'I don't know if I can hide what I feel from him.'

'I don't think you have to,' Seth said.

'No,' she replied, 'you're right. I don't have to. Richie likes you.'

'I think he likes me, too,' Seth said, grinning, 'and you know it's mutual.'

'It's so wonderful to be able to be together like this,' she said. 'To be able to spend the night together.'

He hugged her to him. 'Yes,' he said, 'I can't imagine anything more wonderful. We've got all night. But there'll never be enough time for you and me.'

'We'll have to make time, won't we?'

'Yes,' he said, flipping out the light and sliding under the covers next to her. He embraced her. 'Starting now.'

36

She looked over her sketches for the decorations for what seemed like the millionth time. The party would seal her fate in the lucrative Manhattan party-decorating business once and for all.

She felt a tingle of excitement. She'd just spoken to Matt on the telephone, and he and Thad would be leading a truck convoy into Manhattan from Connecticut. Hundreds of live birch trees and a vast assortment of evergreen shrubbery would be on the trucks, along with hundreds of potted flowers and plants and thousands and thousands of fall leaves.

The party would take place amid a birch forest at the end of fall, in the northern woods of Russia or Finland, as she imagined it, and the guests would stroll in, not on a red carpet as they were used to, but on paths of colorful fall leaves. Among the trees would be primitive small dachas, gingerbread confections she'd had constructed in her warehouse space for the odd tête-à-tête over cocktails. As the evening progressed and dinner came to an end, the dancing would start and snow would begin to fall through the crystal chandeliers she was going to suspend above the dance floor. The crowd, she was certain, was going to be enthralled.

This will make or break my career, she told herself, *but I have the distinct feeling that it's going to make my reputation once and for all.*

'Carolina,' Roxie said, 'it's for you.'

'What?' she said. She'd been so caught up in her sketches of the party that she hadn't heard the phone ring.

'It's the telephone,' Roxie said. 'For you.'

'Who is it?' she asked.

'Guess,' Roxie replied with a mischievous grin.

She knew it had to be Seth, otherwise Roxie wouldn't be playing this silly game. 'Okay,' she said, taking the handset from her.

'Carolina,' she said, after pushing the ON button.

'I love that name,' Seth said.

She felt a flutter about her heart at the sound of his voice.

'I miss you,' he said.

'I miss you, too.'

'What time should I pick you up tonight?'

'About six, I think,' she said. 'I'm going to try to get back home and change by then, and head up early to keep an eye on things.'

'Okay,' he said. 'I'll be there.'

She pushed the OFF button and leaned against the wall. Suddenly the work ahead of her didn't seem like such an insurmountable challenge after all. Yes, she decided. She could handle it. Hadn't she always?

'Okay,' she shouted so everyone in the shop could hear her. 'Let's get this show on the road.'

Payton virtually had carte blanche at the Metropolitan Museum of Art, even if they wouldn't reschedule the party for her. Because her family was so important to the museum and she was on a first-name basis with several of the board members and the most important curators, a single telephone call would gain her admittance to the museum practically anytime she wanted to see an exhibition, with a curator to go along with her if she so desired. Like many of New York's elite, she saw shows before the general public was allowed to, or before or after regular viewing hours so as to miss the crowds. So when she called Cameron Fulham, a curator in ancient Greek sculpture, and told him she wanted to see some recent acquisitions, he immediately agreed to join her and give her a guided tour.

'No, Cameron,' she'd said. 'Thank you anyway, but that won't be necessary. I just want to dash through on my own this afternoon. I thought that if you don't mind you could leave my name at the desk so I could get a pass. I might not get there until a little late, you see.'

'Of course, Payton,' he'd said. 'I'll call down right away. If we're closed, tell the guard to call the security desk. Otherwise, there'll be a VIP pass at the main desk for you. You can go wherever you like.'

'Thanks, Cameron,' she'd said.

Now she hurried through the Greek and Roman sculpture galleries, VIP pass in hand. Not that she thought she would need it. The museum was still open, and she didn't plan on staying after hours. But the pass might come in handy if a guard who didn't recognize her told her she couldn't go into certain areas of the museum, like the Medieval Court, where a certain party was taking place tonight. She knew they would have the area closed off, but she also knew that it would be easy to simply walk around whatever barriers they had erected. Probably nothing more than screens or ropes, she thought. In some ways, security at the museum was a joke.

She saw Carolina's handiwork long before she reached the court. She looked about, wide-eyed, hardly recognizing the area at first. There was a forest of birch trees leading the way into the court, along with several wholesale nurseries of plants and shrubs. *My God*, she thought, *it looks like she's installed a national park.*

In the court itself, she saw several workmen busily arranging shrubbery and repositioning trees. Little gingerbread dachas were being assembled here and there, and at each end of the space, she saw a scaffolding that went all the way to the ceiling. In fact, it looked as if the entire space was surrounded with scaffolding.

I wonder what the devil she's up to? Obviously, she's going to suspend something from the scaffolding.

She strolled on in as if she belonged there, her self-confident air daring anybody to speak, let alone tell her to leave. She could see where the orchestra would be, where the dining tables were being set up, and the dance floor. Then she watched as workmen began suspending crystal chandeliers from the scaffolding overhead.

How trite, she thought. *She can surely do better than that.* However, when she saw the massive collection of chandeliers that was to be hung, she almost gasped aloud. She had to admit that Carolina was taking a slightly different approach. There wouldn't be the requisite dozen or two chandeliers glittering above. She could see that it would be more like a hundred or so.

At one end of the space, she saw workmen gathered around a small forklift and ropes. She walked that way and saw that they were lifting some sort of machine up onto a platform situated on the scaffolding. Gathered in a clump back behind them were a number of other machines. *I see! Fog machines! She's going to use dry ice to create a little atmosphere.*

Payton decided she'd seen enough. She knew exactly what she had to do after she arrived at the party tonight. *It'll be so easy,* she thought, a wicked smile forming on her lips. *So very easy. I can hardly wait to call good old Champers. There'll be plenty of time for him to help me get ready for this party.*

She began strolling back out of the area, her head held high, her heels clicking on the floor. *Yes, indeed. If I hurry, there'll be plenty of time to get ready for this party.*

It'll be so perfect. Carolina Mountcastle's last party. Ever!

*   *   *

'How do I look, sweetie?' Carolina asked, twirling around in front of her son. She had decided to spring for a new outfit, and a very expensive one at that, because she wanted to impress potential clients tonight. Besides, she'd told herself, she could afford it, so why not? She twirled again, and the crimson taffeta skirt with huge ruffles by Oscar de la Renta rustled luxuriously. Its dark gray taffeta shirt blouse set off the thick, rope necklace of ruby beads she wore, along with matching earrings and a bracelet.

She had treated herself to the jewelry, as well, preferring not to wear any of the pieces that Lyon had given her. Those she had gathered up one night recently and locked away in a box that she put on a closet shelf. She had decided to take every piece of jewelry he'd given her to Sotheby's or Christie's and consign it all to auction, including her engagement ring and wedding band. She'd taken them off and put them in the box with everything else.

'You look really cool, Mom,' Richie said. 'Like supercool. You're going to wow the guys tonight. Especially Seth.'

In a dramatic gesture, Carolina placed her hands on his cheeks and planted a noisy kiss on his lips. 'You just made your mom's day,' she said, suddenly realizing that he was as tall as she was. She had to reach a hand up to ruffle that wonderful dark brown mop of his.

'What is it?' he asked. 'You're looking at me like I'm some kind of freak or something.'

'No,' she said, 'I'm just realizing how much you've grown.'

'Oh,' he said. 'I think it's from stretching to hit tennis balls.'

The buzzer sounded. 'That must be Seth,' she said. 'Do you mind letting him in while I check my makeup one more time?'

'No,' Richie said, heading to the vestibule.

Carolina dashed into the bathroom, gave her makeup a final inspection, and then went back out to the living room.

'You look beautiful,' Seth said, looking at her with wide, appraising eyes.

'And you look quite dashing,' she said.

'Ready?'

She nodded. 'I am ready.' She picked up her evening bag and held out a cheek for Richie to kiss.

He smiled and kissed her, and then shook hands with Seth. 'Have fun.'

'I'll probably be very late,' she said.

'Don't worry about me,' he said. 'I've got a bunch of stuff to do, and I'm e-mailing Anja and Monique.'

'Tell them hello,' she said.

'I will.'

Fifth Avenue was bumper-to-bumper with limousines and more discreet Lincoln Town Cars, as well as the occasional chauffeured Mercedes, Bentley, or Rolls-Royce. The steps leading up to the museum's main doors were carpeted in red, as usual, but tonight's decoration was a bit different. Fall leaves in a dozen different colors were strewn along its entire length, all the way up the steps and into the museum itself.

Dozens of cameras flashed as the rich and famous climbed up the steps. Occasionally, photographers would ask a celebrity or well-known socialite to stop so they could get a better shot, and several of them obliged, the women often posing to advantage. Most of these people were so accustomed to the paparazzi that they thought nothing of their presence and tolerated them because the photographers enhanced their egos, despite what many of them might say publicly.

Inside, the path of strewn leaves led all the way through the marble and granite hallways to the Medieval Court, where the party was being held. Jaded partygoers already sensed something special in the air tonight. As simple as strewing a path of leaves might seem, it was unusual in that the decor usually started in the room in which the party was being held. Carolina had already helped set a tone, a mood, from the moment the guests stepped onto the red carpet outside.

As they arrived at the Medieval Court and glimpsed the splendor that awaited them, the *oohs* and *aahs* were audible, even from a crowd accustomed to the most lavish parties. Candlelight spilled from the little dachas' windows, as it did from the beautifully set tables, and the chandeliers overhead glittered like millions of stars.

'It's truly enchanting,' a rail-thin, darkly tanned socialite in Dior couture said to her friend, a vicomtesse from Paris, dressed in a creation of her own design.

'Magical,' the vicomtesse replied. 'Absolutely magical. It's like something Marie-Hélène would have done when she was alive. Do you remember the last ball at Ferriere?'

'Of course, darling. Don't you remember? I stayed with you and Pi—' She caught herself before she used the vicomtesse's husband's name. Everyone knew that he had moved out of their sumptuous *hôtel particulier* in Paris and taken up residence with his mistress, leaving the poor vicomtesse, who was at least sixty-five, high and dry. It was customary to have a mistress, but to leave one's wife for her? Tasteless man.

'Ah, yes. I do remember,' the vicomtesse replied without missing a beat. 'That was the week they had to pump your stomach at the American Hospital. Too much Xanax and champagne, wasn't it?'

They acted as if they weren't aware of the photographer from the *New York Times* 'Style' section taking a picture of them as they chatted, although their lips were virtually frozen in smiles, whether exchanging pleasantries or vicious barbs.

'Oh, hi, Billy!' Payton Fitzsimmons cooed when she saw the photographer. 'How are you?'

'Great, Payton,' he replied. 'And you?'

'Fabulous.' She struck a pose in her new Yves St Laurent with Champers on one arm and a big beaded handbag in the other, waiting for the flash that she knew would come. And it did, after which she and Champers began to circulate.

'Don't look so nervous,' Payton said in a low growl, a smile plastered on her lips. 'And quit fooling around in your pocket with your hand.'

Champers quickly pulled his hand out of his tuxedo pocket. 'I really don't like this idea.'

'Yes, you do,' Payton replied. 'Admit it. You love the idea. You're just a big chicken about being caught.'

Champers smiled. 'I guess you're right, Payton,' he said. 'It's so naughty.'

'You needn't worry,' she said. 'I'll do it myself. When the time comes, you'll give me what you've got, and I'll take what I've got. Then I'll do it. In a flash. Nobody will ever know the diff—' She stood with her mouth open for a moment, staring across the room.

'What is it?' Champers asked.

'I don't believe it,' she snapped. 'It's that low-life scum Antonio. With Libby Cooper.'

'You're kidding,' he said.

'Look,' she said, nodding in the couple's direction.

Champers saw that she was right. Antonio, handsome as ever, in a splendid tuxedo, was squiring Libby Cooper, one of the richest, most beautiful, and most available women in New York – or anywhere, for that matter – about the room.

'They look very chummy.'

'Don't they just,' Payton said vehemently. 'I can't believe that I introduced that creep to her. And they met only for about two seconds.'

'Well,' Champers said, 'from what I hear, that's plenty of time for Libby to make up her mind that she wants something – or some-body. And as we both know, what Libby wants, Libby gets.'

'The bitch,' Payton said. 'I hope he costs her a bundle.'

'If it makes you feel any better,' Champers said, 'from what I hear the last one cost her about two mil. Cash.'

At that moment Antonio looked across the room and smiled widely, nodding at Payton and Champers.

'Oh, the smug bastard,' Payton said. 'This is infuriating!'

'Get over it, Payton,' Champers said. 'Remember, you've got better business to conduct tonight.'

She looked up at him and smiled. 'Yes,' she said. 'I sure do, don't I? Antonio can wait. I'll take care of him another time.'

'Smart girl,' Champers said, nervously adjusting his bulging jacket pocket. 'Very smart girl.'

The dinner had ended, the brief speeches had been made, and now the orchestra was playing and the dance floor was filled with couples. The snow had begun to fall delicately from above the chandeliers, and the fog had begun to swirl in from beyond the trees and shrubbery, causing more *oohs* and *aahs* and applause from the crowd. Before long, the autumn leaves and the forest of birch trees, the evergreens and the chandeliers – everything became encrusted with glittering snow and aswirl in a mysterious fog. The little dachas had become more enchanting than ever as their gingerbread trim glistened with snow. It cascaded down from between the chandeliers, reflecting the light as it fell, exciting gasps of delight from the elegantly clad crowd. Despite their sophistication, the countless extravagant parties most of them had attended around the world, and in some cases their jaded views of the world and the ennui that often accompanied it, the guests couldn't resist the magical effect.

As Carolina had predicted, the effect *was* magical, truly magical, and there was not a single complaint from the beautifully coiffed and gowned women about the unabashedly fake snow that now adorned their hair and gowns, nor from the men in their tuxedos who partnered them on the dance floor. And the fog helped create just the right mystery, she thought, without being overwhelming. Matt and Thad had worked on the machines, making certain that just enough would be released to work. And it did. Time and again during the evening, Lydia Carstairs had sought her out to introduce her to one social lioness or other, and in some cases, a titan of

329

industry. They were eager to meet the woman who was responsible for creating the atmosphere that prevailed at the party.

A stunning beauty from San Francisco who was married to the heir of an oil fortune embraced her warmly, as if they were old friends. 'You have to decorate for my husband's birthday party,' she told Carolina.

A famous movie producer from Los Angeles and his lovely wife gushed compliments. 'You have to do our annual summer party in East Hampton,' he said. 'And our New Year's party in Aspen,' she added.

An ancient doyenne of New York society held one of Carolina's hands in both of hers. 'A bit of heaven,' she said. 'I've heard all about you, of course, and now I'm a believer. I'll be in touch.'

On and on they came, from minor royals to the merely serene, from politicos to designers, from CEOs to famous artists. Carolina could hardly believe her good fortune.

After Carolina and Seth had danced to several numbers in a row, she told him she had to check with Matt and Thad and make certain that everything was under control. Some of the crew was gone, but Matt and Thad would be there until the party was over, remaining behind the scenes and making certain that the snow and fog machines worked correctly, that all the lights worked properly, and seeing to the countless other details that had made the evening such a success.

'Do you want me to go with you?' Seth asked.

'No,' she said. 'I won't be long. Why don't you enjoy yourself in the meantime.'

'I'll meet you at our table?'

'Yes,' she said, and turned and made her way through the crowd to the 'backstage' area where she knew she would find Matt and Thad. She was stopped several times on the way and complimented by guests who had obviously found out who she was.

When she finally spotted her brother and Thad, they both broke into broad smiles as she approached. 'Isn't it great?' Matt said.

'It's fabulous,' she said, hugging first him and then Thad. 'I could never have done it without the two of you.'

'And an army of others,' Thad said with a laugh.

'Oh, yes. We mustn't forget them.'

'You look beautiful,' Matt said.

'Thanks,' Carolina replied.

'You can leave anytime you want to, Sis,' Matt said. 'We've got everything under control here.' He looked at his watch. 'We got a hotel room nearby. Our guys'll have this place cleared out by noon tomorrow. They'll never know there's been a party.'

'It's going to be some job,' Carolina said, looking around. 'I'll be here to help.'

'You don't have to do that,' Matt said. 'You and Seth go have some fun. Don't forget you're paying us quite handsomely for doing our end of the work.'

'That's true,' she said with a laugh. 'But don't you hope it's just the beginning of something really big?'

'You bet we do,' Thad said. 'It's a lot of work, but it's well worth it.'

Carolina gave him a kiss on the cheek. 'I love you for saying that, Thad.'

'It's true,' Matt said. 'We've both loved working on this project.'

She kissed her brother, too.

'Why don't you go enjoy yourself now,' Matt said. 'Go give those ruffles a few twirls.'

'Okay,' she said.

From among the birches and shrubbery that hid them from view, Antonio suddenly appeared, breathless, a frantic expression on his face.

Matt and Thad looked up, and Carolina turned to him, startled. 'Antonio,' she managed calmly, 'I'm glad to see you.'

'Carolina!' Antonio gasped. 'You've got to come. It's urgent.'

'What is it?' she asked, alarmed by his genuine distress.

'It's Payton,' he said.

'What about her?'

'She's trying to sabotage the party,' Antonio said, 'and if you don't hurry, she will.'

'What's she up to?' Matt asked, jumping to his feet.

'I'm not exactly sure,' Antonio replied, 'but she's fooling around back behind the scaffolding by the fog machines, and if I know her she's got something up her sleeve.'

'But what could she do?' Carolina asked frantically.

'I know how to find out,' Thad said, 'if you don't mind a little intrusion into the party scene.'

'What do you mean?' Carolina asked.

'I can throw the most powerful spotlight I've got over there where the fog machines are,' Thad said. 'We'll even be able to see what she's up to from here.'

'Then do it,' Matt said.

'I'm not waiting,' Carolina said. 'I'm going over there right now.'

'I'll come, too,' Antonio offered.

'Let's go this way.' Carolina hurried on ahead. 'It'll be faster.' She led the way to the far side of the great space. She stayed behind the party set, Antonio following closely behind her, maneuvering under and around scaffolding and the trees and shrubbery.

Suddenly they heard gasps from the crowd. At the same time, Carolina realized that the lighting had changed drastically and the music had died. She rushed toward the dance floor and then stopped stone-still when she looked in the direction of the floodlit area.

Like a deer caught in the headlights of an onrushing car, Payton stood poised with some sort of metallic object in her hand, staring into the blinding spotlight. It was obvious that whatever she held in her hand was about to be put into one of the fog machines. Thad had been right, Carolina thought. The spotlight was so powerful that it completely lit the scene. Many of the guests were now watching.

A man in a tuxedo – it was Seth! Carolina realized – followed by two security guards, then a third and a fourth, rushed from out of the darkness, grabbing Payton's arms and wrenching them up behind her, taking whatever she held in her hand in the process. More gasps rose from the crowd. Then the spotlight went out. As everyone began chattering, the orchestra resumed playing.

'I wonder what it was,' Carolina said.

'Some sort of gas is my guess,' Antonio said.

She turned to him. 'Thank you for the warning, Antonio,' she said. 'She would've ruined the party, that's for sure.'

'I'm sure that's exactly what she wanted to do.'

'Do you want to have a drink with Seth and me?'

'I'd like to say hello to him,' Antonio replied.

They went back to the table where she and Seth had dined and found him there, surrounded by a crowd of curious guests, all of them asking questions at once.

'Seth, what was it she had?' asked a tall blond woman of inde-terminate age.

'The guards said it was sulfur,' Seth replied, 'and she had two cartridges of it. Enough to make a hell of a stink.'

'Imagine!' the woman cried. 'Payton Fitzsimmons doing a thing like that!'

'You've got to remember that her mother was a von Hoenhoff, my dear,' another woman declared. 'Doesn't surprise me in the least. It's in the blood, you know.'

'Oh, there you are,' Seth said, seeing Carolina. He stood up and, excusing himself, went over to her. He hugged her to him and kissed her. 'Are you all right?' he asked.

'I'm fine,' she replied. 'But what about you?'

'He's a hero,' the tall woman chimed in.

Seth turned to her. 'I'm not really. The security guards are. And whoever's operating that spotlight. Dee Dee McAllister, I want you to meet Carolina Mountcastle.'

The woman beamed at Carolina, extending a reptilian hand sparkling with many carats of jewelry. 'Darling,' she cooed. 'I'm so delighted.' She looked Carolina up and down. 'Oscar,' she said, meaning Carolina's outfit. 'Divine.'

Carolina recognized her face and name immediately. She was an indefatigable, globe-trotting member of international society who was one of the world's best-dressed women – and she entertained constantly and with a passion.

'I'm glad to meet you, too,' Carolina said.

'You're a genius!' the woman exclaimed. 'An artist! I've got your number and will ringy-dingy soonest. Think Tangier, darling! A sultry summer night! The scent of jasmine!' She trilled laughter; then her voice dropped an octave. 'But New York. In iciest January.' She laughed again. 'Now I'll vamoose! You darling lovebirds tear up the dance floor. I have to go spread the word about that vicious beast, Payton Fitzsimmons. Ta-ta!' She swept away in a rustle of tangerine silk.

Antonio had been standing just behind Carolina, and she turned to include him in the conversation. 'Antonio came to warn me.'

'Hi, Antonio,' Seth said, extending a hand.

'Hi,' Antonio said, shaking hands. 'I saw her back there and knew she was up to something.'

'I really appreciate it,' Carolina said. 'And you!' she said, looking at Seth. 'I can't believe you got caught up in the fray.'

'The instant that floodlight hit her, I went running,' Seth said. 'I was sitting where I could see what was happening perfectly. I didn't know who it was at first, but knew something was terribly wrong. The guards took her away, but I don't know what'll happen to her.'

'Probably nothing,' Carolina said.

'I wouldn't be so sure about that,' a female voice said.

Seth and Carolina turned to see Libby Cooper as she snuggled up to Antonio. He introduced them, although she and Seth had met on more than one occasion in the past.

'Why do you say that, Libby?' Seth asked.

'Because I'm on the board here,' she said imperiously, 'and I've got a lot more clout than she does. Besides, the cow's treated Antonio shabbily. I'm going to see to it that they press charges.'

They exchanged pleasantries with Libby and Antonio for a few more minutes, then watched as the lovers headed to the dance floor, where they plastered themselves against one another and began to move erotically.

'That's the second arrest of the day,' Seth said.

'What?'

'Didn't you know? I heard Leland and Mercedes were picked up by NYPD detectives today. Their investigation proved the letter a fake.'

'Then that means Leland can't press his claim against the estate.'

Seth and Carolina returned to their table, where the crowd that had come to question Seth had dispersed.

'Would you like to dance again?' Seth asked.

'Most decidedly yes. I feel like celebrating.'

As Seth twirled her about the dance floor amid the falling snow, she couldn't help smiling with pride in what she had accomplished tonight. *No more doubts*, she thought dreamily, observing the festivities. *Not after tonight.*

The orchestra was playing 'The Best Is Yet to Come,' and Seth whispered into her ear, 'I have a feeling that the music is for us.'

She looked into his eyes. 'I think so, too.'

They whirled around again, and Seth held her close. 'Will you marry me?' he asked.

Her heart suddenly raced, and she felt little jolts of electricity running up and down her arms. 'I will,' she said. 'Oh, yes, Seth, I will.'

'I love you so much,' he said, stopping and hugging her to him closer.

'And I love you,' she said.

He led off again, and they danced amid the falling snow and swirling fog, staring into one another's eyes, entranced by their love and this place.

'You look very happy,' Seth said to her.

'I am,' she said. 'Everything's worked out like I'd hoped it would, and people really have enjoyed it.'

'I'm enjoying it, too,' he said with a smile. He hugged her closer. 'More than you can know.'

She returned his smile. 'I think I do know.'

When they finally walked off the dance floor, she told him, 'This was a perfect night.'

'For me, too,' he replied, kissing her cheek. 'I only wish we could spend the rest of it together.'

'Oh, yes,' she said, 'but I think I should talk to Richie first.'

'Absolutely,' he agreed. 'I also think we have to set a wedding date – and soon. We can't go on this way. We need to be together.'

'Yes,' she said. 'Together.'

EPILOGUE

It was only a matter of months before Carolina was dubbed the 'Martha Stewart of the flower world' in New York's tabloid press. For a while the media became saturated with news of the latest must-have on the party-decorating scene. She became *the* person to call to decorate for any important occasion, and was even asked to decorate for parties in London and Paris. She was invited to appear on television shows, giving tips on decorating with flowers and demonstrations on arranging. She was asked to speak at national garden club meetings. She secured contracts for books on flower arranging and party planning, one of which she was working on with Sybil Conroy. She became a much sought-after guest at some of the functions that she had decorated.

Her life became peopled with book agents, speaking agents, and publicity agents, and she truly became a face and name in the public domain. Nevertheless, she was somewhat surprised when she was approached about a fragrance bearing her name.

'You wear the smell of success,' Seth teased her.

'It smells a lot like money, doesn't it?' she quipped.

When the rumors began to fly about new developments in her private life, her telephone began to ring with requests of a different nature from those she was accustomed to.

Lydia Carstairs wanted to give her wedding, generously offering her magnificent apartment or her huge shingle mansion on the ocean in Southampton; or, neither of those sufficing, offering to give it at the Plaza or the Pierre.

Matt and Thad wanted to give the wedding, insisting that their magnificently restored colonial home with its acres of gardens, ponds, and beautiful landscaping was the perfect setting.

Everyone, it seemed, wanted a piece of the action, and Carolina and Seth hated disappointing them. But disappoint them they did. Invitations went out to all of these people and a handful of others, naturally, but not for the gathering that many had envisioned. There would be no hungry press, no money-grubbing publicity agents, no mere social acquaintances with big smiles, fat wallets, and expensive gifts. There wouldn't even be limousines, white or otherwise.

The wedding was held under a white marquee ablaze with hundreds of candles, set in the garden at the cottage in the country on Midsummer's Eve. Matt gave his sister away. Richie was the best man. Anja was the only flower girl. Roxie was the maid of honor.

The bride, in a moment of restraint, chose an ecru silk gown of severe cut, in part because it set off the magnificent flowers the groom had given her as a wedding present: they were made of canary yellow and white diamonds and consisted of matching earrings, necklace, and bracelet. They were the same color as the engagement ring he had bestowed on her at Christmastime.

The fiery glitter of the diamonds almost outshone the shimmer of the joyful tears that came into Carolina's eyes during the ceremony, spilling down onto her cheeks before it was over. The groom, quite naturally, had a perfectly pressed linen handkerchief, which he put at her disposal.

Lydia Carstairs, Seth's only relative, was there as his family. For Carolina, there were Richie, Matt and Thad, Anja, Roxie – the closest thing to a sister she thought she would ever have – and the newest addition, Monique Lehnert. She had gradually become a part of the family over Christmas, when Carolina couldn't find it in her heart to exclude her from celebrations with Anja.

The guests enjoyed the delicious dinner and consumed copious amounts of champagne and other wines. Afterward, to the accompaniment of a small orchestra, elegant gowns and tuxedos swirled about the dance floor until the wee hours.

As Carolina and Seth danced together, he murmured into her ear, 'It's going to be so wonderful to be together as a family at last.'

'Oh, yes,' she said, returning his gaze.

'I think I've loved you and wanted to be with you ever since the first time I saw you,' he said. 'It's still astonishing to me that I have you.'

'I'm astonished, too,' she said, 'though it was different for me, of course. I was married when I met you. It's extraordinary what can happen in such a short period of time. We never know, do we?'

'I think the most extraordinary thing of all,' Seth said, 'is that you've forgiven what happened and forgotten.'

'Not forgotten,' Carolina said. 'Not yet. Maybe someday. I don't know. But I really have learned to forgive.'

She smiled. 'I've learned a lot in the last year,' she said. 'From my men. From you and Richie.'

'And yourself,' he said. 'You've learned a lot from listening to yourself.'

'It's opened up a whole new world of possibilities for me,' she said.

He kissed her. 'For both of us,' he said softly.

'Oh, yes, for both of us.'